SPEEDWELL

BOOK THREE
IN THE KATHERINE WHEEL SERIES

By Alex Martin

BOOK ONE - DAFFODILS
BOOK TWO - PEACE LILY

ISBN-13:978-15

ISBN-10:1515

D1472296

All the characters and places in this fictional book are a product of the author's imagination. Any resemblance to people or places is entirely coincidental. The author has endeavoured to research historical facts accurately. Where they are not so, it is hoped the reader will forgive any anomalies and grant the author artistic license.

Please note that this is a work of fiction. Any technical errors are entirely the author's responsibility. While extensive research has been undertaken about the birth of motoring as we know it today, so have many liberties. In particular I have played about with dates of inventions to fit the story. All characters are fictitious. Please forgive any licence taken. It was artistic.

Acknowledgements:

Many thanks go to Phil for his mechanical advice, to Tom for editing, to Phoebe for inspiring me. Thanks too to staff at Brooklands Racing Circuit, particularly Diana Willows for her encouragement and knowledge. I am forever indebted to my writing friends, Judith Barrow and Thorne Moore whose honesty, skill and empathy willed me on to the finishing line. I must also mention Alison Price and her scalpel.

This book is dedicated to my father, Charles Rowe, for teaching me to drive and sharing his enthusiasm, knowledge and excitement from the early days of motoring. And for those spontaneous trips in the car when I was little and we'd stop at dawn and brew up tea on a tiny methylated spirit stove - inside an old biscuit tin - in a lay-by, which took about two hours! He also sings a very good rendition of 'Golden Slumbers'.

Thanks to Jane Dixon Smith of

http://www.jdsmith-design.com/

for her design of the cover. The picture on the front jacket was taken at Brooklands, (and is copyright free, as far as I could find out) which is now a Motor Museum in Weybridge, on the original site of the racing track.

Please note that British spelling is used throughout

SPEEDWELL

CHAPTER ONE
Spring 1920

Katy's spanner slipped. She lunged to catch it, missed, and caught her wrist on a spark plug. She rubbed the bruise already swelling up on her arm. That was the third time today she'd been clumsy. What was the matter with her, dropping things like that? She couldn't get anything right this morning.

She felt so tired, she'd like to curl up next to the workshop cat and doze the day away but it wouldn't do to let Jem catch her napping. The spanner was now lost in the depths of the engine of Dr Benson's Model T Ford. She'd have a devil of a job to retrieve it and she already had a couple of motorbikes queuing for attention against the workshop wall. She hadn't had enough work in the early days of opening Katherine Wheel Garage and now it had all come in at once. She had to prove to herself, as much as to Jem, that she could make a go of her new business; she couldn't relax for a single minute, no matter how out of sorts she was feeling.

There was so much at stake. The garage might be only a Nissen hut with a tin roof, but it contained all her hopes for the future.

Ferreting for the spanner was interrupted by another car drawing up on the garage forecourt. The driver got out and hollered for petrol. Where was Jem? That was his job. Not wholly convinced about her enterprise, her husband was concentrating on building a market garden to pay their way. He must be out of earshot, digging the vegetable patch.

The man shouted again. Damn it, she'd just have to go and serve the customer herself. Katy threw down her greasy rag and stepped out into the spring sunshine, blinking at the glare.

"Fill her up, would you, boy?" The stocky man added, "and be quick about it, I'm off to London and behind schedule. I hope that pump is sealed. I don't trust these new-fangled machines. I can't understand why you don't just use a can."

"We like to keep up to date, sir." Katy's diplomatic skills had improved rapidly since opening her own business.

"Oh, you're a woman!" The man walked over to Katy and stood uncomfortably close; the smirk on his face making him look even uglier.

"Not called Katharine by any chance?"

"At your service, sir."

"Are you now? And I'll bet you're a right firecracker!"

His female companion peered at Katy under raised eyebrows through the car window. Katy smiled back at them both and touched her hand to her cloth cap. She'd learned to ignore this reaction to a woman doing a man's job; if anything, it spurred her on. She hopped out of his way and stood under the shell-shaped glass lamp of the petrol pump.

He watched with narrowed eyes as Katy worked the handle of the pump and the petrol gushed into the tank of his pre-war Wolseley. Built in 1912, it already looked dated, more like a carriage than a car but her customer was obviously very proud of the lumbering beast.

Katy kept her eyes firmly on the nozzle of the hose, fully aware of him staring at her chest through her boiler suit. She was quickly discovering the only downside of running Katherine Wheel Garage were these leering male drivers. Which was why it was supposed to be Jem's job, one he could easily do with his wooden arm. But where the hell was he?

"I'll check the oil for you, sir." Katy lifted the bonnet to check the level.

Sure enough, it needed at least half a pint. Katy fetched the can from the enamel cabinet, just inside the workshop. Her customer breathed down her neck as she poured the oil into the engine. She wrinkled her nose in distaste. He obviously took better care of his vehicle than his teeth.

"So, Katharine Wheel, make sparks fly, do you, eh?"

"Just doing my job." Katy added up the cost of the petrol and oil and held out her grease-stained hand for the cash. "That'll be seven shillings and threepence, sir."

The burly driver loomed even closer, behind the shield of the lifted bonnet. Neatly avoiding another encounter with his smelly breath, Katy brought the bonnet down with a swift click and he sheepishly passed her three half-crowns. She fished for change in her boiler suit pocket, relieved to find a threepenny bit amongst the coins she kept there.

"There you are, sir, threepence change." She nodded her dismissal.

The man threw a guilty look at his passenger before saying, "Aren't you going to wipe the windscreen for me? They always do that at Whitefriars Garage." He put his change in the pocket of his plus-fours and pulled his driving gloves back on, avoiding her eyes.

Katy, unruffled, smiled again. "Certainly, sir." She grabbed the cloth they kept in a bucket on the forecourt and sluiced off the windscreen. The woman passenger glared back at her through the glass. Katy polished it to a perfect shine with a chamois leather and wiped the acetylene headlamps for good measure. There was no way she was letting Whitefriars outdo them. They were only ten miles further down the London road. She hadn't reckoned on such stiff competition within a year of opening. It made it doubly important to give each customer the best service she could.

She caught him giving another glance at her backside, before the middle-aged driver got back in the car, next to his good lady. Katy enjoyed his discomfort when the woman, who must surely be his wife, started a shrill lecture that could be heard above the roar of the engine, as she cranked it back into life. She smiled her satisfaction as the Wolseley lumbered out on to the road, then turned back into the workshop, jangling the coins in her pocket.

She fished out the spanner and was tuning Dr Benson's engine, humming a song as she worked, by the time Jem came in with a slice of her mum's plum cake.

"How's it going, Katy?" Her husband handed her the plate.

"I'm all fingers and thumbs today," Katy replied, taking a bite. Her earlier queasiness had worn off and her sharp appetite reminded her she'd skipped breakfast. "Where were you earlier? I had to serve petrol to a horrible bloke half an hour ago."

"Oh, I was just up in the copse, bringing some logs back for the fire."

"I think we need a bell, or something, out the front for customers to ring." Katy spoke through a mouthful of cake.

"I still wouldn't hear it up in the woods," Jem said, nodding towards the back of their five acre plot. "Perhaps you need an assistant to serve the petrol."

"I can't afford it yet." Katy gave him back her empty plate. "But I need help in here too, lifting the heavy gear when you're not around. You'll have to leave off doing the other jobs until the garage is shut for the day, Jem. You can't expect me to manage everything on my own."

Jem ground his teeth in that new irritating way he had. He did it in his sleep too and it really got on her nerves. "So, is that agreed then?" Katy said, more crossly than she meant.

"And what am I supposed to do when there aren't any customers for petrol? Twiddle my thumbs and watch the road for entertainment? There's so much to do on the other Nissen hut. No doubt you still want me to make those kitchen cupboards. And I've a market garden to build up. We're not going to make enough to live on from a few car repairs."

"Oh, for goodness' sake, Jem! There are enough jobs to do in here, before we think about home improvements and potatoes. The accumulators need checking for Mrs Threadwell's radio for a start and I still haven't sent the bill to Farmer Stubbs for his tyres."

"Alright, Kate. Don't go on. I can't be everywhere at once and we need a dry roof over our heads. I'll have to get up the ladder and have a go at that leak in the home hut sometime today, and I've got to plant the rest of those spuds, whether you like it or not."

Another car pulled up on the forecourt and Jem stomped off to see to the new customer but he was met by their sponsor, Douglas Flintock, who stood in the doorway, pulling off his driving gloves and beaming his usual wide smile at them.

"Why the gloomy faces, partners? Not trouble in paradise, I trust?" Douglas looked from husband to wife and back again, with dancing blue eyes. His American accent was as strong as ever, despite living in Wiltshire for nearly a year, after marrying Cassandra Smythe, heiress of Cheadle Manor.

"There's just so much to *do*, Doug." Katy broke her frown with a smile. "I don't have enough hours in the day and can't catch up with myself with this sudden rush of work."

"You are the victim of your own success, Mrs Phipps." Douglas smiled back.

"Perhaps, but I don't see how I can pay for an assistant, and I'm behind with the books, which is the only way to bring more cash in. I'm just too whacked after a full day in the workshop to tackle the accounts." Katy turned back to work on Dr Benson's Ford. She didn't have time to waste in chit chat and Douglas could chat for hours, having little else to do.

"I could take a look at the accounts for you,"

5

Douglas said.

Katy was surprised. She didn't think her partner was *that* bored. "Well, I wouldn't say no to that, Doug. I haven't much patience for paperwork."

"Excuse me, but I've got to get on in the garden," Jem said.

"Lead me to the paperwork on your way, Jem." Douglas followed Jem to the office by the back door.

Katy returned to Dr Benson's hand-brake, which he'd complained wasn't releasing properly. She had slipped into her usual tuneless humming that should signal to anyone who knew her that she was concentrating, when Douglas flapped some papers in her face. If Jem had done that, she'd have given him what for, but being as it was Douglas and she still relied on him for funds, she swallowed down the swift retort that was on her lips.

"Say, Kate, I can't make head nor tail of these petrol invoices."

"Give it here, Doug." Katy took the paper, leaving a dark thumbprint on its white surface. "See, if I've paid it, I sign it with the date at the bottom but it looks like this one is still outstanding for Shell. You'd better send them a cheque and make sure you log it in the ledger."

"Where's that?"

"Over there, on the shelf above the paraffin stove." Katy tried not to sound as impatient as she felt. "Jem knows where it is. Where is he?"

"Oh, he said he had to mend the roof on your other Nissen hut, I mean your home, next door, while the weather is fine." Douglas wandered back into the office, talking over his shoulder. "I'm sure I can manage on my own, once I learn the system."

Katy watched as Douglas reached for the large book above the stove, then winced as it slipped from his grasp. Over went the kettle, spilling water on to the workshop cat, who had been curled up asleep on the chair next to it.

Felix leapt off his seat, scattering invoices, while the kettle clattered to the floor, creating a puddle on the papers

6

that now littered it. Then the phone rang. Katy threw down her rag for the second time that morning and went to answer it but Douglas had picked up the receiver before she could reach it. Katy picked up the kettle and watched the outraged Felix stalk out into the bright sunshine, his tail held upright and twitching with anger.

"Hello, how may I help you?" Douglas was saying, his Boston accent more pronounced than ever on the telephone. "No, I'm not joking, this is Katherine Wheel Garage." He pronounced garage 'garaage'.

"Oh, give it to me, Douglas, for heaven's sake." Katy snatched the earpiece from him and held it to her ear, but quickly held it further away as Martha Threadwell's loud voice barked at her.

"I want to know how long you're going to take to charge up my radio accumulator," Mrs Threadwell screeched. "Are you sure this is the garage?"

Katy rolled her eyes at Douglas who grinned back and made a silly face. She tried not to laugh into the mouthpiece. "Hello, Mrs Threadwell. No, you haven't made a mistake. Yes, this is Mrs Phipps and I'll have the accumulator ready for collection by five o'clock this afternoon. It's been on charge all night, never fear."

Goodness knows she'd gone to enough trouble to install a generator for the electricity for the purpose. Katy wasn't going to forget it in a hurry.

"So I should hope, Katy," came the reply. "You've had it three days now. That's not Mr Flintock acting as your receptionist, is it? I'd have thought he'd have better things to do up at the manor than being your dogsbody."

"Yes, it is Mr Flintock, Mrs Threadwell. He takes an interest in the garage, as you know and I'm very busy today, so he's kindly helping out." Not wishing to encourage a longer chat with the local gossip, she added, "Do you want us to deliver your radio accumulator or will you be sending young Billy over for it?"

"You can bring it to me."

"Rightio, Mrs Threadwell, but there will be a

sixpence delivery charge."

"Sixpence! For three miles? Hmm, well, I suppose Billy can come over on his bicycle. His basket is big enough and he never stops talking about your garage."

"Very well, if you think he can take the weight of it safely, I'll make sure it's ready for him by five. Good-day, Mrs Threadwell," and Katy hooked the earpiece back on the Bakelite telephone stand. Poor Billy, he didn't get much peace at home and always lingered longer than he should when he delivered their post. He'd have a job balancing his bike with one of those heavy accumulators in the basket and would have to walk those three miles to Lower Cheadle.

It was now eleven thirty and she still hadn't finished Dr Benson's car service.

"Shall I fill the kettle and make a brew? I know how you Brits love your tea."

"If you like, Douglas, but I really have to get on."

Douglas nattered away as she worked. She had to remind him to take the kettle off the hob when she saw clouds of steam issuing from the back of the workshop. Douglas was blithely indifferent to the condensation trickling down the enamel Pratts sign that served as a baffle plate for the paraffin stove. Then her heart sank as he spooned three heaped teaspoons of expensive tea leaves into the pot, before stirring it vigorously enough to splash it on his pale plus-fours.

"Oh, hell, these trousers are new," Douglas said, "still, never mind, I'm none too sure of this new style of showing my socks to the world."

He brought the mug of tea over to Katy and lingered for another chin-wag. Katy ignored him and carried on wrestling with the nut that was causing the handbrake problem.

Douglas yattered on, "Lottie smiled at me for the first time yesterday, you know, just as we went up to the nursery before supper. Isn't it swell that we witnessed that? Cass was thrilled. I must say, Nanny does a mighty fine

8

job of looking after her. I never knew being a father would be so enjoyable."

"That's lovely, Doug." Katy was genuinely pleased that Douglas was happy being married to her old friend and employer, but even more that the nut had freed up with a drop of lubricant.

"Yes, I'd like to spend more time with her, but my dear mother-in-law says it's better to leave Nanny in charge most of the time and of course, Cassandra is busy with Mr Hayes running the estate, so she's happy with the arrangement, though she's insisting on doing the nursing herself. We had quite a broken night."

Katy tested the handbrake. Ah, that was better. It released perfectly. Now for the engine itself.

Douglas perched his tweedy backside on the bonnet. "Douglas, could you move, do you think?" Katy prodded him with her spanner.

"Oh, sorry." Douglas drained his mug. "Hey, you haven't drunk your tea. Aren't you thirsty at all?"

Katy swigged back her drink. It was far too strong and tepid. "Thanks Doug, that was really nice. Now if you don't mind, I must get on."

"Sure thing. Shall I do some more cheque signing in the office? Can you spare five minutes to show me the ropes?"

"No!" Katy almost shouted. "Doug, can't you see I'm busy here?"

Douglas's face fell. "Sorry, I'd help with the cars if I could, but I'm no good with mechanics. I sure love to drive, though. Do you need anything delivered?"

"No, Douglas. Thank you, but I wish you'd offered earlier. Billy will have a heck of time of it with that accumulator; too late now. Now I must finish Dr Benson's car."

The phone rang again. Douglas hurried out the back to answer it. "Yes, you bet, Dr Benson, she's working on it right now. Yes, I'll ask."

"Tell him it'll be ready by tomorrow morning," Katy

called out, and muttered, "if I ever get a moment to myself."

Douglas passed the message on and wandered around the workshop, whistling "Alexander's Ragtime Band", slightly out of time.

He picked up the daily newspaper that lay, still folded on the workbench, where Katy had discarded it earlier that morning. She had no spare minutes to read the headlines today. Douglas leaned against the bench and perused the front page.

"Oh my, that doesn't bode well."

"What's that, Doug?"

"Says here that Sinn Féin supporters and Unionists are engaged in pitched street battles in Derry."

"The Irish troubles never seem to stop, do they?" Katy said, only half listening.

His whistling grated on Katy's frayed nerves and she was glad when he turned the pages and got absorbed in the column he was reading. Eventually, his whistling dwindled into blissful silence.

A few minutes calm descended and she'd managed to make real headway on Dr Benson's engine when Douglas exclaimed, "That Campbell feller sure is the big cheese."

Katy gritted her teeth. Honestly, she was getting as bad as Jem. They would have only stumps for chewing their food at this rate.

"Who?" she asked, her fingers still busy.

"Malcolm Campbell, the racing driver. He's started racing again at Brooklands - you know, the racing circuit in Weybridge? They shut during the war and built planes there instead. Good to see it up and running for racing again." Douglas rippled the paper as he spread it out in front of her and stabbed at the centre pages with his long, clean finger.

"Douglas, I can't see the gaps in the points if you put the paper there and I've never heard of the place," Katy said, with what she felt was admirable patience.

"Look, Kate. See? Malcolm Campbell won the first race - there's a great picture of him - look at that car. Surprised he's racing something from before the war. Says here it's a 1912 GP Lorraine-Dietrich called 'Vieux Charles III'. Just look at those cylinders." Douglas looked at her with bright, expectant eyes.

"That's wonderful, Doug." Katy nodded, then pushed the paper away.

Douglas took the hint at last, and picked it up, holding it wide open in front of him, as he read the small print out loud.

"Yes, it says here, they've finally mended the track and intend to hold regular meetings. I sure would like to see that, wouldn't you, Kate?"

"There's all sorts of things I'd like to do, Douglas, but right now all I want is to make a go of this garage and I never will, if you keep interrupting me!"

CHAPTER TWO
Spring 1920

Jem had never been fond of heights. Being a man of the soil, he preferred his working boots to be firmly planted on a good bit of Wiltshire loam but there was nothing else for it but to get up on the roof and mend the leak before the next rainstorm. The May sun beat down on his uncovered head and he enjoyed its warmth after the long, cold winter they'd endured in the Nissen hut they called home.

"I'm off to Mum's, Jem," Katy called up to him.

"When are you back?"

"About an hour?"

"Alright, see you later."

From his viewpoint on the roof, he watched Katy zoom off on the little motorbike they used for a run-around.

Jem returned to his reflections and as usual, his thoughts were reluctantly drawn to the fraught subject of money. There seemed to be no end to the expense of setting up Katy's garage. There was so much she said she couldn't do without, such as a telephone and the major project of installing a petrol tank and pump on the side of the road.

Thank goodness the petrol company had footed that cost. The council hadn't been too happy about the pump but they'd managed to get away without paying them rent because there was no pavement on this stretch of the London Road.

It would be a few weeks yet before he could sell his vegetables alongside the garage forecourt. You had to grow them before you could sell them and the chickens hadn't started laying enough to produce a surplus either. There was always a ready market for eggs, so they should bring in a handy few bob. He hammered in another nail through the corrugated tin.

Jem had lost count of the number of things they'd

had to buy in the meantime. The ladder he was balancing on, for instance. You couldn't mend a roof without one - or hammer and nails. Douglas had been very generous and had loaned them a lump sum for starting up but Jem was too proud to tell his sponsor that it had dried up long since. He'd thought a tidy amount like that would have lasted years. It would certainly take many a year to pay it back. Worrying about how they'd manage gave him broken nights. It was more cash than he'd ever seen, but Katy's business had soaked it up like a sponge.

The garage had to start earning - and soon - and it seemed work was finally arriving in a rush. He wished he could do more to help her but Katy wasn't the best teacher in the world, so he concentrated on building his own business. In his eyes, a market garden was a much more secure enterprise and suited his skills. Katy was too quick and impatient when Jem struggled to remember all the fiddly components under each bonnet. And fiddling wasn't easy with only one good hand. There again, if it hadn't been for that bloody war, Katy would never have learned her mechanical skills in the army and there would be no Katherine Wheel Garage. He was in two minds if that was a good thing or not, but he kept that under his hat.

Jem pulled the felt across the weak part of the roof with the metal hook affixed to the inside of his wooden hand, and fished in his pocket for the tacks with his good hand. Their bed was directly underneath and they'd both had enough of damp sheets.

Jem looked across the roof to the river valley below his land. His mind flew back to the day he'd got the official set of keys from the solicitor, when Cassandra and Douglas had driven them into town.

He remembered how Katy had looked that day. She'd had one of those short, straight American dresses on, the lavender coloured one with the matching coat and little bell-shaped hat, that Cassandra had bought her in Boston. She hadn't looked remotely like a car mechanic.

"Here they are," Katy had said that fateful morning, as the old Sunbeam lumbered down the drive towards them, with Douglas at the wheel. Cassandra leaned out of the window, and waved.

Jem proudly opened the rear door of the big car and handed his smart wife inside. He felt old-fashioned sitting next to her. He hadn't had a new suit since they were married in 1914 and it looked dated next to the other three, who all wore bang-up-to-date clothes. He felt out of place, as if he belonged to the last century, not this new modern one that raced away from him before he could keep up.

He felt equally at a disadvantage when Mr Leadbetter, the solicitor, read out the legal document that made him an esquire of sorts. Katy listened attentively to the monologue, with her head cocked on one side and her beautiful, almost violet, eyes fixed on the solicitor's glasses, perched precariously on the end of his long nose. Jem didn't understand much of the long-winded mortgage contract and blindly hoped he wasn't signing his life away, as he wrote his name at the bottom of the parchment.

Then Mr Leadbetter folded up the documents with red ribbon and sealed them with wax. He carefully placed them to one side and said they would stay in the vaults of his office, for safekeeping. They all nodded solemnly. Then the solicitor took out a large bunch of keys and handed them to Jem. The cold metal lay heavy in Jem's hand and he stared at them for a moment. A strange sensation swept through his body, brushing away the last traces of his odd black mood of the morning. He couldn't analyse what it meant but it felt like joy and hope mixed together in some unfathomable glue that spelled freedom. Jem looked up at Mr Leadbetter, who removed his glasses and held out his hand to him.

"Congratulations, Mr Phipps. You are now the legal owner of this parcel of land," the solicitor said, with a smile that was also somehow rather serious.

"Thank you, sir." Jem put the keys in his pocket and felt his old trousers sag with the weight of them, as he shook Mr Leadbetter's extended hand. The keys knocked against his leg when Katy turned to him and gave him a quick hug. Douglas and Cassandra were shaking his hand then and all the time those keys had bumped their hello into his thigh, so he couldn't forget the enormity of what he'd just signed up to.

His own land.

And now, from the vantage point of his high perch, Jem surveyed his five acre plot, noting the extensive vegetable patch he'd planted up, divided by neat paths of broken bricks. They saved a lot of weeding, those paths, and kept the slugs at bay. He looked at the copse to the east, where the hens pecked the earth underneath the trees. He'd coppiced a lot of the older ash trees and stacked the logs ready for next winter, when they'd be seasoned enough to burn on the log stove. It was very satisfying to see them lined up in neat rows, drying nicely in the sun.

They'd not had much to burn through this last winter, God knew. They'd kept themselves warm by working until the light faded and cuddling up together through the long nights. A wonderfully happy time, despite the hardships. Another memory, a more intimate one, crept into his mind's eye.

"Our first night alone together since you left for the war, Jem." Katy had said, that unforgettable night, her pansy-blue eyes soft and warm.

"Ay, how many years is that?"

"Must be," Katy counted on her fingers. "Why, it must be four years!"

"Four years too many. Come here."

Katy's body melted into his. Their double bed, second-hand from a cottage on the manor, creaked under their movement.

"This bed's a bit noisy, Jem."

15

"But it don't matter, Kate. No-one in the whole wide world can hear us, whatever we gets up to. That is, if you want to, after..."

She'd touched her finger to his lips. "Don't say his name, Jem. Don't speak of it. I never want to think about it again. I just want to love you, only you, forever. We've been parted long enough so let's make the most of being together again."

And Katy had kissed him then, willingly, lovingly, fully. Jem felt even hotter remembering that passionate night in the bed below him.

Katy's body, once so familiar had tasted exotically foreign, after such a long abstinence. After her traumatic trip to Boston she'd held off from love-making, and sleeping to the sound of her Dad's snores had not helped his attempts to seduce her back, when they'd had to live with her parents. But that night! Oh, yes, that first night, alone in their Nissen hut, they had abandoned all reserve and given free rein to their pent up desire for each other.

Lost and found, he'd called it at the time and so they had been. Both had gone to war in France, both had got lost along the way and now, finally, they were home. Not much of a home, some might say, but neither of them cared about that. However much they might bicker in their tiredness now, Jem knew how much Katy loved him after that glorious night. He'd never forget it. No, he'd never forget that magical time of falling back in love with his wife, with the worries of the world held at arm's length, where Jem preferred them.

A car drew up on the forecourt and Jem watched Douglas swagger out to serve the customer. Jem hoped he wouldn't put them off. Sometimes he despaired of Douglas's bragging. Female laughter tinkled upwards to his lofty look-out and he breathed a sigh of relief. It seemed some customers liked Douglas's charming breezy banter and he smiled as he hammered in his last roofing tack.

A model T-Ford drove onto the forecourt and started beeping its horn impatiently. Jem frowned as Douglas waved them to wait. His lady customer was still laughing up at Douglas and didn't seem at all ready to leave.

The Ford honked its horn again, three times. Jem picked up his hammer and descended the ladder, using his wooden arm to steady him with its precarious grip. He touched earth to the sounds of angry shouts and strode to the forecourt to see what the fuss was about.

The female customer, a fashionable young woman in expensive town clothes, was no longer smiling. In fact, she looked quite upset. Douglas stood between her and the driver of the Ford, who had got out of his car and was pointing at her impressive Bentley.

"If you've finished fuelling, you should get out of the way, young woman."

It was Mr Bartlett, the owner of Whitefriars Garage up the road. He should have guessed.

Douglas looked flustered and greeted Jem with relief. "This man is being very impatient, Jem. I still haven't checked this young lady's engine for oil."

Jem could well believe it, knowing that Douglas hadn't a clue how to go about it.

"Hello, Miss." Jem smiled at the smart woman. "Would you mind just hopping in your car and parking over there? I'll see to your engine oil and my partner can then serve petrol to this customer."

Douglas's brow cleared with a broad smile. "Great idea. That would be swell, if you wouldn't mind, Miss?"

The woman tutted her annoyance but she got back into her big car and revved the engine before gliding over and parking, with expert precision, on the spot Jem had pointed out.

Jem turned to their latest customer. "I'm sorry you've been kept waiting, Mr Bartlett. Was it petrol you wanted?"

"What else would I be here for? You need a system,

17

young Phipps. It's all very well having a fancy pump like this, all lit up like a seashell on fire, but we're better organised with our simple barrels up at Whitefriars." Mr Bartlett had an unattractive habit of jutting his stubbly chin out when talking, making him look as belligerent as he sounded.

"Most of our customers are happy to wait their turn." Jem made a mental note to mark out a separate bay for filling with oil, with its own signpost, but he'd never tell Mr Bartlett he'd pinched his idea. "If you've such a clever way of working, I'm not quite sure why you need to buy fuel here, Mr Bartlett?"

"Just so happens, the tanker's late and I'm almost run dry." Mr Bartlett turned his podgy face towards the workshop. "Your wife not working then? Thought she manned the pump? Sorry, wrong phrase. A woman can't *man* anything, can she?" Mr Bartlett let out a guffaw.

Jem ground his teeth. "How many gallons do you want, Bartlett?"

CHAPTER THREE
Spring 1920

Cassandra heard Douglas's car crunching on the gravel of the drive and went to meet her husband. She hoped he'd had a good morning at Katherine Wheel Garage. He never complained, well not much, but she worried that he still hadn't found a purpose to his life in Cheadle Manor. She had so little time, or energy, to spare since the birth of their daughter, Charlotte, named in memory of her dead brother, Charles.

She strolled towards the stables, where his Buick convertible was housed, and met him as he walked around the stone buildings towards the ancient house she called home. She'd heard Cheadle Manor described as a fine example of the Elizabethan period, with its tall gables in Cotswold stone. Would Douglas describe it as his home, she wondered? She hoped he would, but wished she could be sure.

"Hello, darling." Douglas kissed her cheek.

Cassandra turned her head so that his kiss reached her mouth, not caring if the under-gardener pruning the rose-bed nearby saw them. They climbed the steps onto the welcoming apron of the terrace and walked through the big front door.

"Had a good morning, Doug?" Cassandra asked.

"Mighty fine, thank you, honey," said her husband, giving his coat and gloves to Andrews, the butler.

"I'm glad." Cassandra was relieved. "What have you been up to?"

"I went to the garage and soiled my pampered white hands serving petrol to a smart young lady in a beautiful Bentley. She was bound for Salisbury and had almost run out of gas, so she was mighty pleased to see me," Douglas answered, as they wandered into the drawing room.

Cassandra looked around the large room and knew another moment of blessed relief to find her mother

19

absent.

"Fancy a snifter before lunch, Doug?"

"Don't mind if I do. Gin and IT, please."

Cassandra mixed his favourite cocktail of gin laced with sweet vermouth - one of the best ideas he'd imported from America - and poured herself a glass of soda water. If she had any alcohol she'd fall asleep over her lunch.

They sat with their drinks on the sofa next to the fire and Cassandra relished their rare moment of privacy. She'd never been happier in her life than she was right now but living under her parents roof, no matter how large, had its downsides.

"So, you were flirting with some fashion-plate were you, husband mine, while pretending to be a humble yokel?"

Douglas laughed and stroked her cheek, "I said the car was beautiful, honey; believe you me, its driver had less sleek lines."

Cassandra's warm glow was swiftly quenched by her mother joining them by the fire.

"Drinking already?" Lady Amelia said. "Is that gin I can smell?"

"Fancy one, Lady A?" Douglas rose to greet her with a peck on the cheek.

Lady Amelia sniffed and waved him away. "Certainly not. However, I shall partake of a very small sherry."

Douglas winked at his wife as he turned his back on his mother-in-law and poured out the minutest quantity of sweet sherry into the tiniest glass he could find on the sideboard.

Cassandra, knowing her mother always protested she ate little and drank less, while doing the exact opposite, had a job not to laugh out loud at her mother's expression of irritation, as Douglas handed her the thimble-sized glass with a broad, and thoroughly insincere, smile.

"How is Charlotte today?" Lady Amelia sipped her

20

sherry.

One sip had halved the volume in the tiny vessel and Cassandra struggled to suppress a giggle, as she answered, "Lottie treated us to another smile this morning. I think her eyes are starting to change colour, too."

"Oh? Are they turning brown, like all the Smythes?" Lady Amelia said.

"No, I think they're getting even more blue; more like Doug's, actually," Cassandra said.

The sherry glass was already empty.

"Can I top you up, Lady A?" Douglas made to get up from his chair.

"My name is Amelia," said his mother-in-law.

"I beg your pardon. Can I get you a refill, Amelia?"

"I did not give you licence to use my Christian name alone, Douglas!"

"I apologise a third time, mother-in-law." Douglas didn't wait for permission, but glugged some more amber liquid into her glass.

"Luncheon is served, milady," Andrews announced from the doorway.

"Where is Sir Robert today?" Douglas offered his arm to Lady Amelia, who ignored it and preferred her cane.

"He's gone off to see about some hunt business, something to do with the hounds, I believe." Lady Amelia walked through the double doors.

Cassandra followed her mother's rigid back into the dining room and sat at the long table. Her breasts were over-full and tender and she wished she'd fed the baby before eating. Nanny had suggested bottles of her secret special milk mixture but Cassandra liked to hold her daughter in her arms and share every tender moment she could. She yawned. Those moments seemed all too frequent during the night. She really ought to discuss feeds from a bottle with Nanny and yet she relished those intimate moments when there was only her and Lottie in the whole world.

She attacked her lunch with relish. She'd never known such hunger as she'd had since having her baby. Talk about eating for two. Just as well the current fashion didn't emphasise waists. And Douglas seemed to like her new curves. Cassandra smiled, as she remembered the other reason she hadn't got much sleep last night.

"Cassandra! Didn't you hear what I said?" Her mother's voice penetrated her sleepy fog.

"Sorry, Mother, I was up with Lottie in the night and I'm a bit dozy now."

"It's ridiculous, you feeding the child yourself. You should let Nanny do it all with the bottle. We didn't involve ourselves with the children nearly so much in my day. You were farmed out to a wet-nurse and so was Charles. I was back in corsets at this stage. We gave a ball for each of your christenings and I wore the same size dress each time." Lady Amelia spooned more trifle into her mouth.

Cassandra looked back at her mother, whose stout frame no longer hid her love of sweetmeats, and forced a smile. No, she couldn't imagine lying in those arms as a baby, as Lottie did in hers, and gazing up into loving maternal eyes. She felt sorry rather than angry for the woman who had borne her, but her mind rejected the image when she pictured being on the inside of that boned corset.

Before lunch was over, Cassandra excused herself from dessert and escaped to the nursery. Sure enough, Lottie was crying for milk and Nanny Morgan was glad to see her.

"Ah, there you are, cariad. Tempted to come and find you, I was." Edith Morgan scooped up the child and placed her in her mother's arms.

Cassandra felt a rush of love for her baby, as she sat in the nursing chair, feeding her little girl. Lottie had an appetite worthy of her grandmother and suckled greedily on Cassandra's engorged breast, relieving its pressure.

Cassandra changed sides and settled back into the comfy seat, relaxing in the sanctuary of the nursery. Once fed, Lottie gave a contented burp and drifted straight off to sleep.

Nanny Morgan, a kind woman from the Welsh valleys, popped a padded footstool under Cassandra's feet and gave her a cup of tea. "Have that, dear, and have a lovely cwtch with the little one. I'll leave you to enjoy some peace and quiet together."

Cassandra drank her tea gratefully and placed her cup and saucer down on the side-table. She shifted into a more restful position and nestled her little daughter in the cradle of her arm, supported by the comfy chair, and they both drifted off to sleep in a milky cocoon.

CHAPTER FOUR
Summer 1920

Katy shook her head free of the worries that whirled around her head in a continuous never-ending circle and concentrated on why Cassandra's Sunbeam saloon was roaring like cannon-fire. She wriggled under the chassis into the inspection pit and took a good look at the exhaust, which, as she expected, was riddled with holes. She fished some gum and wadding out of her pocket and started to apply it to the exhaust pipe, glad to focus on inert metal. When she'd plugged every hole, she clambered out of the pit and washed her hands in the basin in the workshop's kitchen-come-office.

It was turning out to be another hot summer, almost as fierce as last year. She went to the two corrugated iron front doors, that gave on to the forecourt, and prised them open as wide as she could, revelling in the flow of air she'd created. Really, she was going to have to rig up some sort of fan. Perhaps she could power one from the generator? It wouldn't relieve her constant nausea though. She wasn't feeling as sick as she had with her first baby, but being pregnant was still a disaster.

Dear, sweet Florence. Had she lived, she'd be starting school now, freeing Katy up to work in the garage but then she'd never have served in the war and tasted a different sort of freedom. Katy had been furious when she'd discovered she was having another child. No wonder she'd been so tired lately.

What would Jem say when he knew? The garage was really starting to garner customers at last. She couldn't stop working now. If only she'd used her cap that time. One slip up and here she was, in the family way, and her the only mechanic to run Katherine Wheel Garage.

She swallowed the acid that rose up her throat and pulled her belt tighter across her still flat stomach, before getting back to work on the Sunbeam. At least Cassandra wasn't in a rush for the car, with Douglas's Buick to fall back on. And of course, Cassandra wasn't out and about as much these days, with Lottie to care for, preferring to stay up at the manor house most of the time. And that brought Katy's thoughts back to square one. How the hell was she going to manage when *her* baby was born? You couldn't have a cradle in a motor workshop.

She thought she might manage to keep a cup of tea down now the morning had advanced and poured some water into the kettle. Suddenly, she felt a little twitch in her belly. No more forceful than a butterfly and yet unmistakable. There it went again! New life quickening inside her. If it wasn't for the garage, it would be thrilling.

How long could she keep working? Would Jem be angry or delighted? How long before he guessed? She couldn't keep tightening her belt forever.

A car pulled up to the forecourt and she watched as Jem served the customer with petrol and oil, then smiled as they pointed to the crates of vegetables on display and he proudly handed over bunches of carrots and spring greens. After the car left, Jem popped his head through the open door. "That was Dr Benson's son, Simon. Seems he's moving back to Cheadle and joining his father in his medical practice. Nice motor, so that's another car that'll need regular services. They're keen on my veg too."

"That's good news, Jem. Old Dr Benson has been looking tired lately." She knew she ought to have seen Dr Benson about her pregnancy but she hadn't even done that yet. It would make it too official.

She felt that little flutter again and Katy flushed with guilt as Jem approached; his brown eyes smiling with love for her.

"You know, you're looking a bit peaky, my love."

"Oh, I'm fine." Katy turned away from him to light the stove. The waft of paraffin oil almost made her heave and she coughed to disguise it. "Fancy a cuppa?"

"Don't mind if I do, even though it's so hot." Jem loved his tea. "Anything I can help with?"

"Yes, actually, Jem. I need to change the tyres on

the Sunbeam. Just the ones at the back. Could you jack it up and lift them off for me?"

"Of course, I'll do it after our tea." Jem spooned tea-leaves into the pot.

Katy noticed how happy he looked, despite the heavy workload they were both shouldering. What would he do when he had to manage alone? Jem was practical and good with his un-matched hands, but he hadn't got her training, or her love of cars.

Again that embryonic butterfly moved in her belly and startled her.

"Are you sure you're alright, Katy?"

"Never better." Katy poured out the tea with an unusually unsteady hand.

Selina glanced up at the painted sign on the Nissen hut and said, with raised eyebrows, "Katherine Wheel Garage will prosper?"

"I sure hope so, Mother."

"So do I, Douglas." Selina lowered her lovely voice, so that Cassandra could barely catch her next sentence. "You see, your father has declined to help with your allowance, you know. If anything were to happen to me, or indeed you, your income from my tobacco plantations would dry up, I'm afraid."

Douglas squeezed his mother's hand, "Oh, Mother, nothing will happen to you, or me. Don't be morbid on this beautiful summer's day. Why, this time next year, Katherine Wheel Garage will be double the size and twice as busy, never fear."

Jem was serving petrol on the forecourt when they drew up. He came up to them and touched his good hand to his chestnut hair. "Good day to you all." He smiled his welcome.

"Hi, there, partner." Douglas jumped out of the driver's seat. "Mind if we show the family around, Jem? This here is my mother, Mrs Flintock, and my youngest sister, Rose."

"How do you do?" Jem extended his right hand but Cassandra noted how both the American women's eyes flicked straight to his false one.

"Oh my, did that poor boy lose his arm in the war?" Selina's whisper was still loud enough for Jem to catch it and Cassandra saw him wince.

She got out of the car swiftly and went to Jem's side. "Jem is the co-proprietor of Katherine Wheel and he also grows all these wonderful vegetables." She gave his wooden arm a friendly pat.

Jem said, "I'm only the junior partner in the garage, you know! Pleased to meet you, I'm sure."

Selina gave a brief, embarrassed nod but Rose shot out her hand and grasped Jem's in a firm handshake.

"How lovely to meet you, sir," Rose said.

Cassandra could have kissed her young sister-in-law.

"Would you like to have a look around?" Jem said, and Cassandra marvelled how Jem was as polite as ever, despite Selina recoiling from him.

"We'd love to, wouldn't we, Mother?" Rose followed him through the workshop's open door.

Discordant humming greeted them within and Cassandra smiled at the view of Katy's backside as she bent over the engine of an Austin Seven. When Katy looked up at their arrival, Cassandra noticed that her usually trim friend was looking a little plump. How odd, when Katy was working so hard. But there was no time to dwell on such interesting developments with Douglas sweeping his arm around the workshop in a grand gesture of welcome.

"Hello, Kate," Cassandra said, hoping to dispel Katy's frown.

"Afternoon, everyone. Didn't think I'd ever see you again, Mrs Flintock. Hello, Rose." Katy wiped her filthy hands on a rag that didn't look much cleaner. She had ditched her habitual tweed cap and her black curly bob was screwed up into a colourful scarf, making her look more like a gypsy boy than a married business woman.

"Good day to you, Mrs Phipps. We meet in very different circumstances to last time. I'm glad you've been able to make a fresh start in your life." Selina's emollient words softened the awkward moment of recognition, but Katy didn't look too impressed.

"Would you care for a cup of tea?" Jem said. Cassandra blessed Jem's pleasant manners for the second time.

"I can't take a break right now, Jem." Katy still looked cross. No doubt her Boston memories were even more vivid than Cassandra's.

"No, don't worry. We mustn't stop the good work," Douglas said. "I can show them around, if you've no objection?"

"Fine by me." Katy turned back to the car she'd been working on. "You know the ropes. Excuse me if I get on, won't you?"

Cassandra hurriedly herded Selina and Rose over to the bank of radio accumulators and beckoned Douglas to join them.

"Do explain about these contraptions, Douglas," Cassandra said. "I still haven't a clue as to how they work."

"Sure thing, honey." Douglas's cheerful enthusiasm filled the hiatus. Jem joined them and explained the finer points of charging the batteries for radios.

"Isn't that simply marvellous?" Selina said. "We have a radio at home now, and it makes me feel so much nearer to you, Douglas, when we hear your British news. I hope that it'll make the world a more peaceful place, if we all learn about important things at the same time, don't you?"

"I'm sure it will, Mother," Rose said, "Why shouldn't it, now they've signed the Peace Treaty?"

"Yes, I saw the picture in the paper of all those important men at that beautiful palace in Versailles," Selina said.

"There's a victory march in London next week," Douglas said. "Would you like to go visit and see the new cenotaph? I could drive you up in the Sunbeam, if you'd like?"

"I don't think so, dear. We've only a fortnight here, after all. What does cenotaph actually mean, Douglas?"

Douglas was pointing something out to Rose, so Cassandra answered for him, "It means 'empty tomb'. I see it as a memorial for dear Charles."

Selina touched her arm. "Oh, yes, your poor brother. I am sorry, my dear. I'm very grateful that darling Douglas came home safe. It's good to see him so happy."

"I'm glad you feel that way, Selina. I hope he *is* content living in my home. It's not always easy."

"I can see that," Selina gave a knowing smile, "but I have no doubt that he loves you very much and now you have sweet little Lottie, too. I just wish you weren't so far away."

"Yes, but the ocean liners are very good now. Maybe we should come over to you for a visit?" Cassandra said, more to be polite than from any desire to return to Boston.

"I think Mr Flintock needs a little more time for the dust to settle, but he'll come round, I'm sure of it." Selina said, avoiding looking at her by pretending to examine some bicycle tyres.

Cassandra felt much less sure and felt a pang for Douglas, still exiled from his home.

Katy had got behind the wheel of the Austin and was revving it loudly, creating a pall of smoke in the workshop. Selina coughed and turned her face away from the fumes.

"Kate! Can't you turn that engine off for a moment?" Douglas peered into through the driver's window.

Katy didn't turn her face to him but said, "No, got to get on."

Cassandra didn't blame her friend for her rudeness but it did pollute the atmosphere in more ways than one. "Come on, everyone, I think we've seen enough here. Let's get back in the motor and take you up on the downs. The view is marvellous from there."

Cassandra looked at Katy who resolutely ignored her.

"Why, that's a lovely idea, Cassandra," Selina replied. "I think some fresh air would be very welcome. Goodbye, dear." Selina said, very directly to Katy.

Katy finally turned her head and nodded goodbye. Any further discussion would have drowned in the noise of the engine and Cassandra ushered her in-laws out into the sunshine with considerable relief.

CHAPTER SIX
Late summer 1920

By the time the Flintocks had returned to Boston and the weather had broken back into drizzly English rain, Katy's nausea had passed. Most of the time she forgot she was carrying a child and, with the return of her energy, worked harder than ever. She bought a bigger boiler suit and stuffed rags in the belt, which muffled her outline nicely. At night, she took to wearing a voluminous nightgown and joked with a still unsuspecting Jem that the Nissen hut was cold, even in the summer. This was far from true and she sweltered in their double bed during the hot weather. Her poor sleep didn't help her temper.

Douglas was a more frequent visitor than ever, after his relatives returned to America, and Katy was finding his constant presence, as unremittingly cheerful as ever, grated on her frayed nerves. She hadn't said anything but seeing Selina Flintock had rattled her. It had taken her so long to let Jem love her properly after Fred's rape and she resented the reminder. Every time she saw Douglas now, Fred's face loomed in her mind. She had to find something for him to do, other than waft about the workshop, getting under her feet. She decided to tackle Jem about it before work one morning.

They were in the home hut, eating breakfast under its curved tin roof, now thankfully free of leaks. Through a slice of toast the size of a doorstep, smothered in her mother's strawberry jam, Katy said, "About Douglas."

"What about him?" Jem riddled the stove so the flatplate was hot enough for another slice of toast.

"Between you and me, he's a nuisance." Katy held her plate up for the fresh toast.

"You wouldn't have a garage without his money, so you'll just have to be more tolerant of the fellow." Jem cut another piece of bread for himself.

"Yes, I know that, and don't think I'm not grateful,

but he needs something to *do*. He's hopeless working on cars and even worse at accounts. By the way - will you help me work on them tonight or I'll be late paying the petrol company, and it's so much easier if you read out the figures for me?"

Jem groaned. "Do we have to do it tonight? I was hoping to dig up the last of the potatoes and make a clamp, once the garage is shut. The nights will be drawing in before we know it."

"We can't put it off any longer, Jem. If we tackle it together, we'll soon get it sorted."

"I suppose so, but I'm not sure how I'm supposed to know all the ins and outs of your business. I just keep a simple ledger for mine." Jem slathered his toast in butter and jam and took a big bite.

She decided not to rise to that but stick to the matter in hand. "I was thinking," Katy began.

"Oh, dear," Jem laughed, but quickly checked himself.

Katy found it hard to see the funny side of things at the moment. She coughed out a crumb of toast. "I was thinking, how about if we sell cars on the forecourt and get Douglas to take charge of it? He's a born salesman and has the patter to match."

"It would be a bit of a squeeze to park several cars out front, with the petrol pump in the way, especially now I've made that bay for checking the oil and tyres. And I'm not giving up the display area for the vegetables."

Katy, pleased Jem hadn't dismissed the idea outright, carried on, "I've thought about that. We could expand the forecourt on the workshop side. There's only a few bushes there and they are overgrown and need tidying up. Douglas could help. I think he's desperate for something to do."

"And who would put the money up for the cars?"

"Douglas, of course! Why don't we ask him? He's bound to turn up later today, like the proverbial bad penny."

Jem protested at that. "I think you need to remember that all your pennies come from Douglas and his mother at the moment, good or bad."

"Don't keep rubbing it in, Jem. Don't you think a forecourt of cars to sell would be a good idea for Douglas? What's the worst that could happen if we ask him? He can always say no, if he doesn't fancy it, but it would add another attraction to the garage and look good to passers-by. Whitefriars don't have any cars to sell - so it would give us the edge over them too."

This was a master-stroke, as Jem couldn't stand Mr Bartlett.

"Alright, we'll ask Douglas today, if he shows up."

"Good, I'll have another slice to celebrate."

"Glad to see you've got your appetite back, Katy. I was worried about you a few weeks ago. You were looking proper peaky."

Katy squirmed at this. "No, I'm just being greedy. I don't need another piece."

"Alright, love, but I'd rather see you with some flesh on your bones, you know."

Jem got up to sluice the dishes in their improvised sink. He'd built a water tank, covered in fine mesh to keep out the leaves, to catch the rain on the roof above their makeshift kitchen, and had reinforced the sloping roof with a flat platform to take the weight of the water. A rubber hose wriggled its way through the ceiling and ended in a tap in the sink. Katy blessed his ingenuity every day she didn't have to ferry to the river and back with a couple of pails, as they'd had to do in the first months of living in the Nissen hut. She had been so excited to have their own place she hadn't minded then, but now she was too busy to waste precious minutes lugging water back and forth.

She looked around their home. They'd made it pretty cosy overall, well, Jem had. She'd concentrated on digging out an inspection pit in the workshop and spending Douglas's sponsorship money on tools, equipment, and most expensive of all, the petrol generator for the electricity supply.

Agnes, her mother, had made curtains for the windows and her dad, Bert Beagle, had lent them a couple of horses from the manor, where he worked as head coachman, to help clear their patch. Jem had built an internal stud wall to separate their bedroom from their living quarters and had made a big wardrobe along one of the galvanised steel walls. He'd even constructed a little privy in the garden, over a deeply dug soak-away. They sprinkled potash from the fire to keep it sweet. Disused tea chests served as cupboards, and they still had the handsome dresser Jem had made in their courting days. Cassandra's wedding gift of blue and white china shone from its shelves. They had no easy chairs, but then, they had no time to sit on them.

Katy loved her strange home, but it was no place for a baby. "Jem, I've been meaning to say something," she turned around to find him gone. Maybe it was just as well.

She went into their bedroom and gazed at her reflection in the chipped mirror above the old washstand. Katy's face stared back. To her critical eyes, it appeared fat as well as tired. She looked puffy around the eyes, and definitely on the plump side. Her breasts had started to swell, as well as her belly, and it couldn't be long before Jem noticed. She was astonished he hadn't guessed already, with no monthlies to regulate her cycle but she'd always taken care to be discreet about them, thank goodness, and she knew he hated it when she looked thin. Agnes had been looking at her through shrewd eyes lately. You could never get much past her, but surprisingly, her mother hadn't said a word.

She shook her head free of worries and bound it up in her bright red scarf, so her black curls wouldn't get caught in any engine parts. It was the only way to keep it clean too, which was important, as washing it in the Nissen hut was a right performance of boiling kettles and filling buckets.

Katy did up her belt, horrified to have to move it on another notch, and went to the workshop next door. True to form, Douglas turned up before she'd finished servicing a motorbike she was working on, and bounced up to her with a smacking great kiss.

"You look positively blooming today, Mrs Phipps!"

Bloom translated into plump, Katy supposed, and she scowled at him. "I've a proposal to make to you, Mr Flintock."

"I'm already married." Douglas twirled his gloves in the air. "Sorry, taken."

Katy couldn't scowl at that and she grinned at him, "Not that sort of proposal, silly."

"I should have known. I am dashed," Douglas said, stooping to kneel at her feet.

"Get up Douglas, you daft bugger," Katy laughed, "What would Lady Amelia say if you went back to the manor covered in engine oil?"

That swiped the smile right off Douglas's handsome face and he got up.

Chastened, Katy said, "Let me call Jem and we'll have a chat over a brew."

"I'm intrigued, and will confine myself to the humble task of putting the kettle on, so I don't break anything. I know my place in the scheme of things." Douglas disappeared into the office at the back of the workshop.

Katy downed tools and went to find Jem. They had rigged up an enormous bell at the back of the Nissen huts. It connected to a pull chain on the forecourt for customers to ring. This had been a major breakthrough for Jem, who was now free to work on his market garden until called to serve petrol. Jem was harvesting onions and laying them out on an old bed frame to dry.

"Fancy a cuppa, love?" Katy called.

Jem straightened up and rubbed his back. "I'd love one." He came over to the outside water trough to wash his hand, stained yellow by the onion skins.

"Douglas is here. I thought we might have that chat about him selling cars on the forecourt."

"Rightio, but I can only spare five minutes."

They went into the workshop together, to find Douglas setting out a tea tray with mugs and teapot.

"Let's sit in the sunshine, out the back, shall we?" Katy said.

"What about any customers who might turn up?" Douglas set the tray down on the old oil drum that served as their garden table. "Shall I be mother?" he added, making Katy's conscience tweak unpleasantly.

Katy explained about the new bell then hitched her upturned petrol can seat nearer the table, to hide her growing bulk. She sneaked a glance at her husband, but Jem was looking at the vegetable patch with a satisfied smile and didn't notice.

They sipped their tea in companionable silence before Jem spoke up. "Katy's had an idea about the business, Douglas."

"Another one? You sure have a resourceful wife, Jem. This bell, for instance - it makes your lives so much easier. I'm glad to see you taking a break from your hard work now and then."

"Thanks, but it was Jem's idea to put the bell here, so he can work in his garden to his heart's desire. No, my idea is to branch out a bit with the garage and sell cars from the forecourt." Katy sipped her tea.

"Now there's a thought," Douglas said. "I'm all ears, boss."

Katy laughed at his unquestioning enthusiasm. "How would you fancy being the salesman, Doug?"

"And the financier yet again, don't forget!" Jem chipped in.

"You mean, I'd buy and sell the cars myself?" Douglas asked, draining his mug.

"That's right." Katy nodded. "You could sell the leaves from the trees, you could. You're a natural, I reckon."

Without a moment's hesitation, Douglas sat more upright and smiled. "I would love to."

A mere two weeks later, at the beginning of September, three cars sat on the newly cleared ground next to Katherine Wheel Garage's forecourt; two small Austins and one large Bullnose Morris.

Douglas and Jem had removed the bushes in record time off the scrap of land on the left-hand-side of the workshop and a new, garish sign adorned the wall, shouting:

"The Katherine Wheel Garage - Agent for all leading makes of Motors and Cycles"

eclipsing Jem's smaller one saying,

"Phipps's Seasonal Vegetables, Fruit and Eggs for sale
- fresh from the garden."

Jem hadn't been too pleased about it when Douglas had hammered the sign into place while he was working in the garden. Jem had whisked his down and put it in a more prominent place on the forecourt. Customers wouldn't miss the vegetable display now. Katy thought she might add another underneath the main sign on the front, emphasising repairs, just to illustrate their diversity, but maybe not in such big letters as the one about car sales.

The expansion gave her mixed feelings. She was proud they were branching out, after all, it was her idea, but her pregnancy might scotch all their plans. She still hadn't told Jem and had left it so long, she now dreaded confessing the truth. He was bound to be angry that she had concealed it from him, so she just kept putting it off, pleading fatigue when he wanted to make love. She

47

pushed the problem to the back of her mind, where it resided permanently, and went to see Douglas.

"If you polish that Morris much more Douglas, it'll blind our customers with its shine!"

"Hi there, Kate." Douglas didn't stop his feverish rubbing. "She sure looks good, don't she?"

"Yes, she does," Katy said, truthfully.

"Hey, Kate," Douglas looked up at last, "you don't fancy a spin up the road in her do you? I'll have to take any prospective customers for test drives and I want to get familiar with the controls - you know, see what she can do."

Katy looked back at the garage. No-one was about in the middle of the day. Everyone would be having their lunch, whether in the fields or the cottages. There would never be a better time to take a little break. Jem was out the back, harvesting runner beans, if anyone rang the bell for attention.

"Just for ten minutes or so," Douglas wheedled.

Katy laughed, "Oh, go on, then. As long as it is only for ten minutes."

"Great! Even you Phipps's can't work all the time. Hop in, boss, and I'll crank her up."

Katy climbed into the passenger seat and revelled in the new smell of the car, a mixture of leather and her favourite perfume of petrol. The car started easily and Douglas clambered past her to the driver's seat.

"Isn't she a beaut?" Douglas revved the engine. "Did you notice the spare wheel and petrol can on the running board - isn't that a good idea? Carries two whole gallons, that gas can. Means I don't have a driver's door, but there's so much room in the cab, I don't think that matters, do you?"

"I'm not sure, Douglas. If I was travelling beside you all the time and had to get out to let you in, and it was raining and I had my best hat on, I would be pretty annoyed."

Douglas's eager face fell. "I hadn't thought of that."

Katy laughed, "But you'll think of some easy way to talk customers around it, of that I'm sure."

Douglas laughed with her, as they turned out of the forecourt and on to the London Road. The road was flat and straight here - a real advantage for the garage signs to be seen from a distance, Katy always thought, but now, she quailed at the way Douglas accelerated along its length.

She resolved to say nothing, guessing that Douglas would be sensitive to criticism at the start of his new enterprise, and willed herself into silence. She gripped the edge of the leather seat for support as the first bend approached.

"Let's take her up on the hill, shall we?" Douglas looked sideways at her.

"Only if you keep your eyes on the road," Katy said, as another car approached in the middle of the road and Douglas had to swerve at the last minute.

He just laughed as he corrected the position of the car and, after sticking his arm out to signal, turned off towards the downland road that rose high up above the manor grounds.

It was good to get out of the workshop, after all. Katy enjoyed the view from up the hill. She'd always loved coming up here, especially when she and Jem had lived in the depths of the valley at Lower Cheadle, before the war. Up here on the downs, the chestnut trees were already turning brown and a few dried leaves swirled across the windscreen. Raindrops joined them and Douglas looked down at the dashboard to find the chamois leather to wipe it.

"Where is the damn thing?"

Katy pointed at it, dismayed he hadn't slowed down first. Neither of them saw the sheep as it jumped down from the Cotswold stone wall and stood, chewing, in the middle of the road.

Katy looked up first. "Douglas! Watch out!" She screamed, before stopping her noise with her fingers,

49

biting them to keep herself quiet, knowing how slow the brakes were. They'd never be able to stop quickly enough to avoid a collision.

Douglas slammed on the brakes and the Morris slewed into a slow skid right across the road, narrowly missing the sheep, who skipped smartly out of the way in the nick of time.

The engine stalled, as the big car shuddered to a halt, and the only sound was the bleating of the sheep, as it clambered back over the wall to rejoin its flock. The silence was broken by the patter of the rain on the bonnet of the car and the wind finding little cracks in the bodywork to whistle through.

Katy's heartbeats almost drowned out the other sounds. With a rush of guilt, she felt her baby move and, for the first time, experienced it as a separate life; one she should be protecting. Finding her voice, she turned to Douglas and yelled at him, "You idiot, Doug! We could have been killed! You were going far too fast. If you drive our customers like that, you'll put them right off, or even *bump* them off. For goodness sake, what were you thinking?"

Douglas held both hands up in supplication. "Forgive me, Kate, please. I'm so sorry. Are you okay?"

Katy put her hands on her belly. They were shaking, but whether from fear for herself or her unborn child, she couldn't tell.

Douglas looked down at her hands, instinctively curved around the swell of her stomach, and blenched. "Kate! Are you? You're not...expecting, are you?"

Katy's resolve broke and she burst out, "Yes, yes I am, Doug, and no-one knows. Please, please don't say anything, will you? Not even to Jem?"

"But Kate, doesn't Jem know? What about the garage?"

"Damn it, Doug! Do you think I haven't been worried sick about the garage? I don't know what we're going to do. We owe money all over the place and I'm trying to send out the bills, as well as do all the workshop work, so it's crucial I keep going. It's only our first year! I didn't mean to get pregnant, but it well, it just happened."

"Oh, I know how these things just happen, believe me, Kate." Douglas stared out of the windscreen at the rain, now driving hard across the chalk fields. "Listen, you have to tell Jem. There'll be a way around this, somehow."

"I'm not sure, Douglas. I've been ignoring it, like a fool, just concentrating on work, getting things established and hoping it'll go away but just now, when we almost crashed, I realised I have a responsibility to this child, like it or not."

"Yes, my dear, you do. Come on, let's get you home." Douglas went to squeeze past her, but Katy got out, and stood in the road, watching him pull the hood up over the wet seats before cranking the engine back into life. She needed some fresh air. She gulped it down, rain and all, and felt better for its bracing effect. Douglas was right. She could no longer put off telling Jem about the baby.

How they would cope, she had no idea, but cope they must, somehow.

CHAPTER SEVEN
Late summer 1920

Jem picked up the heavy basket. It was chock full of carrots and he sluiced them off in a bucket of water. My word, they did look good, considering how new the ground was. The fallow earth was obliging him with an abundant crop. He sloshed the mud off them and went into the kitchen to fetch some string to bunch them, ready for display on the forecourt.

He knew he had some somewhere. Where had he put it? He rummaged in the tea chest by the back door and then stopped to listen. What was that dripping noise?

He looked across at the kitchen and was horrified to see that his improvised tap had given way. A waterfall, flowing freely from the sink, was cascading into a rapidly enlarging lake across the floor. The valve must have gone - but how to stop it? The water tank on the roof was full to the brim with rainwater. September had brought nothing but rain.

Jem strode to the sink and tried to bung the tap with the dishcloth but the force of the water immediately spat it out. He'd have to empty the tank and cut off the supply. He went out to the back garden and wrenched the ladder from the apple tree he'd hoped to harvest that afternoon, shouting, "Katy! Kate! Come quickly!"

She couldn't have heard him but he didn't have time to waste looking for her. He grabbed the ladder and leant it against the home hut, below the water tank. Before mounting it, he ran to the potato patch and picked up the garden hose, detaching it from the other water tank he'd built next to the makeshift potting shed. He grabbed a brick and shoved it into his waistband. Goodness, that was heavy! He hoped it wouldn't slip down and bruise his private parts. Then he coiled up the hose with his good hand, while he ran back to the ladder and scrambled up it, steadying himself with his wooden one and trying not to overbalance from the weight of the brick.

He had a hell of a job to pull the wire mesh off the top of the tank. He'd made too good a job of securing it, but eventually it came free. He placed the end of the hose in the bottom of the tank and carefully drew out the brick from inside his trousers, which had dangled precariously close to his groin, and placed it over the hose, making sure he didn't obstruct the end. Then he descended, letting the hose out carefully, as he went down each rung of the ladder. At the bottom, he took the other end of the rubber pipe and, taking a big breath, sucked as much air as he could out of it, before plunging it into the safe receptacle of the water trough at the back of the workshop. Fortunately, this trough was almost empty, as Douglas had virtually drained it, washing his beloved new cars. It took a couple of goes before he could create enough of a vacuum to make it draw, but eventually the siphon worked and he watched with satisfaction as water began to ooze out.

"Katy!" he yelled again. "Kate! Come and see to the other end of the hosepipe. Katy! We've got a flood!"

No dark head appeared covered in a cheery scarf. Where was she? He ran back to the ladder and clambered up to check on the other end of the pipe. The brick was choking the flow so he lifted it off and held the pipe there. Instantly twice as much water gushed into the trough at the bottom. Jem sighed with relief as the level in the tank dropped more quickly. He'd just have to stay and hold the damn thing. He looked over at the forecourt. There was Douglas's tourer. Why didn't *he* come to his aid?

He pondered over the conundrum, and stared at the workshop, still expecting Katy to appear at any moment. Then another car parked up next to the petrol pump and the driver got out and rang the bell. Jem watched in impotent despair as the woman, smartly dressed and exactly the sort of customer they wanted to attract, paced up and down the forecourt, glancing now and again at her watch. She rang the bell again, really loudly. When the clanging stopped, Jem shouted at her. The woman looked around at the sound of his voice but didn't look up to the roof. It was so frustrating! And where were Katy and Douglas?

He couldn't leave go of the hosepipe until the tank was entirely drained, or the whole hut would be under water inside. He hollered again at the woman but it turned into a curse, as he saw her shake her head and get back in her car. He turned awkwardly on the ladder and watched her drive away, towards London and Whitefriars Garage. Then he spotted the new area of forecourt, where the cars for sale were parked. Only two Austins? Aha, so Katy and Douglas must have gone out in the Morris.

Damn it! They could have told him! Jem could do nothing except watch the water drain out of the roof tank and recite every swear word he'd learned in the army.

The water was draining fast now; gravity from the long drop helping it to gather pace as it spilled into the water trough. Jem had to hold the pipe low in the last bit of water, stretching right across from the ladder to do so. It wasn't very safe but it beat mopping it up from the kitchen floor.

The sound of the Morris returning made him jump and the ladder lurched dangerously to the right. He let go of the pipe and clutched the side of the water tank, just in time to stop the ladder from falling. His heart was going like the clappers as he climbed down. He'd never been so glad to touch solid ground.

When Katy and Douglas strolled nonchalantly around the corner of the workshop, he could have knocked their heads together.

"Where the hell have you been?"

Katy and Douglas stopped in their tracks, looking shocked at his outburst. Jem didn't usually shout at anyone but he'd never felt so infuriated before.

"There's been a bloody flood and where were you two? Out gallivanting in the new Morris! I've been up the ruddy ladder, on my own, trying to organise both ends of the blasted hosepipe single-handed! Didn't it occur to

54

either of you to tell me you were going out? Hmm?"

Katy looked quite white, and Douglas scarcely less so.

"What do you mean, there's been a flood?" Katy said.

"Don't take it out on Kate, there's a good feller," Douglas said, at the same time.

Jem shook his head at them and said, "Follow me," as he went running back to their home.

He glanced back at the others, still too angry to trust himself with more words. Douglas had broken into a trot behind him but Katy followed more slowly, still looking very pale. Jem faced forwards again and reached the hut before either of them. The kitchen was in chaos. The rug they'd made over the winter from rags was a sodden mess, enamel dishes that had been stacked in the sink floated in the dirty water that lapped around the bottoms of the tea chests, themselves staining upwards with damp.

Katy stood behind him, and he heard her whisper, "Oh, no! My lovely kitchen," and uncharacteristically, she burst into tears.

That made Jem madder than ever. He turned to his wife and said, his voice harsh, "We don't need more bloody water! This is no time for tears - grab a mop - some old rags, towels - anything - and let's try and limit the damage."

Douglas put his arm around Katy. "Don't cry, dearest Kate. Come on, you sit down in the bedroom and I'll help Jem."

Jem squared up to Douglas. "Unhand my wife. She is perfectly capable of mopping a floor. What's the matter with you, Kate? This is an emergency! Don't go all missish on me now!"

Douglas put his hand out to Jem. "Jem, don't shout at Kate. It's not her fault, you see..."

"No, Douglas! Don't say any more." Katy grabbed a towel, threw it on the floor and knelt down to soak up the water.

"But," Douglas said, "you shouldn't be doing that, Kate, in your..."

"I said, shut-up, Douglas!" Katy picked up the dripping towel and went outside to wring it out.

"Let me do that." Douglas took it from her.

Jem watched the pantomime in a perplexed daze. Did Douglas fancy Katy? Had they been out in the car to get some privacy? What was going on?

"Douglas, help me move these tea chests outside, would you?" he said.

Douglas left Katy at the door and joined him. The two men heaved the tea chest containing their saucepans and dragged it, through the water, to the back door.

Katy said, "I'm going for a bucket."

"Okay, Kate." Douglas looked more concerned than ever.

"Douglas, what the hell is going on between you and my wife?" Jem was sweating as he pushed the chest along the back wall of the hut.

"Nothing's going on, Jem." But Douglas looked guilty.

"Why did you sneak off in the car just now? Needed a moment alone, did you?" Jem went back into the kitchen for another chest. "One wife not enough for you, then?"

"What? No! Jem, you've got the wrong idea, pal."

"Don't you pal me."

Katy came back with the bucket and began mopping the floor and squeezing the water into the pail.

Douglas turned to her. "I know this is an emergency, Kate, but I think you need a moment alone with your husband. He seems to think we're having an affair."

Kate looked up from her mopping, her mouth hung open in surprise. "Oh, Jem! How could you think that, after all we've been through?"

Jem was sweeping the water out now, brushing great brown waves out of the door. It was difficult to hold the broom with his wooden hand and it kept slipping, making him crosser than ever. It didn't help his temper when Douglas took over, wrenching the broom from him with one competent, fully fingered hand and shoving him in the back with the other.

"What are you doing, Douglas?" Jem felt like hitting him.

"I'll do this, the worst of the water has gone now. Go and talk to your wife outside."

"Don't you tell me what to do in my own home!" Jem shouted.

But Katy took him by his good hand and pulled him into the garden. "Jem, please, love. Doug's right. I need to tell you something."

Douglas bundled them out with his broom and carried on sweeping. Katy drew Jem aside and took him to their improvised garden chairs, made from petrol cans.

"Sit down, Jem, dearest." Katy's voice and eyes were soft, pleading almost.

Completely bewildered by the morning's strange events, Jem sat. He ran his hand across his eyes, suddenly weary.

"Jem, there's something important I've been meaning to tell you, but I didn't know how."

"What?"

"I should have told you long since. I've been so worried about it."

"Worried about what? Damn it, Kate, spit it out. We need to get back to the hut and mop that floor."

"I'm pregnant."

Jem was speechless. Precious mopping time slipped by unnoticed. He looked at her, registering her expanded waistline - how could he have missed it? Now he knew, he could see the difference. He felt duped and stupid that he hadn't already guessed that the woman he loved and lived with was carrying his baby and he knew nothing about it. Then he looked at the workshop, at the market garden, at Douglas emptying the bucket of dirty flood water on to the cabbage patch and then back at his wife again. A baby!

When they had all *this* to deal with?

CHAPTER EIGHT
Christmas Eve 1920

Jem could swear the autumn of 1920 flew by at a faster rate than normal. The garage continued to increase its business and, to Jem's delight, customers often combined buying petrol with their vegetables and eggs and a steady stream of regulars was building up trade nicely. Everything was going to plan. Apart from the baby. With Katy's pregnancy already advanced by the time he knew about it, Katy's belly seemed to swell at alarming speed.

Jem remembered how he'd taken the shock of her news into the garden and dug for England while he'd thought it through. They now had more reason than ever to make a go of things, and despite all his worries, he was thrilled at becoming a father again, but he wanted his child to be born into prosperity and independence, not yoked to the estate like every previous generation.

If the garage failed, and it relied so much on Katy's skills, they *would* be back to begging for a job off the manor and he wasn't going to let that happen. Jem had struggled to find a solution and had many a broken night until he talked it over with his father, George, the head gardener at Cheadle Manor.

"The way I see it, lad, it's just the same as gardening, running a business," George had said, over a pint in the pub.

"How do you make that out, Dad?"

"It's like this - you plant a seed, right?"

Jem nodded and his Dad continued, "Then, you waters and feeds it and it grows. You keep it clear of weeds, like, and hey presto - you're rewarded with a harvest. Can't see that running a garage is so different."

"It's completely different, Dad! Cars don't grow like plants. They're complicated things and changing all the time with all the new inventions coming along and you can't fiddle with those contraptions if you've got wooden fingers."

"That's as maybe, son, and you'll need to train someone up to do the mechanics, while Katy's busy with the baby, but the business itself is no different to organising a garden. Do you know of any youngsters who might be interested in an apprenticeship?"

Jem racked his brains. "Billy Threadwell's always hanging around, asking Katy which bit's what in her engines."

"There you are then." George took a slug of beer. "You can't tell me Billy wouldn't be glad to get out from under Martha's eagle eye. He's got his own transport too, on his pushbike. Martha's got young Susan coming along. She's about to finish school and could take over the post round."

"You may be on to something, Dad." Jem drained his pint. "Billy does seem interested and I suppose if I tackle running the garage as if I was tending the garden, bringing things on, pruning the bits that aren't working, nurturing its growth, maybe I could do the business side. To be honest, I've left most of that to Kate while I was building things inside and out but that's pretty much done now."

"There you are then, Jem. Let's have another pint to celebrate."

Billy Threadwell had jumped at the chance of learning the ropes at the garage and Katy declared him a real boon as her pregnancy advanced. Jem smiled as he recalled how eager Billy was. He hadn't been a quick learner, more like a slow and steady one, but his enthusiasm more than made up for it. Now, with the winter weather halting everything, including all the traffic, Billy was taking a Christmas holiday, and a well earned one at that. Business had stayed brisk and Jem had taken real pride in balancing the books and found the extra wages for Billy without too much trouble. Getting more involved in Katy's enterprise had had an unexpected effect on Jem. He

59

too became infected with the excitement of helping new drivers escape to the freedom of the road for the first time; tasting the thrill of the world opening up in ways no-one could have imagined before the war and witnessing the boundaries stretch far beyond the narrow confines of Cheadle Manor. And he loved it, which really surprised him.

Katy, freed up from the workshop, had spent more time with Jem on the accounts and they now had a system that ran like clockwork. Douglas had played his part too and the profits from the car sales had boosted their joint income, as Douglas insisted on sharing them with the garage.

And now, it seemed to Jem that he'd barely had time to adjust to the situation, but this hushed Christmas Eve found him leaning on his bedroom doorway, gazing at his wife and baby son, both asleep in bed. No sound disturbed the peace on this crystalline winter's day. Not even a bird sang outside in the white, frozen world. Agnes and the midwife had left, driven in the gig by Bert, through snow too deep for any car. Even then, Jem had to push the gig up the slight incline of the garage forecourt to help Larkspur and Chestnut, the two old estate horses, gain a purchase on the ice.

His son, Albert George Phipps, had arrived promptly and the longed-for help had only just appeared in time for his delivery. Jem's second child had come into the world easily and Mrs Armstrong, the midwife, had congratulated Katy on her calm labour. Jem looked at his wife's face. A finger of winter sun played across it; the shaft of light more blue than yellow, reflecting off the silent snow outside, where huge drifts hid the paraphernalia of a working garden, softening the outlines of the petrol cans and buckets that littered it into graceful white sculptures.

In repose, Katy looked as serene as the pure white snow. Lately, the worry of work and childbearing had etched the first lines on her young face and Jem had been reminded of how fleeting life was for them all. Having survived the war, he'd begun to feel immortal. Now, through this tiny child, their lives would carry on, if God spared him. Jem shivered, remembering Florence.

He wanted to kiss his wife awake, have her share this moment of clarity in the short, bright winter afternoon. The daylight would soon fade but this child brought hope of a future. He'd work harder than ever to secure it. There had never been anyone else for Jem but his beautiful Kate. Her eyelashes swept a black band across her flushed cheeks as she slept away the effort of childbirth. Albert lay in the crook of her arm. He looked exhausted too, but healthy.

A healthy, strong son.

Jem slipped down to his haunches with his back against the wall. He couldn't stop staring at his little family; didn't want to ever lose sight of them. He'd been so angry when Katy had told him about her already advanced pregnancy, deeply hurt that she hadn't confided in him. Not having had the usual nine months to come to terms with the enormity of it, he still needed time to adjust.

Now, in the peace of this sacred moment, with no mechanical noise to disturb his thoughts, Jem allowed the arrival of this child, this second chance, to sink in. He looked again at his son.

Brand new, not a mark on him.

A black wisp of hair curled into a question mark on the top of the baby's tender head. He would have some questions to ask alright, wouldn't he? But Jem would spare him the truth. Let that disastrous war, that had stolen his uncle Albert, his namesake, never be mentioned. He'd make sure this child knew nothing of that ugliness; the pointlessness of politicians; the depths to which people could sink. No, this child's life would be filled with light. Pristine light, just like that reflecting off the virgin snow outside that hushed the cacophony this new century seemed unable to live without. Jem had to believe that the 'great war' had been the war to end all wars; had to believe that this tiny baby would not live to fight another.

And with the help of their rich friends, they had built two businesses for young Albert to inherit. God bless Douglas. Jem had wanted to name the baby after him, knowing they'd have no garage or home without his and Cassandra's patronage. But Katy had insisted on naming her child after her lost brother and both their fathers.

The baby stirred and began to mew for food. Jem stood up and gently prised him from Katy, who slept on. Jem wandered around the Nissen hut, crooning "Silent Night" to his son. Albert opened his eyes and stared solemnly back at his father, as if registering his face in his mint-fresh memory. Then, lulled by Jem's soothing voice, he slipped back into a doze, safe in the cradle of his father's only arm.

CHAPTER NINE
Summer 1923

How time flew, Cassandra thought, watching her daughter's first real tantrum and wishing she was still young enough to be put back to bed.

"I want to see Al!" Lottie drummed a tattoo on the nursery carpet with her little feet. Cassandra didn't know what to do with her daughter in this mood. Nanny Morgan had taken a rare holiday to visit her relatives in Wales, her first since Lottie had been born three years ago, so she had no-one to turn to for advice. Should she give in? She knew Nanny would never do so and always counselled her to hold a strict line with her spirited child.

Lottie shouted again, "I want to see Al at the grudge!"

Cassandra willed Nanny's Welsh lilting voice into her head and pictured how she would handle the storm, grateful when the call was answered.

"We'll go to the garage only if you stop shouting and start behaving yourself. If you carry on like this, we're not going anywhere."

Lottie threw her spinning top across to the door where it crashed against the solid oak, making a tremendous noise. The door opened to reveal her grandmother.

"Whatever is going on?" Lady Amelia's hand clenched tight on the brass doorknob.

Lottie burst into tears and pitched straight into her grandmother's skirts, sobbing, "Mummy won't let me go to see my friend! Mummy is horrid, Grandma. Tell Mummy I can go?"

Lady Amelia stroked Lottie's wayward hair and spoke in the soft voice she reserved for her grand-daughter. "Now then, child. There's no need for these tears."

Lady Amelia pinched Lottie's chin and tipped up her red face. She flicked out her lace handkerchief and

63

wiped the child's streaming eyes, before looking over her head to Cassandra.

"Honestly, Cassandra," Lady Amelia's tone was now quite different. "Nanny has only been gone two days and look at the mess you're making of things. The child is quite distraught."

"She's just determined to get her own way," Cassandra began.

"But if she wants to pay a social call, surely that's a good thing?" Lady Amelia rose awkwardly from her stooping posture by leaning on her cane. "Who is this friend Charlotte so wants to see?"

Lottie piped up, "Al at the grudge."

"Who?" Lady Amelia said.

"She means young Albert Phipps, Katy and Jem's two year-old." Cassandra restrained her hands from slapping both her nearest relatives.

"Phipps? Surely you're not allowing her to consort with working class people? It's bad enough that Douglas spends every living minute down at that vulgar garage, without letting my grand-daughter become embroiled in the family." Lady Amelia dropped Lottie's hand, as if it was suddenly dirty.

That decided Cassandra. "Right, young lady, if you are so determined to go, we'll make that social call after all."

"That's it, countermand my wishes the minute I utter them." Lady Amelia sniffed. "Mark my words, Cassandra, if you let Charlotte mingle with working people of a different social standing, she will not turn out well. Who knows where such an alliance may lead in the future?"

But Cassandra was too busy bundling Lottie into her outdoor coat to answer and Lottie, as was her habit, had gone from screaming tyrant to a biddable cherub, now she had her way.

They found Katy in the workshop, even though it was a Sunday. She was working on Douglas's Buick and

Lottie's father was lounging in the office, reading the papers and smoking a cigarette. Cassandra was struck at how relaxed her husband looked. He never wore that expression up at the manor. A little knell sounded in her heart at his oblivious absorption in the newspaper. He looked very at home.

A gentle humming noise emanated from under the car and two boots, small ones, protruded from under the chassis. Neither could have heard Cassandra's car draw up and she almost felt as if she was intruding on a domestic scene, one in which she had no part.

Lottie broke the moment by running to her father and demanding where Al was. Douglas's face immediately broke into a grin of welcome and he scooped her up and threw her into the air, even though she was quite heavy these days. She might only be three years old, but Lottie was a sturdy little girl and Cassandra tried not to compare her to her grandmother, whom she feared the child closely resembled, in more ways than one.

"Where is Al?" Lottie demanded, once she had been returned to terra firma.

"He's out back, with his Pa," Douglas said.

Katy slewed out from under the car on a board on wheels and came upright in one swift and graceful movement. Cassandra supposed being a mechanic kept one fit. Katy had lost her baby curves in record time and now Al was a toddler she looked like she'd never borne a child at all.

Cassandra leaned in to kiss Katy on the cheek.

"Working on a Sunday, Kate?"

"Blame your spouse." Katy winked and nodded at Douglas.

"You wanted to do it!" Douglas protested.

"*Me* want *Al*!" Lottie tugged at her father's hand.

"Then we'd better go find him." Douglas laughed and took Lottie out through the back door and into the workshop yard.

Squeals of delight told Cassandra that Al and Lottie

65

had been united.

Katy smiled at her. "Seems the two angels have found each other."

"My daughter is no angel," Cassandra said, with conviction. "Cigarette?" She'd never been able to give up the habit, since she starting smoking in the war.

"Thanks." Katy accepted the packet and took out a cigarette.

Cassandra flicked a flame at her cigarette and passed the lighter to Katy. "Shall we join them in your backyard and watch the children playing while we smoke them?"

"Yes, I wouldn't mind a break. Your husband is a slave-driver."

"Ooh, I wouldn't use that expression, if you ever go back to Boston." Cassandra immediately regretted what she'd said, but Katy seemed to have forgotten all about Fred Stavely's attack on her in America and simply laughed.

"Douglas wants me to tweak the engine on the Buick so he can go a bit faster. It's all in the tuning, you see. I have to get the mixture just right with the ratio of air to fuel. Even then, it can run too hot, so I have to adjust the carburetor. To get it spot on, the spark has to ignite the mixture at the precise moment the fuel gets into the cylinder and the piston has to be in exactly the right place." Katy flopped down on the bench that had replaced the old cans for seats.

Cassandra didn't even attempt to follow Katy's mechanical explanation. "Douglas is as mad on cars as you are. He spends more time down here at the garage than up at the manor."

Katy looked quickly back at her friend. "Do you mind?"

"No, not really. I just want him to be happy. I don't find it easy living with my parents and I know he certainly doesn't. No, I'm glad he's found a role here, with you and Jem, selling the cars, these last couple of years. It's given him a purpose he sorely lacked and he's pleased that his investment is paying off. Lord knows, no-one could have worked harder to make a go of things than you two."

"Thanks, that's generous of you, Cass." Katy stubbed out her cigarette butt with her steel-capped boot. "But don't you miss him? I know you're still shouldering most of the burden of keeping the estate running."

"To be honest, I get a real kick out of it. We're both independently minded women aren't we?" Cassandra laughed. "I quite like having my own way, a bit like my mother and, for that matter, my daughter."

Lottie was stamping her foot again, this time at Jem, who was trying to explain there wasn't enough room for two in Al's little cart. Katy and Jem had made it out of an old pram. It was propelled by the occupant's feet through a gap in the pallet boards that made up the miniature chassis. Al adored it.

Cassandra took pity and went to help Jem. Douglas wasn't giving much assistance but laughing his head off at his daughter's antics.

Katy gave a wave and shouted, "I'm going back to wrestle with the tuning of the tourer. Good luck with those two!" She disappeared back inside.

Cassandra joined her husband, who now had a wriggling Lottie in his arms declaring - it was her turn - at the top of her young, but very strong, voice.

"That will do, Lottie!" Cassandra felt bold with two male supporters to back her up. "It's Al's cart and we're at Al's house and you are his guest, so you must behave and wait politely."

"Your Mom's right, Lottie." Douglas let his daughter go with a yelp of pain. He clutched his shin. "You little..." Douglas turned to Cassandra. "She kicked me!"

Cassandra tried really hard not to laugh. She didn't want Lottie to think it was funny but it was hard to resist smiling at Douglas's outraged face.

She schooled hers into a stern mask and caught

Lottie by the hand. "If you can't behave properly, Charlotte Flintock-Smythe, I'm taking you straight home."

Lottie's lower lip protruded and started to wobble. Cassandra lost patience. "And don't start crying again to get your own way, because it won't work."

Cassandra looked to Douglas to back her up but his face was turned away as he rubbed his shin and Jem was hanging back with a look that said, 'she's not my daughter'. It was young Al who rescued her. He shifted across his seat in the little cart and tugged at the hem of Lottie's coat.

"Lottie sit," Al said.

Lottie immediately squeezed into the narrow space and kissed Al on his cheek. Still serious, Al pushed the car along with his tiny feet and steered away from the silent audience of adults.

"Well! It seems a two year old has more sense than either of you!" Cassandra said.

"That young man has great presence of mind, Jem." Douglas was still wincing as he practised putting weight on his bruised leg.

"Agnes says he's an old soul." Jem smiled fondly at his son, now driving around the yard with Lottie happily paddling her feet through the gap in the boards beside him.

"Is Agnes still minding him during the week?" Cassandra asked.

"Yes, but she says she's finding it hard to lift him now and he gets bored at West Lodge."

"They get on very well, those two. Would Al like to come up to the manor sometimes and Nanny could look after the pair of them together? I dare say it would be easier than managing Lottie on her own."

"I'm sure he'd love that, but shouldn't we help pay you some of her wages for doing it?"

Douglas chimed in, "No point, Jem, if it means Kate can carry on full-time in the garage. That's worth more than Nanny's wages."

Cassandra wondered for the umpteenth time why Katy never showed much interest in looking after her son. They all knew Katy was obsessed with cars but Cassandra couldn't bear to go too long without seeing Lottie, however annoying she might be. She wandered into the workshop.

Katy was now sitting behind the wheel, revving the engine. Cassandra coughed at the fumes and got in beside her.

"How's it going?" Cassandra said.

"Can't you hear the difference?"

"Frankly? No!" Cassandra laughed.

"How strange. Hear that throatiness? I've tuned it so that slightly more petrol comes through the carburettor. Gives her much more poke."

"Right. I suppose that's what Douglas wanted?"

"Oh, yes, proper speed merchant, your old man." Katy let the engine idle, her head on one side, listening.

"Douglas and I were just talking about your handsome son," Cassandra ventured. "We were wondering if Al would like to spend some time in the nursery with Lottie - with Nanny Morgan in charge, of course. What do you think? Jem said he's getting a bit big for your mother."

"I'm sure he'd love that."

"And you wouldn't miss him?"

"Me? Why should I miss him? He's with Mum most of the time, and you're right, she's not getting any younger."

"It's just that," Cassandra hesitated to broach the delicate subject. "Well, it's just that I love spending time with Lottie, even when she's being a madam. I'm having another baby in December and I can't wait to hold another little one in my arms. Don't you wish you had more time with Al? He's such a lovely little boy - so sweet-natured. He's a good influence on Lottie, so I have my selfish reasons for my suggestion."

"Congrats on the new baby but I don't share your

69

maternal instincts." Katy cut the engine and turned to look at her friend. "You see, I was besotted with my first little girl, Florence. When she died, I almost lost my mind. I'm scared to love Al too much. What if I lost him too? Florence was so healthy and then snuffed out in a week. I couldn't bear it." Katy gave a little shake and said in a stronger voice, "When Al is a strapping young man, I might relent."

"Oh, Katy, you're joking, of course you are!" Cassandra said, ignoring the doubt she felt. "Why don't you have another child, like me?"

"No thanks! I've a business to build and I'm enjoying it too much. You know Douglas is thinking of doing a road trial? I'm really looking forward to that. I'll leave having babies to you." And Katy got out of the car and slammed the door harder than it needed.

Cassandra felt its thump reverberate right through her.

CHAPTER TEN
Autumn 1923

"Listen to this, Doug." Katy was sitting behind the wheel of the Buick and revving the engine to its maximum power.

"Pretty damn good. Sounds like a different car. But I think we should go outside before we die of asphyxiation from all the fumes. Shall we take her for a trial then? I've heard there's one the other side of Woodbury on Sunday, at Denham Park."

"That would be really exciting, Doug. I'd love to see what she can do now, without speed restrictions. I'll ask Jem if he'll look after Al for me. We're due to have Sunday lunch at his parents' house, so I don't suppose my mother-in-law will object to having her son all to herself."

Sunday morning dawned bright, with a fresh breeze, exactly matching Katy's mood. Jem was less happy but she felt a frisson of excitement she couldn't contain when she heard the Buick arrive on the forecourt.

Douglas didn't bother getting out but tooted at her from the car.

"Hey, have some respect for your engineer." Katy gave Jem and Al a kiss each, then scuttled across the forecourt and hopped in.

Douglas laughed and put the car into gear and eased the car out on to the London Road. He whipped through the gears in record time and was soon cruising at thirty miles an hour.

Katy tied her scarf tighter around her hair, and shouted above the roar of the engine, "The speed limit is still twenty, you know, Douglas."

"But who's going to catch us now she's this fast?" He turned off onto another road with a screech of tyres and the Buick tipped towards the nearside as it clutched the tarmac. "She's handling great, Kate. Good job, partner." He gunned up the hill in third gear and by the time they reached the summit, they were doing forty miles per hour.

Katy thrilled to the exhilaration of being on top of the hill, which she'd always loved. The engine was purring along as if it too was loving going fast. She threw back her head and pulled off her scarf, letting the wind ripple through her hair, just for the hell of it. She had made the car roar along like this, no-one else.

"Cass insisted we take a picnic with us," Douglas said, jerking his head back to the wicker hamper on the dickey seat.

"Glad to hear it, I hadn't given food a thought."

"We won't be able to eat it all. She got Cook to ram it full of culinary delights."

"I have to admit, I was more concerned about having enough petrol and engine oil on board."

"Don't worry, I've still got the cans of fuel you donated strapped on the back."

"It's a good job you don't smoke when you drive, Doug." Katy settled herself more comfortably in the front seat. "So where is Denham Park, then?"

"It's on the A46 just north of Bath. Should take us about an hour to get there."

Katy relaxed into the drive, relishing the freedom away from Al's needs, Jem's cautious care and the many demands of Katharine Wheel Garage. They drove in companionable silence until Douglas slowed down near some huge gates. They turned off into the impressive drive, which twisted and turned through woods up a steep hill before swooping down in front of the house. Men, armed with stopwatches and clipboards, dotted the edges of the oak avenue.

A motley collection of cars were parked in front of the handsome Victorian mansion. The angular house was large and built of yellow Bath stone but lacked the charm of Cheadle Manor's mellow old bones.

Katy got out of the Buick and looked around. She was glad to see another woman, who walked straight up to her and extended a gloved hand. She looked about forty, with the red complexion of a countrywoman and eyebrows that badly needed plucking.

"Another female, I see." The well-built woman had a clipped accent. "Jolly good. Driving?"

"No, I'm Mr Flintock's mechanic," Katy answered, in her soft country burr.

The other woman didn't flinch. "Excellent. Name's Constance, Constance Clitheroe and I'm driving this Sunbeam. Pleased to meet you Miss?"

"Mrs." The last thing she wanted was to repeat the disastrous events in Boston a few years ago. "Mrs Phipps, actually."

"Come on. Can't call you that. What's your first name, dear?"

"Kate."

"And a fine mechanic she is. I'm Douglas Flintock and pleased to meet you." Douglas got out of the Buick and shook Constance's hand in turn. "Say, Constance, have you been to one of these meetings before? It's our first time, you know."

"Lord, yes, been coming since the end of the war in 1918. It's the same old crowd usually, good to see some new faces. Let me show you off to everyone." Constance, after nodding to her taciturn Scottish engineer, Bruce, took them over to join the huddle of people admiring a bright red Bugatti.

The Bugatti's driver sat sprawled in the driving seat. He was wearing a leather pilot's hat with the goggles cocked above his forehead. His glasses glinted in the sunshine, making Katy blink. His tie had an unusual pin. She screwed up her eyes to read it. It had BARC written across the enamel and Katy wondered what it stood for.

Constance Clitheroe introduced them in her bluff way. "Lord Finch, meet Kate and Douglas, leading light of the British Automobile Racing Club."

Aha, so that's what the badge meant. She must make sure Douglas joined up too. Lord Finch peeled off his headgear to reveal pale blond hair and good cheekbones. The onlookers stepped back a pace, like a flock of sheep, to allow him to step out of his beautiful car and shake their hands. To Katy's eyes, he looked like one of the film stars she'd seen at the new cinema in Woodbury.

"Charmed, I'm sure," Lord Finch smiled. "Which one is the driver?"

"Hi, there," Douglas said, "I have that privilege. Kate Phipps here is my stablemate and keeps my old Buick running smooth."

"A Buick, you say? American then?" Lord Finch looked back at Douglas after acknowledging Katy with an appraising scan. Was that a glint of admiration in those grey eyes? Katy took off her cap and fluffed up her hair, flattered to be noticed by such a handsome, imposing man.

"You bet. I reckon we can lick your Italian car, alright." Douglas smiled his confidence.

"I doubt that, old chap. Let's have a look at your American import, shall we?"

They sauntered over to the Buick. It did look sadly out of date against the sleek Bugatti, which was as glamorous as its driver.

"Pre-war, is she?" Lord Finch raised his eyebrows.

"1916, as a matter of fact." Douglas's genial smile slipped slightly.

"So, seven long years old," Lord Finch said. "There have been an awful lot of technical innovations since then, old chap."

"But you can't beat class, at the end of the day, can you, *old chap*?" Douglas's habitual smile was now entirely absent.

"Oh, I think you'll find that my Bugatti doesn't lack class. What was your name again?"

"Flintock."

"And exactly where are you from?"

"Boston, in the United States of America."

"Surely, you haven't crossed the mighty Atlantic

simply to join our little throng?"

"Hell, no. I live just down the road these days, at Cheadle Manor, in Wiltshire," Douglas said.

"Cheadle Manor? Isn't that where the Smythes live?"

"Sure is." Douglas was frowning now.

"Ah yes, Charles Smythe didn't make it, I heard. Shame. We were at university together, you know. How is dear Cassandra? I haven't seen her in years, not since before the damn war."

"My wife is very well." Douglas flicked his hand with his gloves.

"Your wife? Good Lord, I had no idea she was married - and to an American! Well, well." Lord Finch looked down at the ground. "We had a bit of thing before the war, dear Cassie and I, you know."

"Really? Cassandra has never mentioned you. Well she's off limits now, buddy, and expecting our second child."

"Cassie a mother! That's hard to imagine. She was always so gung-ho. Full of spirit. Could jump a fence as well as any man on a horse. Drove ambulances in the war, I heard?"

"That's right, and she's just as wonderful now." Douglas shoved Lord Finch aside and climbed back into the driving seat of the Buick. "When does the trial start? I'd sure like to see what your little Bugatti can do. How many horses you got under that shiny bonnet, Finch?"

Katy's heart sank at the way Douglas had dropped the title of this English Lord, whose charms had already worn transparently thin. No-one had thought to include her in the conversation and she decided he was less handsome the longer you looked at him.

Lord Finch turned away and barked over his shoulder, "More than you in that lumbering old heap, I can assure you, Flintock."

"Game on, I suspect," Constance said. "About time Lord Denis Finch had a bit of competition. Give it all you've got, Mr Flintock. See you later, Kate."

Bruce, the other engineer, treated Katy to a conspiratorial wink and followed his mistress back to their Morris Oxford. At least those two had acknowledged her.

A man with a clipboard came up to them and introduced himself as Wilfred Bailey, race official. Douglas passed him the papers on the Buick's statistics and, after licking his pencil, Bailey wrote them down in a fat, childish script. A wind had sprung up and his papers flapped in the breeze, making him swear under his breath. Another official, who looked like a professional gentleman in a pin-stripe suit and trilby, made the calculations for their handicap, after assessing their combined weight.

"The start is over there, sir," said Bailey, "next to the fallen oak tree. You'll see a line of tape on the gravel. It is vital you remain behind that line until I blow my whistle and Manders here will time your departure. The winner will be the fastest car to climb the hill, with allowances made for weight and horsepower. Understood all that?"

Katy turned the crank handle of the Buick, and it sprang instantly into life, as if it wanted to show what it could do. Katy threw the handle into the back of the car and jumped in beside Douglas.

They drove over to the starting line and waited in the queue for the off. Lord Finch was two cars ahead of them and kept revving his engine while he was waiting, so that the car between them was engulfed in petrol fumes and smoke, until Bailey went over and had a quiet word with him. Lord Finch kept the engine ticking over in a more subdued growl until it was his turn for the hill climb. The Bugatti was screaming like a sick child by the time he stormed off up the hill.

"He'll wreck that engine. His revs are much too high for second gear," Katy said. More black smoke issued from the exhaust of the straining Bugatti.

76

"Terrific speed, though, Kate," Douglas said. "He's sure to win."

"Maybe he will, but at what cost? He might not have a car to race next time, if he burns out the clutch."

Constance's modest Sunbeam drew up to the starting line. They watched her wait for Bailey's flag to swish her away and the Sunbeam glided up the hill in a stately roll, contrasting starkly with the previous mad dash of the Bugatti.

Flags waved and it was their turn. Katy steeled herself not to show her nerves and put Douglas off. Douglas revved the Buick gently as they both watched Bailey's flag with intense scrutiny. It came down in a whoosh of permission and they were off. Douglas drove off in first gear, quickly changed into second and took the first incline at twenty miles an hour. Up into third and the big car gained momentum, despite the gradient. The surface was gravelly, with soft verges. There was a tight bend at the brow of the hill and Katy found herself involuntarily leaning into the curve, willing the Buick to accelerate, but it was slow to react and they caught a tyre in the grass, making it spin and lose traction.

"Damn!" Douglas yelled, as the car hesitated, before gaining the gravel and using all four wheels again.

"Lost time there, Doug," Katy shouted, nerves forgotten, desperate to speed up.

Douglas changed down a gear and the car lurched towards the finishing line, shooting across it at about fifty miles per hour, as the chequered flag signalled the end of their climb.

"How did we do?"

"Not great, I fear, Kate. We lost time on that bend and we haven't got the acceleration of Finch's Bugatti." Douglas shook his head as he parked up with the other competitors under the oak trees.

"Well, I think you were brilliant, for a first time, Douglas." Katy gave him a quick hug.

Lord Finch's Bugatti pulled up alongside. "Well,

well, we *are* a cosy team, aren't we?"

Katy withdrew quickly from Douglas's side and straightened her cloth cap.

"Thing is, you'll never do well at a hill climb in such a heavy old car, old chap," Lord Finch said.

"At least I didn't burn out my clutch, pushing my car beyond its limits," Douglas said.

"Nonsense, my Bugatti is designed to perform at maximum stretch. It's what she's built for. I suggest, if you are serious about continuing in these road trials, you get yourself a more suitable vehicle. How about something a little more up to date?" Lord Finch's smile didn't reach his flinty eyes.

"Oh, never fear, Finch, I'm going to stick around and our garage, Katherine Wheel, has many cars to choose from," Douglas said.

Katy was glad of the plug for her garage but not so sure Lord Finch appreciated it.

"Katherine Wheel Garage? What does it sell - fireworks? Never heard of it. I suppose it's buried in the depths of Wiltshire, is it?"

"I wouldn't call the London Road a burial site," Douglas said.

"I'll have to call in some day, on my way back to Berkshire." Lord Finch drove off, leaving a cloud of black smoke behind him.

"Look at the colour of that exhaust smoke. Something's not right there, Douglas, if it's any consolation."

Douglas grimaced, looking unconvinced.

Katy added, "And I'm confident Cassandra never looked twice at that bore, whatever he was boasting about earlier."

"I don't know, Kate. Sometimes I think these English aristos are members of some private club, and I'll never be a member. It's just like when I went hunting. They are so competitive; so insular. There's something primitive and tribal about them all."

"But Cass isn't like that!"

Douglas was silent and remained so for the rest of the trial. They hadn't won. Lord Finch had beaten everyone by a large margin. He didn't even stay for the result. Katy and Douglas ate sparingly of their lavish picnic and drove home shortly afterwards, each deep in their own thoughts.

"You know, Kate, thinking about the garage, and all, I reckon we should race one of the cars we want to sell. Use the race as a showcase, get what I mean?"

"How would that work?"

"I'm not sure, but I think we need to do another road trial using one of the 'for sale' cars and see how it performs. Maybe take it up to Brooklands for a proper race. I would never admit this to Finch but this old Buick *is* too cumbersome to beat the odds and anyway, we haven't any to sell. This could be a winning combination, you know. Show off what we can do as a garage and get people interested. Hell, might even get some sponsorship if we can win. I was reading about it in a motoring magazine. Lots of people do it. Would give the garage a real push. What do you say?" Douglas turned off for the London Road.

"Can we go to Brooklands, just to have a look, first? Maybe Cassandra would like a day out?" Cassandra would soon put that arrogant Lord Finch in his place.

"Now that's a swell idea, Kate. Yes, let's make a day of it - and then enter a race once we've got the lay of the land? We've got two Austin Sevens or that Bullnose Morris we could use. A lot of people use Austins - they're so lightweight."

"Small engines, though Douglas."

"I know, but they're popular and sell well. We might make a packet."

Katy laughed. "Sure you wouldn't rather buy a Bugatti and beat Lord Finch at his own game?"

Douglas grinned at her. "We could work up to that. In time."

CHAPTER ELEVEN
Spring 1924

Oh, so I'm allowed to attend this time, am I? Jem didn't know whether to be flattered or annoyed at Katy's invitation to join her and Douglas at the next road trial, as no-one had thought to include him in the proposed visit to Brooklands. He wasn't convinced that racing would improve sales from the forecourt and thought it a ruse Douglas had cooked up to satisfy his desire for a bit of excitement.

Jem couldn't really spare the time from his garden but he was damned if he was going to be left out at a local event. Katy was constantly working on the new Austin Seven that Douglas had bought specifically for the speed trials, which seemed extravagant to Jem. She'd stripped the extra body parts away from the chassis, and to Jem's mind, it made the vehicle look ugly, and as vulnerable as a skinned rabbit. Apparently it was to lose any unnecessary weight and increase the speed, but he thought it would decrease the safety in equal measure. Katy had been so obsessed with the transformation of a perfectly good little car into a mean racing machine, that poor Billy was left to do all the dogsbody work in the garage. Jem felt sorry for the young lad and tried to help him as much as he could in the little spare time he had between his gardening and parenting duties.

He tackled Katy about the latter one evening, after he'd put Al to sleep in his little bedroom next to theirs. "You know, Al misses you, Katy. Why don't you put him to bed sometimes and read him his story? He gets bored with my voice droning on. You've a way of reading that brings the story alive, you have."

Katy's eyebrows twitched together but she didn't look up from the motor magazine she was reading.

"Hmm, I'll do it tomorrow," she said, flicking the page over, "just got to find out about these new hydraulic brakes that's been invented. There's a diagram here. I'm just wondering if I could change over to this system on the Austin."

Jem got up and put another log into their range cooker. The fire clutched at the new log, sending sparks against the glass door. His wife was just like one of those sparks. Bright, too bright perhaps, and highly flammable if let loose from its confines. He understood why she was excited, even if he couldn't understand all the finer points of the engineering, but he would not, could not, fathom why she wasn't interested in her son. Al was an engaging, lively and polite little boy. Everyone else found him charming, even Edith Morgan, the nanny up at the manor house, declared him a sweet child.

God knew, Katy had doted on little Florence - almost too much. He'd feared for Katy's sanity when she'd died. He sat back down and picked up the paper, sneaking glances at his wife over its thin, wide pages. Katy was looking tired. The fingers that held her magazine were rimed black with engine oil and rough with work, the knuckles ridged like those of an older woman's. He noticed that the crease between her eyebrows didn't recede when her face relaxed any more but stayed, in a little vertical line above her straight nose, like an exclamation mark without a full-stop.

"I'm glad we waited to get the Austin until they'd increased the engine capacity from 696 to 747 cc's," Katy said. "Increased the bore size, see. Technically she should be called an Austin Eight now. The RAC have rated it 7.8 horsepower, it says here, so really it is nearer an eight than a seven but I don't think they'll change the name now. Silly really, and inaccurate."

Jem ruffled his paper and declined to comment. Katy didn't seem to notice.

Still, he felt proud of his wife when he watched her topping up the oil on the little Austin the following Sunday morning. She was attracting a good deal of attention as the lone female mechanic and Jem felt both protective and oddly excluded from the little crowd that hung around their parking space. Douglas had bought himself a leather hood and looked more like a pilot of one of these new aeroplanes than a driver, which seemed a bit ambitious for such a small car. Jem didn't think they'd be flying up the hill climb.

The meeting was only forty miles from the Cheadle villages and right at the top of Salisbury Plain. Jem could see across to the spire of Salisbury cathedral from his vantage point in one direction and the river valley stretched way off towards Bristol in the other. He took in a deep breath of air and, for a transient moment, felt a snatch of the same exhilaration that Douglas and Katy had exuded ever since that first road trial at Denham Park. No-one was taking any notice of him, so he wandered around the other contestants to eye up the rest of the competitors.

Mostly it was wealthy landowners, or rather, their sons, who were testing their cars against their neighbours and a good deal of banter skittered between them on the fresh autumn breeze. Chestnut trees unfurled their tender new leaves, forming a backdrop to the north of the field of rough grass, protecting them from the sharp wind.

"Hello, there! Phipps, isn't it?" someone called out.

Jem turned to see an unwelcome face. John Bartlett, the proprietor of Whitefriars Garage, was hailing him from behind a Model T Ford, the latest version. His pimply son, Gordon, sat behind the wheel and honked his horn. A large hand-painted sign was propped against the radiator on the front of the car, loudly declaiming it came from Whitefriars Garage in big, red letters. Jem wished he'd had the foresight to bring one for Katherine Wheel Garage. His Dad was a dab hand with a paintbrush. They'd bring one next time, that was for sure. Jem straightened his back to lengthen his spine and went over to them, making his lips widen into a smile he could not feel.

"Good morning, Mr Bartlett. How are you?"

"Nothing wrong with me, young Phipps, never is. How's business?" Mr Bartlett placed his hands on his hips, rather than holding one out for a handshake.

83

"Thriving, thanks." Jem shoved his hands, one flesh, one of wood, into his coat pockets and nodded to Gordon in the car.

"Trialling one of yours today?" Mr Bartlett asked.

"Yes."

"Take it you won't be driving yourself, with that gammy arm?" Mr Bartlett laughed.

Jem decided not to rise to the bait. "Nothing wrong with my driving, Mr Bartlett. I just don't race, that's all. Our racing driver is Douglas Flintock, from Cheadle Manor."

"The American chap who married into the Smythe family?"

Jem couldn't see why that was relevant but nodded his assent and starting walking on to the next car but Bartlett joined him, his curiosity still evident. "So what car are you entering, then, Phipps?"

"An Austin Seven." Jem felt annoyed his solitude had been snatched away, particularly by his rival.

"Bit of a piddly little engine for one of these events, I'd have thought?"

"We'll just have to see, won't we?" Jem turned to speak with the policeman who was stewarding the finish line.

"Morning, officer. Here on duty?"

"Ay, sir," the policeman said, with a brief smile.

Jem hadn't had one of those from Mr Bartlett and felt emboldened to ask more. "What are the police required to do at one of these events, if you don't mind me asking?"

"Well, sir, seeing as they're racing on the public road, like, and, strictly speaking, that's illegal, so we issues a license, see, but I have to supervise as well." The policeman looked pleased with his easy Sunday shift.

"What about the speed limit?" Mr Bartlett asked.

"Well, sir, begging your pardon, but if I'm not issued with a stopwatch by my superior officer, I can't rightly tell what speed the cars is doing, now can I?" The policeman winked at Jem, who smiled back, and turned around to return towards the parked cars, hoping but failing, to shake off Mr Bartlett.

"Bit of a rum do, that," Mr Bartlett said. "Either the speed limit is enforced or we have anarchy on our roads. I make a point of never going above twenty miles per hour in any of my vehicles and I impress on all my customers to do the same. Safety is paramount, I always say. Shocking number of road accidents lately."

"Well, I don't suppose there will be any other travellers up on this lonely stretch of the plain on a Sunday morning," Jem said.

"Advocate breaking the law, do you? I'd have a regard for your garage's reputation, if I were you. Wouldn't want it put about that you're flouting the rules, now would you?" Mr Bartlett seemed satisfied with this parting shot, and finally left Jem in peace.

It felt strange, watching from the sidelines, as Katy got in beside Douglas and they drove out on to the road with the other competitors. Jem watched the queue of cars form up. Mr Bartlett, whose son, Gordon, had stalled his Model T Ford, was looking a bit hot under collar. The delayed cars behind him were sounding their horns at the Whitefriars outfit. Mr Bartlett was shouting something at his son. Jem had no alternative but to walk past them and was shocked at Mr Bartlett's red and angry face as he glared at him.

"What are you staring at, Phipps?" Mr Bartlett had got out to crank the Ford's starting handle. He spoke out of the corner of his mouth, twisting his moustache into a comical shape.

"Nothing, Mr Bartlett. I wish you luck and may the best man win." Jem had a job not to laugh.

"Oh, aye," Mr Bartlett said, "those of us who don't rely on our wives to do men's work."

Jem had heard this jibe directed at him before but it had never stung quite so much as now. The Ford's engine kicked back into life.

"I don't suppose *your* wife is allowed out from the

kitchen," Jem retorted, as Mr Bartlett walked past him.

Mr Bartlett pushed his red face up close to Jem's. "You leave my wife out of this."

"Then don't have a go at mine! I'm proud of what Katy can do with cars. She learned it in the war, you know. Where did you fight, Mr Bartlett?"

"What's that got to do with anything?" Mr Bartlett's hands balled into fists.

"Because, Mr Bartlett, I'd be in the driving seat if I hadn't been wounded fighting for my country." Jem immediately regretted his words. He never boasted of his war service, never. It felt like a betrayal of all his fellow soldiers who'd never come home.

"War or no war, I wouldn't let my wife gallivant off with another man."

"Then it's a good job you're not married to my Katy. I know I can trust her so I don't need to keep her on a leash. Good day to you, Mr Bartlett. I'm off to cheer my team on."

Jem nodded farewell and marched past to where Katy and Douglas sat nearer the front of the queue of cars poised for the off.

"What was all that about, Jem?" Katy asked.

"Mr Bartlett was admiring our set-up," Jem answered.

"Really? You do surprise me," Katy began and then stopped, as the race official rapped on their bonnet to signal them to come forward.

Jem stood back to let them proceed. He watched as Douglas revved the little Austin's engine and the car, stripped back to the bare essentials, vibrated with its own power. The official lowered the flag and they roared off up the hill. Jem could see them all the way to the summit before the car disappeared over the horizon. They'd made good speed and looked faster than the others he'd seen. There was a buzz of comment from the officials, who were scribbling numbers on their clipboards.

"That one got away smartish," one said and his

friend nodded as he checked his stopwatch.

"Low handicap for weight, though," said another.

Jem wondered if Katy's stripped down version of the Austin Seven had given them a disadvantage. He stayed to watch the Bartlett team. Gordon Bartlett was at the starting line now, making a huge racket, revving his much bigger engine. His father sat beside him, still shouting the odds at his son, as far as Jem could make out. The Ford jumped forward, backfired and stalled again. With the engine cut, Mr Bartlett's hectoring could be heard clearly in the short silence before young Gordon hopped out and cranked it back into life, as his father switched seats and got behind the wheel. They thundered off, in a cloud of exhaust fumes, and gained speed, but not as quickly as Douglas's Austin, and with the false start, would score poorly when the final reckoning came. Jem grinned, peeled away from the crowd, and ran to the finishing line.

"How did we do?" Douglas called out, as Jem approached.

Katy looked flushed and happy, younger. Jem's heart lurched with love for his wife and he bent over the car and kissed her on the mouth, not caring who saw them.

He reached over and shook Douglas's hand. "You were brilliant, Doug. Got away like a rocket. Young Bartlett stalled his Ford after you and his father took over while he restarted the engine back. You should have seen old Bartlett's face. Red as a ripe tomato!"

"Hey, partner, that's one up to us." Douglas's smile was as wide as his goggles.

"Oh, Jem," Katy said, still rosy-faced, "it was so thrilling. Douglas accelerated round the bends like a natural. I've never been so fast! I'm really pleased with the way the Austin performed too."

Their excitement was infectious and Jem laughed with them.

"Brooklands, next stop, Kate," Douglas said firmly, and Jem felt left out all over again.

CHAPTER TWELVE
Autumn 1924

Despite being six months pregnant, Cassandra was determined to go to Brooklands with the others. She could not face another day stuck at the manor with her parents and Lottie for company. She was due for some fun before she had to return to nursing another child. Lottie was already showing signs of jealousy, as her mother's belly grew, and her first-born had become increasingly hard to handle.

"Don't rise to it, cariad." Nanny Morgan advised. "Take no notice and she'll soon give up."

That was all very well when you weren't her mother. Thank goodness for young Al Phipps. Lottie's face would always light up when the little boy visited. Lottie's moods were always mercurial, but she never lost her temper with Al. They played imagination games together for hours, either in the nursery if it was raining, or in the grounds of the manor house, under Nanny's close supervision.

"I bless that boy from the garage, Mrs Flintock-Smythe, I really do," Nanny Morgan said. "Did you say he's coming for the whole day on Thursday?"

"If that suits you, Nanny. Kate said she didn't want to impose on you, if you didn't feel you could manage such a long visit. It'll be late when we get back, you know."

"Then let the little lad sleep here. Why worry everyone to get back? It's a long drive, isn't it? You could stay at the London house and make a little holiday of it. Once the baby comes, you won't get the chance."

"Nanny, that's a splendid idea. I'll telephone Kate and Jem and ask them if they agree. Thank you, Edith," Cassandra said, before attempting a swift exit as Lottie burst in, wearing her night-dress and clutching her favourite teddy bear.

"I'm hungry!" Lottie said.

"You shall have some breakfast shortly, Charlotte," Nanny Morgan said. "Now say good-bye to your mother,

88

she's busy arranging her trip to see about your Daddy racing cars in London, you know."

"I want to come!" Lottie clutched at her mother's skirts.

Cassandra shook her off. "Don't do that, Lottie. This trip is for grown-ups only."

Lottie immediately began to wail. "Want to go with Mummy to see cars!"

Nanny Morgan said, "I think you should leave now, Mrs Flintock-Smythe. I'll deal with madam here."

Cassandra didn't need telling twice.

As she opened the nursery door, she heard Nanny Morgan say, in a voice that she wouldn't dare argue with, "If you carry on like this, Miss Charlotte, I shall tell young Albert Phipps not to come over and sleep in the nursery on Thursday night."

Like a tap, the tears were turned off. Cassandra smiled and blessed the appointment of Nanny Morgan for the thousandth time.

Cassandra felt sorry for Jem when they picked Katy up outside very early on Thursday morning. Jem stood in the doorway of the garage, with Al on his hip, and waved them off with a determined smile.

Katy clambered into the dickey seat and snuggled down under the travel rug. "Don't mind me, you two. I'm looking forward to a lazy morning while you drive us up, Doug. I've been working really hard to clear the decks, so all Billy has to do is serve petrol and Jem is popping Al up to see Lottie, so they've not got too much to do. I've serviced every car in the queue and we're all up to date. Wake me up if I snore, won't you?"

Cassandra laughed and promised she would, glad to have Douglas to herself for once. She squeezed his thigh as he put the car into first gear and pulled out of the garage forecourt. Cassandra was happy not to talk as they drove along. Katy stayed asleep in the back, curled up like a kitten and Douglas seemed content to concentrate on driving. Cassandra watched the scenery change from sheep farms to dairy and wheat before subsuming into towns and factories as they reached the outskirts of London. The drive took four hours and, having left early, they made it by lunchtime. Douglas looked more and more excited the nearer they were to the racetrack in Weybridge, a surprisingly leafy corner of Surrey.

They parked up on the grassy slope above the concrete banking that encircled the track. Other cars were ahead of them, full of people eating their al fresco picnics in the September breeze.

Katy immediately bounded out of the car and headed off to the edge of the oval race-track. "Catch up with you later! I'm off to those sheds over there. That looks like where the nitty gritty stuff happens."

"Oh, 'bye then," Cassandra called to Katy's rapidly retreating back but doubted she heard her.

Douglas laughed. "There's no stopping Kate's thirst for knowledge. Shall we walk down to the track, darling?"

They wandered down towards the area called the paddock, where most people were milling about amongst the gathering racing cars, next to the red-bricked clubhouse. A steep single-lane track climbed up the hill on the other side, bordered by white railings. "What's that?" Cassandra asked, losing sight of Katy, who'd disappeared into the crowd.

"Test Hill." Douglas's answer was prompt. "It's where they put the cars through their paces when climbing. Means they can time it accurately, knowing the exact distance and gradient."

"Goodness, the banking is very steep when you get near it!" Cassandra said, as they walked towards the race track. More cars were assembling for the race and the noise levels rose. The fumes were beginning to make Cassandra feel a little sick. Just then, a smart red Bugatti car drove by.

"Oh, no, not him."

"Not who?" Cassandra looked at Douglas, then at the sleek sports car.

"Someone who claims an earlier acquaintance with you, honey." Douglas cupped her elbow with his hand.

"With me?" Cassandra followed Douglas's gaze. "Good Lord! Is that Denis?"

"Lord Finch, yes," Douglas said, through a very insincere-looking smile. "Kate and I met him at Denham Park. He told me that you were quite close, before the war, but you've never mentioned it."

"That's because there wasn't anything worth talking about. Denis is not someone you'd want to get close to. He was up at Cambridge, with Charles, and they got sent down, you know and that's why Charles signed up for the BEF in France so early into the war. Lots of loose living at university, I believe. Charles was easily led, so I mustn't blame Denis entirely but there's something rotten at the core of him, Douglas. Be careful." Cassandra stopped speaking as the Bugatti caught up with them.

"Cassandra Smythe! Well, aren't you a sight to behold, in all your matronly glory!" Lord Finch, said, with a wave.

Cassandra clenched her teeth. Denis always could get under her skin. "Hello, Denis. Are you in the next race?"

"Yes, thought I'd try my hand at the JCC 200 Miler. Fancied going the distance instead of those tiddly road trials. So I can't stop now, but I'd love a chat afterwards. See you in the clubhouse?" and Lord Finch drove off, acknowledging Douglas with a very brief nod.

Douglas didn't nod back but turned instead to another spectator and started chatting. The middle-aged man was very knowledgeable and told Douglas that the Talbot-Darracq team were bound to win because of their superchargers, one of which was to be driven by another of Douglas's heroes, Henry Segrave.

"Do you hear that, honey? Segrave's driving. Look! That's his car there."

Cassandra looked across as three powerful-looking cars drove up to the starting grid, followed by a clutch of

91

hangers-on.

"He's very handsome, isn't he?"

"And his car looks even better," Douglas replied. "They'll walk it with those Talbots."

The speed the cars travelled terrified Cassandra during the race. The thought of Douglas going so fast took the edge off her excitement, and she could hardly bear to look when they mounted the curved bank but Douglas looked engrossed as the cars sped by.

"They must be doing over a ton!" he said, his eyes shining.

Cassandra knew her returning smile was feeble but Douglas was too enthralled to notice.

By the time the race was over, Cassandra had a pressing need to use the facilities and a deep desire to sit down. When she came back from the Ladies Room, Douglas had bought her a lemonade and was sitting in a corner seat. Standing over him was Lord Denis Finch, still in his driving gear, swinging his dusty goggles in his hand.

Lots of other men were clapping Lord Finch on the back for coming fourth in the race, after the three Talbots, and offering to buy him drinks but, as soon as he saw Cassandra, he pulled away and drew her to the seat next to her husband, kissing her on both cheeks before he released her. His fans politely withdrew and Lord Finch pulled up another chair and sat opposite Cassandra and her husband.

Lord Finch's flinty grey eyes had lit up with his minor triumph and he looked as young as Cassandra remembered him in 1913. What a long time ago that seemed now. How odd that he looked no different. She wondered what he'd done in the war. Had he been with Charles when he died? She longed to ask him.

Douglas was congratulating Lord Finch on his fourth place. "Fine race you drove, Finch."

"Oh, call me Denis, please," said Lord Finch. "Yes, I enjoyed myself out there today. Topped over a hundred miles per hour but couldn't quite catch up with those Talbots. They had the bit between their teeth today after losing Dario Resta a few weeks ago. Lost a tyre on the Railway Straight and crashed through the boundary fence, you know."

"Really? Do you mean he died here at Brooklands?" Cassandra gave an involuntary shiver.

"Yes, crashed his Sunbeam, fastest grand prix car this season. Well, that's the level of risk you have to accept in this game. So, I shall have to be content with staying alive and coming fourth but I'm definitely going to look into getting a supercharger for my Bugatti." He called the waiter over and said, "Bottle of champagne, please, Peter, and three glasses."

"Yes, sir, right away sir, I mean, your Lordship," the waiter said, and sped off.

"Well this is pleasant, I must say." Lord Finch stretched his legs out under the table so that Douglas had to shift out of the way. "Good bit of driving, and meeting up with old friends."

"Congratulations, Denis," Cassandra said.

"Well, seems congrats are in order to you too, Cassie dear. When are you due to foal?"

"I don't believe I'm giving birth to a horse, Denis. My, *our*, baby is due in December."

Lord Finch laughed, "Touché, Cassie! Never could get much past you, hey?"

"No."

"So, Douglas, isn't it? You're not racing today then? That old Buick not up to it? There is a veteran section, I believe, for older cars. Maybe you should start a club just for Americans?"

"I'll be driving an Austin in the next JCC 200 mile race." Douglas accepted some champagne from the nervous waiter.

"In the 1100 cc category, I take it?" Lord Finch downed his wine in one draught and immediately re-filled his glass.

"That's right," Douglas said.

"Don't fancy something with a bit more poke?" Lord

Finch said, darting a mischievous glance at Cassandra, his double meaning only too obvious.

She flushed, annoyed with herself for betraying her embarrassment and wishing her pregnancy wasn't so evident. She sat up taller, despite her fatigue, trying to minimise the swell of her abdomen and placed her scarf across it. Lord Finch looked at her with a knowing smile that infuriated her even more.

"I'm glad to have seen you, Denis. I wanted to ask if you were with Charles, when he was fighting in France. You did fight, didn't you?" Cassandra schooled her voice so as not to betray her rising anger.

The light in those grey eyes died and Lord Finch closed them, as he took another glass of champagne. "I was here, at Brooklands, working as a test pilot for the RAF, if you must know. I never saw Charles again after that shooting weekend at your place in 1913. Do you remember? I'm sure you must. We danced, didn't we? In the drawing room at your delightful Cheadle Manor. A waltz, wasn't it? Not an evening I shall forget, Cassandra."

Cassandra remembered.

"And now, here you are, all domesticated and breeding happy families. Who'd have thought it?"

Douglas stood up. "I think you've made enough references to my wife's condition, Lord Finch. Don't you English gentlemen have any manners?"

"Oh, sit down, do, Flintock. Don't be stuffy. Thought you Americans were more casual about sex." Lord Finch drained his fourth glass.

"Douglas, let's go," Cassandra said. "I feel a little unwell."

Lord Finch laughed. "Delicately put, Mrs Flintock."

Douglas helped Cassandra to rise and steered her around the little table. Other drinkers were watching from the bar and a little hush had settled around them.

"Whereas delicacy seems entirely alien to you, Finch." Douglas stood between Lord Finch and Cassandra.

"You're the only one who's alien around here,

94

chum." Lord Finch's words slurred slightly.

"I'll see you another time," Douglas's voice had become clipped, "when my wife isn't here and we'll talk again about this."

"Fighting talk! Better get yourself a decent car, then."

Douglas slipped his arm around Cassandra's waist and shepherded her out into the fresh air. She was glad of the drizzle that had set in whilst they were inside the hot clubhouse. It felt clean and pure. Quite a contrast to her mixed feelings.

"Douglas, I think I've had enough for one day. Do you mind if we don't stay for the 1100 cc race?"

Douglas's face fell. She knew how much he loved her when he quickly replaced his frown with a smile, and said, "Of course, darling. Let's find our mad engineer, shall we?"

They found Katy closeted with the other mechanics, sitting on an upturned oil drum outside one of the hangers, swinging one leg and making notes with a pencil and paper. She didn't appear to be the least bothered by any of the men she'd been talking to. Once again, Cassandra felt that familiar stab of jealousy about her clever friend.

"Come on, Kate," Douglas said. "We need to take Cassandra home. She's very tired. We'll take you to the station on the way back."

"Alright, I'll be there in a minute." Katy turned to shake hands with her new friends. She joined them, eyes shining with ideas.

Cassandra listened to Katy's excited babble as she told Douglas all she'd learned. It was strangely silent in the car after they'd dropped her off at Waterloo.

"I suppose you will tell me what all that was about with Finch, someday?" Douglas asked, as they drew up outside the Smythe's London House.

"Someday, Douglas, but not today," Cassandra said.

CHAPTER THIRTEEN
Autumn 1924

Katy flopped back against her first-class seat, a treat from Douglas, and shut her eyes. The train lurched out of Waterloo Station with a loud puff of steam. It was dark and she had the carriage to herself, apart from an elderly gentleman, who smelled of mothballs, and read his book with silent concentration. Good, she wouldn't have to make polite conversation, something she signally failed at anyway. Too excited to sleep, she went over the events of the day in her mind, as the city lights faded into countryside, muffled by the black night and the train pounded out the miles to her home.

"If you want the Powder Room, it's in the clubhouse." The harassed-looking engineer had pointed a grubby finger over her shoulder.

"I'd rather see what you're doing with that Sunbeam," Katy said.

"Look, missus, we're working here. We don't have time for explaining about engines, even to someone as good-looking as you. Why don't you find your husband and go and watch the race?"

"You won't have to explain anything to me, mister. I'm a trained mechanic myself. Got my own garage."

"Got your own what?"

"You heard, and, if you don't mind me saying so, that jack is set too low."

"Oi, Brian, come and hark at this! This young woman thinks she knows better than we do how to change a bloody tyre."

Another man, also in a greasy boiler suit, came over and grinned at her. "What's all the fuss about, Tony?"

Katy was getting irritated now. They were wasting precious time, when she could be learning what went on behind the scenes of a racetrack. "Look, I don't mean to tell you what to do, but I am a proper mechanic. Trained in the WAAC in the war and serviced ambulances for the BEF in France."

Both men went silent and looked embarrassed. They looked about the same age as her and must have served their time in the war.

Katy drove the point home. "Were either of you there? Most soldiers passed through Étaples at some point."

Brian nodded. "Well, then," Katy said. "You'll know I'm not lying, won't you? It's time you men recognised that women can work on cars too, you know. Now, can I just have a look?" And she went to the jack and raised it a couple of inches, freeing the tyre. She spun it round. "Want me to remove it, now it's freed up?"

Half an hour later, they had lent her a spare boiler suit and were listening to her enthusiasm for hydraulic brakes. "You see, it makes it easier for women drivers, like me. Doesn't need brute strength to push the calipers on to the brake drum. Safer too, without so much friction."

"Yes, I've heard that Stockhead have made them but they leak like hell," Brian said, then swore an obscenity after catching his thumb in the spoke of a wheel and forgot to say sorry. She knew he respected her then.

Something shifted in Katy that day. Something important. Respect. That's what she'd seen in those mechanics' eyes by the time she had to leave, and she couldn't wait to return.

Jem was waiting for her at the station. Douglas had phoned the garage to let him know her arrival time. Katy was tired but still exhilarated when she joined Jem on the platform and gave him a kiss. He looked glad to see her; he always did. She felt guilty, then, that he'd had to stay behind.

As they drove home, she told him every detail from her busy day, so that he felt part of it. It was nearly midnight by the time they got home. As they got out of the car - Jem had borrowed one of the Austins up for sale - an owl hooted above them. How quiet it was compared to the noise and hustle of London. The air smelt fresh here, clean and unpolluted, unlike the tang of the petrol fumes from the roaring racing cars at Brooklands; but she knew which she preferred.

"Want a cup of tea before bed?" Jem said, as they let themselves in. The fire was glinting red in the grate of the range and Katy went to warm her hands.

"No, thanks, I'm too tired."

"Let's go to bed, then." Jem led the way to their little bedroom.

They lay in their double bed, arms around each other. It felt strange knowing that Al was up at the manor, with Lottie, and not next door in his little truckle bed. Katy relaxed against her husband when he kissed her. Tired though she was, she responded when he wanted to make love. It was good to be home but she wasn't about to forget the lure of the racing circuit and she fetched her contraceptive cap before yielding to his loving embrace. Another child would scupper all her plans.

Early next morning Katy was back in her own boiler suit in her workshop.

"I'm glad to see you back, Mrs Phipps." Billy Threadwell was an early riser too, and to give him credit, very reliable.

"Thanks, Billy, but you seem to have managed very well." Katy stopped to chat on her way to the office to make an order for a set of hydraulic brakes. She wanted to try them out in the racing Austin.

"Thanks, but there weren't too much to do, just serve the petrol. Mr Bartlett from Whitefriars was here, you know." Billy wheeled a pushbike with a flat tyre into the centre of the workshop.

"Oh? What did that old curmudgeon want at Katherine Wheel?"

"Jem was up at the manor, taking your Albert up to see Miss Charlotte, and I was on my own. I wasn't quite sure what to do, but Mr Bartlett, he says it were alright.

Said you'd given permission." Billy had turned away to insert a tyre lever into the rim of the bicycle wheel.

"Given him permission to do what, exactly?"

"Look at the list of suppliers. Mr Bartlett said he'd been having trouble getting supplies of engine parts and who did we use? I wasn't sure at first if it would be alright to show him the books but when he said you'd given the go-ahead, I didn't like to say no." Billy reached for a new inner tube from the shelf and looked back at Katy with a smile so innocent, she didn't have the heart to wipe it off his face, though she itched to do so.

"Oh, Billy! What were you thinking? Old Bartlett's our biggest competitor. Of course he wants to see our books! He probably couldn't believe his luck when you believed him about my giving permission. I wouldn't give that old codger the time of day, let alone let him sniff around our trade secrets. I despair of you sometimes, Billy, I really do!" And Katy rushed off to inspect the office. She could see no physical evidence of Bartlett's fat fingers amongst the paperwork littering the makeshift desk but she could sense that he'd been there.

Then she spotted a cylinder of cigar ash, lying in a dirty column of betrayal, next to the sales ledger. None of them smoked cigars at Katherine Wheel. Bartlett! He'd seen their profit margins, the bastard. She could murder that buffoon of a boy.

Katy went storming back to the workshop floor. "Billy Threadwell! I could strangle you. Bartlett didn't just look at our supplier list; he's been through the accounts as well. Didn't you watch him? Did you just let him snoop about our paperwork at his leisure?"

"The forecourt bell rang, just as he went in the office. There weren't nothing I could do! I had to go and serve the customer but, as it happens, it were only his son, Gordon." Billy's round, freckly face was now a good match for his red hair.

"Well, there's a surprise. Billy, you witnessed what's called a sting, yesterday." Katy's anger was fast coalescing into a cold rage.

"I thought only bees and wasps give stings." Billy looked mortified.

"I've a good mind to set a wasps nest on your empty head right now, young Billy. It's an American word for a set up. We've been had, lad, and you were a right mug. I'm disappointed in you Billy, I really am."

Katy went out into the backyard to find Jem. He was shocked into sympathy.

"The letter to Glico oil company asking them to back us in the racing was right on the top. I'll bet old Bartlett is on the phone to them now, stealing our potential sponsor. I'll just have to look for a new one," Katy said. "I think I should go to a smaller company anyway. Shell and Castrol are only interested in the likes of Malcolm Campbell or Parry Thomas. We're only small-fry and a smaller outfit might take us on and get more involved."

"You could be right about the sponsorship, Kate, but it makes my blood boil to know that Bartlett looked at your profit and loss ledger."

"Let's go and look through the catalogues."

They went into the office and flipped through the stack of petrol company paraphernalia that kept piling through their post box. They were all glossy and all promised the moon. "How about this company? I like the look of them," Jem said.

"Good name for a racing sponsorship, Jem," Katy said, holding up the poster depicting a racetrack. Underneath, the name 'Speedwell' scrolled across in giant yellow letters. "I'll give them a ring now."

Half an hour later, she had found her backer. Speedwell were delighted to have been picked out from the clutch of petrol companies clamouring for cars to sponsor at Brooklands. Katy put the phone down and looked at Jem. He was smiling.

"What's so funny?"

"It's just the way you left out the bit about not having actually raced there yet."

The following week a representative from Speedwell pitched up at Katherine Wheel Garage armed with placards, postcards, enamel signs and a car load of colourful petrol and oil cans.

"Tim Bluntstone," said the stocky young man, holding out his hand to shake. Too young to have served in the war, Katy felt Tim Bluntstone epitomised this new brave world of motoring. His round face was perpetually smiling, as if he couldn't quite believe his luck in getting a job that licensed him to drive up and down the country, giving out free gifts and attending race meetings.

Douglas had joined her for the crucial meeting and his enthusiasm outshone Tim's. The racing Austin was much admired as Katy showed Tim the finer points she had worked on.

"You certainly know your stuff, Mrs Phipps," Tim's eyes widened to match his smile.

"Call me Kate, Tim." Katy was more pleased than she liked to let on.

"We're going to make a great team," Douglas said, clapping Tim on the back. "The season has finished for this year but let's get her ready for when it re-opens at Easter, shall we?"

Katy couldn't wait for the racing season to start but some local excitement provided a welcome distraction when Cassandra was delivered of another baby girl. Isobel Flintock-Smythe arrived, without drama or mishap, on Christmas Eve, Al's birthday. She took him to visit the new arrival up at the manor.

"I don't know whether it's because the baby arrived on his own special day or because of some strange alchemy, but Al is fascinated with the new addition to your family, Cass," Katy said, silently grateful it wasn't her nursing a brand new baby.

"Well, don't tell Lottie," Cassandra said in a low voice, so her eldest couldn't hear her, and added. "Nanny Morgan's diplomatic skills are being stretched to the limit already."

101

On Boxing Day there was a huge fall of snow. Fifteen feet high snowdrifts walled them in. No car could travel through that, and Katy was forced to close the garage. Afterwards, floods swamped the landscape when the snow melted too quickly, and trade was slow, but the problem was nationwide and London was particularly affected by the Thames bursting its banks. With a little more time on her hands, Katy read the papers every day and they were full of tragic stories due to the extreme weather. The winter continued cold and wet and she was glad when spring brought an increase in custom again.

"Say, Kate, have you read the paper today?" Douglas came into the workshop one windy March morning, looking quite distraught.

"What's happened, Doug?"

"The RAC have banned all speed events on public roads, after that accident at Kop Hill Climb, where a spectator got killed."

"That one in Essex we thought we'd have a go at?"

"That's right, Kate. Makes Brooklands our only hope to test those brakes of yours."

Katy's heart skipped a beat. That meant they couldn't road test the Austin before the race itself, not at any speed. That would make it a lot more risky.

"Best not to tell, Cassandra, I think, don't you, Doug?"

Even by Easter the weather remained dull and damp. Katy was disappointed. She'd looked forward so long to the event through the cold dark days, while testing and refining the Austin as much as she could alongside her other work in the garage. The new hydraulic brakes were working well, although, annoyingly, the brake fluid kept leaking, just as Brian, the Brooklands mechanic, had predicted.

Katy was determined to find out why, being convinced that this type of brake was worth getting right. They used so much less effort on the pedal and the braking was far more even, that is, until the fluid leaked out. She experimented by re-fitting the brakes, then changing the liquid. She tried different mixtures of castor-oil based fluid and alcohol in different ratios, then a mixture of butanol and ethanol, but all to no avail. She decided to focus on keeping the fluid inside, rather than changing its formula. She bought in a different kind of seal, made of rawhide, and fitted it to the brake. She worried if it would hold up over the numerous laps at speed. The trouble was, it kept drying out and shrinking over time and then, the leaking would start all over again, and it was impossible to trial on normal roads, after the RAC ban.

She'd got the seal to fit as tightly as she could by the time the Easter meeting came around. It held up at normal speed, but would it stand the rigorous test of the race itself? Tim and Jem came with her and Douglas to Brooklands for the great day. Cassandra, still nursing Isobel, remained at home and Al had joined her at the manor. Billy had been left with strict instructions simply to serve petrol, answer the phone and not to try and use any of his dubious initiative in their absence. The evidence for his last attempt whilst manning the garage solo was now plastered all over Whitefriars Garage, where Glico placards loudly proclaimed that their petrol was the best in the world and only available locally from Mr Bartlett and son.

In the long months of anticipation she had imagined her great experiment being conducted in brilliant spring sunshine, but the day dawned grey and drizzly. So rainy, in fact, that the faster races, conducted on the Outer Circuit, were cancelled. The adjudicator declared that all cars were only allowed to get up to seventy-five miles per hour. Katy looked around the paddock but there was no sign of their Wiltshire rivals or Lord Finch's Bugatti. She felt almost cheated. She was dying to prove the brake's potential and she would love to get one over on that arrogant Lord Finch, if only for Cassandra's sake. She hoped Brian and Tony were around. She wanted to introduce them to Jem, once the race was over, and demonstrate the improved braking performance of the Austin to people who would really understand how potentially important this trial was.

Douglas watched her touch up the paint on their number, five, on the side of the car. "That number is a good omen. Being as it's 1925, having the number five means it's going to be our year."

Jem and Tim strolled up, bringing tea and biscuits on a tray from the clubhouse. Katy was so nervous her first bite of biscuit stuck to the roof of her dry mouth and she crumbled the rest into her saucer and left it uneaten. The tea was welcome though.

"Good luck, Douglas! Don't fall out on that banking, Katy!" Jem's face lit up with excitement, as she and Douglas clambered into the front seats of the Austin, but Katy could see the dark anxiety at the back of his eyes.

"Can't do more than seventy-five, Jem, no need to worry, pal." Douglas waved as they drove off.

Jem and Tim followed on foot and hovered around the car, making Katy catch Jem's anxiety. She could see the steep banking from the starting point, as the concrete race track curved around the first bend. Spying it from ground level, from the passenger seat of the stripped down Austin, brought home the severity of the gradient. The track was shaped in a huge oval, with its outside rim ramping up on to a bank in the earth. To overtake, any car would have to mount the banking and accelerate at the same time. From here, that looked impossible and for the first time, she was glad of the temporary speed limit.

She fastened the chin strap of her leather helmet under her jaw, tighter than its usual notch, hoping it would stop her teeth chattering, and settled her goggles over her eyes. The race officials waved Tim and Jem to stand behind the spectator's rail and Douglas, after giving her a quick, excited grin, revved up the Austin's 747 cc's into a roar. The other small cars were doing the same, on either side of them. The noise was deafening. Katy instructed her heart to beat more regularly and gripped the side of the open-topped car, as the starting flag swept downwards and the Austin leapt forward.

She looked at Douglas's foot on the accelerator pedal. It was flat on the floor. He changed through the gears quickly and they shot ahead of the pack. Then another car, a bright yellow rival Austin, number eight painted on its side, zoomed ahead and veered in front of them. Douglas changed down a gear, making the engine scream and set the nose of their car into the banking to overtake.

Katy watched the speed dial. Sixty-nine miles per hour. She pointed at the dial with her gloved hand and Douglas nodded. They'd be disqualified if they exceeded the limit. Up the side of the banking they drove, and the car tilted severely to Katy's side, shaking her bones until her teeth rattled inside her head. She looked out at the concrete rushing past beneath them. It was so close, she could easily have touched it and scorched the gloves from her hand. If, as it felt like it surely would, the car tipped up and landed on top of them, they'd be burnt to a crisp by friction alone.

Douglas changed back into fourth, the yellow Austin now safely behind them, and regained the centre of the track, where it was, thankfully for Katy, relatively flat, if bumpy. They drove around the track for a over an hour, switching the lead with the yellow Austin all the time, then, while negotiating a sharp bend, Douglas swerved to avoid a pothole in the concrete, then braked, to steady the car which was threatening to skid. The brakes screeched loudly and smoke billowed out from the tyres.

"I can't hold her, Kate!" Douglas roared above the din as the car veered violently towards the banking, mounting it too fast and high. She could feel the car beginning to tip over.

Kate looked down at the wheel on her side. The smoke was turning black and Douglas was struggled to hold the wheel as the car started juddering. Kate looked behind them. Through the trail of smoke she could just see a stain on the concrete. Damn! Those seals must have gone on the brakes. That rawhide must have got too hot and given way.

"Use the gears to slow her down, Doug!" she screamed back at him.

Douglas changed down into third, and the engine wailed its reluctance. The Austin coughed and jumped as the engine clunked down a gear. Katy could feel the impact on her neck as the car lumped along and slithered down the gradient on to the flatter central bit of track. They had slowed down to sixty miles per hour. Car number eight sailed past them, and the driver gave a snatched wave of triumph.

"I daren't go any faster, Kate, without brake power. We'll just have to cruise home." Douglas yelled.

Katy nodded, miserable that her improvised seal had failed and terrified they wouldn't be able to stop at all.

Katy had never been so glad to see anything as the pit exit. Douglas slowed the car by little stabs of the brake pedal and rapid gear changes. The Austin ground to a crawl in a series of jerks past the finish line, while the other competitors sailed on past. They drove back to the paddock at a snail's pace before he used the handbrake to make the car stationery at last.

"Our first race is over, Kate." Douglas's familiar grin had gone all lopsided and wobbly.

"And we'd have won if I'd got those brakes working properly." Kate chewed her lip.

"Hell, Kate, it was fun though, wasn't it?"

She acknowledged it with a smile but it took a full half an hour for her body to stop shaking.

Then she couldn't wait to do it again.

CHAPTER FOURTEEN
Spring 1925

Cassandra sat in her favourite place in all the manor's gardens, the little love seat in the apple orchard. She lay back against the beautifully wrought iron, one of the local blacksmith, Arthur Radstock's best efforts, basking in the warm May sunshine, contemplating her two daughters. Isobel lay on a rug, kicking her fat little legs in the air while Lottie read aloud to her sister. Lottie's stubby finger marched firmly across the page of her nursery rhyme book. She was reading 'Little Jack Horner' with fierce concentration. Lottie read slowly, but evenly, working out the words methodically if they were new or long. When she got to the bit about Jack pulling out his plum, she popped her own thumb into her mouth and made a 'pop' sound as it came out.

Isobel giggled at the noise and Lottie nodded her approval solemnly. She'd been practicing popping her thumb for weeks, until its tip had become red and sore.

Cassandra clapped her applause, registering the magnitude of Lottie's achievement. "Well done, darling. That was a perfect pop!"

Lottie inclined her head in gracious acknowledgement. "You just have to keep trying until you get it, you see, Mother."

Cassandra suppressed her own giggle and said, "Yes, I do see, Lottie, and look how Isobel loved it, too."

Lottie looked down at her sister, who was blowing bubbles and trying to grasp her tiny toes. "When will she start speaking, Mother?"

"Oh, not for a little while yet, dear, but I'm sure she's listening." Cassandra wished Lottie would laugh like her sibling a little more. She was turning out to be such a serious little girl. The only person who could make her laugh was Al Phipps. He could make her cry too, when he turned his attention to Isobel instead.

Cassandra sighed. Motherhood was far more

complicated than she had imagined it would be. It would be a relief to get away on a trip to Brooklands for the Whitsun meeting, although Douglas was so excited, he was like another child himself. The Austin Seven race at Easter had fired him up. Cassandra hoped he wouldn't do anything silly. She doubted there would be a speed limit this time, with the weather set so fair, and Douglas seemed determined to live up to the name of their sponsor. Listening to Katy's account of mounting the banking during the last race had made Cassandra's hair stand on end.

Lottie turned the page of her book and began reading out the next rhyme. Cassandra leaned back into her deck chair and let her daughter's voice drift over her. The apple blossom above their heads bobbed gently in the breeze, creating a delightfully warm current of air. At this precise moment, life was quite perfect.

Cassandra closed her eyes and counted her blessings. Two beautiful daughters, the estate recovering nicely from the shock of the war, a loving husband and even Sir Robert and Lady Amelia were content, as much as they could ever be. How lucky she was in her own marriage. Her mother kept hinting at the lack of a male heir but Cassandra wasn't worried. She knew she was managing the estate better than her brother, Charles, would have done and had every confidence Lottie could do the same, when her turn came. And she quite liked having babies. Douglas certainly hadn't lost his enthusiasm in making them. They might have a son, given time.

Lottie would be starting school in September at the Dame school in Woodbury. How time flew. Cassandra supposed that Al would go to the local village school. Lottie wouldn't like that.

***

In contrast to the wet weather Douglas had complained about last time they raced at Brooklands, the

Whitsun meeting was conducted in brilliant sunshine. Cassandra lay on the grassy slopes with the other spectators, just as she had in September, but this time blissfully free of her baby bump and her cares. Katy and Douglas were getting the Austin ready by the hangers and Cassandra was enjoying her semi-solitude, amongst the noisy crowd.

She listened to the talk around her. It was all of Parry Thomas and his new car, the Leyland-Thomas. She got chatting to the couple next to her.

"Thomas has been working on this car all winter, I heard," said the man, whose waxed moustache looked like it took up most of his spare time. "He's got a workshop, just over the way there. Lives all alone, with his two dogs. He's obsessed with his cars. He'll be going for the record today, you mark my words."

His wife joined in, "Well, let's hope he doesn't overturn his car like Mr Coe's Vauxhall." She looked as if she'd be more than happy to see another melodrama, with her poached egg eyes wide in anticipation.

"What happened?" Cassandra asked, not really sure if she wanted to know.

"Well," said the good lady, "apparently he pulled off the Member's Banking too sharply."

"Was he hurt?" Cassandra looked back at the race track, squinting to see if her husband was still in one piece.

"Oh yes," said the woman, nodding vigorously.

"But not badly. You mustn't worry about your husband, Mrs Flintock-Smythe, it was only minor injuries." Her husband was obviously more sensitive than his wife to Cassandra's concerns.

Cassandra's carefree mood had now evaporated into the warm sunshine. Instead of a baby in her belly, she now had a snake-pit. Making her excuses to the gossipy couple, she made her way down to the railings next to the race-track and mingled with the rest of the crowd.

The next race was the 100 mph Short Handicap.

109

Parry Thomas's big car was easily recognisable as everyone was pointing to it. Parry Thomas seemed quite an ordinary looking man with dark hair, large teeth and a calm demeanour. Everyone around him looked more excited than he was. There was a stillness to him that drew the crowd like a magnet. Cassandra's eyes were drawn to him too and she followed his car around the track with her opera glasses.

After the cars roared off, Parry Thomas led the pack until he put a wheel over the top edge of the Byfleet Banking and removed a shrub. There was an intake of breath by the spectators, as if they all shared the same set of lungs and only exhaled when he pressed on regardless, lapping at an extraordinary 125.77 mph, she later discovered from Katy.

Then it was the Austin race. Cassandra gripped the railings with her bare hands. It was too hot for gloves. The wood bit into her palm but she didn't feel it. There was their Number Five, shiny from Katy's polishing and glinting its peacock blue paint in the sun. Douglas waved to her. How on earth could he pick her out in such a packed throng? She didn't know, but their eyes connected and she smiled and waved back. She was pleased they'd managed to keep the number five, and she hoped it would remain lucky for them. Was Douglas's heart hammering too? She felt hers was fluttering in her throat instead of where it belonged, safely tucked inside her chest cavity.

The flag came down and Douglas made a good start. Katy looked tiny next to him. She watched her friend lean into the bend. Katy looked as if she'd been born in a car, these days. Round the track they roared. Cassandra could hardly bear to look when Douglas overtook another Austin by climbing almost to the top of the steep banking and accelerating down it's curves in front of the other car. Lap after lap they drove, faster and faster. There was a dicey moment when number five was cut up by that yellow number eight, who'd beaten them in the last race at Easter. She could see that Douglas had to brake but also why Katy

110

always said that the new hydraulic brakes weren't right, as they weren't slowing down nearly quick enough to avoid a collision.

Cassandra gripped the rails, unaware of a splinter piercing her skin. There was a screech of brakes and the cars almost touched. Smoke billowed out from the tyres as the number five skidded off course and careered up the banking. Her eyes were dry from not blinking. Then she breathed out. Douglas had dropped back in the nick of time. He'd lost the lead but he was still on the race track, still whole, still alive.

Afterwards, she met them in the paddock. Both Douglas and Katy were flushed and dusty and both were grizzling about their fourth place.

"How fast were you going when number eight nearly smashed into you?" Cassandra felt angry now they were safe.

"We topped the ton!" Katy said with a grin.

"What? a hundred miles an hour?"

"You bet, honey," Douglas said, "but it still wasn't enough. If we could have braked sharper, I could have avoided him and then accelerated away but instead I had to leave off the accelerator, just to stop the collision and we lost ground and our lead."

"The new hydraulic brakes were leaking again and couldn't get a grip, that's why," said Katy. "I'm sure there must be a better system to keep the fluid inside. The rawhide seals didn't work last time so I tried improvising with flexible hose but they still didn't grip enough."

Cassandra shuddered to think of the speed they'd been going without brakes to stop them, but she schooled her voice to be calm. "Never mind, Douglas, darling. Fourth is really good. Oh, look, here's Tim!"

Tim Bluntstone strolled up. "Sorry I'm late. Bloody good show, Douglas. Nice work, Kate." He acknowledged Cassandra with a nod, making her feel superfluous.

The other three became embroiled in a deep discussion about the braking system. Cassandra couldn't join in because she hadn't a clue what they were talking about. A worm of resentment built in her. If she hadn't met Katy Phipps at the BEF in France and got her that job in engineering while she was serving in the WAAC, none of this would be happening and yet now she was being completely ignored.

"I think I'll have a cup of tea in the clubhouse," she said. The others didn't even notice when she turned away. She watched them drive slowly over to the hangers, Tim walking beside them, all completely absorbed in their discussion.

It was the same for the rest of that summer. Katy was working tirelessly on some new version of the brake seals and Douglas spent most days down at the garage. Cassandra didn't go to any more races at Brooklands, preferring to ride her horse, sometimes with her father, Sir Robert, as they visited the estate farms and oversaw the harvest.

"Timeless, isn't it?" Cassandra's eyes rested on the beloved landscape of the downs above the manor house.

"Let's hope it stays this way, Cassandra, my dear." Sir Robert's horse clip-clopped alongside hers in a placid walk. "All the ruddy changes everywhere since the war. Damned unsettling, if you ask me. Never any peace, these days."

Cassandra nodded. "I know what you mean, Father. I wish the estate could stay like this forever, if only for my lovely girls."

A car whined along the road in the valley below them.

"Can't get away from those dratted cars your husband is so fond of."

A skylark trilled above them, fluttering its wings in the warm autumn breeze. Then a bi-plane roared across the sky, startling the horses.

Cassandra smoothed Blackie's mane and whispered sweet nothings into her flattened ears. How strange that she, who had been so keen to learn to drive and the pioneer

112

of them all with her ambulances in France, now regretted the way the combustion engine drowned out the birdsong.

CHAPTER FIFTEEN
Summer 1926

After the last two unsuccessful races at Brooklands and Tim Bluntstone's polite hints that Speedwell couldn't really support racing failures, however much he liked them as people, Katy worked ceaselessly on her modifications for a better seal on the hydraulic brakes she'd bought from Stockhead. It was a good design and she was convinced that, if only the seal could be sorted out, it would be the method that all cars would adopt in the future, but the leaky seals were a major flaw, and this meant that no serious car producer was buying it.

Even after she locked up the workshop each night and Al was safely tucked up in bed, she would get out her drawings and go over and over them. One evening, as Jem was reading the paper, his feet propped up on the log basket, toasting nicely in front of the fire, Katy was again mulling over the problem. As usual, she unconsciously chewed the tip of her pencil, on the rubber.

And, also as usual, the taste made her spit it out, once it had registered on her unforgiving tongue. "Ugh! I can't stand the taste of rubber. I must buy some pencils that don't have rubber erasers at the top."

"You could always stop chewing them," Jem muttered from behind the paper.

"What would be the fun in that?"

Suddenly, Katy looked at the mashed-up rubber tip of her pencil. Then she stroked it with her finger, prodding it with her black-rimmed nail. The rubber was squishy but it didn't break off. She rubbed it on the paper, releasing crumbs of rubber on to the kitchen tablecloth. Katy picked up the crumbs and rolled them between her fingers, experimenting with the texture of it.

Her mind flicked to the tyres she changed routinely every day. They were tough. They withstood all the road surface could throw at them - stones, tarmac, dung. Of course the pneumatic ones punctured readily if they struck

114

a nail discarded by some poor horses's hoof. But brakes didn't contain nails. There was nothing sharp where the brake seals went, was there? And rubber was impermeable, she was sure of it, otherwise the tyres would absorb every drop of rain that fell from the sky. And then there was her contraceptive cap. That was made of rubber and did a good job of containing bodily fluids!

Katy threw the pencil across the table with a whoop of joy, startling her husband, who was clandestinely dropping off behind his paper.

"What's happening?" Jem blinked, crumpling the newspaper as he lowered it.

"Rubber!"

"Rubber what?"

"Seals, of course!"

"Seals?"

"Yes, Jem, yes! For the brakes!" And Katy got up and kissed his sleepy mouth. She held his face in her oil-stained hands and said, "That's how I can stop the brakes from leaking fluid - with a rubber seal. It's bound to work. It's got to!"

Late as it was, she went into the workshop and unlocked the padlock on the big doors. Switching on the electric light, she went into the office and thumbed through the catalogues of car parts. There wasn't one rubber seal available.

She picked up another pencil and stroked its soft tip. Couldn't be that hard to get some rubber and make her own seal, could it? Who would make the stuff - tyre manufacturers, of course!

It was hard to sleep that night. Her mind was racing with various designs. Should she cut the rubber, melt it into forms or stamp out the right shape? And how could she create a mould of the right size and shape? Perhaps Jem could carve something out of wood? It would have to be perfectly smooth. By dawn she'd come up with the perfect solution. Mr Radcock, the blacksmith in Lower Cheadle, might be able to forge a mould of the right dimensions from iron.

Even though she'd had little sleep, she was too excited to feel tired the next day and spent a good bit of time on the telephone tracking down a rubber supplier, when she should have been helping Billy with the butcher's van, whose carburettor had clogged up.

Eventually she got hold of the Firestone tyre company, who offered to deliver some vulcanised rubber in blocks. It would be delivered by ordinary post, via the train and should arrive by Thursday. The man had been very helpful explaining that raw rubber was too sticky at warm temperatures and the addition of various chemicals and heat - or vulcanisation as he called it - strengthened the rubber and made it much more useful. Katy didn't tell him what she was going to use it for. She was only surprised they hadn't produced rubber seals themselves but then, few people were using hydraulic brakes at all yet, but they just might, if she could come up with the right solution.

As soon as she put the phone down, she got in the Austin and drove down to Lower Cheadle to the smithy.

Arthur Radcock was a mountain of a man and looked as if hewn from one. The sinews of his arms twisted like rope as he worked the bellows and flared the fire hot enough to melt the metal he worked so skilfully. When Katy entered the blacksmith's workshop the heat hit her and made her catch her breath. It was already warm on this June day and Arthur had doors open both front and back but there was barely a draught to stir the beaten earth on the floor. Arthur glistened with sweat and his short brown hair stuck to his wet forehead. Katy had known him all her life. Everyone knew Arthur and relied on his expertise to mend saucepans and kettles, as well as shoe their horses.

"Morning, Arthur, how are you?"

"What you doing here? Shouldn't you be up on the London Road stealing my customers? Martha Threadwell said you mended a saucepan of hers the other day. She

116

brought it in to show me. Rough old weld. Could have done it better here."

Katy saw that this wasn't going to be as straightforward as she'd hoped. She hadn't given Arthur's business a second thought, these past few years. He must be shoeing fewer horses these days. Trust Mrs Threadwell to stir up trouble.

"I'm sure you could, Arthur. Martha only gave it to me because Billy works for us and she knew I'd do it for free," Katy said.

"Hmm. That lad would have made a better blacksmith than a grease monkey, if you asks me." Arthur riddled his fire, sending sparks flying out towards Katy, who backed away.

She decided to try a different tack. "I'm sorry if I've taken farrier business from you, Arthur. Can't stop progress, can we? Everyone's buying a car these days."

"You don't have to tell me that, young woman. Good job I've got Sir Robert's horses to shoe regularly. At least he keeps up the old ways." Arthur drew a poker from the fire and began to beat its white-hot tip. Katy watched, fascinated, as it faded to yellow, then red, under Arthur's hammer. It was impossible to speak above the clanging, so she watched, and learned.

Under the blacksmith's massive fist wielding his hammer, the metal twisted from straight into a long corkscrew at one end, before curving around into a perfect handle. When he plunged the glowing iron into his font of water, great clouds of steam rose up, making the already hot room humid. He laid the poker down on a stone slab, amongst his other creations. Katy looked at the array. They were superb. Arthur wasn't just a practical giant, he was an artist too.

"That's a beautiful poker, Arthur, and you made it so quickly." She put her hand out to touch it.

"Don't put your hand on it, girl! It's still bloody hot. Just because it's gone black, don't mean it's cool enough to handle. Thought a mechanic like you would have known that, at least." Arthur wiped his forehead with a rag he took from his pocket.

"You're right, Arthur, I don't know anything about your work but I have a design here for something I wondered if you might make for me." Katy took out the piece of paper that was burning a hole in her pocket.

"Oh, you did, did you?"

She spread it out on the stone slab and, using her finger, described her idea for a mould. "It's got to be exactly this size, Arthur, and this shape.

"It's an odd looking thing. What's if for?"

Katy explained. "It's a mould for a brake seal. It's got to be completely watertight, as I'll be melting rubber and pouring it in. It's in the shape of a cup see, to sit over the drum and has to have this central pillar to make the hole in the middle. Then, when the rubber is cold, a bit like when your metal has cooled, it goes hard and I'll have to tap it out and leave it to cure. Then I can insert it in the brake mechanism and stop the brake fluid leaking out, the way it does now."

"It would be a damn sight easier to stick to horses, if you asks me. What do you want fluid around a brake for?" Arthur scratched his head.

"It means the pressure from the fluid displaces the brake pads, instead of having to use your foot to push the calipers onto the wheel, which takes a lot of effort. Now women are driving, they're not strong enough to depress the brake pedal sufficiently. This way, they won't have to."

"And are you going to make these new-fangled brakes and all up at your garage?"

"No, it would be too complicated and a company called Stockhead have already produced them but no-one's buying them because of the leakage problem."

"And you reckon you can fix that?"

"Yes, Arthur, I do."

"And sell them on to this Stockhead lot?"

"I hope so, if no-one beats me to it."

"I reckon you might make a lot of money out of

118

that." Arthur looked at her. Was that respect in his eyes?

"Could be. Will you help me, Arthur?" Katy ventured a smile and received a hearty slap on her shoulder with a meaty hand. It almost knocked her over but she didn't mind.

"Leave it with me, young Kate. Come by this time tomorrow and we'll see what I can rustle up."

The next day, true to his word, Arthur had made several moulds, based on her design, each one more smooth than the last. She thanked him profusely and paid him in cash, on the spot, before bringing them back to the workshop and setting them on a bench for Billy and Jem to admire. She couldn't wait for Thursday and the delivery of her raw material of rubber. Katy got Jem to build a firepit in the backyard. Arthur manufactured a metal drum to contain the flames and when she collected it, she also bought a deep, heavy skillet in which to melt the rubber.

It took weeks of work, and prototype after prototype in the workshop, before she was finally satisfied with a circle of rubber that was flexible enough to make a tight seal. If she could prove this worked, she was sure Stockhead would want to buy it for their flawed hydraulic brakes, and her excitement grew as she refined her design until she was confident enough to road test it, before they invested in anything more. If her idea didn't work, there was no point pursuing it, but if it did, they could make a fortune. She decided to leave Douglas out of the first nerve-wracking test on the road, and keep it between her and Jem. If the brakes failed, she'd rather no-one else knew.

Early one morning, when Al had gone to school and before the garage got really busy, they drove up to the downs together. Katy had tested the brakes over and over in the workshop and on the forecourt, but this was the first time at speed. If they failed, she would be putting their lives at risk. She crawled along the narrow lane that led up to the downlands above the manor. Tentatively, she put her foot on the brake pedal and instantly the braking was better. Heartened, she drove it up the hill at a faster rate.

"Keep braking her, Kate," Jem said, his one hand braced against the dashboard.

Each time, the Austin responded quickly, without jarring. It was working! It felt nothing short of miraculous and Katy couldn't help grinning as she drove. She glanced across at Jem whose face showed a similar excitement. They laughed and she drove a bit quicker, confident now she could stop. She got up to twenty five miles an hour and tested it again. The Austin drew to a graceful halt.

"I've done it. I've done it!" Katy crowed.

Jem reached across and kissed her. "You certainly have, my clever wife."

"Let's zoom down the hill as fast as we can, and slam on the brakes, shall we?"

"Only if you let me drive. And brace yourself, just in case you hit the dashboard."

"Alright. I'll be able to observe better that way." Katy got out of the car and they swapped seats.

Jem drove quickly up the incline and let the car swoop down the other side, without braking. At the steepest point, after warning Katy, he applied the brakes. The Austin shrieked to a halt, skidding its tyres on the tarmac to such an extent blue smoke and the smell of burning rubber clouded out behind them.

"A perfect stop! We need to bring a stopwatch and record the braking time," Katy said.

"Yes, I agree, and then we can quote it when we're asking for sales."

Katy got out of the car and looked at the skid mark they'd made on the road. There was, for the first time, no fluid around the tyres.

"That's it. It worked." Katy felt triumphant.

Autumn slunk in with its shorter days but still Katy worked through the evenings, by electric light, trying to perfect her design and come up with ways to make the seals in greater numbers. She could make them, one by one, by hand and Arthur, who was now taking a real

120

interest in the project, had made a spoon-like lever to help pop them out of the moulds, but they would need some heavy equipment to set up a production line, if they were really going to produce them in any quantity, and a work-shed to house it. They would also need to make different sizes for different cars, buy the rubber in bulk and store it somewhere, let alone get cutting tools to stamp out the seals, once formed in the moulds. It would all need a great deal of investment but she was convinced it would be worth it, especially if they could produce them before anyone else hit on the idea.

With the racing season over for another year, Katy asked Douglas to come for a meeting at the garage. She was proud to show him what she had produced.

Douglas listened attentively to her ideas about manufacturing the seal. "I think you're on to a winner, Kate, but before we invest in more equipment, I think we should all go to America. You see, they make Model T Fords close to my home in Boston. The factory is in Cambridge, over the river, near my old college of Harvard. I know someone who works there who might be able to give us some advice about setting up. They have production lines off to a tee, that's why they are so successful. Why, they might even be interested in your invention, Kate, and make it there. Or we could go to Stockhead, see if they want to buy it from you direct."

"I don't agree," Katy said. "For one thing, I'd rather not go back to America. I'm needed here and already spend more time than I should on the racing car and designs than on the everyday work that we've built up here at Katherine Wheel Garage. Billy is complaining all the time and some customers have also grumbled. I must maintain the goodwill I've built up. The garage is still our main business. Without it, we're all sunk."

Jem nodded. Katy's heart leapt. Had he finally accepted that her business was a success?

His next words astonished her. He sounded as committed to her design as she was, and spoke

121

enthusiastically, as if he was a full member of the team. "We've no idea if we can sell it, but we both think it's worth a shot to try and make the component here. We'd have no control over an American manufacturer and would only make a small amount of money from selling the patent to Stockhead. I feel sure that both Morris and Austin would be interested in brakes that performed better but why give away the chance to make it ourselves, under our own steam? We could then offer it to them, under our own brand."

"That would take a great deal of investment capital, Jem." Douglas's face was still very serious. "I'm not sure I could raise the funds."

"Ah, I see," Jem said. "Well, I could approach the bank for a loan. The garage is firmly established now and Speedwell have provided a lot of finance. The sales of Austins continue to increase, as well as the after-sales servicing and repairs. In fact, I think we need to employ another mechanic. Billy Threadwell will never be the sharpest pencil in the box, though he's a good worker."

"I'm not sure about borrowing money from the bank, Jem," Katy said, still reeling from his comprehensive summary of the situation. Jem looked and sounded like a real businessman. While she'd been concentrating on the details of her design, it seemed her husband had also been busy. Recognising the enormity of this change, she now dreaded letting him down. "What if someone else comes up with the same idea and beats us to it? We'll be deep in debt and could put the whole business in jeopardy."

"There's no need to borrow the dough from the bank, Jem. I'll go to Boston and speak with my mother. I'm confident she would want to invest in your scheme and tobacco profits have soared since the war, so she can spare it. I think you should come with me and make the case to her. You'll need more land too. We'll need to involve Cassandra in that. See if you can buy a few more acres from the estate. I can't see why she would find that a problem, the land around your holding is just summer pasture. The cows can graze elsewhere. And, between ourselves, Cassandra might be glad of some extra capital anyway. Sir Robert hasn't lost his taste for flashy hunters and they don't come cheap," Douglas said.

"I could always try visiting a factory in England," Jem said. "Fords have a plant in Manchester."

"But we have no way of introducing ourselves there, Jem. At least I have a contact in Boston."

"But why would you need me to come, Douglas? Couldn't you persuade your mother better than me?" Jem looked thoughtful.

"I think it would look more business-like, more professional, with you not being a member of the family, but co-proprietor of Katherine Wheel Garage. Begging your pardon, Kate, but based on your last visit, I don't think they'd welcome you. And it's time I went back to see my family. Rose wrote me to say Father has been working too hard again and she's worried about the effect on Ma. I'm not sure what that means exactly but it might help her to get involved in funding our new scheme. You've played your part in coming up with the technical stuff, Kate, but Jem is the one who can show the business side to best advantage."

Jem looked pleased at Douglas's compliment. He smiled at Katy and raised his eyebrows in query.

Katy, surprised, nodded her assent. Nodding back, he answered, "Okay, Doug, I'd like to go to Boston actually," Jem said.

Katy gazed at her husband with fresh eyes. Jem had a new confidence these days. She noticed how he sat with his shoulders squared and his back bone straight against his office chair. She looked around at the neat ledgers, labelled and standing to attention on the shelves he'd made. He'd got more involved in running the garage, though she'd hardly noticed, and it had changed him, she could see that now. Yes, Jem would be the right person to approach Selina Flintock. She quite agreed Mr Flintock wouldn't want to see her again, and shuddered at the

123

memory of Douglas's father's stern face when he had been quick to condemn her for a slut. She'd been attacked by Douglas's friend, Fred Stavely, and Mr Flintock had held her responsible, despite having no evidence to the contrary. For a moment, she found herself wondering what had happened to Fred and then discovered she didn't care. The war had long ago taught her to leave the past where it belonged, behind her.

After a meeting with Mr Hayes and Cassandra, it was agreed that she and Jem would buy another twenty acres surrounding their garage for a knock-down rate. They had long ago paid off their dues to Douglas for their initial five acres. This was a much bigger sum and Katy worried that, if they couldn't make the brakes enterprise successful, and quickly, they'd never pay it off.

"You're creating quite a little empire at Katherine Wheel," Cassandra said, with a look that Katy found less friendly than she was used to. Cassandra had so much, more than Katy could ever aspire to, surely, she wasn't jealous?

"Not yet, we're not, Cass, but it makes sense to give ourselves the chance to spread out, if we can." Katy went to kiss Cassandra's cheek only to find her friend's face turned away.

The date for the American trip was decided by Rose Flintock, who wrote to say she was getting married to a Methodist Minister, Cedric Shaw, in November and dearly wanted her brother and his family to attend the ceremony in Boston.

"You can come with us, can't you, Jem? We're taking the girls to meet their paternal family, so Nanny Morgan will come with us too. Lottie will just have to miss school for a short while. She's so keen, I'm sure she'll catch up," Cassandra said, while the children played conkers in the garage backyard.

"Yes, we've agreed it should be Jem who goes." Katy was determined to remain generous, and secretly glad to stay behind, for once.

124

"Don't worry Jem, I'll protect you from the Flintock clan!" Cassandra laughed, "I wouldn't inflict their piety on anyone again."

She looked at Katy, who winced at the memory.

Jem said, "I'm not frightened of them, Cass. I wouldn't mind a bit of exploring though, so staying with Doug's family might tie me down a bit."

"Of course, Jem, I'll get Doug to fix you up with a boarding house nearby and you can be independent. Travel across with us but then you can return home when it suits you. Lord knows how long I'll have to stay but it gives me the option of travelling back with you if I can't stick it."

"That sounds like the ideal arrangement, doesn't it, Jem?" Katy said.

"It does, and you're right, I think I'd be better off staying somewhere neutral," Jem said, with his characteristic smile.

"I'll make the most of the trip, Katy," he added when they were alone. "I'll leave no stone unturned, you can bet on that. I've got a lot of things I want to discover in America."

Katy didn't make much of his words until he was gone. Then she thought about them constantly, wondering what he'd meant.

She missed Jem far more than she'd expected. At first, it was the practical things. Taking the compost bucket up the garden, making the bed of a morning, keeping the fire alight. She realised, with shame, how much she had relied on him to shoulder the everyday chores that kept life running smoothly. Tasks she had previously assumed were hers, he had taken over, without her even noticing, while she'd been focussing on the garage and developing the seals for the new braking system. She felt chastened and selfish as she was forced to remember how much time the domestic routine demanded.

As the days passed, she missed his smile even more; his ever-present smile, no matter how grumpy she was or how pre-occupied. What a cow she had become! He sent a brief letter saying he'd arrived safely and had already fixed up a visit to the Ford factory. He promised he would write and tell her all about it when he could. What a reversal of fortunes. Jem away on a voyage of discovery, going places she hadn't been, and she content to be at home, keeping the business running.

And she was glad he had this chance, even though he'd always said he never wanted to travel. She could trust that he would make the most of it. She could always trust Jem.

The bank wrote and outlined the payments they must now make for the new parcel of land to repay the loan from Douglas. It frightened her. Without Jem's reassurance, his new confidence in his business instincts, she felt lost and small, overwhelmed by the responsibility of the debt they'd taken on.

Her body longed for Jem's at night and, for the first time, motor manuals lost their fascination. Without his loving encouragement, new mechanical knowledge became just that - mechanical.

This is how it must have been for him, she supposed, when she had sailed to Boston before Katherine Wheel Garage had even been a dream. How much had happened in the years since then.

It was strange without Douglas lounging about the place too, filling the air with fragrant blue smoke from his American cigarettes and charming customers into buying another saloon. She wasn't the only one who missed Cassandra's visits with the children, either. Al drooped visibly in the absence of his friends and Katy took to snuggling up with him around the fire in the evenings, listening to his first stumbling efforts to read before she read aloud to him all the favourite stories of her own childhood. She enjoyed putting him to bed, learning about his secrets, and his dreams. It was time, in fact long overdue, she let go of the pain of Florence's death and allowed herself to love her adorable little boy.

Al, at five years old, was the spitting image of his

father and was now attending the village school. He looked so smart in his school clothes and his teacher, Miss Emery, said he showed promise. Katy had loved school and leaving it at the age of twelve had been a wrench. A new grammar school had opened in Woodbury and she had hopes that Al might get a scholarship to go. He was every bit as bright as Charlotte Flintock-Smythe and they had taken to comparing their school experiences like two old professors, puzzled as to why their parents found their serious faces so comical.

Every night Al would ask when his daddy was coming home. How stupid she'd been to deny this intimacy before. Was she using Al as a substitute for his absent father? Perhaps, but it certainly comforted them both and what was wrong with that?

CHAPTER SIXTEEN
Autumn 1926

It was the sheer size of everything that astonished Jem when he reached America. The Atlantic ocean had been large enough. They hadn't been able to see land for days during the crossing. Jem had found that very unnerving. Boston was almost as big, and so built up! He'd been glad to lodge separately from the Flintocks and sleep on solid ground again, although the earth didn't seem to stop swaying for days after docking.

He was content to leave Douglas and Cassandra to their family duties. He had no desire to stay in the States any longer than he had to and persuaded Douglas he could make the research trip to the Ford factory alone. Douglas looked relieved. His friend never was that interested in the details.

"It's easy to get to Memorial Drive, Jem. You could walk it, if you want, it's only about three miles, or take the train. You have to cross the Charles River from the embankment but the Ford Factory is only a few blocks on the other side, next to the river, you can't go wrong." He handed Jem a letter. "See, I've addressed it to the younger brother of my old college pal, Tom Wood. His kid brother Ernest works in the office at Fords and he'll see you right."

Jem left for the factory early the next morning. Douglas was right, it wasn't hard to find, even for a country man like him. There was no mistaking the wide, ruffled Charles River and he enjoyed striding along the bridge above its cold waters. There certainly was plenty of fresh air in Boston but he doubted he'd ever adjust to the scale of the place.

The assembly plant was housed in a tall, surprisingly elegant building, with a stylish curved frontage. It couldn't have been more than a few years old. Jem was impressed. He went through the swish doors and into the wide reception area, clutching Douglas's letter. The receptionist was brisk but friendly and seemed used to visitors turning up. He rang Ernest Wood on the internal telephone and told Jem to wait, so he strolled over to inspect an enormous picture hung on the very white wall.

Jem couldn't credit his eyes when he stood before the scene of the main Ford factory in Detroit, whose two hundred and eighty seven industrial acres stretched across the black and white photograph. Five chimneys soared above the central block in white columns, their rims stained black from the smoke issuing from them. Other huge rectangular buildings flanked the centre on either side and he could just make out the ridged roofs of the factory floor fanning out behind them. The land was flat in Detroit, flatter than anywhere he'd ever seen. Flatter even than the killing fields of Flanders and certainly flatter than that heaving sea he'd just crossed. He questioned why a stretch of plain as level as this was called Highland Park. What idiot had dreamt that name up? The roads ran straight as rulers and everything had a grid-like modernity to it that his countryman's eyes found ugly. There was something about the place that reminded him of the machinery of war.

He was so wrapped up in the picture that he jumped when a young man, only about twenty years old and wearing horn-rimmed glasses, touched his arm. Good job it wasn't the wooden one or he'd never have noticed Ernest Wood's tentative gesture.

"Mr Phipps?"

"That's right, you must be Ernest Wood?"

"Yes, my brother went to college with Douglas Flintock, along the way there at Harvard. I've only just graduated myself. Pleased to meet you, sir."

"Call me Jem, and here's Douglas's letter of introduction." Jem was surprised at Ernest Wood's youth and obvious nervousness. It made him feel ancient but much more at ease. He followed Ernest into a long corridor and then out to the factory proper. The noise on the production line floor was deafening and Ernest had to shout to explain the techniques he showed him. Jem found the streamlined way of breaking down the parts into different areas of work fascinating. Each man had a job to do, but it was the same job, over and over, before the part went on to the next stage of assembly.

The men looked resigned to their fate but Jem couldn't have stood the monotony for one day. He wondered how much they got paid. He'd bought a clipboard in Boston and held it in his wooden claw, scribbling down sketches and notes as fast as he could. He could easily imagine a scaled down model to make the seals Katy had designed and how they could be housed in a comparatively small shed at home. Excitement bubbled in his belly. They'd have to employ more staff of course, but that shouldn't be a problem.

When the tour was over, Jem was relieved to escape the racket. Back in the reception foyer he thanked Ernest, glad not to have to compete with the machinery to be heard.

"Fascinating tour, Ernest, thank you, that was most instructive."

"Glad to help, Jem. Good luck with your project. I'm only sorry Ford are so dead set against changing to the hydraulic brake system but the philosophy here is 'if it ain't broke, don't fix it' and the Tin Lizzie is so popular these days, they don't want to rock the boat. They won't even paint them a different colour, other than black!"

Jem laughed with Ernest, who continued, "My family send their best wishes to Douglas. I'll tell them about his little girls and life back in England. Maybe Tom will go visit, while they're here in Boston."

They shook hands and Jem stepped back into the cool Bostonian air. He made his way back over the huge river to his tall, brown boarding house in Back Bay and spent the rest of the evening working on his notes. It was Rose's wedding the next day and he'd been glad not to have been invited. From what he'd heard Douglas and Cassandra saying about the Flintocks, he considered he was well out of that hornet's nest.

He spent the time writing out his plans in meticulous detail, adding the projected costs in a separate report, ready to show Mrs Flintock after the celebrations were over. Douglas had promised to pop round to let him know when it would be convenient but he didn't expect to see him for a couple of days. That gave him time to do that other bit of other detective work, equally, if not more, important than researching factories.

He'd made enquiries about Fred Stavely as soon as he arrived at his lodgings but no-one had heard of him. He went to the library, that Katy had so fondly described from her visit in 1919, seven busy years ago. For all he knew, Fred Stavely could be dead by now. He hoped not.

As he climbed the steps and walked through the glass doors, he could see why she'd been so impressed with the massive building. He wasted little time in admiring it but went straight to the archive of newspapers the librarian showed him.

His fingers were black with newsprint before he found what he was looking for - an article listing Fred Stavely as a member of the winning baseball team while he was in college at Harvard in 1914. There was a faded photograph too, but how could he pick the bastard out from the smudgy line of beefy players? Even if he could identify him within the rows of athletes, he'd probably look quite different now. He'd have to try another tack.

He went back to the librarian. "Excuse me, but could you help me? I'm trying to trace an old friend while I'm here in Boston. Is there an electoral roll or list of addresses for residents I could look at?"

"We've been keeping the Boston City Directory since 1789, sir. Surname?" The librarian didn't look a bit interested, much to Jem's relief.

"Stavely," Jem said. "Frederick Stavely."

"The 'S's are over there, third shelf." The librarian pointed to a raft of ledgers in alphabetical order in a dark corner near the entrance.

Swallowing his triumph, Jem walked quickly over

and took down the heavy book.

He ran his finger down the page of surnames.

And there it was.

Stavely. Listed under Stavely, Percival, were his wife, Mabel, and their three children - Frederick, Gertrude and Jane.

"34, Chestnut Street," Jem read aloud. "Such a rustic name for this huge city."

He closed the big book and held his hand on the hard cover for a moment, unable to believe how easy his discovery had been. Then he carefully replaced it in its correct position on the shelf with the other identical ledgers. He nodded his thanks to the librarian before returning to the vestibule, where he had spied a large map of Boston framed in an ornate scroll of plaster on the back wall.

Some thoughtful bureaucrat had listed all the streets in alphabetical order. Such a methodical community. Jem silently blessed their attention to detail and looked up Chestnut Street's grid reference. Tracing the lines across and down, he found it was not so far from where he was staying. He memorised the street layout without difficulty and marched swiftly out into the November drizzle.

Boston was much colder than Wiltshire at this time of year and he was glad of his hat and gloves. Glad, too, of his anonymity. He'd bought a trilby hat for the trip, egged on by Katy. Jem had always worn a flat cap, like every other working man he knew, but Katy had insisted that he was a business owner now; one going on a business trip and he must look the part. He felt conspicuous in his new hat but no-one took any notice of him as he strode down the busy streets, too pre-occupied with his mission to window-shop. Douglas had shown him how to use the tram and he hopped on, using his good hand to steady himself. The tram-car was crowded, so he stood all the way to Beacon Hill, and having recognised the rounded dome of Massachusetts State House, got off to get his bearings.

He found Chestnut Street easily and knocked on the door of the tall brownstone house with his wooden hand, before he had time to be nervous.

His rap was loud. Wood on wood.

Jem waited a full ten minutes before his knock was answered. He'd almost given up and was about to turn away, when it creaked open. A young, heavily built woman stood there, looking harassed and a little breathless. Jem assumed she'd had to navigate a lot of stairs. When she spoke, she had a strong Irish accent. Jem hadn't expected that.

"What are you wanting?" No smile of welcome.

"I'm sorry to bother you." Jem tried to infuse warmth into his words with his own smile. "I'm looking for Fred Stavely. He's an old friend and as I'm visiting Boston, I wanted to look him up. I believe he lives here?"

"Fred's not been here for a long while." The woman looked more hostile than ever.

From the depths of the house came a querulous voice. "Who is it, Kathleen? Who's at the door? Did I hear Fred's name?"

The disembodied voice sounded ancient to Jem's ears.

Kathleen frowned and muttered something under her breath, but she opened the door wider to allow him in.

"You'd better come in and see the old fellow, but I warn you, he's very weak and you can't stay long."

"Thank you." Jem crossed the threshold, wondering what on earth he would find inside.

Kathleen showed him in to the front parlour. The drizzle outside had been bordering on sleet and Jem welcomed the fire at first, but this room was so hot, he soon felt almost faint. A bank of red coals blazed in the hearth and a wizened old man sat hunched over it, swathed in blankets and scarves, looking like a beggar living on the streets, instead of the owner of the rich furnishings surrounding him.

Jem took off his hat and loosened the buttons of his

133

overcoat. Sweat prickled on his brow and neck within seconds.

The old man turned to Jem. His face was lopsided, with his mouth and left eye drooping in a downward slant. His eyes were rheumy and watered so much he constantly mopped them with a large, damp handkerchief.

The old man spoke again in the same reedy, weak voice. "Who are you? No-one calls these days. What do you want with my Fred?"

Jem cleared his throat, which had dried up. "Good day to you, sir. I'm sorry to bother you, but, yes, I am looking for Fred Stavely."

The old man shook his head from side to side. A real tear squeezed out of his wet eyes and plopped on to the blanket on his lap.

"You mustn't upset yourself, Mr Stavely, now." Kathleen went over and fussed the old man's blankets.

She looked at Jem. "Fred hasn't been here in a long while. This here is his father and you can see he's not well."

"Yes, I'm sorry, but do you know where Fred is living, if not here?"

The old man uttered an unearthly wail. It was soft, in keeping with his lack of strength but Jem could recognise grief when he heard it.

"Forgive me, but Fred is alright, isn't he?" Jem said.

Mr Stavely pressed his handkerchief to his eyes and started to actually sob.

"There, there, Mr Stavely, don't take on so." Kathleen looked cross. "I'll show you out." She got up and nodded Jem in the direction of the door.

"You're just upsetting the old man. I've enough to do without that. Fred disappeared some years ago and his father suffered a stroke soon after. Mrs Stavely died at the same time. No-one knows where Fred went or what he's up to. It's broken his father's heart. Both his daughters have moved away. One's gone to Italy and the other has gone to New York. Not that they're much missed. I'm sorry,

134

mister, but we can't help you. Good day."

Jem was on the pavement before he'd registered the finality of her dismissal. Frustrated, he went back to his boarding house.

Up in his fifth floor bedroom he tried to ignore the argument coming through the walls from the bedroom next door. He went over his notes for the umpteenth time but he couldn't concentrate. He might be stumped so far, but he wasn't about to give up his search for the man who had almost wrecked his marriage.

He'd just have to try a different tack, that's all.

CHAPTER SEVENTEEN
Autumn 1926

"Oh, Doug, I didn't think this visit would be easy, but I never expected it would be quite this hard, either." Cassandra was profoundly grateful for the privacy of Douglas's old bedroom.

Their daughters were asleep in the room next door, with Nanny Morgan watching over them, and they finally had a moment alone. It had been a long day of preparations for the wedding, with all the Flintocks at home together for the first time since they'd arrived in Boston a few days ago.

"I thought our beautiful girls would melt your father's heart but I've never seen such a stony face. How could he not love his own grandchildren?" Cassandra felt defeated by her father-in-law's indifference and close to tears. She so rarely felt like this, it shocked her.

Douglas looked rattled too and came and sat next to her on the double bed. He put his arm around her. Cassandra relaxed into its familiar security and leant her weary head on the curve of his neck, her favourite resting place. Her stomach unknotted the ball of nerves that had resided inside it all day and she let out a sigh. Douglas kissed the top of her head and took her spare hand in his. Warmth from his body crept through her veins.

"At least Rose looks happy," Douglas said. "That fiancé of hers seems a fine feller, if a little dull."

"But don't you think Rose has lost her bloom?"

"Maybe, she's certainly thinner than she used to be, but then, she was a little on the plump side, you know," Douglas said, with the honesty of a brother.

"I always thought that was part of her charm." Cassandra wriggled down the bed and let her spine stretch flat. Douglas joined her, so they lay prone together. "Her Cedric does seem awfully *good*, if you know what I mean.

"Douglas chuckled, his blue eyes dancing with affection. "I sure do, honey, but then, so is Rose, if not

136

quite so pedantic. Takes all sorts to make a world, I guess."

Cassandra snuggled closer to her husband. "I'm so glad you're my sort, Doug, darling. I don't know what I'd do without you, or how you became such a wonderful human being when your family is so, well, so *unhappy*."

Douglas kissed her mouth and then the tip of her nose. "I doubt I'd be happy if I hadn't met you, my love."

Cassandra thought he'd kiss her more deeply and she wanted the intimacy of love-making but Douglas drew back a little. A frown played across his forehead. "I'm worried about Mother, Cass. She's always been slender and dreamy but today I thought she looked ill. Those shadows under her eyes, you know, and her hands were so restless. They looked almost transparent, she's so thin. That agitation's not like her, she always used to have the gift of stillness. Do you think she's drinking again?"

Cassandra pulled back from succumbing to the sensuous magnet of Douglas's body and pictured his mother instead. He was right. Selina Flintock had exuded charisma when she'd first met her, here in this very house, seven long years ago. She'd been impressed by her blonde grace and the beautiful timbre of her deep, slow voice with its rich southern drawl, so different to Mr Flintock's clipped Bostonian tones. Today her mother-in-law had been distracted and had barely noticed her new granddaughters. Isobel, whose tiny blonde head resembled Selina's, had gurgled delightfully while playing in the parlour and Lottie had recited a poem, painstakingly learnt for the occasion, but Selina had barely even smiled at them.

And, on an entirely pragmatic level, she and Douglas were here, not only to celebrate Rose and Cedric's marriage in due solemnity, but to ask Selina for a hefty sum of money. Douglas's mother had hardly strung two words together. How would she be able to listen to Jem's careful plans and make a business decision? And they couldn't involve Mr Flintock. His answer would be an inevitable flat 'no'.

"Maybe, Doug, or maybe she's just a bit down in the dumps. It can't be easy, living with your father, and Cheryl is so sarcastic too. Cheryl didn't mention Fred once, I noticed. I doubt she's forgiven us for bringing Katy last time and driving him away. She must be very busy now she's a qualified doctor. She's probably never at home. Selina will miss Rose dreadfully, when she moves into her marital home. Maybe your mother is lonely, or suffering from depression?"

"I'm sure she is lonely, darling, and I can't sit idly by and not do something about it. We'll invite her to come home with us for another visit, shall we?" Douglas kissed her willing mouth again, little butterfly kisses of invitation.

Cassandra nodded, not wanting to talk, in case he stopped caressing her lips. Flickers of desire shot through her and she pressed her body into his.

Such a perfect fit.

Douglas's kisses deepened and she opened her mouth to let him in. All thoughts of his family soon faded into the black night.

***

Rose and Cedric's wedding was a simple one, held in the Methodist Chapel where Cedric had his new living. Being November, there were few flowers, which Cassandra thought a little dreary but Rose looked so joyful, it was impossible not to feel happy for her. Rose looked lovely in her white dress and her new slimmer frame made her look both older and more elegant, but Cassandra remembered her fuller figure and rosy cheeks with nostalgia and worried about the bride's careworn face, underneath that glowing smile. Rose's eyes shone when she made her vows. There was no doubting how much she loved the man she was marrying.

Douglas and Cassandra exchanged their own loving glances, when the pair were announced man and wife, and

138

held hands below the level of the pews, linking their gloved fingers in a secret troth. Isobel slept peacefully through the ceremony, too young to understand it, but Lottie drank in every detail of the marriage vows with wide-open eyes and a little frown of concentration, as if memorising the sacred words.

The elder Mr and Mrs Flintock stood in the pew in front of them. It gave Cassandra ample opportunity to study her in-laws. Douglas's father looked little different from how she remembered him. There was a little grey in his sideburns and a few more lines around his mouth, all in a downward direction. They had the effect of making his severe, craggy face look harsher; even more unforgiving than before, if that were possible. His wife, in contrast, looked pale, almost ethereal. She had finally given up those wide-brimmed hats in a concession to the fashionable clôche. Her long elegant neck rose like a swan's from the white fur stole around her shoulders, and her pale blue coat could not disguise her wraith-like figure. Once, Selina swayed, looking like she might faint. Cheryl, ever efficient and alert, caught her mother's arm, tucking it inside her own and holding it firmly, almost clamping it to her navy blue outfit, which reminded Cassandra of a policeman's uniform, so severe was it.

The wedding breakfast was served next door, in Rose and Cedric's new house. Cassandra was hungry and thoroughly enjoyed the break from the housekeeper's cooking at the Flintocks'. Maureen's meals were both heavy and bland and had not improved in her absence. In contrast to the modest dressing of the church, the wedding feast was quite lavish and full of Bostonian seafood.

Cassandra loved the taste of the fresh dressed lobster, the salads of clams and prawns slathered in rich mayonnaise and garnished with cucumber out of season.

"I could do with a glass of champagne to wash this down, Douglas," Cassandra said in a low voice to her husband.

"Couldn't we all, darling, but there'll only be

cordials here. It's always been temperance for the Flintocks, even at a wedding and don't forget, alcohol is prohibited everywhere nowadays. You won't catch my lot breaking the law." Douglas winked at her.

"Still, give them a toast, Doug. I doubt your father will celebrate the happy couple otherwise." Cassandra winced at the sweetness of her drink, and longed to relax with a cigarette.

"Good idea." Douglas tapped his glass with his fork for silence.

"A toast to Cedric and my lovely sister, Rose; the new Mr and Mrs Shaw! May they always have health and happiness together."

Everyone dutifully sipped their insipid drinks and smiled at the bridal couple.

Douglas continued, "Rose is the best of sisters, and I'm sure she'll be the most loving of wives. You're a lucky man, Cedric, and you are both always welcome to our home in England. All the very best, always!"

A genteel cheer went up and shortly afterwards guests started to peel away. Cassandra kissed Rose goodbye in her turn. "Good luck, darling Rose. I can see you have a good man there. I hope you will be very happy. Time to take my little ones back home for a rest now."

Rose kissed her in return. "Thank you, Cassandra. I hope we can come and visit some day."

"I'd love that. Have a lovely honeymoon in the summerhouse at Falmouth. I loved it there so very much."

"Come and see us. Bring the girls before you go home," Rose said.

"Oh, no, you won't be wanting company on your honeymoon! No, we'll come another time." And Cassandra rounded up her sleepy daughters.

The next day, everyone was a little tired and out of sorts. Cassandra found the atmosphere oppressive and persuaded Douglas to take the girls to the park for the afternoon, despite the threat of snow.

Dinner was turgid and the conversation, never very

fluid, listless.

"It was a lovely ceremony, yesterday." Cassandra could think of nothing else to break the silence.

Mr Flintock always chewed his food thoroughly and swallowed before replying. "Yes, simple is always best."

"I thought Rose looked very pretty."

"Did you, Cassandra?" Cheryl took a sip of water. "I thought she looked rather tired, though I can't think why, when she doesn't work."

"Weddings can be exhausting." Cassandra cut her chicken.

"How would you know? You barely had one." Cheryl's white teeth dispatched her meat with precision.

"I hope they'll be warm enough at Falmouth." Selina's melodic voice broke the tension, which was just as well, judging by Douglas's tense face.

"If Cedric wasn't so tight with his money, they could have gone somewhere warm. It'll be a wonder if Rose doesn't catch pneumonia. It isn't called a summerhouse for nothing." Cheryl looked at her brother. "Not like when you were there in the hot summer of 1919."

"I think that episode is best forgotten, Cheryl." Mr Flintock got up from the table, signalling the end of the meal.

It was a relief when Monday dawned and Cheryl and her father returned to their normal workaday routines.

Cassandra wasn't sorry to see the back of either of them. "Shall we ask Jem over to talk to your mother, while the coast is clear, Doug?"

"Good idea, might as well get it over with and seal our fate. Oh, my, that was a terrible pun. I'd almost forgotten that humour existed. Yes, as soon as we have the business side of things sewn up, we'll be able to go home. I don't know about you, Cass, but that would suit me just fine. I'll go and fetch Jem and you ask Mother when would be a good time for her to see him."

Cassandra knocked on Selina's door. There was a rustle of silk and a clink of glass before the door was

141

opened. She fancied she could smell gin on Selina's breath. It was only nine o'clock in the morning. She wondered how she got hold of the stuff, with Prohibition in force. They had better not delay their meeting.

"Selina, hello. We were wondering if it would be alright if our friend Jeremy Phipps came to see you today, to talk about that business proposal?"

Selina smiled, and nodded, "Of course, darling. Give me a moment to get ready. Shall we say, eleven o'clock?"

Cassandra smiled back, "Lovely. See you in the parlour at eleven, then," she said, adding privately, "and please be sober."

Jem was already downstairs and chatting with Douglas in the hallway, when she found them.

"It's so lovely to see you, Jem." Cassandra had never given a more sincere greeting to anyone. Jem represented the sanity of Wiltshire and the promise of a brighter future. Both sorely missing in this brownstone terraced house. How Douglas had turned out to be so cheerful, growing up here in this gloomy place, remained a mystery to her.

"Hello, Cass." Jem kissed her cheek. "How are the girls?"

"Fine, come and say hello to them. They're downstairs in the kitchen, having their milk and biscuits with Nanny. I'm sure they'd love to see you." Cassandra led the way down the servants' stairs.

Both the little girl's faces lit up at the sight of their old friend. Jem seemed to bring the winter sunshine indoors, even in the basement kitchen, which was even darker than the upstairs of this narrow house. Jem picked Isobel up and swung her round, then listened to Lottie's solemn account of Rose's wedding.

Much to Cassandra's surprise, Maureen, the Irish housekeeper, didn't complain about these liberties. She seemed instead to take a shine to Jem.

"Won't you sit down and have a cup of coffee, with us now, Jem, is it?"

Nanny Morgan looked at Cassandra with a querying lift of her expressive eyebrows and Cassandra winked at her behind Maureen's broad back.

"Thank you, I'd like that. The coffee at the boarding house is more grey than brown," Jem said, with a light laugh.

"Where are you staying?" Cassandra asked him, sitting down at the table and taking Isobel on to her lap.

"On the corner of Clarendon Street in Back Bay." Jem took the cup of coffee Maureen held out to him. "Thank you, Mrs?"

"You can call me Maureen." Maureen treated Jem to the glimmer of a smile, something she had yet to bestow on Cassandra.

"Thanks. Mmm, this coffee is delicious, Maureen."

"Can I taste it, Jem?" Lottie said, sniffing his cup. "It smells nice."

"No, you can't, Lottie," Nanny Morgan said. "Coffee is for grown-ups. Drink your milk like a good girl now."

"Don't see why the mite can't be allowed a sip. How's she going to learn anything if she doesn't try it? Folks say that my coffee is the best in Boston," Maureen said.

Cassandra hid a smile. Nanny Morgan had been complaining about the housekeeper's dreadful cooking from the moment they'd met.

"Can I let her taste it, Nanny? On educational grounds?" Jem said, with a mischievous twinkle.

"Oh, go on then, just a sip, mind." Nanny Morgan looked quite put out.

Jem helped Lottie hold the heavy cup, and she took a large swig.

"Ugh! It's horrid! It tastes like smoke!" Lottie screwed up her face.

Maureen's triumphant smile disappeared and Nanny Morgan's broke out.

Cassandra judged it time to change the subject. "So, what have you been up to, Jem, whilst we've been

143

celebrating Rose's wedding?"

"Oh, this and that, you know. I went to the Ford factory in Memorial Drive, across the river at Cambridge. Got lots of ideas there."

Maureen sat down heavily at the table and joined them, hefting her bulk on to the seat with an exaggerated sigh. "My Patrick works there, you know. Good money. Terrible living conditions on the outskirts, you know, not fit for a pig, but with the steady income, they'll soon get something better."

"Does he? How does he find the work, Maureen, if you don't mind my asking?" Jem showed polite interest on his pleasant face.

"Work's work at the end of the day, isn't it? Making motor cars is as good as anything else. It's better than domestic service, I can tell you. I wish I could persuade my Kathleen to work in a factory but she's a housekeeper like me and her old boss is too mean to have other staff to help run the place. We've got a new, younger man-servant here and he's worth his weight in gold. Works twice as hard as the last feller, Gallagher."

Cassandra stole a glance at Douglas at the mention of Gallagher, who's eye he had blackened over the fracas with Katy on their last visit, but he didn't seem to be listening. She decided that was probably just as well.

Maureen was still talking. "Oh yes, Kathleen's place is as big as this house and her old master's no joke to look after." Maureen folded her arms across her enormous bosom with an air of martyrdom.

Cassandra looked back at Jem, expecting him to jolly Maureen along. He'd been doing so well in diffusing the mutual animosity between the two older women. She was shocked to see the expression on his open features. Jem was staring at Maureen with intense curiosity. In a different, tight sort of voice, he said, "Is Kathleen your daughter, then, Maureen?"

"She's the eldest of six daughters. I've only the one son, Patrick, that I told you about. My three oldest girls are

144

all in service. That's all anyone thinks Irish are good for. I just hope Kathleen gets remembered in the old man's will. She's devoted to him, you know. His daughters don't give a fig about him; never visit." Maureen got up to help herself to more coffee from the enamel pot steaming away on the top of the range cooker.

Douglas was playing a noisy game of snap with Lottie and didn't seem to notice when Jem got up to help Maureen by the stove. Cassandra did, and watched him carefully but she couldn't make out what he was saying to the housekeeper, as he spoke so low, and his voice was drowned out in the racket.

"Hey, look at the time, Cass! It's a quarter to eleven. I guess we'd better head up to the parlour," Douglas said. "Come on, Jem."

Cassandra kissed her daughters and joined the two men on their way upstairs to the parlour. Jem, looking every inch the businessman in his new suit, acquitted himself well in front of Selina's bemused stare. Cassandra listened attentively, impressed with the way Jem set out his plans for building a small factory at Katherine Wheel Garage. He'd got all the figures worked out, down to the last penny, and had even drawn diagrams of the shed they hoped to build. He showed Selina all the drawings and explained the designs Katy had provided.

Cassandra was fascinated by his ideas, but when she looked up at Selina, to see if she was taking it all in, her mother-in-law's eyes were glazed over and unfocussed.

When he had finished, Jem fell silent and Douglas took up the thread. "So, Mother, dear, do you think you could invest in our little scheme?"

"Oh, Douglas, darling, I'm not sure if I understood all of your clever friend's plans but it sounds like a lovely project. I'd be happy to give you any amount you need, with one condition."

"What's that?"

"That you tell your father nothing about it. Not a single word, dear, and say nothing to your sisters, either.

145

This shall be our secret, Douglas, Jeremy and Cassandra. It'll all be happening in England, so they don't need to know anything about it. I'll tell Mr Sanders, my lawyer, to deal with all the papers and you can correspond with him, once I've given him the go ahead. And, my dears, you should know that this is my own money, from my tobacco plantation in Kentucky. It has nothing to do with Mr Flintock - please remember that, won't you? People seem to smoke more and more these days. Why, even ladies are taking up the habit, though I don't like it myself, so there's plenty in the pot. "

"We will, I promise, Mother." Douglas got up and kissed her thin cheek. "Thank you, Ma, darling. We'll make a go of it, you'll see. You'll get your money back, with interest."

"I don't want it back, Douglas, dear." Selina smiled but still managed to look sad. "Have it now, while I can give it to you. Who knows what the future holds? And another thing, Jeremy here is married to Katy Phipps. Now *I* know that they are a happily married couple in England with a respectable business, but your father, and especially Cheryl, still regard Mrs Phipps as the girl who drove Fred Stavely away. Just because they don't talk about it, doesn't mean they don't remember. Cheryl will never, ever forget it, or, I'm sad to say, forgive. I'm sure that's why she works so hard. Maybe all doctors do but, deep down, I think she'd rather be married to Fred. We've never seen him since, you know. So, Jeremy, I think it best if you don't visit again. I'm not sure I could give you this capital if the family realised your surname and connections. I hope you understand?"

Cassandra felt sorry for Jem then. He'd done so well with his presentation and achieved the funding it needed but this rejection was harsh, and so unfair. Katy seemed doomed to be misunderstood forever in this corner of the world. She watched him struggling with his anger, his flushed face giving him away.

She felt proud of him when he said, "Of course Mrs

146

Flintock, I do understand. My Kate was entirely innocent, you know, but that's not always how the world works, is it? Neither she nor I have done anything to be ashamed of but I'll not visit here again, you can be sure of that."

"Thank you, Jeremy, I do think that's best. It's a long time ago, after all and we're here to think about the future. I hope that my investment will go some way to recompensing your wife for any injustice she received from my family. It is all I can do. Now, forgive me, but I'm a little tired after all this chat. I think I'll have a little lie down before lunch."

Selina rose from her chair, tottering a little, until Douglas went to her side and steadied her. Cassandra didn't think it was the booze, looking at her mother-in-law, but illness. That speech had taken all her strength. Douglas escorted his mother from the room with tender care.

Alone with Jem in the overstuffed parlour, Cassandra turned to look at him. "That was a wonderful summary of your plans, Jem. No wonder Katherine Wheel Garage is such a success. I was so impressed."

"Don't patronise me, Cassandra. I feel that Mrs Flintock is giving us this money as a charitable gesture now, because of the wrong done to Kate, not because of anything I've said about the business," Jem's face, usually so sunny, had gone dark.

"Oh, Jem! I'm sure that's not true." Cassandra was aghast at this turn of events.

"Isn't it? Kate's always being criticized by snobs who don't know her properly. It's not fair. We wouldn't have a garage if it wasn't for her. I'm not sure I want to take this money at all now."

"Don't say that, Jem. This is your future! Our future - Douglas's dreams are caught up in it too, remember. And how would Kate feel if you went home empty handed? How could you tell her the reason for refusing? Just think how she'd feel if she thought she was the cause of your failure?"

"Failure? The only damn failure around here is that bloody Fred Stavely." Jem turned away and stared out at the street.

Cassandra found his back somehow very poignant. She changed tack. "Jem, dear, both Douglas and I love Kate. We love you, and young Al. You are like family to us - far, far more than any of Douglas's relations living under this roof. Take this money. Turn it into something *positive*. Build a future for Kate and Al with it. She does deserve it, Selina's right about that. Why shouldn't she be compensated for the wrong done her by that wretched man? Selina wants to right that wrong by her gesture and that's not charity."

Jem folded his arms across his chest and let out a sigh before turning back to Cassandra with a set face. He nodded. "Very well, Cass. I take your point and I'll take this money and put it to work, but I won't visit here again. I've some more research to do and then I'll head home alone. I'll send a note round to let you know when."

Cassandra stood up and went to him but Jem turned away before she could embrace him.

"I'll see you back in Wiltshire, then, Cass. Give my best to Douglas," and Jem was gone.

CHAPTER EIGHTEEN
Autumn 1926

Jem wasted no time in reflection after quitting the Flintock residence for the first and last time. He wouldn't be sorry not to return to the miserable place. Instead, he marched swiftly on to Chestnut Street and, without any of the hesitation that had stayed his wooden hand last time, rapped once more on the door of number 34.

Kathleen opened it swiftly. Jem gave her his best smile.

"Hello, Kathleen," he said. "I've been thinking about you. I met your mother, Maureen, the other day at a friend's house, where she works, and she said what a tough job you've got. I wondered if you fancied coming out with me for an ice-cream soda?"

Kathleen's wide face went from white to pink in seconds. Two red patches bloomed on her cheekbones and her mouth gaped open.

"What do you say, Kathleen?" Jem was determined not to take no for an answer. Kathleen was his only lead. "Everyone deserves a break now and then, don't they? Your mum thought it was a good idea, or should I ask her out instead?"

"I'll get my hat." Kathleen shut the door against him.

Within ten minutes they were walking down the street towards the centre of town. Jem explained how he had met her mother and had taken a liking to her, and her daughter. Kathleen seemed to accept the legitimacy of this and visibly relaxed. She stopped next to an ice-cream parlour and Jem followed her in.

"What's your fancy, Kathleen?" The cold cabinet showed various flavours of Italian ice-cream.

"Sure, I only ever have vanilla."

"I'm going to have that stripy one."

"Eez, from Naples." The swarthy man behind the counter said with a strong foreign accent. "Like me, you know. We Italians, we know how to make ze best ice

149

cream in ze world. One vanilla, one Napolitan, coming up. Take a seat, I'll bring them over."

They sat by the window, which was steamed up by the contrast with the warmth inside the cafe and the freezing cold out on the street.

"Seems daft to be eating ice cream when it feels like snow outside," Kathleen said.

"Got to be daft sometimes, or you go mad," Jem said. God knew the world was crazy enough. His mum's voice suddenly floated through his head. 'Two wrongs don't make a right'. One of her favourite sayings. Stuff that.

The ice-cream slipped down his throat easily. It had become a little sore from all the talking he'd done. The cold sweetness lubricated his voice.

"So, Kathleen, old man Stavely is a bit of a taskmaster then, your mum says?"

"Right, so." Kathleen shoveled her ice-cream down in an unbecoming rush. She didn't look starving hungry, not with those stocky legs.

"Can't be easy, working alone, with that great big house to clean." Jem spooned the pink stripe of dairy sludge into the white one.

"You're not wrong there." Kathleen wiped her mouth with her sleeve. "I feel sorry for the old feller. That's why I stay. I doubt anyone else would put up with it. And there's only the one mouth to feed. He sleeps a lot, even in the day, so I have plenty of time to call me own."

"And you said his daughters have moved away? Was it Italy? Maybe she's married to an ice-cream maker, like this one!" Jem laughed, amazed at his own acting ability.

Kathleen smiled back, darting a look at him under her stubby lashes. "I wouldn't know about that. She only sends a Christmas card every year and that's only to check the old man hasn't died. The other one's no better, even though she's only a train ride away."

"Ah, yes, New York, wasn't it?"

"That's right, you've a good memory, but I thought it was Fred you were friends with?"

"Yes, I really want to see him," Jem said, completely truthfully. "Say, Kathleen, you wouldn't have the address of his sister in New York, now, would you? I might be able to trace him through her. Me and Fred, we go back a long way you know. I've travelled all the way from England - on a business trip - and it would be such a waste not to see him before I go home." Really, that wasn't a lie at all.

Kathleen's face fell. "So, you're buying me ice-cream because you still want to find Fred, not because you like me at all?"

"Did I say I didn't like you? I can find out about Fred and get to know you at the same time, can't I?" Jem clung as near to the grain of truth running through his questions as his compromised conscience allowed.

Kathleen smiled again. Even that didn't make her pretty. "As it happens, I always keep the family addresses in my handbag. Old man Stavely's so ancient, I always worry he'll peg it and I'll have to contact them. Wait a minute while I find it."

She rummaged in her bag and brought out a little notebook. She licked her finger and thumbed the pages, opening it near the beginning. "Here you are, do you want to write it down?"

Jem still had his paperwork from the garage plans in his own bag. He picked out a piece of paper at random and noted down the address in New York carefully, in ink.

"Thanks Kathleen, that's really helpful. Would you like another ice?"

Walking back from Chestnut Street to his digs, Jem congratulated himself on escaping kissing Kathleen at the door, when he'd walked her back home. It had been a close run thing and he knew she'd be disappointed when he never called again but needs must. He hadn't raped *her*, after all.

The next morning was equally cold, but thankfully

dry and sunny, despite a glacial north wind.

Jem was getting familiar with Boston now and walked at a brisk pace to the train station and bought a ticket for New York, popping a postcard to Katy in the Post Office box on the way. You couldn't say too much in a postcard. He just let her know that the money was assured and that he was missing her. She didn't need to know about anything else.

***

The train to New York was crowded but the journey only lasted a few hours. Jem ignored the other passengers and gazed out at the scenery, dusted here and there with snow and dotted with little farmsteads hugging the coast. Boats bobbed about in the harbours along the way and the whole landscape looked placid with prosperity.

By contrast, New York astonished Jem. Surrounded by water, its incredibly tall buildings shrouded in mist from the low cloud rising from the sea, the city dwarfed him, making him feel like a scurrying ant who'd lost its sense of direction. Hardly any sunlight illuminated its streets, wide though they were, due to the high rise towers piercing the sky above. Dozens more were under construction. When he dared to look up, he was horrified to see men on swaying scaffolding so dizzyingly high, some of them disappeared into the clouds.

He hadn't liked the bustle of Boston. He hated New York.

Yellow taxis criss-crossed the grid of streets like wasps, ready to sting you if you crossed their path. Noises bounced off the concrete and amplified into a crescendo that tore at his nerves. He wouldn't waste time looking for the address in his pocket. Never normally reckless with money, he gritted his teeth and hailed a cab, giving the driver the directions before sitting back in the sanctuary of the car.

"What's the fare?"

152

"50 cents a mile, bud."

Sometimes it was worth splashing out, if it was important enough.

The cab drew up outside a street of houses in Brooklyn, indistinguishable from the others they'd passed on the way. He parted with his dollars and got out directly in front of Fred's sister's terraced house. Tall and made of dark brown brick, just like those in Boston, it had bay windows and a run of steps up to the glass front door. Jem trotted up them to find a list of names next to a set of bell buttons. Gertrude Stavely had married Harrison Peabody, a middle-aged insurance salesman, in 1922, Kathleen had told him. She'd added that Gertrude, never too fussy with men, had accepted his offer as a means of quitting Boston, rather than from sentiment. He scanned the nameplates, and pressed number six, once he'd found the name he'd been searching for.

A bent old man, presumably the caretaker, let him into the lobby and pointed upstairs. The stairs were wooden, their rails polished by the traffic of many hands, and wound around a central pillar in a long spiral. He counted the six flights as he mounted them. Mr Peabody couldn't be that wealthy, he reckoned, judging by the motley collection of neighbours he glimpsed through open doors.

He was breathless by the time he reached the sixth floor and took a moment to steady himself before ringing the doorbell. A maid opened it, dressed in a white frilly pinny, like the one Maisie wore at Cheadle Manor. It seemed old-fashioned in this most modern of cities and the face behind it also belonged to the last century. The housemaid looked at least fifty, her wrinkles incongruously framed by less-than-white lace.

"Can I help you, sir?" Her twangy accent was quite different to any he had heard in Boston.

"Good afternoon." Jem removed his trilby hat. "Is Mrs Peabody in?"

"Who shall I say is calling?"

"My name is..." Jeremy hesitated. If Fred *was* here, he wouldn't want to meet Mr Phipps, husband of Katy, would he?

"My name is Beagle, Jeremy Beagle." On the spur of the moment, Katy's maiden name had sprung into his head, unbidden. Just as well, as his mind had gone blank.

"Wait there." The elderly maid pulled a chain across the door and went away.

Friendly and trusting in New York then.

The maid returned and unhooked the chain. "Follow me, sir."

Jem trooped after the woman, looking about the apartment as he went. Why did these Americans love brown so much? Little light penetrated to liven up the sepia room, as most of the windows were either swathed in heavy net or obliterated by aspidistra plants in large Victorian pots, redolent of an earlier era when the British empire still ruled Asia.

They entered a drawing room without a change of decor. A younger woman, heavily made-up with vermilion shiny lips, lounged, feet up, near the window, smoking from a long cigarette holder. The room was fusty and stale, with a gas fire sputtering out a moist heat in one corner.

"If you're selling anything, I'm not interested," Mrs Peabody said, without getting up or introducing herself.

"Good afternoon, Mrs Peabody." Jeremy was determined not to be put off his quest by anyone, however rude. "My name is Jeremy Beagle. I'm here on a business trip from England."

Mrs Peabody lowered her silk stockinged legs to the floor from the chaise longue.

"Gertrude Peabody." She spoke in the same nasal tones her aged maid employed. The scarlet lips widened to a half-hearted smile before clamping themselves around the cigarette lighter again. "What do you want, Mr Beagle?"

"I'm looking for an old friend. I believe he's your brother, Fred Stavely?"

Gertrude Peabody exhaled a long cloud of blue smoke, narrowing her eyes as she did so. Jem tried not to cough in the airless room. His eyes prickled with irritation.

"What do you want to see Fred for?"

"Just to talk about old times, you know the sort of thing."

"How do you know him?"

"Oh, Fred and I go back a long way."

"You do, huh? Well, he isn't here, if that's what you're expecting. Fred don't come home till late, if you get my meaning." Gertrude's cigarette ran out of tobacco and she stubbed it out into an onyx ashtray that teetered on a stand at table height.

Less effort, Jem supposed. Wouldn't do to move off that couch.

"He owes you money, is that it?" Gertrude Peabody reached over to a cabinet, next to her seat and drew out a fresh cigarette. "You don't look like a heavy, I must say. What's the real reason you want to see Fred so much?"

Jem racked his brains. He'd stick to the same principles, if you could call them that, he'd used with Kathleen and sail as close to the truth as he could. "I've got an old bit of business to finish up with him. What I owe him is long overdue and would be worth his while, you know. He'd be a different man, once he's heard what I'm going to tell him."

"Is that so? Well, Fred sure could use a little help and I could use the back rent he owes me. I don't know when you last saw my brother, mister, but he's not what he was. I guess none of us are. When d'you last see him?"

"Years ago, now." Lies that were white were alright, weren't they? "Like I say, we go back a long way."

"Yeah, you said. I shouldn't trust you, mister. I don't know you from Adam, but I like your face. It's an honest face, the type you don't see no more. You'll find Fred at the corner of 157th Street. There's a Speakeasy there he goes to every night. You do know what a Speakeasy is don't you?"

155

Jem shook his head.

"Jeez. Okay, it looks like a barber shop, see? But it ain't no barbers. You go in and ask for a haircut from Stan. Remember the name Stan. Then you say, you've heard Stan serves iced tea while he's cutting your hair. Then you get to the Speakeasy. Do you like music, Mr Beagle? You'd better, nothing but jazz there, every night of the week. Fred's addicted to it and I don't just mean the music. Yeah, you find him, Mr Beagle, give him a leg up, if you can. Like I say, he sure could use one."

***

Jem passed the waiting hours wandering around the area. He didn't want to stray too far and get lost in this concrete jungle. Hunger drove him indoors as the long night fell. He drank some Coca Cola in a diner and ate a hamburger drowning in mustard and onions and some strange, strong pickled cucumbers the waiter told him were gherkins. The whole combination gave him indigestion.

"Excuse me asking, but what time does the barber's across the road open? I'm only in New York for a day and I need a haircut," Jem said.

"Listen, mister, if I were you, I'd pipe down about only being here for the day, you know? Some folks might take advantage. It ain't your normal sort of barbers, you know," the waiter said, out of the corner of his mouth.

Jem flushed. The man was right. This was no time to drop his guard. "Understood, and thanks."

"And the answer is nine o'clock, but it ain't no place for greenhorns. Watch your back, okay?"

Jem bought another soda, even though he didn't really like them, to say thank you, and told the waiter to keep the change. At this rate, he'd have to go home sooner rather than later or he'd be out of cash. He fingered the coins in his pocket, their shapes still alien to him. For a moment, his mind flashed back to Wiltshire; to Katy and Al, innocently getting on with their lives back home. Was

156

he doing the right thing? What if Fred had become a prize boxer and flattened him? He must be careful; spy the bugger out before introducing himself.

He'd come this far. No point giving up now.

CHAPTER NINETEEN
Autumn 1926

At half past nine that evening, Jem crossed the road to the Speakeasy. Flakes of snow eddied down from the black sky, catching the lamp light in white flurries. The snow lay on the grimy pavement, clean specks of frosted water against the dirty grey flags. The ice crunched under his boots, staying frozen and pure. The air was so cold he could feel his skin shrivel.

The barber's shop didn't look open. One electric light-bulb gleamed above the door and the stripy blind hung down across the window. The wooden door's bland facade was dissected by a tiny trapdoor at face height.

The waiter in the diner - what a guardian angel he'd turned out to be - had told Jem to knock twice quickly and twice slowly, next to the little door. He did so, using his wooden hand in careful repetition.

The trapdoor opened immediately and a disembodied voice said, "Yeah, what d'ya want? The shop's shut."

Jem followed the script he'd been given by Gertrude Peabody. "I need Stan to give me a haircut."

"I told ya, we ain't open."

"Someone told me Stan makes great iced tea."

"That's right, fella, okay, you're in," and, miraculously, the main door opened.

There were two big men inside. The ugliest men Jem had ever seen. The room was indeed kitted out like a real barber's shop, with combs, soap and razors arranged, almost too neatly, on a shelf in front of a row of chairs, each facing a large mirror. Jem caught sight of himself in one of them. His face was as white as the snow falling in the street. He cracked it with a smile.

The door men appeared unmoved. The tallest one watched while the other frisked Jem for weapons. Looking at his ear, a large part of which looked like it had been bitten off, made Jem realise you didn't always need to be

158

armed to do someone a damage.

"He's clean," said the one-eared thug.

"This way for iced tea." The biggest one led him to another door at the back of the shop. A muffled rumble of noise lay behind it. Nothing could have prepared Jem for the sight on the other side. A crush of noisy people filled the dark room to capacity. A bar ran along one wall and a stage, just a little higher than the rest of the floor, stood in the corner, but he couldn't make anything else out in the dim light or think straight in the babble of chatter competing with the loud jazz music.

His immediate sensation was one of stifling heat, even worse than at old Stavely's house. He felt instantly overdressed. A young woman, very curvy, a detail impossible to ignore due to her low cut dress, offered to take his coat.

"Want to take something off, mister? Let me know if you want me to do the same, later, you know what I mean?" Jem was torn with keeping his coat on and melting with sweat or parting with it, never to see it again.

"Don't worry, honey. Everybody puts their coats in the lobby. See, you even get a ticket." The girl waved to a rack of coats on hangers behind her.

Jem still wasn't convinced. "No, thanks." He brushed past her.

"Suit yourself, bud." The girl shrugged.

Jem undid his coat buttons and folded his trilby hat into one of the pockets. He'd rather sweat in his coat than take it off and lose it. The sheer press of people propelled him to the bar, and a vacant stool. He sat on it and tried to catch his breath. The barman, who had a face like leather underneath a thatch of red hair, said, "Iced tea?"

Jem nodded; it seemed the safest response. The barman poured amber liquid from a whisky bottle over a tumbler full of ice-cubes and told him the price, which seemed steep. Jem passed over some change, hoping it was enough. It was so dark in the speakeasy he could hardly make out the coins. The bar was lit up by electric lights along its mirrored backdrop but the rest of the place was illuminated only by candles on the tables.

Jem took a sip of the icy liquid and gasped. The man on the next stool laughed loud enough to be heard over the thumping music.

"Never had iced tea like that where you're from, I'll bet?"

Jem shook his head. He couldn't have said anything, even if he'd thought of it, because his throat was on fire. This stuff tasted more like petrol than whisky.

"Where are you from anyways? Ain't New York by the looks of you."

"England," Jem croaked.

"And straight off the boat, I'll be bound. You look as green as an apple. Here on business or pleasure?"

"Business."

"Is that right? What line you in, boy?"

"Cars. I've just been to see the Ford factory in Boston."

"That accent sounds more like country to me, than city."

"That's right. I live in Wiltshire."

"Farming country, I'll bet."

Jem nodded.

"Have another on me, country boy. The second one ain't so painful."

"No, thanks, it's alright," Jem said, his voice still hoarse.

"Listen, mister, I don't offer to buy strangers drinks any day of the week, you know. Come on, have another."

There was a challenging look in the man's eye Jem thought wise not to ignore.

"Thanks."

"Gotta drink up the first, then. I'm Pete, by the way, Pete Curley. What's your name?"

"Jem Beagle." Jem decided to stick to the name he'd given Gertrude Peabody.

"Pleased to meet you, Jem. Come on buddy, drink

up. Hey, Ginger, two more teas over here!"

"Coming right up, Pete," said the barman.

Jem took another sip. He never drank spirits at home but was pleased that the first swig had anaesthetised his throat. The second slug *was* easier.

He looked around the dim room, unable to make out its size, as the edges blurred into darkness. The only strong light came from the stage where a small band was playing jazz. All the musicians were black; their dark faces dripping with perspiration. Jem started to relax to the sound of the music. Unconsciously his foot began to tap on the lower rung of his bar stool.

They struck up a new song, unlike the others, that began with an electrifying introduction. "What's that tune?" Jem had never heard anything like it.

"Oh that's Gershwin's new number. Think it's called 'Rhapsody in Blue' or some fancy name. Different ain't it? Everyone's talking about it." Pete grinned at him. "They ain't bad, are they? They mostly play Dixieland stuff, from the south. Warms up a New York snowstorm real well, don't ya think, Jem?"

Jem nodded at his new friend and listened. They were playing "Mammie" now and improvising freely. Jem had never heard anything like it on the radio. A black dancer got up on to one of the tables at the front and started swaying her hips to the beat. She was wearing the new Charleston style of dress, with a fringe that swung in time to the music. The dress was so short it exposed the entire length of her shapely legs, and its sequins sparkled in the candlelight. The men sitting around her started thumping their hands on her table-top in time to the beat, egging her on. She moved well and Jem was amazed at how her little feet could tap in perfect time and still avoid the greedy hands trying to grab them.

Now his eyes had adjusted to the murk, and the whisky had calmed his indigestion by sheer alcohol, he remembered why he was here. He scanned the other drinkers' faces in the subdued candlelight. There must have been at least fifty people squashed into the room, which he could see now, wasn't so big after all. Jem reckoned they were all sweating as freely as he was, judging by the animal smell.

"Who's that dancer?" he asked Pete.

"She's swell, ain't she? That there's Lulu. She can sure sing too, but I wouldn't get too friendly, she's spoken for."

"Who's the lucky man?"

"Fred, and he don't take kindly to Lulu's admirers, get my meaning?"

Jem's heart skipped a beat. "Fred what?"

"Stavely, I think it is. He's here every night, making sure Lulu don't get fresh with other customers, not that he treats her right," Pete added, in a lower tone, glancing over his shoulder to see if anyone else was listening.

Bingo! This was too easy. Speak*easy*. Jem almost giggled. He was light-headed from the whisky mixing with the adrenaline pumping through his system in a dangerous combination.

"You'd better point him out to me, Pete. Wouldn't want to get on the wrong side of him, by the sounds of it."

"You betcha life. He's that fat feller, facing the stage, sitting at the table where Lulu's skipping her pretty black legs."

Jem's eyes locked on to the seedy looking bloke, who's piggy eyes never left his girlfriend's lithe body. Fred Stavely. There he sat, in the living flesh. And there was plenty of it. To think those pudgy hands had been all over his Katy's body. Jem's remaining fingers tingled with the desire to punch the leer off his ugly face. He took another gulp of firewater and tried to think of a way to get Fred alone in this crowded hellhole.

Several songs and whiskies later, Jem was still stuck on his barstool while Pete, now very drunk, told him rambling stories about bootleg liquor coming off the boats and being smuggled into the back of the bar, which got Jem nowhere. Cigarette smoke lay in streaky strands across the room, creating a blue haze. The band was playing much louder now and Lulu, having danced on most of the tables, was sitting next to Fred, whose meaty hand lay on her thigh, signalling ownership. If Jem made a move, Fred was bound to think he was after his girlfriend. He was at a complete loss as to how to proceed. He was so damn close, too.

Then everyone stopped moving and talking in a comical, freeze-frame moment. A piercing whistle had sounded, an octave higher than the jazz music and easily heard above the comfortable low roar in the room. The band ceased playing immediately and the musicians grabbed their instruments and whisked out of the back door with the speed of a hurricane. A few women screamed. Chairs clattered to the floor, as people clambered upright and followed the band to the exit.

"What's happening?" Jem said to Pete.

"Raid," Pete said, his voice slurred. "Get the hell out, bud. Go on! Run for it!"

Jem tried to help his new friend. "No, leave me here, son. I can't run so fast these days. Just go, Jem. I mean it. Run like hell!"

Jem got off his stool. The floor seemed to sway under his unsteady feet, and he thought he'd fall, but the rush of people around him swept him along to the rear exit. Carried by the force of the crowd, he squeezed through the back door, and out into a dark alleyway, gasping at the cold air that rushed into his smoked-filled lungs and jarring the whisky blurring his brain.

"Come on feller, don't stand there waiting for the pigs to find you," said a woman's voice. It was Lulu. Jem followed her blindly. The sequins on her short dress jiggled in front of his eyes but at least they caught the lamplight and helped him to see where she was. Everyone else seemed to have melted away down the narrow streets that criss-crossed on either side. The sound of a bin being knocked over clanged out but their own feet were muffled by the white carpet underneath them. Jem had never known snow settle so fast.

Lulu grabbed his hand, slippery with sweat. The cold hit Jem's head, making it contract painfully. His ears still rang with the loud jazz music. He hadn't a clue where he was going. They rounded a corner and Lulu leant back against the brick wall, under a street lamp. Now he was up close, Jem could see that, under her heavy make-up, one eye was bruised and swollen.

They were both panting heavily. As soon as he could, he thanked his rescuer.

Lulu laughed. A rich, full uninhibited laugh. "Couldn't leave a poor baby like you to get arrested, honey."

Jem grinned at her. "Is it so obvious I've never been to New York before?"

"Yeah, baby, it sure is," and she laughed again. "You look so innocent, I'll bet you ain't never even heard jazz before or drunk moonshine. That right?"

Jem nodded. He liked her and couldn't take offence at her frankness. After all, she was right. "How did you hurt your eye, Lulu, if you don't mind my asking?"

A guarded look came over her lovely, dark face. "Best not to ask, sonny, then I can't tell no tales."

"Who's telling tales?"

A bulky silhouette loomed in the darkness, out of the sphere of the street light. Jem sensed Lulu's body stiffen with fear, before she peeled away from the brick wall and went towards him.

Fred. It had to be Fred.

Jem's quest was over.

CHAPTER TWENTY
Autumn 1926

"I am," Jem said. "I can't tell you how pleased I am to meet you at last. I wanted to give you this."

He made contact with Fred's soft belly, making hardly any impact on the soft expanse of his midriff, which acted as a shock absorber. Fred looked surprised and a little winded but otherwise unscathed, and hit back in a reflex reaction, catching Jem's eyebrow with a glancing blow. Jem had almost got out of the way in time to avoid being hit at all because Fred moved slowly. Jem could see that punch had made him breathless with effort. Fred's pugnacious eyes widened in horror as Jem recovered quickly and swung his wooden arm at Fred's head, sideways, catching him on the ear. Fred fell to the floor, blood trickling out of his ear.

Lulu started screaming then. Jem turned around and whispered, "Shut up, and clear off. This has nothing to do with you. This bastard raped my wife. Get yourself lost, Lulu. Leave him - permanently."

The big brown eyes in Lulu's ebony face stared at him but she stopped screaming. She looked back at Fred, now squealing like the coward he was and then nodded at Jem.

"Thanks mister, you're right. I'm going, but watch your back. He fights dirty," and Lulu scarpered into the black night, her little tap shoes making no sound on the soft crystals of snow.

Where the police were, Jem had no idea. It was just him and Fred now.

Fred had thrown one arm across his face, to shield more blows, and still lay on the pavement. It would have been easy to kick him into a pulp but that wouldn't have been nearly satisfying enough. Jem wanted the brute to know why he was here. He wanted Fred to remember Katy and what he'd done to her.

"Get up, you bastard," Jem said.

Fred lay immobile.

"I said, get up, or I'll kick your head in. I've got something to say to you." Jem held his boot poised above Fred's head.

One bloodshot eye peered over the prostrate arm and saw Jem's boot. Fred rolled on to his side, then on to his knees. When he stood up, he swung for Jem's face, but Jem had been a soldier. He'd been trained in hand-to-hand combat and his wooden arm instinctively came up to block the blow. He forced Fred's arm back easily, with his good one, and pinned him against the cold brick wall.

Fred's greasy face was lit by the feeble street light. Sweat mingled with the blood dripping down his neck from his ear. Jem shoved his face in front of Fred's, who started to shake. Jem was shaking too, but not with fear. Anger thrilled through his body. He could barely contain it. He'd waited a long time to meet Fred Stavely.

"I think we should introduce ourselves. You're Fred Stavely, is that right?"

Fred didn't respond. Jem punched his face with his wooden claw. A new trickle of blood oozed from the corner of Fred's thin-lipped mouth.

"Sorry? Didn't catch that?" Jem wanted to be quite sure he had the right man before he carried on.

"Yeah, I'm Fred Stavely. Who wants to know?"

"I'll tell you who I am. My name is Jeremy Phipps. My wife, my beautiful, lovely wife, is Katy Phipps. Remember her?" Jem's anger rose further at the thought of this ugly mug kissing Katy's pretty one.

Fred frowned and looked confused.

"Shall I trigger your memory?" Jem raised his claw.

Fred shook his head. "Cape Cod, 1919. I remember. She was with Doug Flintock. She was the servant of that posh English woman."

Jem slapped him. Hard. "That's right. My friends, Douglas and Cassandra Flintock-Smythe. You know, the people who trusted you to behave like a gentleman? Well, we can see what kind of a man you are just by looking at

166

Lulu's swollen eye. Do you remember what you did to my Katy at Cape Cod? I do, she told me all about it. Do you have any idea, Fred Stavely, how you ruined her life? She couldn't get a job, or a house, after what you did to her. She was miserable and frightened and chucked out of the Flintock's, who blamed her and ruined her reputation at home, as well as here. All because of you. She'd done nothing wrong. But she's still got me, see? I made a vow, Mr Stavely. I promised her I would come and find you and treat you like you treated her that day. Get it? And that's just what I'm about to do."

"No, no, mister! Please! I didn't mean no harm to your girl. I just got carried away. You're right, she is a beautiful woman and I really liked her but she didn't want me. She deceived me. I thought she was a lady but..."

That was enough. "She *is* a lady!" All the anger welled up in Jem at that.

He lunged at Fred with his good hand and caught him cleanly on the jaw but, in doing so, had to release his grip on Fred, who immediately hit him back. Fred was a heavy man and he put his full weight into the blow. Jem went reeling back on his heels but managed to steady himself and avoid falling over. Fred had relaxed, and was leaning back against the wall, panting. Jem turned and kicked his legs behind the knee, making Fred crumple to the ground, but not before he'd grabbed Jem's wooden claw. Jem couldn't feel the contact on the wood and was caught off balance. He fell on to his wooden arm, which cracked in two, sending a shaft of pain up his upper arm from the impact. Jem picked up the broken piece and used it as a club on Fred's head, several times.

All the pent-up anger of the intervening years powered his good arm into whacking Fred over and over again. Only when Fred's big body went inert did he stop. Jem drew back, terrified that he'd killed him, and frightened of his own uncontrollable rage.

Snow began to float down again, settling immediately around them, soaking up the blood on the stained pavement, so it resembled the sodden cotton wool he'd seen too many times in the war. Jem shivered at the cold; at the thought of what he'd done. If he'd murdered Fred, he could go to jail. He might even hang. That wouldn't help Katy. What the hell had he done?

With panicky fingers, he knelt down and felt Fred's pulse, which throbbed in his neck in thick, but irregular, beats. Thank God! Jem sat back on his heels. He must think. He'd had his revenge. He didn't want anyone to die, not even a rapist scumbag like this.

With shaking hands, Jem felt his own lumpy face. Bruises were already swelling. His fingers came away red and wet. He must look a sight. In all conscience, he couldn't leave Fred here. He might bleed to death or die of the cold. Somehow, he'd have to alert someone to shift him, without being caught for assault. But how? Who?

A dark shadow, grotesquely enlarged by the street lamp, crept up behind him. It was impossible to make out its shape. Jem's heart sank. It must be the police. He was done for!

"Have you killed him?"

With immense relief, Jem recognised Lulu's rich, deep voice. The tremble in it betrayed her emotion, but whether it was from hope that he had seen Fred off, or grief, Jem couldn't decide. He whirled around to look at her.

"Did you see the whole thing?" Jem asked, almost, but not quite, ashamed of his violence.

"No." Lulu didn't take her eyes off her lover, "I walked away, like you said. I done the sensible thing for once but then, I thought, Fred's no match for you. He's fat and drinks too much. Hell, he sniffs cocaine most nights. I could tell you was strong and you looked like you meant business. The further I walked, the more I knew Fred didn't stand a chance. And now he's dead." A sob escaped her and she stopped it with her hand. Her bracelets jingled musically, too delicate a sound for the bloodied street.

"No, he's not dead, Lulu." Jem stood up. "He's still

168

breathing, I checked his pulse. It's faint, but I think he'll live. Listen, I don't do this sort thing all the time, you know, but he had it coming, after what he did to my wife."

Lulu nodded. She didn't look a bit surprised. Jem was. Why would anyone come back for a fucking git like that? He watched as Lulu knelt down next to Fred and touched his battered face. Jem knew he should feel remorse but he didn't.

Lulu looked back at Jem. Tears coursed down her attractive face. Jem realised she was much younger than he'd thought. "Go now, mister. I won't tell on you. I know what Fred's like. Your wife is a lucky woman. I'll get help from the club. The police will have gone by now. Get going. I ain't going to leave him to bleed to death but I won't split on you either. Jeez, I don't even know your name and I don't want to. Disappear, why don't you? Hey, and take this with you or you'll be identified, sure as hell."

She passed him the broken piece of wooden arm with its hooked false fingers at its tip. She was right. It was a dead giveaway.

"Are you sure you'll be alright?" Jem fingered the prosthetic and found it sticky with Fred's toxic blood. He couldn't wait to wash himself clean.

"Sure, baby. Get going. I'll fix him up. Help is round the corner but if those guys turn up before you're gone, you'll be dead meat. Get right out of the city, tonight."

"Thank you, Lulu. He doesn't deserve you."

"I know that. Now, beat it!"

Jem went. He stuffed his broken wooden limb in the deep pocket of his trench coat and rammed his trilby back on his head, wincing as his bruises complained. He walked to the main road, following the sounds of the traffic, and hailed a cab, amazed they were still looking for trade at this hour of the night, or probably morning by now. The snow kept falling, turning to grainy slush at the edges of the streets. He averted his face when the driver stopped and he asked him to take him to the train station. Katy had insisted he bring good linen handkerchiefs with him for the trip and he blessed her foresight as he drew one from his suit pocket. Licking its edge, he dabbed his cut lip, using the cab window as a mirror, and smoothed down his soiled clothes.

The car drew up outside the pillared Grand Central train station.

"Here we are buddy, Grand Central Terminal, 42nd Street. That'll be four bucks."

He shoved some notes at the driver with a hand that still shook and walked swiftly away from the man's curious stares at his empty sleeve. Jem was fazed by the size of the marbled interior of the vast station and stood in a daze until he sighted the washroom. He went straight to the lavatory and washed his face, now livid with bruises. The cut lip, though grossly swollen, was already healing up and had stopped bleeding. His dark grey coat was covered in red splashes and he used the handkerchief to sponge it down, not caring how damp it made him. There was nothing he could do about his amputated arm, which was aching worse than his face. He took off the remaining piece of prosthetic, undoing the strap with difficulty as his fingers were swollen and sore. His upper arm had swollen too and the strap was cutting into him in a painful tourniquet. Underneath, his stump was red and bleeding from the force of his fall. He put the two wooden pieces in his pocket, where they knocked against his thigh, not letting him forget how nearly he had killed a man.

The mirror told him he would pass muster, just, if he kept the brim of his hat pulled down. He went to the station platform and found that the next train to Boston wouldn't be until the early hours. That wasn't so long to wait. It was now three o'clock in the morning and the first train was due to leave at six. He sat down on a bench in the darkest corner he could find in the cavernous station, praying the cops wouldn't come looking for him. His three hour vigil was cold and eerie in the alien marble building. Every noise echoed in the hollow space under the huge domed ceiling. The big station clock crawled past the

170

hours, each second marked out by a loud clunk as the hand edged forward. He couldn't sleep, he was too terrified of being arrested. He prayed the slow minutes away instead.

A few bleary eyed passengers turned up just before six, even before it was light, along with wagons of post and newspapers. He bought one from the news stand. As soon as he could, he boarded the Boston train, using his return ticket, and hunkered into a corner seat like a fugitive, opening the newspaper wide to obscure his sore face.

When he arrived in Boston, he found it covered in a deep layer of snow. Thank goodness the train hadn't been cancelled. Curious stares followed him as he hurried along the white streets. There were no cabs working here, the snow was too deep and, thankfully not many people were about. A few kids played in the park as he strode past, chucking snowballs at each other and shrieking with a joy he could not feel.

An icy hush enveloped the residential street where his boarding house stood. He walked quickly past the receptionist and let himself into his tatty room. He shrugged off his stained coat, and threw his hat on the rickety table by the window. Kicking off his shoes, Jem lay on the lumpy bed, fully clothed, dragged the edges of the bedspread over him, closed his eyes and fell instantly asleep.

CHAPTER TWENTY ONE
Autumn 1926

Katy read Jem's postcard. It didn't take long, being composed of only two meagre lines.

"Money secured from Mrs F. Home soon, miss you, love, Jem."

She stared at the picture of Boston's Faneuil Market and felt annoyed, not for the first time, that she hadn't gone with him.

Susan Threadwell, Billy's younger sister, looked at the picture over her shoulder. "Wouldn't catch me on a boat going all that way." Susan hitched her postal bag higher across her flat chest. "By the way, Mrs Phipps, Mum asked if you could solder this teapot. The handle's come adrift, see?"

Susan held up the enamel teapot. It was an ugly mustard yellow and chipped. Katy wouldn't have given it houseroom. "Here's the handle, come right off, it has." Susan passed it over. "Mum said she can't do without it long. Asked if you could get Billy to bring it home with him tonight. That alright?"

Katy nodded. Mrs Threadwell was her most impatient customer. Well, she'd get her son to do it for her. "Billy!"

Billy shambled over. He was as slow as his mother was quick. "Yes, Mrs P?"

"Solder this handle on your mother's teapot for me, would you?"

"I'll tell Mum you're doing it then, shall I?" Susan said, mounting her bicycle again.

"Alright." Billy took the bits from Katy without enthusiasm.

"Any post to send, Mrs Phipps? Nothing for America?" Susan stood, one foot on the pedal and her whole body leant forward, ready for the off.

"Not at the moment." Katy knew full well the postcard would have been scoured for gossip by Susan's mother and was determined not to fuel any false fires. Just as well Jem hadn't put much detail in the card but Mrs Threadwell would have noted the comment about money and be agog for details. Well, she wouldn't hear it from Katy, who now wished Jem had put the card in an envelope and paid the difference.

"Sure?" Susan had obviously been primed by her mother to find out more.

"Quite sure, Susan. Mustn't keep you from your post round. Other people will be waiting, you know." Katy nodded her dismissal. Thing was, with Billy working at the garage, his mother usually was the first to find out their plans and from there, it would be round the village faster than Douglas drove around the Brooklands track. Well, at least he'd have a decent set of brakes next time.

Katy was excited about her progress with the new braking system. She couldn't wait to see Jem, find out how much money they had got and get started on making the rubber seals here at Katherine Wheel. That would put old Bartlett's nose out of joint. She hated the way he kept sniffing around the place while Jem and the others were away. Billy didn't give her much protection. She'd taken to locking the office door, when she wasn't in there, just in case Mr Bartlett dropped by and tried snooping around again.

The next Saturday was Billy's twenty-third birthday and she gave him the day off.

Billy's eyes were round with surprise when she told him. "Really Mrs P? The whole day?"

"Yes, Billy, you always work hard and you deserve it. Me and Al will cope, I'm sure," and she'd given him an extra ten bob note with his wages. Billy had gone home on his bike whistling, *'Daisy, Daisy, give me your answer, do',"* that Friday afternoon, making Katy speculate on whom he might be sharing his birthday with.

Saturdays were always busy. Customers seemed to concertina in droves to fill up with petrol before the weekend got going. Katy regretted letting Billy off, ruefully realising that manning the pump was a full time job. Al was a great help though, running out to the forecourt to tell her if the phone rang or running back the other way to tell her if a car pulled in for petrol. She'd hoped to get Dr Benson's Model T Ford engine oil changed and back on the road before lunch but between one thing and another, she didn't know how she'd make time.

There was a welcome lull at ten thirty. "Come on, Al, let's have a cuppa and see if we can't get that oil changed on the doctor's old car, shall we?" Katy said, as her latest customer pulled out of the garage forecourt with a wave and a belching exhaust.

"Shall I fetch water, Mum?"

"Can you carry it?" Katy smiled at her son.

"I can, if the bucket is only half full."

"Go on, then." Katy ruffled his chestnut hair. It was starting to wave, like Jem's. She ought to cut it really but she'd miss those curls.

By the time Al staggered into the office with his bucket of water, the floor was as wet a river and he was red in the face with the effort.

"Thank you, Al. You're a little treasure." Katy poured some water into the kettle on the paraffin stove. "Now fetch a bottle of milk from the home-hut, will you, love?"

Al nodded and trotted off happily to get the bottle from the cold bucket of water in the kitchen. Katy still hadn't got used to the novelty of Express Dairies delivering their milk every day. Being on the busy London Road had quite a few benefits, and not just for the business.

Katy watched him go, one sock up and the other down, then lit the stove. She'd have a ten minute sit-down before tackling that oil change. She'd be glad to shut the garage and put her feet up later. Maybe she and Al could listen to the radio for an hour, before they set off for the lodge house where her parents still lived. One of Agnes's dinners would set them both up and save her cooking. She could use a night off, alright, and it would be good to have the company. These weeks before Christmas, with their short, dull days, were always the hardest of the year, doubly so without Jem's cheery face to brighten them.

The door of the workshop creaked open. She poked her head out of the office to see who'd had the cheek to let themselves in without knocking or ringing the forecourt bell.

Bartlett and son. She might have guessed.

"All alone, Mrs Phipps?" Old man Bartlett looked around at the workshop, rather than at her.

Katy came out of the office and shut the door behind her. Gordon Bartlett, pockmarked from his acne-ridden adolescence but still just as snotty, nudged his father and pointed to the doctor's Model T Ford.

"See, told you, Dad, she's working on Fords, even though we're the agents," Gordon wiped his nose on his sleeve.

"Exclusive agents, don't forget." Mr Bartlett came towards Katy. "Thought you dealt with Morris and Austins, Mrs Phipps?"

"We do, but Dr Benson is an old customer of ours. I suppose it's a question of loyalty."

"Typical female response. Business isn't about sentiment. We are the agents for Ford, not you. How would you feel if we started selling Austins on our forecourt?"

"I'm not selling Dr Benson's car, just replacing the oil, and anyway, you don't have a forecourt, just a backyard, despite all your hoardings plastered all over the front."

"I don't like your tone, young woman." Mr Bartlett was now uncomfortably close. His son leered behind him.

Katy suddenly felt very vulnerable.

"Oi! Leave my Mum alone!" Al came through the back door, clutching a bottle of milk. He took one look at the situation and marched straight up to Mr Bartlett. Al

175

was less than half the man's height but he glared up at him.

"Oh dear, young man. You don't frighten me with your bottle of milk."

"How about this then." Al kicked him on the shins. Mr Bartlett hopped about clutching his leg.

"Well, don't just stand there, Gordon, you useless lump. Punch the little brat!"

"You touch my son, Gordon Bartlett, and I'll take a spanner to that stupid head of yours." Katy picked up the nearest tool, a wrench, and waved it at her unwelcome visitors.

Al ran at them, waving his milk bottle.

"Alright, alright, we're going! But don't think you can get away with stealing our business."

Katy bundled them out of the door, poking their backs with her heavy wrench. Once outside, Mr Bartlett turned around and pointed his finger at them. "You might think you've got the better of me this time, Mrs Phipps, but this isn't the end, you know."

"Get lost, Mr Bartlett." Katy pulled the big door shut and released the latch inside.

"Al, I'm so proud of you." She pulled her son to her and hugged him until he complained she was squashing him.

"I think we've earned that cup of tea, don't you?"

"Come on, Mum. Come and sit down. I'll always look after you, you know."

***

Later, sitting around the familiar table at the west lodge, eating shepherd's pie and cabbage, Katy let herself relax and gazed on her family with genuine fondness, while Al told them all about their set-to with the Bartletts. Daisy, no longer the inquisitive teenager whose curiosity about their private life had driven her mad when she and Jem had lived here after the war, looked like she had some secrets of her own these days. Jack, now a strapping lad of

176

eighteen, worked full-time at the stables with his father, Bert, the head coachman of Cheadle Manor. Only Emily was still a child, and as noisy as ever.

Agnes, completely grey now, had lost none of her energy, though Katy had feared for her health when Lady Amelia had threatened eviction after the scandal of her American trip.

"So, Daisy, what's the latest gossip from the manor then?" Katy asked. "With Douglas and Cassandra away, I'm out of touch."

Daisy, as blonde as her mother had once been, flushed and clammed up.

"Daisy's been courting," Jack said, through a mouthful of food. His mop of hair was dark and curly, like hers and their father's, though Bert's was also streaked with white these days. Sometimes Katy wished time would stand still and give them all a break.

"Don't talk with your mouth full, Jack," said his mother, tutting.

"Sorry." Jack took a slug of barley water. "'Tis true, though, isn't it Daisy?"

Daisy just smiled and fiddled with her fork.

"She must have it bad, if she's off her food," Katy said.

"You ought to tell your sister who it is, by rights," Agnes said.

"Why's that?"

Everyone paused in their eating and stared at Daisy, who squirmed in her seat. "I been seeing Billy Threadwell, if you must know."

"Have you now? So that's why he was singing that song when I gave him the day off yesterday."

"What song?" Daisy said, all pretence of eating gone.

"You know," and Katy sang, "*Daisy, Daisy, give me your answer, do,*" and the others joined in until Daisy went beetroot red and ran out of the kitchen.

"*I'm half crazy, oh, for the love of you,*" they

177

chorused, then stopped, laughing too much to carry on. Katy laughed too, but then, feeling sorry for Daisy, she went out into the parlour to have a chat.

"Is it serious, then Daisy? With Billy, I mean?"

Daisy could only nod.

Katy drew her in, back to the others, still sitting in the kitchen around the table, and said, so the rest of the family could hear, "Billy's a good choice. He's got steady prospects with us at the garage. We're hoping to expand, you know, and Billy's a hard worker. If he wants to, he's welcome to stay working for us for as long as he wants."

Daisy peeped under her lashes at her older sister, her cheeks still pink and her eyes full. "He's asked me to marry him, but he was worried about whether the garage was a goer, if it had a future, like. He said, he wouldn't wed me if he couldn't provide me with a good home." Daisy's words came out all in a rush.

"Good for Billy. Let's see what happens when Jem comes home. It's early days but I think I've got a design for rubber seals on hydraulic brakes we can produce at Katherine Wheel. It's ambitious, but if it comes off, we should be home and dry. As it is, we're doing alright, but we've got to pay off this new bit of land. Jem's researching factory production at Ford's in Boston and raising some money. If all goes to plan, we should be in production ourselves by next year. We'll have to build a big shed to house it, and get more staff."

Daisy's eyes were shining but Bert's looked clouded. "That's a lot to take on, Katy, my girl. You sure you're doing the right thing?"

Agnes added, "Isn't it enough to have a garage, without a factory to manage and all? The countryside won't be green much longer, with all these cars puffing away, choking the air and drowning out the birdsong. I don't hold with it. Why can you never be content, our Katy?"

Katy had been half expecting this and felt sorry for Daisy, sensing she'd stolen her thunder by eclipsing

Daisy's news with her own. "Well, it hasn't happened yet, Mum, and if Jem's research doesn't work out, maybe it never will, but we'll be careful, honestly we will. And, in the meantime, Billy's got a job with us and I think we should raise a toast to him and Daisy!"

Daisy rewarded her with a flash of a smile, then blushed all over again as they all stood up and raised their glasses. "To Daisy and Billy!"

Daisy said, "Thank you, but I haven't said 'yes' yet!"

They all laughed and got back to eating Agnes's delicious pie, now gone cold. Agnes was just putting an apple crumble on the table with a dish of cream, when the door burst open and Maisie, the housemaid from the manor, stood there, so out of breath, she could barely deliver her message.

"Mr Beagle, you're wanted up at the house. Lady Amelia said for you to fetch the doctor." Maisie took a gulp, glanced at Katy and managed to blurt out the rest. "See, Doctor Benson's car's at Katy's garage and he've got no transport. Sir Robert's been took bad!"

So, how did you break it?" The doctor loomed over him. "Must have given it a hell of a crack."

Jem didn't feel like explaining. His black eye would have to speak for him. "Just caught it on something."

"Your stump is grazed and badly bruised. You did the right thing to leave off your prosthetic. Don't worry, we'll fix you up with a new one, right here in Boston."

"Really? That would be good." Jem couldn't believe his luck.

"Sure thing, we have a prosthetic department in the Massachusetts General. They've got all the latest ideas. Your new arm will be miles better than this worn out, broken one."

Jem looked at his false arm. Now in two pieces, it lay on the doctor's desk in silent testament to its encounter with Fred Stavely's fat head. The wood had splintered right up the shaft. Stupidly, he felt a part of his living body was missing. He'd got fond of the old thing, once so foreign, now so familiar; it had become part of who he was and he felt he'd betrayed its loyalty. How daft. He pictured Fred Stavely's body lying like a dead man on the cold pavement in New York. Yes, it had been bloody worth it.

Jem turned to the young doctor, who was watching him thoughtfully.

"Want to talk about it?"

"No."

"Fair enough. Let's pack you off to the artificial limb department then. You know we have a veteran's programme, so you might even get a subsidy, although you not being an American might be an obstacle, but I guess you still fought in the war."

Jem looked at the medic. Pictured him an old man, still in a white coat, years from now. He'd go far, he was sure of it. He'd already learned not to ask questions.

Douglas was waiting for him in the corridor. A

180

nurse gave them instructions on how to find the prosthetic department and they set off. "So, what did the doc say, Jem?"

"Said they can fix me up with a new arm. Could even be a better one."

They stepped out into the deep snow covering the quadrangle between the buildings. The hospital was quiet, presumably due to the weather. Some men were clearing the entrance road as they walked past, so Jem doubted the peace would last.

The sun had ventured forth this morning and glinted off the snow in diamond clusters. It couldn't lift the temperature above freezing, though, and their breath came in steamy white clouds, as they walked along the path, following the painted signs towards the main reception hall.

Inside, a group of medics were gathered within a shaft of sunlight beaming down through the big skylight in the foyer. They were studying a notice-board of rotas, grumbling about their shifts in low voices.

As they walked past them, the only female doctor disentangled herself from the group and smiled. She had a severe face, with a strong, protruding nose above skinny lips. Jem had the impression that mouth wasn't used to smiling but he supposed you didn't need to be pretty, if you had enough brains to be a doctor. He was surprised when Douglas stopped and embraced her bony frame.

"Hello, you, and good morning! Nice to see you in your natural domain. You look every inch the doctor these days, my dear." Douglas kissed her on the cheek in a very informal way.

The woman doctor kissed him back. They were obviously good friends. Perhaps her looks belied a friendly nature.

"Won't you introduce me to your handsome friend?" She looked directly at Jem, who held out his good hand.

Douglas's friend glanced at the sleeve that should have housed his absent one and her face slipped into a professional, polite indifference.

"May I introduce my sister, Cheryl? Dr Flintock, I should say," Douglas said, laughing. The group of other doctors had moved off to the various wards where their duties lay and the three of them stood alone in the foyer in the bright winter sunlight. "This is Jem Phipps, my business partner in England."

Jem didn't know who froze first, but it had nothing to do with the arctic weather.

"Phipps? Did you say, Phipps?" No trace of her earlier smile remaining on Cheryl's sharp, intelligent face.

Douglas's easygoing, ever-ready smile had also slipped. Jem could see his brain catching up. Sometimes he despaired of his friend's casual attitude to life, both business and personal. And this couldn't be more personal.

"I would say 'pleased to meet you' but I don't believe in telling lies," Jem said, unable to stop himself.

Cheryl's already pale face blanched to white. "How dare you!"

"Oh, I dare alright. Just as you dared to write that wicked letter to Lady Amelia and nearly ruined my wife's life. My innocent wife."

"You're Kate Phipps's husband?"

"I am, and proud of it."

Cheryl turned to her brother. "How could you bring that woman's husband here, to Boston! He hasn't been to the house, has he?"

Jem answered for him. "I have, as it happens, though you'll be pleased to know I spent most of my time in the servants' quarters, but I also met your mother again. She at least seems to have some manners and a sense of justice."

"Jem..." Douglas held his hand out, gesturing Jem to pipe down.

Cheryl's already small eyes narrowed. "Why are you here, Mr Phipps? You didn't come for Rose's wedding, so what's the purpose of your visit?"

"My private business is no concern of yours, Dr

Flintock," Jem said, and added, with force, bringing his face close up to hers, "and it *never* was. Excuse me, I've got to go," and he walked away, leaving the siblings facing each other.

Their raised voices followed him down the echoing corridor, their anger bouncing off the pale green walls of the massive institution. Jem didn't want to hear them. God, what an ugly witch Cheryl Flintock had turned out to be. He supposed he shouldn't be surprised. No wonder Fred didn't fancy her and preferred his beautiful Katy. He never thought he'd sympathise with the bastard but he couldn't have kissed that hideous, bony mug either.

He'd thought he'd expunged all his rage but it shocked him how nearly his hand had reached out and strangled that scrawny neck of hers. Maybe it was just as well he was one-handed, or he might not have been able to hold back.

CHAPTER TWENTY THREE
Winter 1926

"Hello, darling." Cassandra was busy buttoning up Lottie's wool coat, ready to go out and build a snowman in Copley Square. Nanny Morgan was minding Isobel, saying she wasn't 'one for the snow' and happy to stay indoors in the warm, even if it meant holing up in the children's tiny bedroom while little Isobel had her nap.

Douglas looked blue around the mouth. Maybe it was too cold out there for Lottie. "Is it freezing outside, Doug? You looked chilled to the bone."

"Yes, it is. Are you taking Lottie out in it?"

"Well, I was, but I'm not sure now, looking at you!"

"Oh, Mother, you promised," Lottie said.

Cassandra looked at her daughter and quailed at fighting her strong will on foreign soil. "Yes I did. We'll go, but if it's too cold, we'll just have to come straight back. Is that a deal?"

Lottie nodded and submitted to her hat and gloves.

"I'll come with you," Douglas said.

"Are you sure, darling? You look frozen already."

Douglas did indeed look unwell. "Nonsense, a jig around the park is just what I need."

They set off at a brisk pace. The depth of the temperature shocked Cassandra. She had never experienced anything like it. They crunched along; their boots breaking the film of ice encrusting the snow. They walked as fast as they dared, one on each side of their daughter, and swinging her between them over the drifts. Lottie squealed in delight. Where the snow had been shoveled away, the pavement was notched with ridges of ice, too slippery for anything but tentative steps. Cassandra worried she had made the wrong decision and gripped Lottie's mitten too hard, until the little girl complained.

"Sorry, darling, but it's so slippy!" Cassandra checked that Douglas had Lottie's other hand, glad to see the park gates just ahead. Ominous black clouds foreshadowed another fall of snow all too soon. She longed for the green fields of Wiltshire and its mild, damp air. This air was so raw, it hurt your lungs.

It was easier once they reached the park and they let go of Lottie's hand. The snow here was soft, with grass underneath it, albeit frozen. If Lottie fell over, she'd have a safe landing. The little girl went up to a group of children who were building a snowman. Douglas went with her and chatted to the parents who were watching them. Cassandra expected him to join in. He loved games. His child-like enjoyment of life was one of his charms, so she was surprised when he came back to her, his face still serious and drawn. She hoped he wasn't sickening for something. Quite apart from any suffering he might endure, she desperately didn't want to extend their stay in Boston.

"I know some of those parents, vaguely," Douglas said. "She'll be alright with them."

Cassandra nodded her agreement, glad of a moment alone with her husband. "What is it, Douglas, darling? You don't look right at all."

"I've had a difficult morning. Look, Cass, I might as well tell you. I didn't want to worry you before, but I have a nasty feeling you're going to find out anyway, from the wrong quarter."

"Find out what? You're worrying me now, Doug."

"It's Jem. You mustn't tell Kate about this, Cass. He swore me to secrecy and he never wants her to find out."

Cassandra nodded her assent and focused all her attention on her husband.

"He went sleuthing and managed to find Fred Stavely, in New York, apparently. He beat him up and broke his wooden arm. He wasn't going to tell me about it but he can't manage without a new artificial limb, so I took him to Massachusetts General Hospital this morning, to see if I could get him fixed up with a new one."

Cassandra was shaken by the news. "But Douglas, Jem is always so genial, so unassuming and gentle. I can't picture him hurting anyone, but then, Fred *is* a man apart.

185

And, I suppose, we must remember, Jem fought in the war. A lot of people got hurt then."

"Jem's a lot tougher than he looks. He's tougher than me, I'm sure of that. I just hope it doesn't come back and bite him. He said he hadn't killed Fred, but by that, I assume he came close."

"Oh, Doug! That's awful! He does love Kate so. To think he's been that angry for all these years. Well, let's hope that's the end of it. He's had his revenge and if the police haven't caught up with him by now, perhaps they never will. Did it happen in New York?"

"Yes, two days ago. He looks a bit battered himself, quite apart from his false arm - that's broken clean in two. But Cass, that's not the worst of it."

"How can anything be worse than that?"

Douglas grimaced. "It can, because very unfortunately we bumped into Cheryl at the hospital. Such bad timing. What are the chances? But, there you go, it's happened now. As you can imagine, it didn't take her long to guess Jem's identity - especially as I, well, I let it slip. God! I feel so stupid. I *am* so bloody stupid!"

"What do you mean? You didn't introduce them? Oh, Doug!" Cassandra's blood, already almost chilled to a standstill, drained out of her hands and feet and she felt quite faint. A muscle twitched in Douglas's face as she watched him wrestle with his conscience. Douglas was always so carefree, she could picture his blunder all too easily.

"Cheryl doesn't know about him beating up Fred, does she?"

"No, no, she doesn't, and that's one good thing, but you can bet your bottom dollar she'll not let it go that Jem's here in Boston. It might be freezing cold, my darling, but you can expect fire and brimstone at the dinner table tonight."

And so it proved. Even Lottie was glad to get back to the brown terraced house before the snowstorm broke but Cassandra remained unthawed, despite standing before

186

the roaring parlour fire, hours later, after the children had gone to bed. The rest of the family had gathered around it, as they always did, but earlier than usual. In deference to the severe weather, they'd all hurried home from work, before they got stranded. Cassandra found the heavy snowfall suffocating, trapping her in this constricted house, sandwiched between rows of others just like it; swamped by the muffler of white ice smothering the streets, blocking her exit.

Cheryl, by contrast, looked overheated. Two perfect red circles inflamed both her thin cheeks. Cassandra pondered the absurd conundrum of how pale blue eyes could look hot with pent-up anger. She braced herself for the coming eruption, knowing from previous experience, it would be volcanic.

Selina went to the window and drew back the curtains. "Look outside! It's coming down heavier than ever! The whole of Boston will be snowbound by morning."

"Let the drapes fall back, Selina," Mr Flintock said. "You're making the room draughty."

Selina gave a low laugh. "It's silly of me, I know, but I hardly ever saw deep snow till I came to Boston. It's never lost its fascination. A winter wonderland. I wonder if we'll have a white Christmas? "

"Seems likely, if it keeps up," Mr Flintock said.

"Oh, Douglas." Selina let the curtains fall and turned to her son, her once-lovely face lit up by a rare smile, and said, in her lilting voice, "Why don't you stay for Christmas? It would be so perfectly charming to have your little girls here to celebrate with us."

Cheryl broke in, "Oh, yes, Douglas, why don't you stay? In fact, why not invite all your English friends to join us? Half of them seem to be here already, after all."

Cassandra glanced at her mother-in-law who looked crushed, and guilty. If only Cheryl would shut up. She'd ruined their plans once before. She mustn't let her get away with it again, but it was so awkward with Selina swearing them to silence about her generous offer. Cassandra willed Douglas to speak, and then wished he hadn't. When would he learn?

"And it's a shame you can't be civil to them, Cheryl," Douglas said.

"What's this?" Mr Flintock's fierce eyebrows drew together in a v-shape, furrowing his heavy brow.

Cassandra just knew their father would winkle out any whiff of confrontation between his children. Really, he seemed to thrive on it, whereas Selina looked as if she might crawl under one of the splindly tables that littered the cramped room.

"It's hard to believe, Father," Cheryl said, "but Douglas has brought over that little slut's husband. You remember - Kate Phipps - the one who accused Fred of assault."

"She's no slut!" Cassandra burst out, unable to resist or accept the insult to her friend.

Douglas sighed. Cassandra could see he knew this wasn't going to end well but not how it could be avoided. "No, Cheryl, Katherine Phipps is a respectable married woman and her husband, Jem, is pure gold. I am proud to be in business with them and to call them friends. Always was, always will be."

"Huh! And what was this golden boy doing in Boston, precisely? He was very coy on the subject when I asked him," Cheryl said.

"How did you meet him, Cheryl?" Selina said.

"At the hospital of all places. I didn't know why he was there, at first, so I checked with the records and found he's being fitted with a new prosthetic for his left arm. Now why on earth would he come all this way for that?" Cheryl looked triumphantly around the room, waiting for an answer.

"Jem Phipps didn't come here for a new artificial limb but to research a business project. He just had an, um, unfortunate accident and broke his wooden arm. It was, er, just one of those things that happen sometimes. No, the

188

real reason he's here is that we are embarking on an expansion of the garage where we both work, with his clever and enterprising wife. I've been racing cars in Britain and selling them from Katherine Wheel Garage. The sponsorship for the racing has brought some money in and Kate has invented a new sort of brake seal that we're hoping to produce. Jem went to Boston, to look at the Ford factory," Douglas said.

Said too much, in Cassandra's opinion but she held her breath and waited.

"You've been racing?" Mr Flintock his frown now lifted by raised eyebrows.

"I can't see how anyone can have an accident severe enough to break a wooden arm on a trip to Boston. How did he get it in the first place?" Cheryl said.

"He was wounded in the war, Cheryl. He's an honourable man, an ex-soldier. And just like Cassandra, Kate served in the WAAC, while you stayed home and kept safe," Douglas said.

He seemed to have touched a nerve there because Cheryl looked embarrassed, for once. "I was studying medicine by then. Anyway, how can you afford this ambitious project?"

"Yes, Douglas," Mr Flintock said, "Cheryl has a point there. She usually gets to the meat of the matter. How are you funding this expansion and why haven't you told us before about this dangerous racing racket?"

Selina shuffled in her seat, looking undecided. No, don't tell them, Cassandra wanted to shout at her but Selina had made up her mind. "I'm funding it, if you must know, Theodore." She looked directly at her husband. "I think it's an excellent idea and I'm happy to get behind it."

"How do you know about it, Selina? Why on earth haven't you told me that you're involved?" Mr Flintock's powerful voice started to rumble.

The volcanic lava was beginning to flow and Cassandra dreaded the explosion she sensed was coming.

Selina impressed her then with her bravery. "I met

Mr Phipps, here in our house, and he gave me a very professional break-down of his plans, which were meticulous in detail. Why, he is the most genteel of men, reminded me of the manners down South, before the war, you know. I liked him enormously, and I'm happy to provide the means for his project with Douglas."

"He was here? In our house? After what his wife did with Fred?" Cheryl's cheeks were an even more hectic shade of puce now.

Cassandra said, "Kate didn't *do* anything with Fred, Fred did something to her!"

"And it's high time we put the nasty incident behind us," Douglas said. "It's completely irrelevant!"

"It's not irrelevant if my wife is lending money to people without morals," roared Mr Flintock.

"That is hugely unjust and untrue, Father," Douglas said, looking steely and not unlike his father, Cassandra realised, with a shock. She'd never noticed the slightest resemblance before.

"I shall lend money where and to whom I choose." Selina shocked them all into silence.

They all stared at her, she who rarely gave an opinion, if she could avoid it. Where was this new strength coming from, Cassandra wondered? Selina looked like she might float away if the wind blew in her direction and yet there was a determination about her she had never seen before.

"But, Selina, my dear," Mr Flintock began.

"No, Theodore, it's my money, from my family in Kentucky, and whilst I have breath in my body, I shall do what I like with it. Douglas has his heart set on this enterprise and, having met both Mr and Mrs Phipps at their garage in Wiltshire, seen how hard they work and heard their good ideas, why, I feel honoured to be able to help them." Selina sat down abruptly and rubbed her temples with her fingertips.

Cassandra noticed the black shadows under her eyes and went to her side. "Thank you, Selina. You are very

190

kind but you've exhausted yourself. Can I get you anything?"

Selina patted Cassandra's hand. "A glass of water, dear, please."

Even Cheryl was moved to silence. Shortly afterwards they went into dinner and confined the conversation to the extreme weather that kept them all locked together inside the narrow walls of the Flintock household.

CHAPTER TWENTY FOUR
Winter 1926

Jem couldn't believe how quickly the Prosthetic Department at the Massachusetts General had made his new arm, or what an improvement it was on his old one. Apparently things had moved on in the intervening years since the war, they'd told him yesterday afternoon, when he'd called at the hospital for his final fitting. This new artificial limb was far more comfortable and the expert staff made sure it fitted him perfectly. The old rasping sensation around his stump was gone and the new hand had fingers that articulated, making them far more useful; far more human. Stronger too, with metal rods and cable pulleys inside each finger and joints that actually worked, or locked together by a little mechanism, if he chose to apply it. He could even oppose his finger and thumb again, by a simple rotation of his upper arm.

All he had to do now was think of a reason, other than the real one, why he had broken it. One that would convince his wife.

He'd paid for it in cash drawn on the garage bank account, after going to the bank to check there was enough, and drew out some extra for the passage home and settling up at the boarding house. His new arm hadn't been cheap but it had been worth it. He was experimenting with it in his lodgings, while eating his breakfast. It had been five days since his fight with Fred and so far, he'd seen no sign of reprisals from the authorities. And why should there be? That was the question that woke him every morning and the one that kept him awake at night. Now he had his new arm and his bruises had faded, there was nothing to keep him here. If the cops hadn't traced him to Boston from New York, they certainly wouldn't find him in Wiltshire. It was time to go home.

No new snow had fallen and, gazing out of the grimy window, Boston looked pretty much back to normal. Drifts lay in lumpy piles on the sidewalks but traffic flowed noisily again on the streets. Jem fiddled with the food on his plate. He was tired of Boston beans with pork followed by stodgy pancakes for breakfast. It would be good to taste proper Wiltshire bacon again and what wouldn't he give for a pint of proper ale!

His thoughts were interrupted by the hotel receptionist schlepping, in his carpet slippers, into the dreary room. Jem wouldn't care if he never saw beige again. To his surprise, the receptionist, Mr Long, one of the shortest men he'd ever met, was wending his way to his table.

"Mr Phipps, sir?"

"Yes?"

"Telegram for you," Mr Long said in his odd piping voice, retrieving an envelope from his greasy waistcoat pocket.

"Thank you." Jem reached out for it. The little man hovered and Jem tipped him a dime. The coin was received with an ungrateful grunt but it disappeared into the waistcoat pocket in a flash.

Mr Long still lingered while Jem ripped the envelope open, looking curious and trying to read the words upside down.

Jem looked at him. "If I need to send a reply, I'll go to the Post Office." He folded it away from view.

Mr Long grunted again. "Okay, mister, whatever you say." The little man shuffled off, tutting loud enough for everyone to hear.

Jem didn't like telegrams. They never brought good news. This one was no different. It was from Katy.

"SIR ROBERT DIED TODAY STOP HEART ATTACK STOP UPROAR AT MANOR STOP TELL CASS AND COME HOME SOON STOP LOVE KATE"

Jem abandoned his sickly breakfast and went to the desk. "I'm checking out today," he told Mr Long. The reception counter was tall and Mr Long could barely see above it. He looked at Jem over his pince-nez and said, with a hint of hope, "Bad news, I guess?"

"How much do I owe you, Mr Long?" Jem took out his wallet, hoping there would be enough money inside it. He hadn't reckoned on leaving quite so abruptly.

Mr Long sucked his teeth and got out his ledger. He ran his knarled finger down the columns. From behind his ear, he drew a stub of pencil and began laboriously to add up the figures, licking the pencil from time to time and muttering under his stale breath.

"Listen, Mr Long, I'll go and pack while you make up the bill." Jem couldn't bear to waste more time. He'd needed no excuse to hurry home and now he couldn't wait.

"Say, I won't be a moment," Mr Long called up to Jem, who was already halfway up the first flight of stairs.

"Neither will I!" Jem took the treads two at a time and arrived, panting, on the fifth floor. He threw his clothes, and the little presents he'd bought during his stay, into his suitcase, brushed his teeth, and grabbed his coat and hat in record time. He dashed back down the many stairs within five minutes, only to find Mr Long still hadn't written out the bill but instead was chatting to the fat woman who sat at the next table to Jem every morning in the drab dining room.

Jem was itching to get away. He didn't know the time of the boats but he did know they didn't turn up every day. What if the ship he needed was in the dock now, getting up steam?

"So, I said, to him, Mr Long, I says, it won't do, young man!" The fat woman had embarked on one of her rants. "And do you know what he said?"

"Look, I'm sorry to interrupt, " Jem said, without a grain of truth, "but I've got a boat to catch. Mr Long, how much do I owe you?"

"Well! How rude!" The fat woman, wobbled her chins.

"Excuse me, Mrs Trump." Mr Long raised his eyes to the ceiling. "I must attend to this impatient young man."

"Oh, don't mind me, I'm sure." Mrs Trump peered at the invoice total.

Jem handed over a good chunk of the notes in his wallet. Anything to get out of the dingy place.

"Thank you, Mr Phipps, that'll do nicely." Mr Long thumbed through them with a speed Jem had never before witnessed.

"Good day to you both." Jem tipped his trilby at the pair, who were never going to go anywhere else. Feeling a little lightheaded at his extravagant gesture, and thankful for his freedom, he quitted the boarding house for the final time. A sense of profound release chased his heels as he jumped on a passing tram into the centre of town where he stopped to buy a copy of the *Boston Advertiser* and a pie from Faneuil market.

He went to the Post Office and dashed off a reply telegram to Katy, saying he would be home as soon as possible. Then he wrote another, to Douglas, explaining about Sir Robert and sending sympathy to Cassandra. He didn't want to call at the Flintock household in person, after duping Kathleen into thinking he would call again. He wouldn't like to get on the wrong side of her mother, Maureen. Just thinking of all these deceptions, all the risks he'd taken, made him long to board the boat home, and leave it all behind.

He almost ran along the slippery, icy streets to the dockside and couldn't believe his luck when he saw the ocean liner lined up against the quay. He went straight to the ticket office.

"What time does she sail?"

"Three o'clock this afternoon, sir." How could the ticket man know how joyous that information was to Jem? He almost hugged him through the glass window.

"I'll have a one-way ticket to Liverpool, please."

"What berth do you want, sir?"

"I'll sleep anywhere, just so long's I'm aboard."

"Third class do you?"

"Yes, anything, how much?"

Jem paid for the ticket, pleased he still had enough. He had hardly any dollars left after.

"Can I board now?"

"Yes, sir, go right up the gangplank and give your ticket to the sailor at the gate. Have a safe trip."

"Thank you." Jem's heart was light as a bubble.

Once aboard ship, he found his quarters cramped and airless. He was sharing with three other men in bunks, two deep either side of a gap so narrow he could hardly turn around in it, but he didn't care. Just so long as the prow pointed towards England, he'd sleep on a bed of nails, if he had to.

Katy wished, for the umpteenth time, that she had more than one pair of hands. Billy did his best but he was no good at tuning engines and this magnificent three-litre Bentley, brought in by one of Cassandra's influential friends, deserved her full attention. Al would be in from school in half an hour, wanting his tea, and she had nothing prepared, again. If only Jem were here, he'd have fetched the spuds already, and got them peeled.

The forecourt bell rang out. "I'll go, shall I?" Billy said.

"Yes, please, Billy, and don't forget to check the oil, once you've filled up with petrol. Or charge for it."

Really, she shouldn't have to keep reminding him about these basic things. At least he was happy these days, after his engagement to her sister, Daisy, but it had made him even more easily distracted.

Everyone else in the local community had long faces, since Sir Robert's death last week. Katy wasn't sure they were mourning for the old fellow out of love and affection, rather that his going meant the end of an era and the beginning of uncertainty for all the tenants and farmers who relied on the estate for their living and their homes. Just like her's and Jem's parents. At least she and Jem had a freehold property to call their own.

She hoped Cassandra had got the message about her father by now. She'd had no word from anyone, except to say Jem was on his way, but she had no idea when.

The office telephone rang. "Damn," Katy said. There was no sign of Billy. The telephone kept up its insistent clamour. "They're not going to give up, are they?" Katy muttered to Felix, the cat, who didn't have an answer. She jogged to the office, wiping her hands on an oily rag, before picking up the earphone and speaking into the mouthpiece.

"Katherine Wheel Garage. Can I help you?"

197

"I reckon you're the only one who can, or ever could," came the reply.

"Jem! Oh, Jem! Where are you?"

"Woodbury station, waiting for you to come and pick me up, of course," Jem's crackly voice said.

"You're home? That's wonderful! I'll come and get you right now. Just wait, just wait there, Jem. Oh, how lovely! I'll be there as quick as I can."

"Drive safely, then, my love," Jem said, and the line went dead.

Katy was all of a fluster. Should she change? What about Al? "Billy, Billy!" she called. Billy came in to the workshop and put the money from the petrol customer in the till, just inside the door.

"Yes, Mrs Phipps?"

"Oh, Billy, Jem's home. I've got to go to the station and collect him. Would you mind Al for me when he comes in from school?"

"I could, but I'll have to manage the garage as well. What about this baby Austin I'm working on?"

"It'll have to wait." Deadlines no longer seemed important. "Give Al something to eat, forget about the garage, unless it's petrol. Put up the closed sign for the repairs workshop. You don't even need to answer the telephone if you can't get to it. People will just have to wait. I'll be as quick as I can, Billy, I promise, but don't go home until I get back, or I'll set Daisy on to you."

Billy blushed and laughed, "Alright, Mrs P."

"And Billy?"

"Yes, Mrs Phipps?"

"Call me Kate, like everyone else, won't you? After all, you'll be family soon."

Billy nodded, too tongue-tied to use the permission she'd just given him.

Katy patted him on the back and dashed into the home-hut to glance in the mirror. She wrenched off her headscarf and threw it on the table, dipped a flannel in the pitcher of water by the sink and scrubbed her face. She dragged a brush through her hair and wondered if she should put on a skirt. Not enough time. It would have to do. She took off her boiler suit and grabbed her coat. If she didn't get out of the car, who would see her trousers?

Katy grabbed the keys of the Austin they were using as a runabout and got in the driving seat, waving to Billy as she drew off on to the London Road. She felt a bag of nerves. She had missed Jem so much. She couldn't wait to see him; kiss him; tell him all the gossip about Sir Robert's death, share everything again. The early December afternoon closed in as she drove. She could barely see in the gloaming twilight, even with her headlights on.

At last the lights of Woodbury appeared. She stuck her hand out to signal left and turned in for the station. And there he was, standing under the wooden eaves, looking out for her.

As soon as he saw her car, he stepped down from the platform and came to meet her, smiling. Katy had never been so glad to see anyone. She forgot all about wearing trousers and leapt out of the car, into the drizzle that had now set in, and wrapped her arms around him.

"God, I've missed you!" she said into his overcoat collar.

His answer was to kiss her, hard and deep, oblivious to the porter wheeling his trolley past them.

Katy kissed him back. She felt like a fish who'd returned to familiar waters and could breathe again, come alive again, swim again.

"Why Jem! Is that a new arm? It looks amazing. Where did you get it?"

"Tell you later."

The drizzle became rain, heavy rain, laced with the threat of sleet.

"Oh, I can't wait to get you home." Katy's hair was already clamped to her uncovered head. "Al's missed you too."

"How is he?"

"Fine, enjoying school and doing well. We've been

199

reading together every night at bedtime." Katy glanced at Jem; caught his pleased smile. "Tell me everything you've done in Boston and all about that new hand. Do those life-like fingers actually work?" Katy looked at his arm then screwed her eyes up to see through the drumming rain, washing across the windscreen.

"You concentrate on getting us home, Mrs Phipps," Jem said, still smiling but looking a little anxious. "We can talk all night if we want to. I'm not going anywhere else."

Katy nodded. Seeing the road through the teeming rain demanded all her attention. Billy had waited with Al until they got back and insisted on cycling off in the downpour, wearing his gabardine waterproofs. She would have given him a lift but he was keen to see Daisy and tell the family Jem was home safe. As the lodge was only a couple of miles away and young love was as good as any engine, she let him go.

When they got inside, the rain was beating a tattoo on the tin roof and they all had to shout to be heard above the din. Katy kissed Jem again and left him to catch up with Al, who wouldn't let go of his father for a minute. Katy left them to catch up, and fetched some potatoes and carrots from the clamp and threw them in a pot with some onions and bacon. She stirred some flour and water together with a few herbs and bundled them into dumplings to go on top. It would have to do. They had some cheese and apples for afters, if they were still hungry.

Jem had already made a difference. The fire was banked up and chucking out a good blaze, Al was sitting on his knee, thumb in mouth, listening to stories about America. Katy felt the gap in her heart fill up again.

She found a couple of bottles of beer in the lean-to larder and they washed down the hotpot with them.

"I'll put Al to bed, then, shall I?" Jem said.

"Not yet, Dad." Al clung to his father's shirt tails, now hanging down outside his trousers in a relaxed at-home manner.

"Come on, Al, it is bed-time, my lovely." Katy stacked the dishes into the sink. Such bliss not to have to return to these after putting Al to bed but to get straight on with them.

"Only if you show me how your new fingers work again, Dad." Al trotted off with his hand in Jem's.

"Again?" laughed Jem, ruffling Al's hair.

"Just once more?" And they disappeared into Al's little separate bedroom.

Kate plunged her hands into soapy water, and rattled through her chores as fast as she could. She had butterflies in her tummy, just like a lovesick girl, waiting for her first kiss.

Jem came back half an hour later to a tidy living room. Katy sat by the fire, waiting, smiling, anticipating. He took her in his arms and held her, silently, and then kissed her until she was breathless.

"Come and sit down, Jem. Let's sit either side of the fire or we won't get much talking done!"

He laughed, and did as he was bid. "Tell me about Sir Robert, then."

"Well, I was up at Mum's when we got the news, and we were teasing Daisy about Billy - they've got engaged."

"Never!"

"Yes, so he's more in a dream than ever, but very happy. Anyway, Maisie turned up saying Dad was to fetch the doctor up to the manor house. His car was here, having a new tyre, you see. But it was too late, Sir Robert was stone cold by the time Dr Benson reached him. It happened when he was out riding, apparently. Luckily, Colonel Musgrove was with him and brought him home across his saddle. They laid him in bed but he died an half an hour later. Dr Benson told my Mum and Dad he couldn't have saved him anyway, not after such a big heart attack." Katy shook her head, remembering.

"Poor old feller, but if you've got to go, it's not such a bad way, I suppose," Jem stared into the fire.

"No-o, but no-one saw it coming."

"But Cassandra said he'd been drinking enough for an army ever since Charles died. That's a lot of booze over the years, bound to take its toll."

"Yes, he never got over that, really." Katy shivered despite the glow from the fire.

"So, how's Lady Amelia taken it?"

"She went a bit doolally, Dad said. Mrs Andrews had to take over everything. Lady Amelia hasn't left her room, by all accounts. Just keeps saying she won't make any funeral arrangements until Cassandra's home."

"Typical. Those who shout loudest are the weakest, in the end. That'll mean Cass will have to do everything." Jem stretched his legs out to the warmth.

"Now, that's the local news - tell me all about your trip to America, and how you got fixed up with your new hand." Katy sat back in her chair, impatient to hear every detail.

She listened attentively as Jem described the Ford factory in Boston, saying that despite the sheer scale of it, he thought they could copy some of the production techniques here, and showed her his rough sketches, and how he could turn the pages with his new articulating fingers.

Katy touched the new hand, finger by finger.

"Doug told me about the prosthetic department at Massachusetts General Hospital and how they had set it up for war veterans. It seemed too good an opportunity to miss, but it wasn't cheap." Jem looked very apprehensive when he said that and Katy rushed to reassure him.

"We're spending enough on everything else, Jem. What could be more important? But what did you do with the old one? I was rather fond of it. We could have put it on the dresser as a trophy."

Jem laughed in an odd way, but looked so relieved Katy decided to let it drop. It was enough to have him home.

When Jem told her about Selina Flintock agreeing to

fund the expansion of their business and that they could go ahead and build a shed on their extended land, she could contain herself no longer, and got up to hug him. He didn't say much after that, because they were too busy in the bedroom.

Three times they made love before they were satisfied, each time more loving, more passionate than the last. It was only when Katy lay back, exhausted, her head on Jem's dear chest, that she remembered her contraceptive cap. Too bad, what was life for, if you couldn't love your husband when he came home? She snuggled closer to his warm body, tucking her legs into his and letting her breath relax into sleep, matching his rhythm and synchronising perfectly.

Everything seemed easier once Jem was home, and Katy swore she'd never take him for granted again. To share the responsibility for the business and their family; to halve the workload, was nothing less than blissful.

Katy hadn't been idle while he was away and was desperate to show him her refined design for the hydraulic brake seal. She'd finally managed to make one she was satisfied would be completely effective. They road-tested it together again up on the downs.

"I think you've cracked it, Kate, I really do," Jem said.

"Yes, Jem, I think I have. I honestly think we can make a go of this."

"And with all I've seen in America, Kate, I know how to make the production smooth and efficient. Once we get a production line going, I'll write to Fords and see if they'll buy them. No point making the seals perfect, if we've no buyers."

His words tempered her confidence. Jem was right, they had a long way to go before they could be sure this gamble would pay off.

Within three days of Jem's return home, news came via Billy's mother that Cassandra and Douglas had also come back from America.

203

"We should soon know about the funeral," Katy said. "Poor Cassandra, she'll have her hands full. I think I'll drive up there tomorrow and see if I can help out."

"Good idea," Jem said. "I'll come with you."

Cassandra looked drawn when she saw her the next day but pleased to see them. "I can't get Mater to venture downstairs. I feel I've lost both my parents overnight."

"Have you got a date for the funeral?" Katy asked

"Yes, next Wednesday. Father's been dead so long, there's no point delaying it further. His body has been kept at the funeral director's up till now, but I've seen the vicar first thing this morning and we've agreed it's best to crack on with it, now I'm back. So long as Mother will emerge from her self-inflicted purdah."

"I'm sure she will, honey, now we're home," Douglas said.

"Poor Father. Well, I suppose he's with Charles now."

"Yes," Katy said, feeling uncomfortable. "You must let us know if there's anything we can do."

"Actually, there is," Cassandra said, once more in charge. "Can you sort out the cars for the funeral cortêge? It's not far from the house to the church but we should have cars with drivers for the great and good. The coffin will go with the pall bearers in the carriage with Mother's matched horses. No doubt the entire county will turn out. And they'll all need feeding and watering."

"Yes, there's a lot to do. You leave the cars to us, Cassandra," Katy said.

The door of the drawing room opened, slowly. Lady Amelia, dressed entirely in deepest black, entered and then stopped on the threshold, once she caught sight of Katy and Jem.

"Phipps! And in my drawing room. I might have known you would trespass here, the moment my back was turned; the minute I am left alone in this world, here you are, like vultures, pecking at the corpse."

"Mother! Don't be so melodramatic. Jem and Katy

have kindly offered to help with the funeral cars," Cassandra said.

Katy watched Douglas get up, teeth clenched, and escort his mother-in-law to one of the sofas. "Come and sit down by the fire, Lady Amelia."

"Unhand me, Douglas, I'm not a horse to be led. I know the geography of my own house."

"We'll leave you to it," Jem said.

He and Katy got up and murmured goodbyes. As they were leaving, Katy heard Lady Amelia say, "And why have we got tradespeople in the drawing room? I see standards have slipped in my absence."

She didn't wait for Cassandra's reply.

"She's on the mend then," Jem said.

"God help Cassandra," Katy said, glad to get outside and back in their car.

Cassandra's hunch was right. Sir Robert's funeral was indeed a grand affair and hundreds of people attended it, despite the frost not melting all day. From simple smallholders and tenant farmers, to the Bishop of the diocese and the Mayor of Woodbury, it seemed to Cassandra that the entire county had turned up to mark her father's passing. She hadn't had time to think since coming home from Boston and the sombre ritual passed in a blur of faces she hardly recognised. The whole thing had been very expensive but her mother had insisted on providing a reception after the service at Cheadle Manor and ordered Mrs Biggs, the cook, to lay on a lavish buffet. Mr Andrews, the butler, served wine to the gentry and beer to the others. Barrels of both had to be bought in, along with hams, turkeys, sides of beef and salmon. The vegetables were supplied by the estate, so that expense was spared at least and some of the local farmers had given pies or rounds of cheese, in honour of Sir Robert.

"It's a pity your father isn't here to do justice to the food, he would have loved all this," Douglas said quietly, as they stood in line to receive guests into the large drawing room.

"But Mother would never have allowed him to enjoy it whilst he was alive." Cassandra was too tired to reply with anything but the truth.

Lady Amelia had made a remarkable recovery, once the funeral arrangements gathered pace. She'd ordered her dressmaker to make her several new outfits, all in black satin, all long and unfashionable. That hadn't made them any cheaper, sadly. Cassandra signed cheque after cheque, appalled at the cost of hosting the event.

Only Jem and Katy refused payment for the cars. They were the one bright spot in the whole sorry affair, as far as Cassandra could see. That, and her little girls, both dressed in dove grey for the occasion, both polite and

206

quiet, subdued by the sheer number of people in their home, and Nanny Morgan's close supervision.

When they had waved off the last car from the Manor house steps, Cassandra turned inside and went back to the drawing room. The servants were clearing away the piles of dirty dishes.

"I think I'll go up to the nursery and see the girls," she said to no-one in particular.

Her feet ached and she longed to throw off her tight shoes, fling herself down on the comfy nursing chair and enjoy one of Nanny's cups of good strong Welsh tea.

"That's right, Cassandra, leave the rest of us to cope, now the real work must begin," Lady Amelia said.

"Real work? You have no idea what real work is, Mother! I haven't stopped working since I got off the boat from America. While you were lying upstairs in state, the rest of us were making today happen!" Cassandra was furious and surprised she had enough energy to feel this angry.

"Might I remind you, Cassandra, that I have just lost my husband?"

"Might I remind you, Mother, that I have just lost my father!" Cassandra quit the room before more home-truths slipped through her lips.

She was so tired she didn't linger in the nursery after all. She kissed the girls goodnight and retreated into her bedroom instead. Maisie relieved her of her black dress and jet jewellery.

"Could you bring me a cup of tea, please, Maisie?"

"Yes, Ma'am." Maisie put the dress in the wardrobe.

"And, then just leave me in peace, would you? I don't need any supper after all that food. Tell Mr Douglas I've gone to bed with a headache and don't let anyone else disturb me. We have the solicitor coming in the morning and I'll need my wits about me."

"Yes, Ma'am. It was a lovely service, Ma'am, if you don't mind me saying. Sir Robert would have been that proud of you."

It was the longest sentence Cassandra had ever heard Maisie utter and she was touched. "Maisie, that's so kind of you. I *was* feeling a little under appreciated. Thank you, my dear."

Maisie bobbed a curtsey and went to fetch her tea. Sometimes the little things that lifted your heart came from the most unexpected places.

Mr Leadbetter arrived promptly next morning at the arranged time of ten o'clock. Ever a punctilious man, it would have been out of character for him to arrive late for such an important meeting. Lady Amelia however, didn't usually finish breakfast until half past, and she evidently wasn't prepared to change her schedule, whoever was kept waiting.

"Ah, you're finally here, Mother." Cassandra knew her comment to be unwise and didn't care a jot.

It took Lady Amelia another good ten minutes to settle her folds of black satin into her favourite wing armchair, the one nearest the fire, with the best light behind it. Mr Leadbetter bore it all with great courtesy and patience, patting his papers and sorting them into neat piles. Cassandra sighed, that looked like a great deal of paperwork to plough through. Douglas squeezed her hand in sympathy, mind-reader that he was. What would she do without him? She gave him a quick smile, before Mr Leadbetter cleared his throat and began reading out her father's will.

The first few paragraphs contained instructions for predictable legacies to servants and other dependents on the estate. Bert Beagle, custodian of Sir Robert's beloved horses, got a special mention. Cassandra made a mental note to tell Katy how much Sir Robert had valued her father.

"Now we come to the main beneficiary of the bulk of the estate." Mr Leadbetter looked over his reading glasses with a piercing stare first at Lady Amelia, then her daughter. Cassandra had a moment of foreboding before the solicitor's neutral voice read out, "The bulk of the estate of Cheadle Manor will go directly to my daughter, Cassandra Victoria Smythe, in perpetuity, for her sole benefit and thence to any offspring she may have, now or in the future. "

Cassandra was confused. Surely the estate should go to her mother? Lady Amelia's gasp next to her confirmed that her mother was thinking exactly the same. They all remained silent while Mr Leadbetter intoned the rest of the will.

"For my wife, Lady Amelia Margaret Hepworth Smythe, I bequeath a yearly allowance to meet all her needs for clothes and subsistence, until her death, unless she predeceases me."

"Is that it?" Lady Amelia, not usually one to move swiftly, had jumped to her feet and crossed the room to an astonished Mr Leadbetter. She snatched the large piece of parchment from his hand and scanned the beautiful script, stabbing a plump finger at her name when she found it.

"This cannot be right! This isn't correct? How can this be true?" Lady Amelia said, after a moment of intense scrutiny.

Cassandra concurred with her mother, for once. "That's right, Mr Leadbetter, surely the estate should go directly to my mother?"

She looked at Douglas, who was struggling to keep a straight face, but this really was too serious for laughter. She turned back to Mr Leadbetter, whose own face was normally the same colour as the parchment documents he wrote all day, but the poor man had gone an unbecoming shade of dull purple, right down to his neck inside his old-fashioned upright collar.

"Won't you sit down again, everyone?" Mr Leadbetter spoke with surprising authority.

Stunned, Cassandra sat back down, next to Douglas and, after a minute's hesitation, her mother also returned to her seat. They all looked at their legal advisor.

"I can assure you that, unusual though this directive is, it was Sir Robert's firm and solemn intention. I queried it myself, when he drew up this final will but he insisted that the estate should be left in Mrs Flintock-Smythe's hands. Capable hands he called them; I recall his words distinctly. He said he couldn't wish for a better daughter or a more sensible one. He felt that you had proved yourself many times over, since your brother, Charles Smythe, died so tragically in the war, and that he had every confidence Cheadle Manor would be cared for by your goodself and remain in the family for generations to come. That was his dearest wish, you know. That the traditions he upheld would remain in perpetuity and continue to support all the many people who depend upon the estate for their wellbeing. 'Couldn't have wished for a better successor,' I believe were his exact words."

The rest of the will was read out, but Cassandra doubted any of them listened.

When Mr Leadbetter had finished, there was a profound silence for a few minutes. Then Lady Amelia broke it with a sob.

"I've never been so insulted in my life! How could Robert not think I would take care of the manor? I've been a faithful wife to him for all these years, despite his looking elsewhere for, for..." and she stumbled out of the room in great haste.

Cassandra got up to follow her, but Douglas restrained her.

"Leave her go, Cass. Let her cry it out of her system. You'll have to supply tea and sympathy in buckets soon enough."

"I think that would be best, Mrs Flintock-Smythe," Mr Leadbetter said, shaking his head. "It was bound to upset Lady Amelia but I think, for what my humble opinion is worth on this private family matter, that Sir Robert knew exactly what he was doing. You will make an able mistress of Cheadle Manor and you know you can rely on me for any legal advice you may need over the coming years. I shall always be honoured to be in your service, Mrs Flintock-Smythe, always."

"Goodness, thank you very much, Mr Leadbetter. I'm sure I shall need your support." Cassandra was surprised and flattered to have his respect, as well as her father's.

"You may well need it." Mr Leadbetter looked grave. "Your Estate Manager, Mr Hayes, will confirm this, I'm sure, but I understand that, as you have inherited the estate, not Sir Robert's spouse, Lady Amelia, as would be more normal, there will be substantive death duties to be paid."

"Death duties?" Cassandra said.

"Indeed. Mr Churchill, the Chancellor of the Exchequer, spoke about the change to inheritance tax last year, you may remember. I fear it will be a hefty sum that you must pay to the government. However, it is a variable percentage and we, as trustees, will have to have the entire estate valued, which will obviously take time. Please feel free to discuss it at a future meeting, perhaps with Mr Hayes, after you have had time to digest the outcome of your father's will."

Mr Leadbetter then took his leave.

Douglas turned to face her. "I think your father knew you very well, darling Cass. Whether he knew his wife as well, I'm not so sure. You can bet she won't take this lying down. There are bumpy times ahead, my love."

He shook his head and took her in his arms.

Cassandra leaned her head on her husband's shoulder. "At least I'll have you as my rock to lean on," she said, still absorbing the enormity of her father's trust in her.

A great weight settled on her shoulders and she was glad of her husband's support, or it might have flattened her.

CHAPTER TWENTY SEVEN
Winter 1926

"How's it going, then, Doug?" Jem asked, over the noise of the children's party. It had become a ritual that marked the beginning of the Christmas holidays for Isobel and Al to celebrate their joint birthday on Christmas eve up at the manor house. Little Isobel had turned three today and, unbelievably, it seemed to Jem, Al and Lottie had somehow already reached the age of six.

"Oh, you know, it's not easy with Lady Amelia."

"I can well imagine. I suppose Cassandra is very busy all the time?"

"You bet, and I've got involved too, overseeing the farms, travelling round to make sure all the tenants are happy and paying their dues. Sir Robert did that before he died. I've been surprised to discover just how *much* he did. We all thought he was only out riding for his own pleasure, but actually he was providing an excellent support service to everyone on his estate. It's no wonder his funeral was so well attended and he was held in such affection. I'm not sure they view my Buick turning up with quite the same fondness as Sir Robert's big bay hunter."

"I was wondering about the hunt. What's going to happen to all the horses?"

"That's one of the first things we've got to tackle in the new year, Jem." Douglas batted a balloon back to the children. "Cass says we can't afford to keep them on. Puts Katy's father into a different situation, you know. Keep that under your hat for now, pal."

"Of course. We'll be putting our plans into operation in January too. I've found a builder, Mr Wood, who's come up with some good quotes for building the factory shed. He wasn't the cheapest, or the dearest, come to that, but I could tell he knew what he was talking about."

"Good, that will be exciting. Nice to hear about something positive, for once."

"What do you mean?"

"Well, Jem, the death duties from Sir Robert's willing the estate to Cass, not his wife, are going to be horrendous, Mr Hayes fears. Could be between one, or up to ten percent, of the value of the whole estate. We're just waiting to get the place valued and hear the government's decision. Might have to make some harsh decisions of our own, if it doesn't go our way." Douglas took a cup of tea from Maisie.

"I'm sorry to hear that." Jem was very aware that, if it wasn't for Douglas's mother's generosity, he wouldn't be expanding his business at all.

"Well, let's hope they'll be kind to us." Douglas put his empty cup down so he could operate the radio for the children in a game of pass-the-parcel.

All went smoothly until the last unwrapping.

"The music didn't stop with you, Isobel!" Lottie said, looking hot and bothered. "That's cheating!"

Isobel gave Lottie the parcel. Lottie tore off the paper. It was the last layer. A new set of colouring pencils sat in her small, triumphant hands.

"Oh, pencils," Isobel said, in a small voice so only Al and Jem could hear. Al was, as usual, sitting next to her. "I really wanted some new ones."

"It was you who cheated, Lottie," Al said. "You snatched the parcel from Bella after the music stopped."

Jem watched as Nanny Morgan, her antennae bristling, despite being deep in conversation with Katy and Cassandra, turned around and broke up the imminent fight with as little fuss as anyone could hope for.

"Another round, I think," Nanny Morgan said. "Mr Douglas, if you would oblige with the radio?"

Douglas switched the music back on. Jem smiled as he watched Douglas skilfully let Lottie undo several layers before making sure the last layer was opened by her sister, to reveal an identical set of pencils.

Jem walked over to Douglas. "I take it you wrapped the parcels, then Doug?"

Douglas laughed his easy ready laugh. "Mum's the

213

word, pal!"

"Understood. By the way, if you want to work off your Christmas excesses, I'll be clearing the land on the other side of the car sales display over the holidays. Bert's coming with the heavy shire horses to fell the trees. We could use another full pair of biceps, if you've a mind."

"Sure thing, bud. It would do me good to slave over some hard labour and get out of the house."

"Who's getting out of the house?" Cassandra said.

Jem was sad to see her usual smile couldn't hide the worry in her eyes. He sympathised. He wouldn't like the weight of so many people's hopes on his shoulders. "You can come too, Cass. We're clearing the land ready for building the factory over the Christmas holidays. All hands on deck."

"I might just do that, Jem." Cassandra's tired face lifted a little. "Could be just the antidote to too much cake and sherry I'll need by then."

"Good. Merry Christmas, then," Jem said, as Katy had come up to say it was time to leave, before the short afternoon became really dark.

As it turned out, there was no shortage of willing hands to help with the land. Jem mightn't be able to wield an axe himself, but his brother-in-law, Jack, could. So could Douglas, who was less skilled but as, if not more, willing. Jem smiled as he watched young Jack show Douglas how to swing the heavy blade over his head and bring it down with a wallop on the felled tree trunks. Bert had chained up the shire horses who pulled the big trunks away from the woods and laid them in a long pile at the back of the Nissen huts.

"Plenty of firewood there, Jem," said his father-in-law.

"Yes, should last us years, that lot."

Billy had come to help too but spent most of the time following Daisy about as she picked up the smaller branches and laid them in a separate pile. Still, it all helped. Katy, unusually, had stayed indoors to help her

214

mother, and his, prepare food for the workers. It wasn't like her, she normally opted for outdoor work, given a choice, but it was a cold, grey sort of day. No snow this year, thank goodness. It wasn't even raining, which meant they could use every minute of the short winter's day. Mr Wood was due to start the foundations on the third of January, the first working day of 1927. Jem had a feeling it was going to be a good year.

By the end of February, the footings were down. He and Katy stood looking at them on one of those February days when a false spring steals in, pretending the winter's over.

"You can really imagine the walls going up now, can't you?" Jem said, counting his paces around the periphery.

"Hmm. We might have a little problem getting into production." Katy shuffled her shoe in the exposed soil from the diggings.

Jem looked up. "Oh, why's that?"

"Because I'm going into production myself - in the family way."

"Katy!" Jem came over to her and enfolded her in a hug.

"It's your own fault for making me miss you so much when you were in Boston. I threw caution to the winds that night you came home. The baby's due at the worst possible time - history repeating itself."

Jem laughed. He knew it was crazy and irrational but he couldn't have felt happier. "Katy, we'll manage. We always do, and I'm delighted, my love, my dearest, beautiful love." He kissed her lips, her full, luscious, wonderful lips and let his hand stroke her tummy, in the delicious knowledge that another child lay safe within it. Katy kissed him back, but once he'd let her go, she looked far less happy about her pregnancy than he felt.

Douglas came to see how the new project was getting on a few days later. Car sales had been slow during the winter, so Jem had hardly seen him, but knowing he had other duties to attend to, he'd let it go.

"My, you can really see the size the shed's going to be now, Jem!" Douglas said, as they stood together watching Mr Wood's men graft away.

"Looks quite big, doesn't it? Are we being too ambitious do you think?"

"Not at all, partner." Douglas slapped him on the back. "You gotta think big, to make it big. Say, why don't you and Kate come on a trip with us next week? You look like you could use a break."

"Where to? I can't leave the site for long."

"I fancy going to Pendine Sands. We could do it in a day, there and back, no problem. Have you heard of it?"

"That's in Wales, isn't it?"

"Sure, Parry Thomas is going for the land speed record. He and Malcolm Campbell have been trying to outdo each other since 1924 over that wet sand. Last month Campbell managed over 170 miles per hour and Parry is determined to beat that. Wouldn't it be something to see a car go that fast? I can't even imagine it. Thomas has a workshop at Brooklands and I chatted to him last season. Quiet, unassuming sort of guy, but very knowledgeable. I liked him enormously. I'm not sure which day he's going to attempt it but Tim Blunstone's gone up there and he said he'd call me on the telephone on the day. It all depends on the weather, you see. I've a mind to take a picnic and go watch. So, do you fancy coming?"

"Fancy coming where?" Katy had joined them, bringing a tray of tea for the workmen.

"Pendine Sands, in Wales," Douglas kissed her on the cheek. "Watch the land-speed record get broken again. I read about Malcolm Campbell's attempt last month and I'd love to see Parry try and beat it. We could take some flyers for the garage, do a little advertising. It all helps attract sponsors and Tim's going to tip me off for the right day."

"Douglas, I meant to talk to you about racing this year," Katy said. "Are you planning to do another season?"

"You try and stop me."

"It's just that..." Katy hesitated and looked at Jem.

"Katy's expecting again, Douglas," Jem said, unable to keep the pride out of his voice. "I've told her I don't want a repeat of her running risks like before. I'm in on the secret this time, and I've said she's not to race with you. I hope you understand, Douglas, and there's no hard feelings?"

Douglas's face, always an open book, was a comical mixture of emotions. "Congratulations, both of you. I must say I'm surprised at your timing, but sure, I understand about not wanting to race. Maybe I'll get Billy to ride alongside, or just go solo."

"I can still come and be your mechanic, Doug, at least for a while," Katy said.

"Why not give Billy a chance, Kate?" Jem didn't want her out of his sight until their baby was born in August.

"Listen," Douglas said, "we don't have to decide all this now. Let's have our day out to Wales first. Hell, we're all overdue for some fun, aren't we?"

CHAPTER TWENTY EIGHT
Spring 1927

As they drove away from Cheadle Manor, Cassandra let her tired brain switch off and slip into neutral. Firmly placing her many cares behind her, just for this one day, felt enormously good. Douglas was driving the Sunbeam, so they all had a proper seat to travel in to Wales. No-one wanted to go that far on the dickey seat in the back of the tourer.

Katy and Jem seemed to catch the carefree mood. Jem told them that Mr Wood had already begun building the walls of the factory shed and Katy chattered away about ordering up the parts they would need to build the brakes.

"So, it's all taking shape then." Cassandra turned round to see her friends in the back of the car.

"Yes, thankfully, though I still have sleepless nights about it," Jem laughed.

"And how are you feeling, Katy?" Cassandra said, half wishing she was pregnant too.

"Sick as a dog in the mornings. I always am, but it won't last and we're so busy I don't have time to think about it very much."

"Well, don't be sick in our car," Douglas said.

"Already got it over with before we left, Douglas." Katy grimaced. "I'm nibbling plain biscuits as we go along, so there should only be crumbs left behind and nothing worse."

Cassandra gave her a smile of sympathy.

"You know, Malcolm Campbell's car is a Sunbeam," Douglas said, negotiating a bend.

"What, 'Bluebird'?" Jem said.

"Yes, maybe I should put this old girl through her paces today?"

"Don't think you'll get over fifty in this old thing," Cassandra said.

"And you'd have the police after you if you did,"

Katy said.

"Why do they attempt the land speed record on a beach?" Cassandra asked.

"Well, as Katy just pointed out, you can only go at twenty miles per hour on the roads, so a beach is speed limit free, and quite frankly, flatter than any road I've ever driven on, except perhaps back home, in America," Douglas said.

"And there are strict rules, Cass," Katy said. "Now that record-breaking speeds are around 150 mph, and they have to reach that within the measured mile, they need enough safe braking distance afterwards, which means they need a smooth, flat, straight surface of at least five miles."

"I see, so not every beach is that long, either," Cassandra said.

"No, that's right," Jem said, "and they have to take account of the tide times as well."

Cassandra laughed, "Yes, just think if the tide came in and swallowed the car."

Cassandra enjoyed the drive to Wales with her friends. She had made her mind up not to think about the exorbitant tax demand she now knew she had to face, but this wasn't the day to dwell on it. They stopped at an old coaching inn for coffee on the way and arrived at the enormous beach in good time to catch the low tide.

"Goodness," Cassandra said. "Pendine beach is as big as the one in Étaples."

"That seems a lifetime ago." Katy took her arm as they walked towards where a group of men were watching the big car get ready for its sprint across the wet sand.

Jem and Douglas wandered off to chat to the other blokes. A keen wind whipped across the bay, making Katy shiver.

"Come on," Cassandra said, "let's go back and watch from our car. I've a thermos of hot chocolate in the hamper."

"Good idea, it's freezing. I've primed Jem to ask

219

about the mechanical bits so, just this once, I'm going to take it easy and let him investigate."

"Good for you." Cassandra was surprised that Katy wasn't more interested in the nuts and bolts of 'Babs', Parry Thomas's powerful racer.

"I'm always so tired at this stage of having a baby," Katy explained, once they'd reached the refuge of the Sunbeam. "It's the worst bit for me. Once I'm through these early weeks, I'm fine again, but right now I could sleep for England. It couldn't be worse timing, with all that's going on with building the factory shed. Sometimes, I wish I was a man."

Cassandra looked at Katy's weary face. "I'm very happy to stay here with you, in the warmth. Are you too tired to explain your invention for brakes, Kate? I'd love to know what you'll be making in that new shed."

"Alright, if you really are interested. The brakes on most cars are calipers at the moment and just mechanical - that is - directly applied from the brake pedal."

"How?"

"Well, they squeeze outwards from the action of the driver's foot on the brake pedal. That pressure applies friction which restricts movement of the wheel through the brake drum, but that's also why it's so damned exhausting to press the brake pedal. It's the action of your foot directly impacting on the drum."

"I think I follow you."

"Good." Katy was now in such full flow, Cassandra doubted she could stop her continuing. "Stockhead's idea is to use fluid - that's why they're called hydraulic."

"Sorry, you've lost me now. I have no idea what hydraulic means."

Katy's face looked brighter now, as she warmed to her theme. "It means it's liquid - a mixture of ethyl and water - passing through a pipe or channel. When the driver depresses the brake pedal in a hydraulic system, it displaces the brake fluid which increases the pressure to the brake drum via cylinders and pistons. This makes the braking both safer and more effective than calipers, which can wear out, and get very hot under friction. And, of course, you don't have to apply so much pressure with your foot. Should make it easier for women to drive."

"So, the fluid sort of expands?" Cassandra was still struggling with the concept.

"Sort of, more displaced towards the brake cylinders, which then press on the drum."

"I'm not sure I've quite grasped it still, Kate, but I am, as ever, very impressed with your knowledge. But how are you going to set up a factory and have a baby at the same time?"

"I wish I had the answer to that much more difficult question. But, as long as I can get the production line going, I don't have to make the components myself, only supervise. And Mum will help, she's already promised. She's past having more babies of her own, but she loves to look after them, luckily for me. I just hope all goes smoothly with the birth. I'm a lot older than when I had Al."

They sat in silence after that, with the odd bit of chat, as only old friends can. Cassandra found it very comforting not to talk. She tried to picture the mechanical process Katy had described but quickly gave up and idly gazed instead at the huddle of spectators around 'Babs's' gleaming white hulk and long, tapering tail. The car had such a modern silhouette, it looked like something from the future, which in a way, she supposed it was.

The preparations for the speed record seemed to be taking ages and Katy dropped off to sleep, snoring gently, with her head lolling to one side on a rolled up car rug. Cassandra relaxed and let her eyes rest on the beautiful scenery. Spears of acid yellow gorse flowers drifted around the marsh grass on the sandy edges of the beach, promising spring. Looking out on something other than accounts and ledgers was a welcome respite and the distant view across the sea gave her a sense of perspective. Lord knew she needed it, living under the black cloud of the tax bill.

At last, the big engine gunned into life. Cassandra nudged Katy awake and they both sat up to watch.

"She's a beautiful car, isn't she?" Katy looked transfixed as the white, streamlined 'Babs' lined up at one end of the seven mile beach, ready for its sprint. They could hear the roar of the engine reverberate across the wet sand. "See that high engine cover? That's because he's got drive chains to power the engine. I reckon he'll need them too, if he's going to get such a heavy car up to the speed he needs." Katy's words were drowned out by the roar of the engine.

"Goodness me!"

"Wow!"

'Babs' streaked across the beach at a terrific speed, blue smoke streaming out behind.

"I've never seen anything so fast. It must have broken the record." Katy's mouth gaped open in awe. The whole attempt passed in a flash before the big car drew to a halt and the crowd on the beach ran towards it. Then it slewed round and turned back towards them.

Jem went to join the other on-lookers, exchanged words with a few of them, then came over to their Sunbeam. "Didn't beat the 'Bluebird's' record of last month of 174.22 per hour. Or Segrove's 203 mph at Florida's Daytona Beach."

"Didn't that kill Segrove, I heard?" Cassandra had read about the crash in the newspaper with a sense of foreboding.

"Yes, it did, but Parry's much more sensible. He's going to refuel and have another go."

"How fast was he going, Jem?" Katy said.

"Over 160 mph, I think."

"That's incredible." Cassandra shivered at the risks these men were taking, grateful it wasn't Douglas at the wheel.

She watched the gaggle of men around the racing car preparing for another attempt. She didn't want to think about all the things that might go wrong, and instead leant back against the leather seat and dozed for a bit, like Katy, who was looking a little green. "Here, darling, have this, just in case," and Cassandra gave her friend a bowl from the picnic hamper.

Katy gave her a wonky smile, "Thanks, Cass, takes a woman to understand!"

They sat back in companionable silence.

Cassandra broke it, saying, " You know, it's only when you relax sometimes, that you realise how exhausted you actually are."

"I know, it's nice to stop, isn't it?"

Another roar from the beach signalled Parry's second attempt. Cassandra and Katy sat up to watch. Parry Thomas drove up to the same starting point and revved the engine.

"He's off again."

"Yes, even faster than before, I think, if that were possible."

Cassandra kept her eyes fixed on the white car blurring across her vision at rocket speed. It looked impossibly fast and she held her breath.

Suddenly, the car lurched violently and tipped up, dug into the sand, then whirled into a couple of complete somersaults.

"Oh, no! I can't bear to look." But neither could she stop looking, appalled at the car crash. "Oh, Katy. You shouldn't be witnessing this, in your condition."

She looked at her friend, who had covered her eyes, obviously finding the scene unbearable.

Cassandra looked over to where Douglas and Jem were standing a few yards away. Jem was running towards the broken car, shouting something but Douglas just stood, as still as a rock, staring and staring. Cassandra felt a frisson of fear ripple through her, looking at his rigid body. He was rooted to the spot instead of following Jem and the other men, as they ran to the crash site. He alone stood there, a pillar of immobility; if he had been lying down, you would think he was dead.

A chill hand squeezed Cassandra's heart, as the thought struck her. Douglas might not drive as fast as Parry Thomas at Brooklands, but neither did he go at a sedate pace. Without Katy's good sense next to him in the passenger seat, would he take more risks, like Thomas just had? There was no way the driver was getting out of that broken car alive.

Jem came running back and she and Katy got out of the car to meet him.

"Is Parry Thomas alright?" Katy asked, her hand on Jem's arm.

Jem's face was white; he shook his head;, "Killed outright. They think the right hand drive chain came loose, hit his head and decapitated him. Grim business."

Cassandra looked across to Douglas. Her husband turned around slowly and her eyes met his. Douglas's eyes were nearly always alight with fun and dancing with his ready humour. She had never seen that look before. His eyes had gone dark and hollow like two huge black holes. He still didn't move but neither did he look away. Cassandra went cold all over. She felt sick and giddy. What was happening to her?

Seeing her stumble, Douglas finally broke his petrified stance and came to her.

He folded her in his arms and held her tight. Cassandra heard his heart beating, too fast. She clung to him for dear life, afraid to say anything at all; afraid she could never let him go.

The mood was sombre as they drove home. Katy, Douglas and Jem went over and over the details of the crash, theorising about what might have happened, until Cassandra thought she would scream.

CHAPTER TWENTY NINE
Summer 1927

Maybe it was her pregnancy making her over-sensitive; maybe it was witnessing Thomas Parry's fatal, dreadful crash; or maybe it was Mr Wood himself, but Katy couldn't stand their builder. Mr Wood was forever making snide remarks about women taking over men's work and asking Jem what he was going to have for supper. When Jem didn't have an answer, Mr Wood would tell him, in elaborate detail, what his own long-suffering wife was cooking up for him when he got home.

"So, what's Mrs Wood got on the menu tonight then?" Katy asked Felix, the cat, one evening after work when she was too tired to think what to cook. Mr Bartlett had been in the garage again, wanting to see her new greasing bay and of course, snoop around the building works. The workshop had been busy too and she'd had a difficult time with a Bullnose Morris whose radiator had needed welding. She was no longer feeling sick, just bone weary. She'd be glad when her energy returned. Men didn't know they were born.

She stood staring at the larder, an improvised lean-to just outside the kitchen door of their hut. Jars of her mum's pickles stared back but she could barely look at them. The thought of sour vinegar could still make her stomach churn. She could make a cheese pie, she supposed, but oh, the effort of making pastry! Jacket potatoes would have to do. Her stand-by. They could grate cheese into them and have some of that lovely purple-sprouting broccoli standing ready for its first pick in the vegetable patch.

She picked up three big potatoes from the basket. They would be eating new ones soon and the mint was spearing up, green and tender, ready to go with them. Spring was early this year and the birds celebrated the good weather by trilling their songs with full throated gusto. Katy scrubbed the potatoes, pricked them with a fork and popped them in the range oven. She shoved some more logs into the little furnace and left them to it. Grabbing an apple from last year's store to keep the hunger pangs at bay, she went outside to the wooden bench Jem had made and listened to the blackbird wooing his love from the apple tree. The buds on the trees were fattening up nicely. Soon their garden would be garlanded with blossom, with all the promise of a new crop.

Katy eased her aching back against the bench and lifted her face to the lingering sun. She loved it when the days lengthened and stretched out to greet the coming summer. Traffic rumbled on the road behind her. She'd put the closed sign up on the forecourt, so, as far as she was concerned, it could rumble right on past. Distant hammering told her that Jem was still working on the factory shed, even though the dratted Mr Wood and his crew had gone home for the day. Presumably Al was with his Dad, he usually was. Al took a great interest in the building going up, little by little, and as soon as he got home from school, dashed off, a slab of bread and jam in his hand, to find his father and follow him like Peter Pan's shadow.

Katy gently rubbed her tummy, just to say hello to the baby. Not much outward sign yet, thank goodness. She closed her eyes and, behind them, saw rainbows of light from the sun's last rays, playing across her under-lids. Her cheeks were warm, sun-kissed. She knew a moment of rare peace in her busy day. How welcome that was.

And yet, there was much to be thankful for. Deep down, she was secretly as pleased as Jem about the child she carried. Here at the garage, on their own patch of land, they were building something that would outlive them; become a legacy. What would be the point, if they didn't have children? Some days it seemed as if nothing but more hard work lay ahead but at least she was doing a job she loved and was good at. How many people could say that? The general strike last year had shown how tough other people's lives were. The miners had protested when national rates of pay were removed and the mines were privatised. For eight days the entire general workforce withdrew their labour in support. London had almost ground to a halt, the newspaper said, but the army and some posh volunteers had rallied and kept essential services going. And it had all ended in defeat. Hunger drove the miners back underground seven months later, having gained nothing. Just like the war all over again. Sometimes she wondered what they had all fought for in that awful all-encompassing battle. How Albert would have loved Katherine Wheel Garage. She'd never accept the waste of her brother's life. He would have been the perfect recruit to manage the new factory.

Al and Jem broke her reverie, coming from the direction of the factory, chatting together. Al looked like a miniature version of his father, with his wavy chestnut hair and warm brown eyes. Katy's heart swelled with love for them both. Yes, she had much to be grateful for and a cowardly part of her wished they hadn't embarked on the expansion of the business, but settled for just being an ordinary family. Her mother was sure of it. And the image of Parry Thomas's crash was a constant reminder of how short life could be.

"What's for supper, love?" Jem asked.

"Been talking to Mr Wood have we?" She smiled to take the sting from her words.

"Just hungry, that's all."

"Me too, Mum," Al chirruped beside him.

"Jacket spuds and cheese. Just need to pick some of your new broccoli to go with it, Jem."

"I'll do it now, before I wash my hands."

"Lovely, I'll put the water on to boil and you can grate the cheese, Al." Katy prised herself from the bench.

Over supper, Jem said, "It's getting dark now, but you must take a look at the factory shed, Kate. One more day, and we'll be putting the roof on."

"Really? That's great news. I must start thinking about workbenches and the rest of the equipment and parts. How long do you think before it's ready for occupation, Jem?" Katy wiped the rest of the butter from her plate with her finger and licked it. So nice to have an appetite again.

"I think the roof will take the best part of two weeks."

"That long? It's only corrugated iron, isn't it?"

"Yes, but it all needs nailing down. I've told Mr Wood that I'll do it, if he leaves one of his lads behind to help me. Keeps the cost down, you see, and Mr Wood is itching to make headway with his plans to build a row of semi-detached houses on the other side of Woodbury. In the new Arts and Crafts style, he said, whatever that may be." Jem finished his last mouthful of broccoli. "This is tasty and promises a good crop. It'll keep us going till the other veg comes in."

"The factory roof is a big job to tackle, Jem. Surely we've enough left from Mrs Flintock's fund to pay for more labour?" Katy got up and started clearing the table.

"Is there any pudding, Mum?" Al butted in.

"Um, we've some tinned peaches and I could make up some Bird's Eye custard, if you like?"

"Can I mix up the custard?" Al loved watching it turn from white powder and milk into a deep yellow paste.

Katy laughed, "Of course you can, little chef."

Jem said, "It's surprising how much the building has cost, actually, Kate. We tried to keep to the least expensive materials but, as you say, we need to buy a lot of equipment to set up the production line and install water and electricity. That won't be cheap."

Katy knew a moment of sheer panic. What if her idea didn't take off? What if they couldn't sell the new brake seals? Everything was resting on it. And they'd have to employ staff, especially with the baby arriving at just the wrong moment. All her complacent contentment of half an hour ago swirled down the plughole, with the dirty water, as she washed up the dishes.

CHAPTER THIRTY
Summer 1927

Cassandra read the newspaper article again. That was the fifth time.

Lottie got down from the breakfast table and came to look over her shoulder at the fuzzy photograph, taken at Brooklands, the previous day. "Is that Daddy?"

"Yes, darling. Doesn't he look handsome?"

"Who's that man standing next to him? Why's he got goggles on as well as Daddy?"

"Oh, that's Tim Bluntstone, Lottie. He works for Speedwell, the oil company, Daddy's sponsors. Kate's too busy at the garage to go racing this year, so Tim's going to be your father's passenger in the Junior 500 race, next week." Cassandra peered at Tim's photograph. "I can't help thinking he weighs a lot more than Kate Phipps, though."

"Won't that slow them down, Mummy?"

"It could well do, yes." Cassandra never failed to be impressed with her daughter's intelligent, quick mind. "Now, run along and get ready for school or Nanny will be cross."

For once, Lottie obeyed without protest. Thank goodness for the dame school. She obviously loved her lessons there and Lottie had been much easier to handle since she'd started attending. Cassandra supposed a bright girl like Lottie needed more stimulation than could be found at the manor. In sharp contrast, Cassandra never ran out of things to occupy her on the estate. However busy she was, she always made time to chat to Lottie before and after school, and to enjoy some precious time with her other, more gentle daughter. Isobel reminded Cassandra of her sister-in-law, Rose Flintock. They both shared the same, sweet temperament and were equally undemanding of others. After Lottie's tempestuous babyhood, it made for a restful change and it was doing Isobel good to have some time with Nanny and herself, without Lottie's dominating personality to overshadow her.

Apart from these cherished moments with her girls, and even fewer private times with Douglas, when he was home, Cassandra's days were crammed full of estate duties. When she wasn't with Mr Hayes trying to balance the books and contrive ways of paying the death duties still outstanding from the unfinished probate business, she was out visiting tenants and farmers. There was no end to the problems she had to deal with. The wives worried about their family's ailments or the cost of feeding them, while their husbands needed advice over crops or house maintenance, to which she rarely had an answer. And then there was always the matter of extracting the rent.

Today, she had a difficult meeting with the hounds-man. Colonel Musgrove had found another Master of the Hunt, after Cassandra declined to take it on since her father's death. Tom Beamish had a cottage on the estate that came with the job, but he would have to lose both and he wouldn't like it. They simply couldn't afford to keep him on, or his dogs. Cassandra folded up the newspaper with a sigh.

After her visit to the nursery, she joined Mr Hayes in the Estate Manager's office above the stables.

"Well, Mr Hayes, we can put it off no longer."

"I suppose you mean old Tom?" Mr Hayes took his reading glasses off and laid them down on the pile of papers on his desk.

"I do. Colonel Musgrove has found another Master of the Hunt. Lord Pendlebury's estate is a good fifty miles on the other side of Woodbury and I've agreed to sell the hounds to him."

"Poor old Tom." Mr Hayes sucked on his empty pipe.

"Can't be helped, Mr Hayes." Cassandra itched for a cigarette herself. Maybe afterwards.

"Then, let's get on with it, Miss Cassandra." Mr Hayes had never adopted her married name. Cassandra quite liked still being called Miss; it made her feel younger. Didn't make her responsibilities weigh any less heavily today, sadly.

"Has Tom got any other family who could provide a home for him, do you know, Mr Hayes?"

"Aye, as it happens. He's a daughter in Lower Cheadle. Married to the farrier, Mr Radcock."

"Would they have room for him at the blacksmith's?"

"Reckon they'll have to find room. Tom's too old to look for work elsewhere. Between you and me, Miss Cassandra, he's getting too old for the job anyway."

Cassandra nodded. Tom used to take the hunt in his stride but he got quite fretful these days at the beginning of the season and looked worn out by the end.

They could hardly hear themselves talk above the baying hounds, once they reached the kennels on the north side of the stables. Tom's cottage, a meagre one-up, one-down thatched affair, stood within sound and fury of the dogs.

Cassandra would have preferred to talk softly to the old man, explain gently to him why he had to go, but instead she had to shout his dismissal above the racket.

Old Tom slumped in the one greasy armchair next to the open fire. Cassandra scuffed her foot in the earth floor. The cottage smelt of damp and a black, ancient fungus decorated the walls, rising upwards to meet the low ceiling in streaks of mould. This was no place for anyone to live. She felt ashamed her father hadn't improved it. It couldn't be healthy. No wonder Tom's wife had died straight after giving birth to his only daughter.

Mr Hayes was asking about her now, at the top of his voice. "So, do you think your Margaret will give you a home, Tom?"

Tom was staring at them, his mouth open, in a perfect 'o' of surprise.

"Mrs Radcock, the blacksmith's wife, your daughter? Can you live with them, Tom?"

"But what about me dogs? They can't live down in Lower Cheadle village. T'wouldn't suit at all."

"No, Tom," Cassandra butted in. "The dogs are going to the new Master. Lord Pendlebury's taking them on. They're going to join his dogs and he's already got a hounds-man."

"But is he sound, Miss Cassandra? Do he know what he's doing, like? Dogs need proper care." Tom's voice caught. "What will I do without 'em?"

"There, there, Tom. They'll have a good home, and I'll go over and check they're alright. You could come with me, and make quite sure of it, once they're settled in." Cassandra could see that sorting the dogs' new home was far more important to Tom than his own.

"Could I? I've looked after those dogs all my life and my father before me, and his before that. To have them sold, as if they was a sack of potatoes. 'Tis a sad day." Tom shook his head.

Mr Hayes drew them back to more practical matters. "Miss Cassandra will take you to see the dogs, Tom, but I'll take you to see your daughter, Margaret, and we'll ask her if she can find room for you at the smithy. Come on, we'll go now, shall we? We'll walk down and talk on the way. Get your coat, there's a good fellow."

Mr Hayes turned to Cassandra. "Leave him with me, now, Miss Cassandra. I'll come and let you know the outcome with Mrs Radcock. They've a spacious house down in the valley. I can't see it being a problem."

Cassandra, knowing how difficult it was living with an ageing, bereaved parent, couldn't share his faith but she gladly left him to it.

There was a letter on the hall table, when she returned to the house. It was addressed to Douglas. That left her in a quandary. Should she open it and read it, or forward it on? Douglas was staying at the London house for a week or two, while he was racing at Brooklands, and trying to garner more money from sponsors. With the factory now completed, Katy and Jem were busy recruiting staff and equipping it with all the paraphernalia for making these new brake seals Katy had designed. Money was tight and Douglas had offered to drive in more races at Brooklands on the basis that Speedwell upped their sponsorship money and he might attract others to do the same.

Cassandra loved Katy dearly, and Jem barely less so, but there was no escaping the fact that this new enterprise was putting them all under pressure and there was no guarantee that they or Douglas would recoup their investments. She wished she could offer to help but it was taking all her brainpower to come up with ways to keep Cheadle Manor afloat. She just hoped Douglas would be sensible and not take any silly risks for the sake of winning. A fleeting image of Parry Thomas's huge white car, 'Babs' somersaulting on Pendine Sands, over and over with that sickening crunching sound, flashed across her mind. She shut her eyes but couldn't erase it.

The letter, postmarked Boston and written in Rose's round, flowing hand, couldn't be that important. Best not to worry Douglas and distract him from his racing. She'd give it to him when he got back, next week.

CHAPTER THIRTY ONE
Summer 1927

Jem decided to hold the interviews in the new factory shed. Why not? They might as well see what their working conditions would be like. Spartan, he'd call it, but not as bad as being down the mines or labouring in the fields.

Mustn't be soft-hearted.

Twenty people had applied in writing. He and Katy had whittled it down to six interviewees before the Easter weekend. They held the interviews on the first Tuesday afterwards, as Jem was eager to crack on and get production started. The sooner the better. He wore his suit for the occasion. Noting this and approving of it, Katy had decided to wear a dress but had what she called a 'clothing crisis'. None of her dresses fitted anymore.

"Jem, I'm huge," had been the wail from the bedroom that morning. Jem was so used to her spending every day in her boiler suit, he'd not noticed how much her girth had increased and it had come as a shock. In the end she had found a baggy tunic top, that she used to wear with a belt that nipped her waist in, and wore it over a skirt whose buttons she could leave undone without it falling around her ankles. Seeing her juggling garments made getting the right employees more urgent than ever.

By half past nine, the first applicant arrived. He'd cycled from Woodbury, and, being rather plump, was red in the face with the effort. It didn't take Jem long to decide his brain was as little used to exercise as his body, and he crossed his name off the list. The second one promised far more than he could deliver. Under close questioning, they discovered that his experience of cars extended to travelling on the omnibus from time to time and his written claims had been pure fantasy.

"Oh, Jem, will we ever find anyone?" Katy shifted in her seat. She looked very uncomfortable in her tight skirt. He wished those shadows under her eyes would lift.

When the third and the fourth job seekers also fell short of what they were looking for, Jem knew a moment of sheer panic. Katy couldn't carry on working for much longer, three months at the most, though knowing her, she'd resist giving up until the labour pains started.

The penultimate interview was with a man, older than the rest at nearly forty years old, but Jem had been prepared to ignore this in view of his history in the Royal Engineers during the war. Len Bradbury had a family to support and a lined face to prove it. What Jem hadn't reckoned on was that Len only had one foot.

The fact that Len had walked from a neighbouring village to arrive exactly on time was testament to his determination. He had a limp and a stick.

Jem reminded himself he'd sworn not to be soft-hearted over this business. "How far have you walked to get here, Mr Bradbury?"

"Barely two miles, sir. I live in Bassettbourne."

"And you didn't find your bad foot a problem?" Katy asked, her voice gentle.

"No, ma'am. I like to walk. Does me good."

"I see," Jem was unconvinced. "How about your stamina? We were hoping for someone younger but your engineering experience looks relevant. Can you tell us a little more about what you did in the war?"

"Certainly, sir. I can assure you that I'm in good health. As for my experience, I was in charge of the guns. Maintaining them, making sure they were greased up and ready to go. Sorting out any mechanical issues."

"And your leg?"

"Potato masher caught my ankle, sir."

"Grenade, eh?"

"Yes, sir. Begging your pardon, but looks like you didn't come out unscathed yourself."

"No, lost my lower left arm. I've got an artificial one now, a new one as it happens, got it in America recently. Forgive me asking, but we need to know. Have you an artificial foot? How far down was your wound?"

Len Bradbury clenched his teeth visibly. He had a kind face, but right now it was strained. He was very thin.

"I've lost my right foot, Mr Phipps. I have a prosthetic with a hinge to enable me to walk. It's made of an aluminium and copper alloy, so it's very lightweight and I find it completely satisfactory," Len Bradbury's answers were refreshingly succinct and to the point. The last interviewee had waffled on without conveying anything relevant.

Katy asked the next question. "How many children do you have, Mr Bradbury, if that's not a personal question?"

"Three living, Mrs Phipps."

Jem saw the effect of that answer on his wife's face and the way she stroked her round belly.

Mustn't be soft-hearted. This was a business, not a charity.

"What was your previous employment, I mean, since the end of the war?"

"This and that. Mostly self-employed, doing odd jobs. Whatever I could find. Len Bradbury shuffled on his seat. Jem could picture his post-war years only too well. He had seen enough discarded ex-servicemen begging on the streets in Woodbury to demonstrate the situation.

Business, not charity.

Len Bradbury spoke out of turn then. "Can I say something?"

"Of course," Jem and Katy said in unison.

"I need this job. I'm a good mechanic, I've got references from the army to prove it. I've a family to feed and, quite frankly, we're desperate. No-one seems to want a one-footed engineer, however experienced he might be. If I get this job, Mr and Mrs Phipps, I'll work as hard as three men. I'll work all the hours you want and more. I won't look for work elsewhere. I'll be loyal, trustworthy and do everything I can to make your business successful. There's not much I don't know about engines and how to keep them sweet. I promise you that my lack of a foot won't stop me doing a full day, every day." Len Bradbury had become breathless through his long speech. Jem could almost see his heart pounding through his threadbare shirt. He looked at the man's hands, gripped together with white knuckles. There was no doubting his sincerity.

Jem looked at Katy and she spoke for them both. "Thank you, Mr Bradbury. We've one more person to see this morning and we'll write to everyone who has attended with our decision. Will you be alright walking all that way back?"

"Aye, ma'am. I'm strong enough and it doesn't bother me. I take it I've not got the job then?"

Jem hastened to reassure him. "That's not what my wife said, but we need to discuss all the applications and then decide. We'll be in touch as soon as possible, be assured of that. If you have a telephone number, we could ring you?"

"No sir, no telephone, but I could ring you, if that's easier?"

Katy shook her head. "No, we'll write to everyone - tomorrow - you won't have to wait long for the verdict."

"Very well, good day to you," and Mr Bradbury stood up like the soldier he'd been. Jem was sure he would have saluted them, if requested.

The door shut behind him.

"What did you think, then, Jem?" Katy asked, her head cocked to one side, as she always did when she was thinking hard.

"I liked him enormously."

"So did I."

Their verdict was truncated by the sixth applicant scraping open the corrugated tin door and entering their empty factory.

"Gordon Bartlett! What on earth are you doing here? I haven't got your name on the list. It says here, John Waterman." Jem was astonished to see someone from Whitefriars Garage.

Gordon's pockmarked face cracked open with a

sheepish grin. "No, sir, but that's because I gave a false name on the letter, like. Made it up out of me head, I did. Knew you wouldn't want to see a Bartlett but truth to tell, my Dad's a stick in the mud and I'm frustrated back at ours. This new factory of yours, well, it's the future, I reckon. I'd like to be a part of that."

"We're not here for your benefit, Gordon. And how are we to know you won't go running straight home to your father and tell him everything you've learned?" Jem felt a slow burn of anger ignite in his stomach. He'd bet ten bob old man Bartlett had put his son up to this.

"And giving a false name is not the way to make us want to employ you, Gordon," Katy said, quite justifiably in Jem's opinion. "We have an honest business here and we pride ourselves on being open and trustworthy. How can we trust you as an employee, if you start by deceiving us?"

Gordon had taken off his flat cap and now twisted it round and round in his spatulate hands. Maybe he was more nervous than he looked. Maybe he was being sincere?

Business not charity.

"I'm sorry about that, Mrs Phipps. I can see it was the wrong thing to do now, but I thought it was the only way I could get to see you both about the job. Everyone who comes into Whitefriars is talking about what you and Mr Phipps is doing. My old Dad just wants to run a repair shop and sell petrol. He's quite happy with things as they are. He might be working with cars, but sometimes I think he'd rather it were horses, as if nothing had ever changed. Everything I suggest he says a flat 'no' to."

"Look, Gordon, what goes on between you and your father is none of our concern. You'll have to sort it out between you. If you want to expand your garage that's up to you, but I don't think we can employ our nearest competitor." Jem felt certain Katy would agree with his decision and looked over at her. Her face was wearing that customary frown he'd grown too familiar with.

"But Mr Phipps, sir, I know how to service an engine, all sorts of makes. I can change a tyre, tune up the carburettor, change the oil - everything. I'll work hard, I promise I will. Give us this chance, please?"

"Gordon, does your father know you are here?" Katy said.

Round went the cap in his hands. Gordon mumbled something into them.

"Speak up, boy!" Jem was getting impatient.

Gordon couldn't quite meet his eyes. "No, sir."

"I've heard enough." Katy struggled up from her hard seat, and stood, leaning on the back of it. "Your Dad put you up to this, didn't he?"

Gordon Bartlett had suffered terribly with acne in his youth. Now the old scars flushed a deeper red than the rest of his wide face. It made him look as if he had the measles. And, as far as Jem was concerned, his mottled complexion gave the game away.

"I'm sorry, Gordon, I don't think it would be right for you to work here. Come on, time you went back up the road to your own place." Jem got up to escort the young man out of the shed. The corrugated iron door had been left slightly ajar. Jem had moved so quickly that the person standing on the other side of it didn't get out of the way soon enough to avoid it bashing into him when Jem opened it wider.

"Mr Bartlett! Why am I not surprised to see you here? Gordon hasn't got the job and we're not impressed by your deception. Take him home. If you want to know what we're doing, just ask, instead of this ridiculous farce of pretending to look for work. Of course, that doesn't mean I'll give you an answer."

Mr Bartlett put one hob-nailed boot and an elbow inside the factory and leaned forward into Jem's face with his chin. Jem gave the bulky older man a shove.

"Oi, lay off me, you!"

"No, you lay off my premises, Bartlett, and shove off. And don't bother coming back! Sort your own business out, instead of wasting my time!"

Jem felt the warmth of Katy's body standing behind him. He put his arm out to protect her, as Bartlett shoved his face closer. So close, Jem could smell his putrid breath.

"Gordon has every right to apply for the job in your factory, same as anyone else. And what are you going to make here, anyway?" Mr Bartlett's eyes were darting looks in every corner.

Jem's temper rose, as it had when he beat up Fred. Aware of Katy's vulnerable state, acutely aware of their child inside her, but forgetting how far his anger had driven him before, he said, "Go inside, Katy. It's time this was settled, once and for all."

"But Jem..."

"I said, go! Now. I mean it." Jem turned around and gently pushed her back into the furthest reaches of the shed.

Mr Bartlett and his son were now fully inside the building, and Jem prodded them both in their portly stomachs. "I've had enough of this. You're forever snooping around seeing what we're up to. Well, let me tell you this, Katherine Wheel Garage already knocks spots off Whitefriars and it always will. Yes, we're expanding and going into production of a new component. You'll have to find out for yourselves what that is. The whole world will know soon enough, but we don't need you lot hanging by our coat-tails. So bugger off and see to your own affairs."

"Now don't you take that tone with me, young man, and you can take your hands off," Mr Bartlett began.

But Jem pushed them again until they were fully outside the factory shed, and ignored their shouts of protest. He could see their Model T Ford, parked out in front of the petrol pumps, blocking any customers who might want fuel.

"And you can take that heap of junk with you and park it elsewhere. And know this, Bartlett, you are never welcome here again. Do you hear me? Never again! Now piss off!"

CHAPTER THIRTY TWO
Summer 1927

Katy had looked forward to Saturday lunch at her parent's west lodge all week and the savoury smell on entering her mother's kitchen didn't disappoint. Now she had her appetite back, she could never satisfy it, and her mum's cooking couldn't be beaten. Not that she had time to try. Katy tucked in to her meal like a woman starved, after liberally pouring hot onion gravy over her pile of greens.

"Oi, don't nick all the gravy," Jack said, snatching the jug away.

Katy ignored her brother and concentrated on plunging her fork into the pile of buttery mashed potato, paying scant attention to Jem's tale of the interviews.

"Well, I never," Agnes said. "The cheek of it. Them Bartletts never was no good. His old father was a coal merchant in Woodbury and his sacks was always lightweight, Aunt Maggie said. 'Course no-one could lift the sacks to weigh 'em theirselves so he got away with it, the old swindler. His son, and sounds like his grandson too, takes after him.

"It won't help them in the end," Jem said. "If you want a good business, you got to be straight with people."

"That's right, Jem," Bert said. "I'm that proud of the way you and our Katy have built up Katherine Wheel."

"Hmm," Agnes said. "It's all very well, but if all you've got is a one legged middle-aged ex-soldier to help you in this new enterprise you're so determined on, how's Katy going to have time to have this babe? You'll have to put a cork in and cross your legs, my girl."

Katy was startled out of her gluttony. "Mum!" She had never known her mother say anything so crude before.

Her brother Jack spluttered out his mashed potato. "That's funny, that is, Mum."

"Be quiet, Jack and eat your sausages," Agnes said, looking embarrassed.

"You're right, though, Agnes," Jem said. "We still

need at least one more member of staff."

"I've a mind to apply," Jack said.

Katy looked at her brother, then at her father, whose jaw had dropped. Jack worked with Bert up at the stables. Her father wasn't getting any younger and everyone expected Jack to succeed him as head coachman.

Bert couldn't hide the hurt in his voice. "You ain't leaving the horses, lad?"

Jack swallowed a big bite of sausage. "Thing is, Dad, I've heard that they're all going to be sold off, like the hounds was. Rumours is flying about amongst the other staff in the house."

"First I've heard about it and I'm in charge of the bloody stables!" Bert laid down his fork.

"Language, Bert," Agnes said.

"You mind your own, woman, with your corks," said her husband. "What have you heard, lad, and from whom?"

"Seeing as Tom Beamish has gone down to Lower Cheadle to live now his hounds is sold off, and Sir Robert is gone, everyone is saying as how there's no need for the estate to keep the hunters on. Miss Cassandra only ever rides Blackie and never hunts no more, and Lady Amelia barely goes anywhere these days. The carriage horses haven't been out since the funeral."

"Yes, Jack, but that's just speculation." Katy joined in, having taken the edge off her appetite.

"Ay." Her father picked up his fork again but didn't really eat. "I asked you who said it?"

Jack looked serious for once. He said, in a sober voice, "I overheard Mr Hayes, Dad. He was talking to Miss Cassandra, when I was cleaning the tack. I don't think they realised I was there and I made sure to keep quiet when I heard what they was saying."

"Which was?"

"Miss Cassandra was saying that she still hadn't paid all the death duties after Sir Robert's passed away and, although she couldn't bear to part with Blackie, most of the others could go. She asked if Mr Hayes knew of anyone who'd want them."

"Why's she bloody asking him? *I'm* the head coachman!"

"Don't take it out on Jack," said his mother.

"I'm sorry, Dad," Jack said.

Katy had finished her delicious meal and was thinking. If this was true, it put her father's job in jeopardy. Cassandra must be more hard up than she realised. She knew that Douglas was doing extra races this year, but she thought that was for the garage. Maybe he needed to raise funds for the estate, too.

Bert threw his cutlery across his half empty plate. "I'm going over to Hayes's cottage right now. This calls for some straight talking, this does."

The lodge back door slammed behind him.

Into the silence, Agnes said, "It's his favourite pudding too, steamed jam roly-poly."

Al piped up. "With custard, Gran? Say it's with custard?"

"Ay, with custard, young Albert. And I suppose you wants to make it?"

Al got down and went to help his grandmother at the range cooker. Daisy was out having supper at the Threadwell's house above the Post Office in Lower Cheadle. Emily, always a slow eater, was still preoccupied with her sausages.

Jack looked from Jem to Katy and back again. "I mean it, you know. Horses is over. There ain't going to be another coachman after Dad. Them days is gone. I love the horses, of course, but not as much as Dad does. If I go, maybe they'll keep him on for the few that's left, but I'd rather go before I'm pushed. I'm a quick learner, you know that. Kate, Jem - will you have me at the factory?"

Katy and Jem exchanged glances. They'd argued all week over the appointment of Len Bradbury. Katy didn't think the man was physically strong enough but Jem asserted his expertise and experience cancelled it out. He'd won in the end but they still needed another pair of hands and they had agreed that none of the other applicants had been good enough.

Katy nodded her assent.

Jem turned to her brother. "Better the devil you know, I suppose, but don't think you'll be let off the hook, just because you're Kate's brother, or anything."

"Does that mean you'll take me on then?" Jack's face was a perfect picture of astonishment.

"Yes, brother mine, it does, but Jem's right - no privileges for family members, mind," Katy smiled at Jack.

"Thanks, Jem, thanks Kate! I won't let you down! Oh, wait till I tell the other lads at the manor. They'll be green with envy and, oh please, can I learn to drive?"

"You might have to, Jack," Jem said. "We going to need a van driver. Len won't be able to do it with his gammy leg."

"Quite," Katy said.

"I'll give my notice in tomorrow. I only has to give a week, because I'm paid weekly. I'll see Mr Hayes first thing. Can I start the following week?"

Agnes returned to the table with the custard jug. "Don't you think you owe something to your father, Jack? If the horses is to be sold, that'll take a mite of sorting out and he'll need all hands on deck. Don't desert him now, lad."

"Mum's right, Jack," Katy said. "See what Dad thinks first. This will come as a blow to him."

***

A fortnight later, Jem opened up the big doors of the factory shed. Katy, already bulky, was slower in the mornings these days and he'd left her in the home-hut to have a lie-in before getting Al off to school.

It was very early in the morning, just after dawn. White mist rose up in gauzy streams from the river valley, far below their garden. Drops of dew spangled on the cobwebs between the trees. Jem was sorry they'd had to cut so many down to make way for the big building. A robin sang out his good morning, blithely unaware of the importance of the occasion.

Jem felt nervous. Douglas had brought worrying news from America that his mother had been taken ill. Jem supposed that shouldn't have come as a surprise, she'd looked so pale and fragile last November. He hardly knew the woman but he'd taken a liking to her, and not just because she was his sole investor. They'd only received half of the promised sum from her. He couldn't pay Mr Wood until he received the rest. It made it imperative that they made a go of things, and soon. He would like to give her some return on her investment; prove she was right to believe in his ideas. He hoped she'd recover soon and even come and visit again. He'd like to show her what her money had bought.

He brewed a mug of tea in the workshop and took it, steaming like the river mist in the fresh morning air, into the factory. Inside, the huge shed looked unready for its big day. Crates of rubber stood in piles in one corner, the workbenches, as yet unmarked by cuts and spills, appeared both expectant and too pristine. Jem looked forward to the day, he hoped not too far away, when Jack and Len had perfected the system they had yet to develop and the only piles of boxes were ones marked for despatch.

Len turned up first, well before his appointed time. "Morning, Mr Phipps," Len Bradbury said, limping only slightly as he knocked and entered the cavernous space.

"Morning, you're nice and early. How about we drop the formalities and you call me Jem and I'll call you Len?"

"Be glad to, Jem." Len gave a shy grin. "Point me in the right direction, and I'll get stuck in right away."

As they began to sort the bales of rubber into graded piles, Jem encouraged Len to talk. It took a bit of prising out of him but eventually Len told him about his three daughters and his wife, Edith, who was often poorly with asthma. Jem gathered from the things Len left out, that they were desperate for some steady money and the war had brought them nothing but misery. Despite the flecks of grey at his temples, and his artificial foot, Len worked like a man possessed.

"It's alright you know, Len, you've got the job. It's not the interview now. Relax and pace yourself," Jem said, when he saw beads of perspiration on Len's brow.

"It's alright, Jem, I'm enjoying it, to be honest," Len wiped his forehead with a spotless but threadbare handkerchief and carried on at the same relentless pace.

They'd nearly finished stacking the bundles when Jack turned up on his bicycle. "Started without me? It's not even half past eight!"

"Morning, Jack. This is Len Bradbury, your new colleague." Jem introduced Jack and they shook hands.

"Jack here is Kate's brother but he'll get no special treatment. Now, as you're the eldest with the most experience, Len, I'm putting you in charge of the production line. Jack, you'll be in charge of deliveries. I'm going to look at a van later and you can come with me. It's the old bread van from Carruther's Bakery, an old Tin Lizzie. Bartletts have been servicing it, so it's probably a bit run down, if I know them, but we'll have your sister give it the once over and see if it's worth what they're asking for it. Then we'll have to teach you to drive. I'll get Douglas on to that."

Jack shook Len's hand; his eyes shone with excitement. Jem wondered if he'd been rash saying Jack should drive the van, before he'd even learned how, but someone would have to take it on. Had he done right in employing a disabled man and an untried youth? He was glad to see Katy waddle in with a tray of mugs of tea.

"Hello, Kate," Jack said.

"Tea's up! but don't go thinking that's how it's going to be all the time. This is a special occasion. We'll take turns from now on. I'll be working alongside you, showing you how to make the seals. As you can see from the state of me, time is pressing!" Katy laughed, but Jem could see the anxiety in her eyes. She turned to Jack. "How's Dad?"

"He's down in the dumps, Kate. The hunting horses got sold so quick they was all gone by last Friday. The stables echo without them. We've still got the shires for the plough and that, and old Chestnut and Larkspur for trips in the gig. Miss Cassandra's got Blackie and Lady Amelia has her carriage bays but that's the lot. It's odd without the constant racket from the kennels. Think we'd all got used to them dogs barking their heads off all the time. It's downright eerie up there now."

"Things are bound to be different, with Sir Robert gone." Katy eased the hollow of her back with the flat of her hand. Jem wished she'd sit down more often and upturned a crate for her. She sat down with a grateful smile.

"Yes, and I'm that glad to have this job, Kate. Reckon I'd have been out on my ear anyway, like old Tom Beamish, and down the Labour Exchange today, if it weren't for you."

"Right then, Jack, we'd better get started on making a few seals, seeing as how we're all banking on it," Katy said.

Jem silently acknowledged at the truth of this. God help them if they couldn't make this enterprise pay. It wasn't just him and Katy depending on it now, there was Len and his sickly wife, and young Jack with no other job to go to. Douglas was the only one making a profit from his racing, as they had to plough any money made at the garage straight back into the factory. If something happened to him or his mother, they would be done for, unless they could start turning a profit too - and the sooner the better.

CHAPTER THIRTY THREE
Summer 1927

"Do you think I should go over to Boston, Cass?" Douglas stroked her arm as they lay under the covers of their big double bed. Her refuge.

"What did Rose say again?"

Douglas picked up the second letter he'd received from his youngest sister in a fortnight from the bedside table. "She says, *'Mother's in hospital. They think an operation will remove the tumour and she'll be well again, once she's got over it. Father's going to take a vacation and they're going to Falmouth, to the summerhouse, for a few weeks while she convalesces. Cheryl said not to worry; that these operations were quite routine these days and that she knew the surgeon personally, and says he's very good.'* I suppose Cheryl knows what she's on about but so often, she's a bag of hot air. Rose is so uncritical of everyone, she believes everything my dear elder sister says but, as we know to our cost, Cheryl doesn't always tell the truth."

"But not about something like this, something so important and so, well, so medical?"

"Hmm, I'm tempted to go and find out for myself, but I can't really give up the racing so early in the season. Speedwell have already shelled out a fair bit on the sports Austin and I've spent most of my allowance from Mother this month putting the word around about these new seals of Kate's." Douglas twirled her long hair around his finger.

She loved him doing that. It made her feel like a princess from a fairy tale. Sleeping Beauty perhaps; not that she ever had enough sleep or felt particularly beautiful these days.

"Then leave it a while. Selina has to undergo this operation anyway and there would be nothing you could do in that situation. You'd be a spare part in Boston, you know you would. No, darling, carry on racing for now. See if you can beat that rat, Denis Finch for me. How's it going with Tim as passenger?"

"If I could beat Finch, no-one would be happier than I, honey, but Tim, well, he's not got the same feel for the car as Kate, but I guess he weighs about the same as she does now she's eight months pregnant, probably a lot more. It doesn't help my speed."

Cassandra giggled. "I know what you mean, if Tim were a woman, you might think he was in the same condition."

"I've got to get some wins up at Brooklands and demonstrate that Kate's brake seals work. It would be the best advertisement. Word would soon spread amongst the drivers and mechanics and, from them, to the big guys like Austin and Morris."

"But, Doug, hasn't Jem written to them and asked them if they want the seals? Surely it doesn't all depend on you?"

"No, honey, not yet. We've all agreed that it would be best to announce the invention after successfully testing it in public. If I can demonstrate the effectiveness of the brakes on the track, and win a few races, I'll get some press coverage. Then I can say it was all down to the brake seals, and people, particularly Stockhead who make the hydraulic brakes, will come flocking. That's the plan anyway, and it will take Kate and Jem most of this season to perfect the production line. That way, if I can generate the interest, they'll be ready to supply in quantity at the perfect time." Douglas kissed the top of her head.

His kiss was as light as a butterfly's wing but still had the power to send a shiver through her body.

Cassandra snuggled closer to her husband. "But, Douglas, darling, that puts you under so much pressure! I don't like to think of you feeling you absolutely have to win every race you enter."

"Sweetheart, these new brakes work like a charm. Kate really has come up with something special, you know. If anything, they make racing safer."

"I'm glad, Doug, because I'm fairly sure you're to

become a father again and I'll soon be stouter than Tim."

"What? Really? That's marvellous, Cass darling, it really is. And are you well? Do you feel alright?"

"Never better, and do you know, I fancy it'll be a boy this time. You'd like a son, wouldn't you, Doug?"

"As long as I have you, my love, everything else is a bonus. So you'd better look after yourself. No riding, for a start!"

"And what if I was to forbid you to go racing again? It works both ways you know. This child needs a father just as much as a mother."

Douglas brought his face down to lie facing hers on the same pillow and, this time, he kissed her mouth, drowning out her worry with his warm, urgent desire. Cassandra let her mind relax into oblivion while her body took over.

She loved the weight of Douglas's tall frame when it lay on top of hers; loved the familiarity of his touch, his skin, and their deep intimacy. She succumbed to his insistent caresses with delicious abandon, marvelling that even after two children and with another on the way, every time they made love was different; still exciting, still fresh.

This time they were slow and took their leisure in building up to a climax. Their room was in a separate wing at Cheadle Manor, on the west corner, gilded each night by the evening sun. With a dressing room flanking each side, no-one could hear them and Cassandra gave voice to her ecstasy. Douglas groaned with pleasure too, before they collapsed into a tousled heap of bed covers.

He quickly fell asleep but slumber eluded Cassandra. She lay amongst the twisted sheets, listening to his steady breathing, smiling as he twitched in his dreams. How relaxed she felt, lying next to her husband. All the doubts about his fidelity and his home-sickness for America had been laid to rest. She now knew, deep in her heart, that she could trust him absolutely and that he loved her in the same all-encompassing way. There had never been anyone else for her, not really, despite what Lord

Finch claimed, and there never would be. Douglas completed her; he had become her other half, just like all the old jokes said. She hadn't even known she'd been missing this portion of wholeness before her marriage. Life without him would be soulless.

Was this how her Mother was feeling without Sir Robert? No, they had never been close. She couldn't remember them even touching each other in public, though they must have done in private in order to produce her and her brother. She shut her eyes against the images of how she had been made in this old manor house. If only her mother would relent in her constant criticism, she could love her as she wanted to, but, if she was honest, she didn't, not really. She had loved her father and missed him more than she had expected to, but Lady Amelia only showed affection to her grand-daughters. Even then, her mother divided the girls by preferring Lottie to little Isobel, who felt the distinction keenly, even though she was still so young.

And Lottie was so strong. However often Cassandra told herself not to compare her eldest child to her mother, there was no denying it. Lottie and Lady Amelia both had sturdy frames, lusty appetites and fierce tempers but to Lottie's credit, the little girl was much more serious, studious even, than her grandmother and intensely loyal to those she loved. She defended Al Phipps against any disapproval Lady Amelia threw at him about his roots but she also protected her little sister against their grandmother's favouritism. Cassandra couldn't help but be proud of her eldest daughter and, secretly, a little in awe of her.

Isobel, by contrast, was a restful little person, promising artistic rather than academic potential, and she enjoyed spending time with her. Isobel was taller and slimmer than Lottie had been at that age; Cassandra suspected she might grow into a beautiful woman. For all Lottie's qualities, even her own mother couldn't expect that from her.

What would this new child look like, she wondered? Having children was a fascinating business, never knowing how the combination of genes would develop into a unique individual. She hoped it would be a boy, just to balance things up, but then, Lottie would be displaced as heiress. That wouldn't go down too well.

A fox barked in the grounds outside. He or she must be revelling in their freedom from persecution. No doubt they would breed in numbers now, with no hounds to chase them from their lairs. Tom Beacham had looked miserable when she'd visited him in Lower Cheadle last week. Oh, the Radcocks looked after him well enough and his daughter, Margaret, despite her sharp tongue, had him looking sprucer than he'd ever done when living alone amongst his hounds. It had been a shock to see him clean and dressed decently. So much so, Cassandra hadn't recognised him at first. Margaret had allowed him one dog, who followed old Tom around like a mournful shadow, as if it too, missed being with the pack.

The night was totally still, without a single rustle of leaves outside the window. So still, Cassandra could hear the faint rumble of a car on the main road, in the far distance. Peace was hard to find these days. Oh, they were all at peace of course. No war threatened, thank God, but the old quiet had gone with her father. Cassandra knew that the one constant in life was change but she couldn't remember a time when it had been so rapid. The war had catapulted them into a mechanical world and Cassandra was none too sure she liked it.

At all events, here, in the bedroom she had slept in all her life, she had sanctuary, and not least because of the man who slept beside her. Her eyelids drooped. It must be long after midnight and tomorrow would bring just as many demands as today. She rolled on to her side, facing Douglas, and with one last peep at his beloved profile, closed her weary eyes and yielded to the velvet night.

CHAPTER THIRTY FOUR
Summer 1927

Katy ignored the dull ache in her back and told Jack to restart the motor. He must have stalled it a dozen times over the last couple of hours. Jack's mood was as bleak as the drizzly day.

"I thought learning to drive would be fun," he complained.

"Driving will be fun, Jack, but you must learn to do it properly. It'll be no good if you crash the van and lose our deliveries. Come on, try again. It's not the engine because I've got her running sweet as a nut now. You've got to get that clutch control right. Feel for the bite as the engine engages." She rubbed her back.

Thank goodness this van had a push starter or Jack would have spent most of the morning outside cranking it with a starting handle. Katy peered through the rain at the deserted road. She'd driven the van up to the downs, where she could be confident there would be little, if any traffic. Jem had offered to give Jack his first lesson but was fully occupied in the factory shed, installing the stove and its chimney. He'd said it was vital they got the big second-hand range to draw properly or they wouldn't be able to control the heat. Katy would far rather be there, helping him to work it out than having her patience tried by her brother, but Jem had insisted she did a sitting down job.

She'd had to concede because she could never resist getting stuck into an engineering project like the installation of the vital stove and would have wanted to heave it about with the men, despite her huge belly. She and Jem were just rubbing each other up the wrong way these days. She wanted to be in charge and he wanted her to rest. All it caused was friction.

"Right, concentrate, Jack. Put her into first gear, now, handbrake off, ease up the clutch, check your mirror, and off we go!"

"There's so many things to do all at once!"

"I know, but soon it'll be second nature and you won't even have to think about it. That's it! Good, now you're getting it. Well done, Jack. Into second gear now, down with the clutch first, that's it, good. Keep checking your mirror. Good, ouch!"

Jack took his eyes off the road and looked at his sister.

"Jack! Eyes front!"

Jack yanked the wheel back and the van brushed the grassy verge before straightening up.

"What's the matter, sis?"

"Your driving! *I'm* fine," Katy lied. The ache in her back had spread around her entire abdomen.

Jack managed to get up to fourth gear and was cruising along at twenty miles per hour. A wide grin stretched across his face and he let out a whoop. "Hey, I'm doing it! I'm really driving!"

"Well done, Jack." Katy tried not to let her breathlessness show. Then, the next contraction kicked in and she groaned.

"Kate?"

"It's the baby, Jack. You'll have to drive down the hill and get me home. Can you do it?"

"I'll have to!"

"Take it slow," Katy said, gasping with the pain. "I'll talk you through it, oh, God!"

Jack, as if by instinct, changed down into third gear and braked gently as they went downhill, back towards the busy London Road.

Katy gripped the dashboard as another wave of pain swept over her swollen body. Sweat broke out on her forehead. She couldn't think about Jack's driving. She couldn't think about anything at all.

The engine screamed in second gear but words failed her. She could hear it and yet felt she wasn't there at all. She was in another place entirely, in a world where all she could do was endure the overwhelming sensation of pressure enveloping her in rapid cascades. This baby was coming so fast, much faster than either of the others. They'd never make it. The van lurched violently to one side as Jack swerved to the wrong side of the road.

"Bloody hell, that was close! Are you alright Kate?"

"Baby...coming... quick," she gasped.

"Hell! Look we're coming to the London Road junction. What do I do?"

Katy could only groan as another contraction consumed her. There were hardly any gaps between them now. A gush of water poured out of her, pooling on the leather seat. She could feel the baby's head pressing. She opened her legs, not caring if Jack was watching, unaware he was even there, unaware of anything but the pressure bearing down inside her.

"Oh God, Oh God, I don't know what I'm doing!" Jack wailed as they bumped along for another quarter of an hour.

Then the van lurched awkwardly to the right and lumped down a slope. Katy didn't look up, didn't care where she was. The van came to a juddering halt and Jack heaved up the handbrake and turned to her.

"We're home, Kate, we're back at the garage, I've got you safe!" Jack pressed the palm of his hand on the horn and kept it there.

Kate was aware of hands holding her, pulling her about. She heard Jem's voice, felt him lift her legs on to the bench seat of the van. She had to push, she just had to. Someone stuffed a cushion behind her back. She gave one more push and opened her eyes. Jem's face, white and tearstained smiled at her. He was holding a baby, their baby. The child was bloodied and slippery but he lifted her onto her lap, on to her empty, deflated belly. Katy held out her arms.

"It's a girl, Katy. You've done it, my love! We've got a daughter!" Jem climbed into the cab and kissed her.

Katy started to shake uncontrollably. Jem put his arm around her.

"It was so quick," Katy managed to say.

"We must get the doctor, at once." Jem wriggled away and got out of the driver's door, shouting to Jack who was standing, his mouth open, watching from the garage forecourt.

"Get on the telephone, Jack, ring the doctor, then the midwife, then your mother. Tell them all to come and see to Katy urgently. I don't know what the hell happens next!"

Within the hour, Katy found herself in her own bed, clean and washed and sipping sweet tea. Everyone had turned up at once and she had quite an audience.

"Shock, you see," Dr Benson was saying to her mother, Agnes. "When a child comes that quickly the mother often goes into shock. Good job your son got her back safely in that van." The doctor laughed. "Delivery van - it certainly was that today!"

"It's nothing short of a miracle, Doctor." Her mother shook her head and smiled at the same time.

Mrs Armstrong, the midwife, whose tiny frame disguised her toughness, scooped up the baby and replaced the cup of tea with her warm bundle.

"She needs some colostrum, dearie," Mrs Armstrong said. "Can you manage that?"

"I think I can remember what to do." Katy laughed and took her daughter in her arms.

The doctor nodded his approval. "I'll leave you capable ladies to it. Well done, Katy. You've a fine daughter there." And he left, looking very pleased with himself. Not that he'd had anything to do with it.

The baby's rosebud mouth puckered up over Katy's nipple and latched on, as if it wasn't the first time, as if she knew exactly what to do. Katy hadn't yet got used to the baby being on the outside of her body, instead of tucked up safely inside her, and could only gaze at her in wonder and study her new little face. She looked like a determined little character, busily sucking away.

"What will you call her, Katy?" Agnes, said watching her new granddaughter greedily drinking.

"Little Piglet seems appropriate," Katy said, chuckling.

Jem popped his head around the door. "Can I come in?"

"Aye, lad, come and see the little one. I'll get Katy another cup of tea. She still looks a bit shaken up." Agnes patted him on the shoulder.

Jem sat down on the bed. Katy reluctantly drew her eyes away from her daughter's fascinating features and looked at him.

"Another little girl, Jem. That makes me fear for her."

"There's no reason why history should repeat itself, Kate. Look at Al, he's as strong as an ox. I'm glad it's a girl. I've got a name for her too."

"Have you?"

"Yes, I've been thinking about it. I want to call her Lily, after the plant, the Peace Lily. And that's what I want for us all, Kate, my love. Peace. It's the most important thing; more important than the garage or the factory. Do you agree?"

Katy looked at Jem's solemn face. "Lily it is." Katy leaned across their new child to kiss him.

CHAPTER THIRTY FIVE
Summer 1927

Jem hadn't realised quite how worried he'd been about Katy until Lily was safely in her mother's arms and it was a huge relief to know they'd both come through it.

But that meant it was now up to him to make sure that the demonstration of the brake seals was a complete success. They would only have one stab at proving it to the reps from Austin, Morris and Stockhead at the next race. The first available date had been cancelled due to bad weather, unusual for an August Bank holiday, so it all rested on the JCC Four-Hour Sporting car race on the thirteenth of August, later than he'd hoped.

And time was pressing. They had to create a market for the seals and start turning a profit very soon, or he would be forced to borrow more from Mrs Flintock, in order to keep Len and Jack on. He still hadn't paid Mr Wood's final invoice for the building work because the last instalment of the money she'd promised had not come through. He didn't understand it. It had been due to arrive two weeks ago, and Mr Wood had reminded him of the overdue payment in very forthright terms only yesterday.

Lashing out on a buffet at Brooklands clubhouse was another extravagance he could do without, especially when Len looked as gaunt as ever and Jack's different hunger for work nagged him night and day. They had a steady trickle from his market garden produce but the garage work wouldn't bring in as much with Katy out of action. Billy, reliable as the seasons, worked steadily but oh, so slowly. There was already a backlog of cars to be serviced and customers wouldn't wait forever. He'd have to get Len working on them too and Jack would have to learn the mechanics as well as Billy. He at least was a good student, as swift as his sister to pick up the details of how to make an engine run smoothly and Len was a good teacher. While he was away at the race, he'd get Jack to man the petrol pumps. The factory could lie idle until the orders came in, if they ever did. He shuddered inwardly at the prospect that all their plans could backfire. He had to make it work!

Everything rested on the race and therefore on Douglas. Jem grabbed his jacket and told the others he was going up to the manor. He drove carefully, as he always did, having no choice with his wooden makeshift fingers, and arrived to find Douglas getting in his tourer to come and find him.

"Hey, Jem, congratulations on the baby, pal! Bert Beagle gave me the news. I was just coming to see you with these flowers. Cassandra's not feeling too well, but she said she'd come down later. We, um, we're having another kid ourselves. She only told me last night. Baby's due next spring. We're building quite a dynasty between us, aren't we?"

Jem laughed, glad to see Douglas was relaxed and not fretting about the race. "Thanks, Doug. The baby came so quickly, she was born in the new delivery van while poor young Jack was having his first driving lesson. The lad did well to get them safely back to the garage but he didn't make it in time to get her into the house, so Katy had her on the front seat!"

"Guess you've got a new mechanic in the making there, if she was born in a truck." Douglas clapped him on the back.

Jem laughed back. "You could be right, Douglas, but it means that Katy's not available for the race next week. I came to tell you that all the reps from Stockhead, Austin and Morris have confirmed they are coming to watch your demonstration of the brake seals. I hope you don't mind?"

"Hell, no. That's what we planned, isn't it? The more the merrier. That sports Austin flies around the track now and I can let her go as fast as she can, because I know I can rely on the brakes. Makes a big difference, means I can push it as hard as I like and show them I can stop any time I want to, whatever the speed."

"That's great, Doug, it really is. And you're going to have Tim as your passenger?"

"Yeah, I think so. He's on the heavy side but he's used to it now and I'm used to compensating for his weight. Hey, what's this? I thought Cass was having a lie-in."

Cassandra came running down the drive, looking distressed. "Douglas! Thank goodness I've found you before you left. Cheryl's on the telephone, from Boston. Your dear sister is insisting that she speaks with you and only you and she won't wait. You'd better come. Sorry, Jem, didn't mean to be rude. Congrats on the birth of your little girl. Is Katy well?"

"Yes, thanks, and lovely to hear your news too," Jem said, but Cassandra was already dragging Douglas away, tugging at his sleeve.

Jem watched them jog back to the house. Strange. He decided to follow, on the pretext of seeing his father. George Phipps had just come around the corner of Cheadle Manor, wheeling a barrow. Jem strode up to meet him. They hadn't had a chat in ages and he wanted to tell him all about the baby.

"I like the name Lily, Jem. Your mother would approve but I think she'd appreciate it if the middle name could be Mary, the same as hers," George said.

"Oh, I'll have to ask Kate about that." Jem was confident that Katy would reject the idea outright.

"Yes, of course. We'll have to come over and see them. How's Al taken to having a baby sister?"

"Yes, come whenever you like but make it after work, so I'm there too. As for Al, he seems to have taken it in his stride. Feeling very important, he is, fetching and carrying for his mother when he's home from school. It's a big help, as I'm so busy with the garage and this big race coming up next week." And Jem told his father how much rested on the reaction of the guests they'd invited to Brooklands.

Just then, Douglas appeared on the terrace, smoking

one of his American cigarettes and looking quite distracted. Cassandra hovered in the big doorway, watching her husband and biting her nails. A chill crept into Jem's bones at their white faces and he called out to his friend.

"Douglas?"

But Douglas walked away from him with a negating wave of his hand and disappeared into the orchard on the west side of the house. Cassandra went to follow but seemed to change her mind and instead came to join Jem and his father at the bottom of the terrace steps, where they stood on the immaculate lawn.

George doffed his cap. "Good-day to you, Miss Cassandra."

"Hello, George. Do you mind if I have a quiet word with your Jem, in private?"

George immediately nodded to them both, picked up his wheelbarrow and walked smartly away out of earshot.

Jem turned to Cassandra, who still looked very pale. "Are you alright, Cassandra? Can I get you anything?"

"I, I'd like to sit down, Jem, if you don't mind. We've had a bit of a shock and it affects you, too. Let's sit on the terrace steps, shall we?"

"Of course." Jem took the liberty of taking her arm. She looked like she needed some support and Cassandra didn't refuse it.

They sat down together. Jem looked up at the sky and hoped it wouldn't rain. They'd rarely had a dry day all summer long.

Cassandra cleared her throat and turned to look at him. Her hazel eyes were red from crying. What had happened? It must be that bloody Cheryl telephoning from America. Jem never heard of that awful woman without it being connected to trouble somehow. His stomach contracted into painful knots.

"Jem, we've just heard that Selina Flintock has died."

The knots in his stomach tightened into a solid ball,

261

as Cassandra spilled out the tragedy and the implications sunk in.

"We knew she was ill, well, you saw her yourself in Boston before Christmas, and no-one could fail to notice how thin she was. We thought she was drinking - she used to - but apparently she was taking morphine tincture - it's a painkiller preserved in alcohol - that's what I could smell on her breath. That's why, I suppose, she was so dreamy but then, she was always like that. Oh, dear, I'm sorry Jem, I'm not telling this very well. The thing is, dear Jem, that it was cancer, of the breast. Two days ago, she had an operation to remove the tumour but she died on the operating table. That blasted Cheryl said the surgeon was so good too. Oh, why did we believe anything she said? I suppose it meant she didn't suffer, if she was under the anaesthetic and I'm glad about that." Cassandra's jagged speech finally tapered off.

Jem could hardly take it in. Selina had looked peaky back in November, in frozen Boston, but he'd been so preoccupied with the business proposition and his revenge on Fred Stavely, he'd not dwelt on the state of his sponsor's health too much. And if he had, he was honest enough to admit he would have ignored it, because the fate of the factory had hung on her generosity.

Jem studied the flagstone path in front of them. A red spider - a money spider - scuttled across in front of his booted toe. Ironic. His mind grappled with the full ramifications of Selina's death. Not only was she too nice a person to die at her age, but they were all relying on her to see them through the birth of the factory. No wonder the money hadn't come through for Mr Wood. What would he tell *him* now?

Jem became aware of Cassandra sitting so still beside him. He wrenched his mind away from his business worries and slid his arm around her shoulders.

Cassandra leaned into him and sighed. "She was such a beautiful woman - in lots of ways."

Jem nodded. He couldn't quite trust himself to speak

262

yet. His mind darted about thinking through all the disastrous consequences of this news. Would Douglas have to go to America for the funeral? Would he have to miss the race? Would he want to drive at all, and if not Douglas - who? Should he attempt the driving himself, despite his arm? Would he be disqualified on grounds of his disability? Who would host the reps then? Katy couldn't leave Lily yet, surely?

Cassandra patted his leg and drew away. She cleared her throat. "I realise this will have an impact on everything."

"How's Douglas taken it?" Jem ventured.

"He's completely distraught. He adored his mother."

"I think I'd better leave you to it, Cass. Douglas needs you right now."

Cassandra nodded; didn't attempt to make him stay.

Jem stood up and pulled her upright before kissing her on both cheeks. He held on to her ice-cold hand and squeezed it. "We're here if you need us, Cass. Anytime. You know I mean that, don't you?"

She nodded again and treated him to an uncertain smile. "I do know, and thanks, but you've the new baby to think about. A girl this time, isn't it?"

Jem's stomach, already so busy that morning, flipped over, but he managed a nod of assent. So many people depending on him, including his brand new child. "Yes, we're calling her Lily. Give my love to Doug, won't you? If he needs to chat, just ring the garage and I'll come straight up, day or night."

"I will, Jem. Thanks again. That means a lot."

Jem walked down the drive, so deep in thought, he almost forgot he used to trim it when a lad. His brain teemed with questions he couldn't answer until he spoke to Douglas. Everything depended on that race, even more now their sponsor had gone. And how would he pay the wages this week, or Mr Wood? Or the clubhouse buffet for those reps? Or demonstrate the brakes at all, if Douglas had to go away? And how could he burden Katy with all this when she had so recently given birth? She still didn't look right. He hadn't a clue about women's stuff but had a hunch that the speed of Lily's birth had traumatised Katy somehow. He knew she was worried about losing her but the baby looked healthy enough to him and not a bit like Florence. Lily resembled her brother, Al, if anything; more like Jem himself. Their father. The man they all depended upon to protect them.

He got in the car and drove home. Shadows chased him all the way.

CHAPTER THIRTY SIX
Summer 1927

"You see, I didn't know how much I loved her until she'd gone." Douglas was chain-smoking again.

Cassandra was sitting next to her husband in the orchard a few days later, to the same spot he'd gone when he first heard the news about his mother's death. It was one of Cassandra's favourite places. The love seat under the Bramley apple tree was small and they had to sit tight up against each other.

"I'm surprised the girls aren't more upset," Douglas was saying, for the hundredth time. "Didn't they love her?"

And for the hundredth time Cassandra replied. "They hardly knew her, darling. They only met her a few times, last year. Just remember she wasn't in pain. She would have known nothing about it."

"She'd been in plenty of pain before. Why didn't we realise she was taking morphine, instead of assuming she was drinking again? Why didn't I take more time, more trouble, to talk to her, instead of manipulating her for money? Why didn't she tell me she was ill?"

Cassandra schooled her voice to be calm. She wanted to scream. "She did drop hints, when she was here that summer, do you remember? Saying about your allowance drying up if anything happened to her? I think she knew then, looking back. Hindsight is ever a marvellous thing."

"Yes, and another thing is that allowance. How are we going to manage if it's discontinued?"

"We'll manage, Doug. As long as we have each other. That's all that matters."

"It's not though, is it? There's Katy and Jem depending on me driving this race next week. And I've borrowed a bit from the bank against my projected winnings. I'll have to telephone Father, find out when the funeral is. I doubt he'll bother to ring me. It's been five days now and I've not heard a word from him." Douglas lit another cigarette from the butt of the last one.

Cassandra coughed as the smoke blew across her. She always hated the smell of cigarettes when she was pregnant. Strange when she could never break the habit any other time. She looked away, towards the downs, trying not to breathe in the smoke, or retch.

It was a relief when the bulky form of Andrews, the butler, blocked out the sun, so little seen during this damp summer. He was holding out a silver tray on which lay a thick envelope, bordered in black ink.

It bore an American stamp and was addressed to Douglas in a fierce, bold script, entirely in capital letters, making it look more like a telegram.

"Letter for you Mr Douglas, sir," Andrews intoned. How did he always keep such a neutral voice, whatever the circumstances?

"Thank you, Andrews. I'll let you know if I need to send a reply when I've read it."

"Very good, sir." Andrews melted away towards the house. His feet might be big, but they were uncannily silent on the terrace steps.

Cassandra shivered, even though the fitful sun still shone. "Shall we go inside to read it, Doug, darling?"

"No, this is written in Father's hand. I'd rather be outside. Excuse me a moment?"

Cassandra gladly withdrew and went inside for a cardigan. When she returned, she found Douglas had stopped smoking; had stopped breathing almost, by the looks of him. He sat, still as a stone statue, staring out at the English countryside, his letter scrunched into an awkward mess. The stiff paper crackled under his fist.

Cassandra stood at the foot of the terrace steps, uncertain whether to approach. She'd never seen Douglas like this, he was always so quick to make light of any situation. Now his profile reminded her of the writer of the letter he clutched in his hand. Douglas looked older, sterner, utterly miserable and thoroughly unreachable. While she hesitated, Douglas jolted up on to his feet and threw the letter away from him, with a shout of rage. Paper flew in all directions, and landed on the grass, still wet from a recent shower.

Instinctively, she ran to him and gripped his arms, searching his eyes for an explanation. As he met hers, all the rigidity left him and he sank back on to the little bench.

"What is it? What on earth did your Father say in that letter?" Cassandra kept hold of his hands, still bunched in fists.

"Read it yourself," Douglas said, dashing his hand across his eyes, then leaving it there so she couldn't read his expression. He turned his face away, brought up both hands to cover it and hung his head, the picture of despair.

Cassandra's heart fluttered in panic. She picked up the scattered scraps of paper. Some of the ink had run at the edges, making it hard to place it into the correct order, until she realised Mr Flintock had methodically numbered each one, in tiny figures at the right hand top corner of each page. A lawyer's touch and, in truth, it read like a lawyer's letter - dry as dust - at least, to start with.

"*Dear Douglas,*" she read. "*It is with deep regret that I write to confirm the death of your mother, Selina, on the 2nd of August 1927, as Cheryl informed you via the telephone the following day, the 3rd of August. Your mother was suffering from breast cancer and was undergoing an operation to remove the tumour but unfortunately died during the procedure. The funeral will be on the 26th of August 1927 in the Methodist Church and Rose's husband, Cedric Shaw, will conduct the ceremony.*

You are welcome to attend, if you must, but do not feel it to be imperative. It will be a small, private ceremony with as little fuss as we can manage. Your mother left no instructions to the contrary and I do not wish to invite the world to witness our grief."

Then the letter changed tone entirely. Up to this

point, Cassandra had been fuming at the formality, the coldness, the business-like nature of Theodore Flintock's legal style on such a matter to his only son. As she read on, her relatively mild anger was overtaken by a burning rage against the injustice of Douglas's father's intransigent attitude and her hand shook as she tried to hold the crumpled paper steady enough to read through eyes blurring with tears.

"Now we come to the matter of how your Mother's death affects you personally. I was aware, though you appeared not to be, that your Mother was unwell at the time of your last visit to us in Boston, just before Christmas. In view of that fact, and in deference to her delicate state of health, I forbore to comment at the time at the callous audacity of you, and your so-called business partner, Mr Phipps, in manipulating your Mother into lending you what I now discover is a considerable sum of money.

Had I been party to this transaction, I would have utterly forbidden it. It was a cowardly and deceitful act on your behalf to conduct this business behind my back in this unforgiveable manner. You knew I had no control over your Mother's fortune and could do nothing about how she spent it, but I still deserved to be informed of your proposals and yet I was completely excluded from every meeting. It was only uncovered by Cheryl accidently meeting Mr Phipps at the hospital and telling us about his visit, or we'd have known nothing of it. I was deeply shocked at your mother's announcement about her financial involvement but could say nothing after the event, for fear of upsetting her in her worrying state of health.

Now your dear mother has departed this earth, the truth can be said, plain and simple. You are, and always were, an ungrateful son who has exploited a sick and fragile woman, who loved you, who would have given you anything - and apparently did so, with no advice, no input

268

*from **me**, her loving husband and your **father**.*

*How could you do this, and in **my** house? How could you invite the spouse of that sluttish servant girl, Katherine Phipps, who ruined every chance of Cheryl's happiness? For I have told Cheryl all about this dirty trade and she condemns you as soundly as do I.*

As for your racing cars - how can you be so reckless? You have two young children to think of and Cassandra has numerous dependents on her estate in England. Since her father died, she is responsible for the lives of many people and yet, you play around on race-tracks like an irresponsible child with a toy, without a care for your family or your reputation.

Indeed the only thing you seem to care about are these wretched Phipps and their pathetic little business! Well, I have discussed it with Cheryl, and we are both agreed that the allowance from your Mother should cease, as of her date of death. Furthermore, no capital monies, with effect from the same date, the 2nd of August 1927, should be paid to you or your business partner, Jeremy Phipps, even if it was previously owing.

From this day forward, I do not call you my son. As previously stated, you may attend your mother's funeral if you so wish, but you will have to find accommodation elsewhere than our family home. Perhaps Rose and Cedric will offer you a roof over your head, but I shall not.

Let this be a termination to our correspondence. I do not expect, or desire, a reply.

I do send kind regards to your wife, Cassandra, and your daughters and wish them good health.

Sincerely,
Theodore Flintock"

An entirely irrelevant thought struck Cassandra as she finished reading the excoriating letter. They say hell has no fury as a woman scorned. Neither has it for a man who's ego has been ignored. His arrogance knew no bounds. The man was an imbecile. She looked across at

Douglas, who sat on the bench in a heap, his head low, his face obscured by his nicotine-stained fingers.

She squeezed into the tiny space left on the little love-seat and reached out to touch his hands. He slapped hers away. He wouldn't look at her. That vile family of his. They had destroyed him.

"Look at me, Doug, look at me," she said.

Douglas turned further away. She grabbed his hands and prised them from his face, using all her strength.

"Look at me!"

Douglas opened his eyes, and shut them again.

"Douglas, I love you. This is nonsense. This is your Father's grief for Selina coming out all wrong. I've seen it often enough in my own mother. It's just bitter anger, directed at the wrong person. You are doing a good thing for us and the girls and Kate and Jem. You are a good man, a wonderful man, a loving father and the best husband in the world. This is rubbish. You *must not* believe it. Even though this stupid man is your father, you must not believe a word he has written. None of it is true.

"Look at me. None of it is *true*, Douglas!"

Katy was still in bed when Jem got home. She looked flushed, but not with a healthy glow. Her cheeks were hectic, with a high colour alien to her. He didn't like it. Lily slept peacefully in the cot beside the bed. He took a peek inside. The baby, *his* baby, looked quite normal and her breathing was regular.

He kissed Katy. Her face was hot on his lips. "Hello, my love," she said.

Her beautiful eyes were dark, their pupils dilated, and glittery.

"Where have you been?" Katy's restless fingers fidgeted on the covers.

In that instant, Jem decided he could not tell her the news about Selina. Katy needed Doctor Benson, not a shock.

"Just popped out for some supplies. Len needed more screws and cement for the factory stove," he lied. "How are you feeling, Katy? It's not like you to stay in bed this long?"

"I should get up, you're quite right, but I can't seem to get the strength somehow and Lily is so peaceful, I didn't like to disturb her, so I thought I'd just lay here awhile longer. You don't mind, do you?"

"No, not a bit, but you seem a bit hot to me. I'm going to get Dr Benson to have a look at you."

"Oh, no, Jem. There's no need for that. Mum said she'd pop in this afternoon and I'll get up then."

Jem had never forgotten, never would forget, the pneumonia Katy had suffered from before the war, during that black time of grief for Florence. He wasn't taking any chances now.

"No, Katy, I insist. You don't look well and I'm going to ring him right now. I'll come straight back and make you a cup of tea after I've made the call."

Jem got up from the bed and knew a moment of real

271

concern when Katy didn't dispute his decision. She must be ill.

She gave him a wan smile of consent and closed her eyes. Not a good sign. He strode straight over to the garage office and picked up the telephone earpiece. Martha Threadwell's unlovely voice answered and put him straight through to Dr Benson, who was, for once, at home.

"I'll come right away, Jem. Now, you mustn't worry, it's only a few days after the birth. My son is doing my usual rounds these days and I'm more at leisure, but I've a soft spot for your Katy and I'd like to see her myself. Now you're on the London Road, it only takes me quarter of an hour to get there."

Jem found the doctor's sensible old voice hugely reassuring. True to his word, he drew up in his old Model T Ford within fifteen minutes. Jem showed him into their bedroom in the Nissen hut. Lily was still sleeping. Jem couldn't remember Al's infancy. Was it normal for a child to sleep so long? He'd get the good doctor to check his daughter over while he was at it.

Jem lingered in the kitchen next door, fiddling about with things that didn't really need doing, while he waited for Dr Benson's verdict. The doctor appeared after an interminable wait. His face, framed by its shock of white hair, wore a frown. Jem had learned to dread that expression over the years.

"Katy has a puerperal fever, Jem."

"What on earth is that?"

"It can happen after childbirth from an infection in the womb. She needs bedrest, lots of fluids and no anxiety. I'll get Emily Armstrong to visit with some of her herbs. They'll be the best thing for her right now. I wish you had a proper bathroom here, Jem. She needs to bathe her lower half, twice a day, to rid it of the infection, preferably with some lavender oil. Can you rig something up?"

"Of course, I'll get the zinc bath from outside and give it a good scrub. I'm sure we can manage that. And, I'll keep any problems from her," he added, knowing that would be a far harder task than lugging the bath.

"Good. I'll get on to Emily Armstrong. And you'd better get Agnes to come over and help with the nursing. Katy mustn't get tired in any way. Her body needs to recover from that traumatic quick birth." The doctor clicked the clasp on his case shut.

"I understand, Dr Benson. Is the baby alright?"

"Oh, yes, the baby's very well. Quite perfect. No worries on that score."

"That's a relief anyway. Agnes is visiting this afternoon, as it happens."

"Good, make it a daily visit for a week at least." Dr Benson clapped him on the back. "Good man. She'll come through this, never fear. Your wife is a remarkable woman and very strong. A bit of careful nursing and she'll be fine."

"Thank you Doctor. I'll show you out."

Jem went back to the bedroom after the doctor had left. Katy was asleep and Lily was gurgling happily next to her. He'd be glad when Agnes was here to watch over them. Reluctantly, he turned away and went to the workshop.

Billy was pumping up a tyre on a pushbike and Jack was serving petrol to a customer on the forecourt. He found Len putting the finishing touches to the fire cement around the stove. He told them all he needed a meeting and they gathered around him in the tiny office.

Jem looked at the three expectant faces, all depending on him, and swallowed. "Katy's not very well. I've had to call the doctor out and she's going to need bed-rest for a couple of weeks at least, so she's out of action. Now, you all know we've got this race next week at Brooklands and I've got to go up there with Douglas. I'm hoping to secure a contract with Stockhead, based on the brake seal performance during the race.

"What you don't know is that Douglas's mother has died. I'm hoping that he will still be able to drive but can't be sure yet. If he rings or visits here at the garage, you must come and find me immediately. In the meantime, we must continue as if the race is on."

Jack piped up, "I could drive the sports Austin, if Douglas can't."

Jem smiled and shook his head, "Sorry, Jack, but you're just not experienced enough. I'd do it myself but I can't trust myself to go fast, with my gammy hand."

Billy shuffled his feet, and mumbled something Jem couldn't catch. He still hadn't learnt to drive, always preferring his pushbike.

Len cleared his throat. "I can't drive either, because of my foot, Jem, but if there is anything I can do, anything at all, even if it's outside normal hours, you only have to ask."

"Thanks, all of you. I know I can depend on you. We'll just have to hope that Douglas won't cancel. I doubt he will, he knows this race is crucial for Katherine Wheel. So, back to work everybody. Let's show Katy we can keep things running without her."

Over the next couple of days, each of his employees demonstrated their loyalty by working twice as hard as normal. Jem would have found that heart-warming, if Douglas had only showed up to confirm he would be driving in the race and if only he wasn't distracted by Katy's fever getting worse.

Agnes had moved into Al's room, who had been despatched up to her lodge house. Jem couldn't help but be relieved when his mother-in-law said, "Our Emily's now of an age to look after young Albert and they go to school together anyway. That lad is no trouble, Jem. It'll do our Emily good to have a bit of responsibility."

Agnes spoke with the authority of years of mothering and Jem was glad to have the decision taken from him. Katy improved from the minute her mother moved in but she was still very weak. Jem hadn't told her about Selina's death and swore anyone who came within her hearing not to mention it.

With Katy tentatively on the mend, he turned his

full attention to the all important race, now in only three days' time. He was confident Douglas would have let him know if he wanted to cancel but was desperate to have it confirmed. Bereavement or not, he had to find out. He drove up to the manor house, where Andrews informed him that Douglas was in the old barn, next to the stables, which now housed the cars.

Douglas had the bonnet up on the Sunbeam and didn't hear him enter the stone building. Jem cleared his throat and his friend looked up. Jem hoped the shock he felt on seeing his friend's face didn't show on his own. Douglas had aged ten years since he'd seen him last and he looked like he hadn't slept a wink since that fateful telephone call from his spiteful sister, Cheryl Flintock.

Black shadows ringed Douglas's blue eyes, and new, deep lines furrowed either side of his mobile mouth, usually upturned and smiling. Now it curved the other way, making his face severe. How could a man change so much in such a short space of time?

"Jem. Hello, pal." Douglas wiped his hands on an oily rag. "Just checking over the old girl, ready for Saturday's race. I thought I'd take the Austin up on the trailer, like I did last time. Keeps her sweet for her big moment, don't you think?"

"Err, yes, good idea. How are you, Douglas? I was so sorry to hear the news about your mother."

Douglas clenched his jaw, emphasising the new lines on his face. "Yes, it was a shock about Mother. My dear Dad has withdrawn all funds, Jem. I'm sorry, I should have come and told you. I've, well, I've been in a bit of a state, to be honest."

"That's understandable, Doug, but did you say *all* funds?"

"Afraid so, pal. I'm pretty much destitute, apart from Cassandra's money. A kept man, you might say. Not a nice position to be in." Douglas let out a long sigh. "I guess I'll just have to win that race, right?"

Jem's mind was spinning with the realisation of

Douglas's words. Damn it! Why hadn't the man come and told him this straight away? His friend was bereaved and upset but this ruined everything. He had to know more, even if it meant trampling all over Douglas's raw grief.

"Douglas, forgive me, but does that mean no money will be forthcoming whatsoever? It's just that I haven't paid Mr Wood's final invoice, as the money I was expecting didn't come through a couple of weeks ago and I've spent a lot more on equipment since then."

Douglas threw down his rag and turned to face Jem. "Yes, buddy, that's right. You got it. My father has seen fit to cut me off without a cent - or a penny, you might say." Douglas gave a hollow laugh. "But don't worry, Jem, I'm going to win outright on Wednesday. You just watch me. I'll whizz around that Brooklands track as if my blasted father was on my heels. You won't see me for dust. Then the guys from Stockhead and those car makers will snap up your seals and you'll be in the money for good. Think of it merely as a temporary cash flow problem."

Jem couldn't share his confidence but he couldn't destroy it either. Neither did he trust that reckless look.

He attempted a laugh. "Good for you, Douglas. I'm sure you'll win. We'll manage somehow. Bring the Sunbeam down with the trailer tomorrow and we'll load up the Austin and get off to London, shall we? Is Cassandra coming?"

"You bet, she is. We're all going to stay at the London House overnight. You too, bud. We'll have a swell time."

"Right." Jem was determined the doubt that consumed him wouldn't show in his voice. "See you tomorrow then, bright and early."

"See you then, partner. Make sure that Austin is ready for the race of her life!"

Jem promised he would and left, wondering how Douglas could sound so positive and look so miserable at the same time. His forced cheerfulness had jarred as much as his devastating news. Rather than feel reassured, Jem

276

was more worried than ever. If Stockhead didn't come through with a contract, they were truly done for. He had no idea how they would pay off the debts that had already accrued. The misgivings in his stomach lodged there like lumps of lead and refused to budge.

CHAPTER THIRTY EIGHT
Summer 1927

Cassandra found the journey up to London tedious. She elected to drive, so that Douglas could rest. Normally she would have enjoyed navigating the familiar roads, but the weather was wet and blowy and she had to strain to see beyond the bonnet. The tiny windscreen wiper hardly helped at all.

Too distracted for chitchat, all three of them were largely silent in the car. Most of the noise that accompanied them was the rattle of the trailer from the sports Austin bouncing along behind them, ensuring that none of them could forget the reason for their trip.

Jem didn't help to ease the tension in the car. He'd been deep in thought the entire way. She tried to draw him out but the only subject which he'd been willing to chat about was his new daughter. Lily, apparently, was the most exquisite child that had ever drawn breath.

"Katy's on the mend, I'm glad to say."

"Thank goodness for that, Jem." At least she needn't carry that anxiety to the race track.

"Yes, I was really worried about her but she'll soon be up and about again. She sends you her best wishes for the race tomorrow, Douglas." Jem's voice floated through into the front of the Sunbeam.

Douglas gave a brittle smile. "That's swell, Jem. I'm so glad Katy's out of danger."

The conversation dried up again after that and Cassandra was relieved to draw up in front of the London House overlooking Hyde Park. She had telephoned ahead and Hewitt, the butler, had obviously been looking out for them, as the door swung open before she'd applied the handbrake.

"Let's have tea here and then you can take the Austin over to Brooklands and store it in one of hangars overnight. Then we'll know it's in place, ready for the off tomorrow," Cassandra said. "I'm parched."

Jem checked the Austin was securely attached to the trailer, before following them inside. He looked uncomfortable in the elegant drawing room and remained quiet. Douglas's overbright veneer had also slipped. Cassandra decided to give up with the sympathy and concentrate on the tea, which as ever in this house, was excellent. She wasn't sorry when Douglas and Jem took the Austin over to Brooklands without her, She decided to luxuriate in a long, hot bath, with no daughters or mother to claim her before her skin wrinkled like a prune.

Some of the tension had left all three of them by supper time. Cassandra had washed her cares away and the two men appeared to have left theirs at the racing circuit. They each had a glass of wine and enjoyed the delights of Mrs Hewitt's delicate cuisine, such a blessed relief from the heavy hand of Mrs Biggs, the cook at Cheadle Manor.

"Now if this was my last supper, I couldn't wish for a finer meal than that," Douglas said, sitting back in his chair and patting his stomach. "All my favourite things. Smoked salmon blinis, stuffed artichokes and a thoroughly juicy steak."

"Don't forget that magnificent raspberry meringue, darling," Cassandra said.

"I shall never forget that meringue. Don't leave us for the port, Cass. Do stay while I enjoy a cigar, won't you?"

Cassandra laughed, "Alright, I can't refuse tomorrow's conquering hero anything on the eve of his glory, but don't blow the smoke in my direction."

"Fancy a cigar, Jem?" Douglas said, looking much more his normal urbane self.

"Not for me, thanks, Doug. Never liked them. I might indulge in a little glass of port, though."

"Not too much partner! We'll both need clear heads tomorrow." Douglas's face lit up by the flare of his match. Fragrant Cuban leaves curled into ash, exuding their foreign scent. Cassandra wouldn't admit it to her husband, but she actually quite liked the rich smell of a big cigar, even when pregnant, and anything that helped Douglas relax tonight had to be a good idea. She felt her anxiety lift a little as she gazed on his familiar features, whose harsh new lines were softened by the candlelight, making him look younger, carefree.

"I'm looking forward to the race, you know," Douglas said, through a blue haze. "I don't find it stressful on the track - just exciting. Driving at speed means you can't think about anything else. It's both liberating and exhilarating. You're the one that will have all the worries, entertaining that crowd and trying to persuade them to buy Kate's brake seals, Jem. I shall be free as a bird, flying around the banking doing what I do best - showing off."

They all laughed, even Jem. "It's great you're not nervous, Doug. I wish I could say the same."

They all retired early, aware of the importance of tomorrow. Cassandra watched Douglas undress, marvelling at his still flat stomach, the strength of his buttocks, the length of those long, muscular legs. He came to bed naked, joking that she was a voyeur.

"I am looking at you, it's true," she said. "It's a sight I shall never tire of. Would it sap your warrior strength to make love to me before the race?"

"Never," Douglas said, kissing her nose. "It would fortify me against anything, always has, always will."

Cassandra laughed and opened her arms.

***

The next morning, the day of the race, dawned as wet as its predecessor. The wind hadn't abated either. In stark contrast to the previous black week, Douglas seemed determined to be cheerful. Almost grotesquely so. He wore a rictus grin the entire morning, despite Jem's despondent comments about the weather. Cassandra had dressed with care, in an outfit she knew Douglas liked, but he didn't notice. It was irritating, but she decided to let it go and take her cue from him.

"Far from ideal conditions, Doug." Jem poured himself a cup of coffee from the silver pot on the breakfast table.

"It'll be the same for everybody."

Douglas's thin veneer of confidence couldn't disguise the fact that his appetite seemed to have deserted him since last night. Cassandra's was absent too. Butterflies flitted around her stomach. It couldn't be the baby, it was too soon. She buttered some toast and took a bite. Sawdust.

"I hope it won't be cancelled like the Bank Holiday meeting," Jem said.

Cassandra was beginning to wish it would, but that would be unfair on Katy and Jem. This was a crucial day for them. She tried to focus on that when they arrived at the Brooklands race track and met up with the bunch of representatives from the motor industry. She forced a smile on her face and extended her gloved hand in friendship, trying to remember each of their names and failing utterly. Her mind remained elsewhere, with Douglas, still unusually taciturn, who had quickly gone off to the hangars to check on his car.

"Would anyone else like to go to the hangars, and look at the brake system more closely?" Jem gave their little assembly a confident smile but Cassandra wasn't fooled.

There was a murmur of agreement and the group wandered over to the workshops.

One of the representatives, a tall, thin man dressed entirely in brown, Cassandra couldn't remember if he was from Austin or Morris, said sheepishly, "I see Malcolm Campbell isn't racing today? I was hoping to meet him. He's a hero of mine, especially now Parry Thomas is gone."

Cassandra pulled her blue coat tighter around her and resisted a shiver. "No-one would think it was August, would they?"

The safe topic of the unseasonal weather brought

them to the shed where Douglas's Austin was housed. Cassandra wished Katy was there, checking it for safety, being cheeky to the men who gathered around the wheels of the little sports car and looking too pretty to be a mechanic. She'd take a bet Jem was thinking exactly the same thing at this precise moment.

"Nifty little car. Who stripped it down like this?" The eldest of the motoring experts poked his nose into the engine. Cassandra vaguely remembered he was the man from Stockhead and therefore the most likely to want the seals.

"My wife, Kate Phipps. She's our chief mechanic and the one who designed the seals."

"Your wife, eh? Not here today?"

"No, we've, she's, um, just had a baby, actually." Jem shuffled his shoe in the gravel.

"I see," said the older man, looking non-plussed.

Cassandra decided to step in. "Mrs Phipps will be back at work very soon, gentlemen. She will oversee the production of the brake seals, isn't that right, Jem?"

Jem took up the theme. "Absolutely, you can rest assured on that. We've taken on more staff in readiness too and the machines for their manufacture are already in place. If you like what you see today, with the brakes performing under the stress of a race, the next step will be to come and see our new factory at Katherine Wheel Garage."

"And remind me where you are based?"

"Wiltshire, Mr Mayhew, near Woodbury."

"Ah, yes. Not too far from London then. Use the trains for delivery would you?"

"Yes, sir, that shouldn't be a problem and we've got a van to take them to the station, with a driver already employed."

"You have thought of everything, Mr Phipps." Mr Mayhew looked impressed.

Jem looked less strained after this conversation but Cassandra felt more so. All the pressure was on the driver's performance. Too much pressure.

Douglas was deep in conversation with Tim Bluntstone from the Speedwell company, his racing sponsor, in the corner of the big shed. She hovered around them, leaving Jem to deal with the potential brake seal buyers. Seeing her, Douglas broke off and gave her a quick peck on the cheek. Her first and only kiss of the day from him.

"Say, Cass, looks like it'll just be me in the car today. Tim's been telling me that it's a drivers only day today."

Cassandra wasn't sure which man looked more relieved at this news. Douglas wouldn't have to worry about balancing the car with Tim's heavy weight on the nearside and Tim, who'd never been an enthusiastic passenger, wouldn't have to career around the track as hostage to Douglas's mercy. She had mixed feelings about it. No-one would be advocating caution to her husband. Could she trust his judgement, when driving solo? If only Katy were here to give her wise counsel. Douglas always listened to her.

"Sorry you're missing out, Tim." She decided to be diplomatic, in case Tim hadn't realised she knew he was terrified.

"Yes, shame, really. Quite fancied a spin today." Tim truncated further debate by wandering off to join the group around the car.

Cassandra grabbed Douglas's arm, already encased in his white boiler suit. "Now listen to me, Doug. This doesn't mean you can go mad on your own, alright? You don't have to win, just show these motoring gentlemen how well the car can brake."

Douglas frowned, all his earlier hubris now vanished. He had that stern look again, the one that reminded Cassandra of his bloody awful father.

"I mean it, darling Douglas, please be careful, won't you?"

"Hell, Cass, I'm not on a suicide mission, you know.

It's just a race. I know what I have to do."

Just then, another man walked into the hangar. He was a head taller than the other men but Cassandra would have recognised him a mile away in any case.

He walked straight towards her, ignoring the gaggle of males who flocked around him.

"Cassandra Smythe! As I live and breathe. How charming to see you here, in my lair. How are you?" Lord Finch's grey eyes were fixed on her. Cassandra was annoyed he'd singled her out, as if she meant more to him than he had a right to.

Douglas turned and saw Lord Finch coming over. He stood closer behind her. She was glad of the ballast. Lord Denis Finch had always been unpredictable. It had been part of his charm, all those years ago.

Without preamble, or warning, Lord Finch leaned in and kissed her on the cheek, just managing to brush her lips with his in passing. Douglas stepped even closer behind her, and slipped his arm about her waist, thankfully still slim. Even Lord Finch couldn't possibly guess she was pregnant again.

"Morning, Flintock." Lord Finch gave Douglas a brief, not entirely friendly, nod.

"Good morning, Finch. Driving in the four hour race too?"

"Yes. You?"

"Yes."

"Well, let the best man win, eh, Cass?" Lord Finch drew on his driving gloves. "Still puttling about in a baby Austin, Flintock?"

"Not yet changed your flashy Bugatti?"

"How can you improve on perfection? You should know all about that, being married to Cassandra here."

"Oh, Denis, you always did exaggerate," Cassandra didn't like the tension that fizzled between the two men. Calm, that's what was needed now.

"Not a bit of it. You know I never had eyes for anyone but you and now you're taken." Lord Finch didn't drop his stare.

"That's right, pal. She's taken." Douglas drew her tight towards him. Cassandra leant against his tall body, drawing strength from the protection it always gave her.

"If it wasn't for that damn war, Cassandra would be wearing my ring, not yours. Her family were all for it, you know. I wonder how Lady Amelia feels about an American living at Cheadle Manor?" Lord Finch looked at their entwined hands and frowned.

"Denis, a lot of things might have happened if it hadn't been for the war. Don't be silly, now." Cassandra knew she had hit the wrong note, the minute the words left her mouth.

"Good God, I don't think anyone's accused me of silliness since I was three! Is that a favourite Americanism, Cassandra?"

"Oh, for goodness sake, Denis. The world has moved on, even if you haven't." Cassandra's patience had run out. Hadn't the war taught him anything?

There was an awkward silence. Lord Finch's face blanched white. "Thanks for the advice, Cassandra. I'll see you on the track, Flintock. We'll see who's moving then."

"Oh dear." Cassandra watched Lord Finch walk back out into the rain; a clutch of mechanics trotting behind him, like a pack of fawning dogs. "Denis always makes me so cross. He's such an arrogant bastard, always was, though I couldn't see it that way when I was younger."

"Yes, and exactly what did happen between you?" Douglas watched his rival depart, then snapped his eyes back to her face.

"Just juvenile nonsense, you know the sort of thing. Seems like a lifetime ago now."

"Don't brush me off with that vague dismissal. I want details."

"Good God, Doug, does it really matter?"

"Yes."

"It's such ancient history, but if you must know, we

were sort of engaged but I broke it off after Charles died and went to France. He never accepted it and insisted we were still engaged throughout the war but I thought I'd made it quite clear that it was over. I felt I had to grow up by joining the fight. I suppose I naively felt I could avenge Charles's death. Impossible, of course. And then, as you know, right at the end of the whole ghastly business, I met you and recognised the real thing."

"And it wasn't the real thing with Finch?"

"Lord, no. Of course, you don't know that at the time, do you?"

"And did you, I mean, how far did things go between you?"

"Oh, Douglas, do we have to do this?"

"I think we do, yes." His blue eyes were dark now and those furrows around his mouth deep and unyielding.

"It's an unwritten law, isn't it? Well, it was then, in my circles. Getting engaged did mean that a certain license was granted to one's fiancé." Cassandra could see from Douglas's fierce expression that even that wouldn't do. Nothing but absolute honesty would. "Alright, yes, we had a physical relationship, but we didn't have full sex. You must have realised that, when we were at the summer house in Falmouth. Now are you satisfied?"

"I see. You could have told me before."

"Why? I didn't ask about your life before you met me! How could I know that the love of my life was waiting for me on a French battlefield?" Cassandra felt really angry now. How could playing around with Lord Finch have been a sin, when she hadn't known Douglas even existed? Though, she could see now what a narrow escape from misery she'd had. It wasn't her fault Lord Finch still held a candle for her, was it?

"And did you formally break off your engagement?"

"Not precisely." Even to Cassandra's ears, that sounded weak.

"No wonder he's fuming. I think you might have handled that better, Cassandra."

Something in Cassandra snapped. "Oh, do you? After that bloodbath? All the carnage I'd seen? And falling in love with you? Maybe loving *me* wasn't such an overwhelming experience, Douglas? *I* forgot about everything else after I met you. Or had you forgotten? It seems to me you're becoming as stuffy and narrow-minded as your stiff-necked prude of a father!"

She walked away. She'd had enough for one morning. Jem looked across and beckoned her over. She joined his group of tweed-suited middle-aged men and parked her brightest smile on her face. "Shall we seek some refreshment in the new Clubhouse, gentlemen? I don't know about you, but I could use a glass of bubbly." She tucked her hand inside the arm of a startled representative; she still couldn't tell one from the other, and marched him out of the hangar, without looking back.

Jem had gone to great lengths to provide a substantial buffet for his guests but Cassandra wasn't hungry. Neither Douglas nor Lord Finch showed up and she wondered what they would eat before the race. She was still too angry to organise anything on their behalf. No doubt they'd grab a sandwich on the run. When Tim Bluntstone joined them he more than made up for their abstinence, putting away far more than his fair share, until she whispered in his ear and offended him. Offending people seemed to be the order of the day and she'd be glad when it was over.

The race was due to start at half past one. Feeling slightly giddy from the wine, Cassandra applied lipstick to her face in the mirror of the Ladies Powder Room. She looked tired and no amount of rouge could rescue her. She shrugged. It would have to do. Douglas hadn't noticed anything about her today. He wasn't going to now, with the race about to start. She joined Jem and the others. Mr Mayhew helped her on with her coat.

"No let up in the downpour, Mrs Flintock. Shame that."

She nodded her agreement and clamped her clôche

hat on her head, tucking her wayward strands of hair under its brim. "I suppose we have to go and stand by the track?"

"We've all agreed to a soaking, at least at the start, Cassandra." Jem looked more anxious than ever.

She'd just have to put up with it. She could always go to the grandstand later.

"They want to see how the brakes operate, close up, you see," Jem added.

"Let's brave it, then, shall we?" Cassandra smiled at the group and led the way outside.

She immediately regretted it. The wind had picked up, rather than lessened and the rain came in swirling gusts. It was far more like October than August. She remembered the drive up to London and the poor visibility. With the spray from other cars, it would be hell out there today. As quickly as it had arisen, her anger with Douglas evaporated. Cassandra picked up her pace and almost ran to the paddock where the cars were assembling for the off. She was too late to give her husband the good luck kiss that hovered on her painted lips. He was already lined-up at the starting point, wearing his goggles and wiping his windscreen on the inside with his gloved hands. She couldn't see his face at all; couldn't make the eye contact she so desperately wanted to. She didn't want him driving for four hours, thinking she was still furious with him, but even the mechanics had been shooed off the track now, leaving just the cars with their single drivers exposed to the inclement weather.

"They're not going to be able to see a thing, Jem."

"Visibility is poor, it's true. I hope the brakes perform in the wet or it'll all be for nothing." Jem pulled the rim of his trilby hat down over his eyes and squinted through the rain.

Cassandra waved to Douglas but he still didn't see her. The cars were lined up in a row, with Douglas at the centre and Lord Finch's red Bugatti on the far side. The flag was raised and the cars revved up to their full throated maximum, drowning out the thrum of the rain with their louder roar.

"At least the bridge supports have gone now." Tim Bluntstone nodded to the footbridge that spanned the track.

"Oh yes, that's a big improvement. Those struts were a menace and with the rain making it so hard to see, it's one less hazard for them to negotiate." Jem's words would have reassured her but just then the flag descended and with a tremendous din from the engines, the cars careered away, with Douglas's Austin a nose ahead of the pack.

"Terrific start, Doug." Jem's face was a picture of conflicting emotions but Cassandra wasted no time studying it. Her eyes were fixed on the little blue Austin number five, still nudging ahead of the other cars. At least that meant he wouldn't be blinded by spray.

"Oh look! That red Bugatti's gaining on Douglas. Yes, he's secured second place. They're establishing a lead." Tim Bluntstone pointed his finger at the two cars now distinctly ahead of the pack and the other men nodded, looking quite excited, if a little damp.

Cassandra strained to see the leaders but they were round the bend now and out of sight.

"Come on, let's go to the grandstands. We'll see more from there now." Jem gathered up his wet guests, who were very willing to follow him undercover.

Cassandra, though soaked through herself, was reluctant to leave the track side and be at a remove from her husband. She wished they had passengers in the race. She would have volunteered. Then she could have told Douglas how sorry she was; how the row was stupid; how it meant nothing; how much she loved him.

Tim cupped her elbow. "Come on, Mrs Flintock, you'll be able to watch in comfort from there and have a bird's eye view of your husband. The race is four hours long, remember."

She nodded and accepted his arm. They strode quickly to the grandstands where everyone shook the rain from their overcoats. Cassandra couldn't be bothered to take hers off. The fur collar was ruined anyway and there was no saving it now. She shouldered her way to the very front of the stand and tried to locate Douglas by the direction of the thunderous noise of the cars. Through the drizzle she could just make out a red and a blue blur on the far side of the track, by the members banking, which curved steeply before sweeping down and becoming flat again alongside the railway line. The two cars were a couple of lengths ahead. She dreaded to think what speed they must be doing.

"Anyone have any idea how fast they're going?"

She supposed Tim knew what he was on about when he said, "At least a ton, I should think."

A hundred miles an hour? Surely that wasn't safe. The cars thundered past underneath them, convincing her that Tim had been right about the speed. Almost as fast as Thomas Parry that day at Pendine Sands. Her empty stomach stopped growling and knotted up instead. Four hours seemed a very, very long time.

Lap after lap she stood there, until her drenched coat was only damp and she was cold and shivery.

"Fancy a nip?" It was Mr Mayhew, obviously a man of some experience at these events. She took a sip from his hip flask. The brandy warmed her; stopped her shivers. The rain didn't let up, as had been predicted.

"Why don't they stop the race, Mr Mayhew? Surely it's too wet?"

"Not up to me, Mrs Flintock. I suppose they know what they're doing. Shows off those brakes to advantage though, I'm most impressed."

"Have you told Mr Phipps that?"

"Not yet, but I will."

"I'm glad, Mr Mayhew. They are a really good set up at Katherine Wheel Garage, you know. You won't be disappointed. Which company are you from?"

"Stockhead. We've been very disappointed with the performance of these hydraulic brakes. Couldn't get the damn things to stop leaking but by Jove, I do think

Katherine Wheel have cracked it."

Cassandra couldn't resist. She stood on tiptoe and pecked him on the cheek. He smelled of damp wool and stale tobacco and rewarded her with a surreptitious wink.

At that moment, the crowd let out a collective moan.

"What's happening?" Cassandra had only looked away for a moment. Trust that to be the very time when something exciting occurred. She looked at the faces of the other spectators. They didn't looked excited, but shocked.

"What is it?"

Jem came to her side. "There's been a crash, Cassandra."

"Which car? Who is it?"

"I don't know, no-one knows. Look, they're stopping the race."

Sure enough, as she looked below all the cars that had been racing past in a fog of smoke and rain, slowed down and came to a halt. She scanned them all. Not one was blue, or red for that matter. Then around the bend came Lord Finch's scarlet Bugatti. He was still travelling at speed and only braked just in time to avoid the stationary vehicles, now bunched up by the pits. He skidded into the fence, narrowly missing a race official who had to jump out of the way. He obviously hadn't got hydraulic brakes.

But where was the blue Austin? The knot that had resided in her stomach all morning now rose to Cassandra's throat, threatening to block her airway. She put her hand on her throat, then over her mouth, to stop the scream building up inside.

"Jem," she whispered, grabbing his arm. "Where is he? Where's my Douglas?"

Jem shook his head and pinched Tim's binoculars, using them to scan the whole track. All the other spectators were doing the same, crowding on to the banister, craning their necks to see through the rain that still whirled down. The track was laced with puddles.

"Let's go down, Jem. We must find out." Cassandra

291

managed to say.

She snatched his hand and he followed her down the wooden stairs. They ran to the paddock. She lost her hat on the way in the wind and left it to blow away. She accosted the first official she ran into.

"Tell me what's happened? Where is Douglas Flintock's Austin?"

"Sorry, miss but I think it's had an accident."

"No! It can't be him."

"Come on, Cassandra." Jem took her arm. "We mustn't panic until we know the facts."

She nodded, blinded by the rain in her eyes and followed him to the pits.

Lord Finch had a crowd gathered around him, as usual. Everyone was clamouring to know what had happened. When he saw Cassandra he clambered out of his Bugatti and came towards her.

"I'm so sorry, Cassandra. It was on the far banking. Douglas was driving like a mad man. I'd overtaken him fair and square, you see, but then he drove up the banking to get past me again and after that, I couldn't see him. I kept going. I was going too fast to stop but I think he's come to grief."

"You idiot!" Cassandra slapped him as hard as she could across his face, hurting her hand on his goggles. She bent the nail back on her wedding ring finger. It started to bleed.

"Jem, we must go there. I must find out if he's alright."

Jem nodded and started running to the Byfleet banking, in the direction Lord Finch had pointed.

Cassandra ran beside him, too lightheaded to think, quickly out of breath and panting. Many people had got there before them and were crowding around the blue Austin. Its bonnet had concertina'd like an accordion against a large beech tree. Steam escaped and mingled with the rain in a white cloud. The engine was dead; silent. As silent as the huddle of people standing by the car. A strange eeriness hung over the scene.

She knew then.

White clouds issued from their mouths as they ran, adding to the steam from the broken radiator, their rasping breath announcing their arrival. Pale faces turned towards them as they approached.

Jem went ahead of her and talked to an important-looking man. "I have Mrs Flintock with me." She heard him say. "How's the driver. Is he badly hurt?"

The man looked blankly back at Jem and shook his head.

It couldn't be. She ran to the car, shoving the onlookers out of the way with all her strength, ignoring their protests.

Douglas had been thrown out of the car and his long body was sprawled out on the grass next to the impervious tree. He lay face down and still, so still. Cassandra ignored the shouts from the men and ran to him. Hands pulled at her coat to restrain her but she couldn't feel them. She crouched down next to him so she could see his face, turned towards her. It was unmarked; perfect. Someone had removed his goggles and unhooked the strap of his leather hood. He looked as if he was asleep. She'd watched him sleeping so many times. The other people stood back, sensing her loss, respecting her privacy, muttering words that didn't mean anything. Nothing meant anything now. Nothing ever would.

An earth shattering wail pierced the odd silence. She looked around to see who had made it. A grey-haired man, carrying a doctor's bag, came running up. He didn't stop her hugging her husband but inspected him with professional skill and speed, working around her. When he had finished he looked at her.

"I take it you know this driver?"

Jem spoke for her. "This is Mrs Flintock, the driver's wife."

"I see. I'm very sorry, Mrs Flintock, but there's nothing we can do. Your husband has died from a broken neck. If it's any consolation, he would have felt nothing. Death was instantaneous. I'm very sorry."

That wail again. Who kept making such a terrible noise? Jem had his arm around her and someone else was waving the others away. The doctor patted her shoulder. This couldn't be happening to her. This was a dream. A nightmare. It wasn't, mustn't be real.

"Douglas!" That voice again, screaming his name now. Why didn't they shut up?

The doctor had a pill, he was pushing it in her mouth, getting Jem to tip brandy down her throat but her throat was too tight. It wouldn't open. Ugh, the fiery liquid burned her gullet. The tablet stuck, then slithered down, helped on with more brandy.

They were pulling her away, she wouldn't let go. Oh, give me one more look at his dear face. Please God, let me see him again. More hands clutched at her wet sleeves. She couldn't see him. She wanted to see him. She wanted to look at him every day, every minute for the rest of her life, but he just lay there.

Douglas! Help me, *Douglas!*

"I love you, Douglas, I love you. Don't leave me, oh, Douglas, my darling, don't leave me alone."

CHAPTER THIRTY NINE
Summer 1927

"I'm feeling much better today, Mum," Katy said, flinging the covers off her bed. "I think it's high time I got up."

Agnes felt her forehead. The frown she'd been wearing for well over a week cleared from her brow. "Reckon you could get up for a spell. You'll feel different when you're dressed and it would do you good, but no going over to that dratted garage, mind. I know you, young Katy, you'd have your head in one of them oily engines within five minutes. So, up you get, but back to bed early tonight and I'll take no nonsense."

Katy laughed. Her mother could read her like a book. She was itching to go to the workshop and find out how they were managing with Jem away. And desperate to find out how the race was going at Brooklands. Had Stockhead liked her design? Would one of the car makers also want supplies? Could they work together to arrange it? The questions in her head all vied for urgent answers. Patience had never been her strong point.

Lily cried and Katy leant over her crib and picked her up. "She's getting heavier by the day, the little guzzler."

Agnes smiled. "Yes, it's good to see her thriving but that's another reason you mustn't overdo it, whilst your nursing her. You're still feeding two, remember, and we don't want that infection to come back."

"Stop going on, Mum, I got the message the first time. I'll just give her a feed, then I'll have a wash and get dressed. And I promise not to go to the workshop, not today at least."

"Hmm, alright, I'll put the kettle on and get those nappies out on the line. Then we'll have a bit of lunch together, with a proper sit-down at the table, shall we?"

"Sounds lovely."

Agnes bustled off and Katy sat in the old rocking

armchair that Cassandra had lent her from the manor nursery. Its arms were just right for cradling a newborn, taking all the weight of the baby and the ache out of a mother's arms. Lily latched on with her usual gusto and she smiled at her busy little mouth sucking away, letting all her worries about the garage fade into the background for a few contented minutes. She'd forgotten how disorientating a new child made her feel. Lily only woke a few times in the night but it was enough to blur the boundaries between night and day. She'd be glad when she settled. Maybe when her milk came in a bit more, and Lily wasn't so hungry. Greedy little thing.

She hummed a nursery rhyme to her daughter and rocked her gently. 'Golden Slumbers' was her favourite. Agnes had sung it to her when she was a little child. How lucky she was to have a mum like that. She wondered how Al was faring up at the lodge. It would be nice to get back to normal when Jem came home. He was missing these early tender moments with the baby. So was Al. It would be good to have her own little family all back together again, however supportive her mother was. No doubt Bert was missing his wife, and her cooking, too.

Lily finally appeared to have had enough. She patted her tiny back to wind her and placed her back in her crib. The baby went straight off to sleep and Katy took pleasure in getting dressed for the first time since Lily's dramatic birth in the delivery van. Agnes had made a cheese and onion tart and baked bread. It had been the irresistible smell of fresh bread that had got her out of bed.

The living area in the hut had never looked cleaner. Every surface shone with polish. Fresh flowers graced the rickety old table, which was laid for two.

"I'm going to miss you when I have to shift for myself again. What a pity Jem isn't here to be spoiled too." Katy sat down, gingerly, on the hard chair. Some bits of her were still sore.

"We've got potatoes and greens from your garden to go with the tart. I've done a bit of weeding of the veg patch this morning. Jem's done well this year. Can't fault his gardening, I must say, Katy, but the rain brought me in. I've had to put those nappies on the airer over the range to finish off. Want some butter on your tatties?"

"Lovely, thanks." Katy licked her lips. Her mother had better not stay too much longer or she'd be the size of a house.

They managed to get through lunch before the baby stirred again. Katy was just picking her up for another feed when there was a sharp rap on the door. Agnes went to answer it.

Over the baby's cries, Len spoke in his deep voice. "Begging your pardon, Mrs Beagle, but Jem's on the telephone in the garage. He wants to speak to Mrs Phipps."

"It's not very convenient at the moment, Len. Did he say it was urgent?"

"Yes, he did. I think she'd better come, if she can. He's holding on."

"All the way from London? That'll cost a fortune. You'd better go, Katy. Give me the baby and I'll give her my finger to suck. Come straight back, mind."

"I will." Katy grabbed a shawl and followed Len outside. The rain had turned into a determined drizzle that looked like it meant to stay for the day. "Did Jem say what all the fuss was about, Len?"

"I think I'd better leave him to tell you himself," was all the answer she got.

"You'd better sit down, love," came Jem's voice, sounding serious even through the crackles. "Is the baby alright? And you? Are you better?"

"Yes, we're fine. I got up today for the first time. Look, what's happened? I can tell by your voice something's up?"

"I'm at Brooklands. The race has been cancelled because there's been an accident. A serious accident."

"Is anyone hurt?"

"Yes, Douglas. Katy, my love, he's been killed. Broke his neck after leaving the track and hitting a tree. He

297

was thrown out of the car. The doctor said it was instant. He wouldn't have suffered."

"Oh, my God! Dear Douglas. Oh, God. Jem - did the brakes fail? Was it anything to do with that?"

"No, I'm sure it wasn't. The weather was dreadful. There was talk of cancelling but they'd already cancelled the Bank Holiday race and it went ahead. Douglas was overtaking Lord Finch's Bugatti - you know him, don't you - I think they might have had words before the race. There was some sort of row, I don't know. Anyway, Douglas shouldn't have gone so high on the banking. He was going much too fast for the steep gradient." Jem's voice cracked and it had nothing to do with the telephone line.

Katy couldn't take it in. "It must be the brakes. Surely he could have slowed down? But we tested and tested them. I can't understand it."

"He was going too fast Katy, I told you. And he went too high on the curved banking. Shot right off the edge of it into this blasted tree. The Austin is stoved right in at the front."

"I can't believe this. Not Douglas. How's Cassandra?"

"Terrible. Just terrible. She's beside herself. Having to be sedated. The Hewitts at the London House are looking after her. Katy, I'm going to come home tomorrow. I'm going to drive the Sunbeam and bring the Austin back on the trailer. At least then Cassandra won't have to see it and I'm no help to her here."

"Can you drive all that way with your hand?"

"I'll have to. Don't worry, I'll go slow. I'll be careful. Don't want two accidents. You mustn't worry."

"Oh, Jem, This is so awful. Poor Cassandra. How's she going to come home?"

"I don't know. The Hewitts will look after her for now. She's in no fit state to go anywhere. I've never seen anyone so upset, not even in the war. Listen, I've got to go. Someone else needs the telephone kiosk. I'll see you tomorrow."

And he was gone.

She hadn't even thought to ask about the contract with Stockhead. That all seemed totally irrelevant now. Katy replaced the receiver into its cradle and buried her face in her hands. She didn't know how long she wept but after a while, Len poked his head around the office door, handed her a glass of water and the balm of silent sympathy.

CHAPTER FORTY
Summer 1927

"Don't forget to allow for the length of the trailer, Jem." Tim Bluntstone's round, kind face peered in through the driver's window of the Sunbeam saloon. "Take any corners wide and slow. Listen, why don't I come with you?"

"Thanks, Tim, but I'll be fine." All Jem craved was some time alone. He wanted to take the journey slowly. He needed to think; maybe not even think, just absorb Douglas's death.

"If you're sure?"

"I am. I'll ring your office at Speedwell when I get home, if it'll put your mind at rest."

"No, I trust you, but I don't suppose I'll see you for a while, not after this."

"Come and visit anytime, Tim, you'll always be welcome at Katherine Wheel but I can't see us racing for the foreseeable future, or maybe ever again. It all depends how it goes with the seals and I've no idea what any of the reps thought. Everyone disappeared after the accident, so I'm none the wiser. I just don't know what lies ahead for any of us now."

Tim wound the starting handle and the Sunbeam growled into life with a slow, reluctant rumble. He passed the handle back through the window, saying, "No, I understand, Jem. Good luck, mate. Safe journey. Give my best to Kate and the baby. At least you have that."

"Yes. " Jem was too choked to add more and revved the engine. Not trusting his voice, he said goodbye to Tim with a wave, turned the big car round and exited Brooklands over the river bridge. He'd written down the directions for the road home in big capital letters and propped it on the dashboard. He didn't want to stop to consult a map. He just wanted to drive and drive and drive.

He had to take a break for lunch and pulled up at a coaching inn. Not that he could eat much. Half a pint of bitter relaxed him and he snoozed in a lay-by afterwards for half an hour. It had been horrible waking up and remembering that Douglas was gone. His best friend. Cassandra's husband. Laughing father to those beautiful little girls. Who was going to tell them about his death, with Cassandra still in London?

He'd have to go up to the manor and see Nanny Morgan. She'd be the best judge of that. And try to avoid Lady Amelia. Jem was quite sure he couldn't cope with that old bat right now. He rubbed his tired face with his hand and ran his fingers through his hair, pulling it hard to wake himself up properly. He'd like to pull all his black thoughts out too. He'd willingly pull all his hair out, make himself bald, if it would erase yesterday's events.

How could they go on without Douglas? Quite apart from any personal loss, which threatened to overwhelm *him*, let alone Cassandra, where would the money come from now? Selina Flintock and her son were - had been - their only sponsors, along with Speedwell, and they had been entirely dependent on Douglas's racing. Both had suddenly gone, out of the blue, leaving Katherine Wheel high and dry with no contract or even acknowledgement from Stockhead, Austin or Morris about making the brake seals.

The whole thing had been a disaster on every level. He couldn't think about it whilst driving, so he cranked the engine back into life and climbed back behind the wheel. The crushed Austin was covered with a tarpaulin and strapped down to the trailer with rope, which was just as well, because Jem didn't think he could bear to look at it ever again. Was it only yesterday Douglas was roaring around Brooklands' track in that death-trap?

He pulled out onto the main road and concentrated his entire mind on gear changes and negotiating bends. Anything to blot out the pain in his heart.

He arrived home at about three o'clock in the afternoon. One part of him longed to see his new baby, Al and Katy, but the other wanted to drive past, keep driving and never stop, never have to face this sad, new reality. He turned into the garage, down the gentle incline to the forecourt, past the petrol pumps and parked up alongside the workshop Nissen hut, now bedecked with signs boasting of their prowess with cars, cycles, petrol and oil, servicing and sales.

Sales. Douglas's domain. Another source of income dried up. And no cheery face showing off the cars to new customers.

He switched off the engine and laid his forehead against the steering wheel. He couldn't go in. Couldn't face them. Couldn't face going over the details of the accident.

But he had to. He owed it to them. Owed it to Douglas. He brushed his good hand against his tired eyes, clamped his hat on his bedraggled head and climbed out of the car, slamming the door to signal his arrival. Better get it over with.

Jack saw him first. He opened his arms and enfolded Jem in a bear-hug. It undid him immediately and he let out a sob. Jack, still so young, somehow knew what to do and held him until he regained his composure. Only then did he look at him and give a silent nod. Jem went into the workshop first. Seeing Katy would be even harder. He'd leave that till last. Len shook his hand and Billy clapped him on the shoulder. None of them said anything for a full five minutes.

Jem cleared his throat and broke the silence. "I want you all to know that he didn't suffer. It was over in a second. Broken neck. The Austin's on the trailer but just unhook it and park it round the back, would you? I don't want to look at it just yet but we'll have to check it over at some point. See if it was the car's fault, but I don't think so. He just overshot the steep banking while trying to pass the lead car."

"Any takers for the brake seals, Jem?" Len had so much at stake with his new job.

"I don't know, Len. The race was abandoned and everyone shoved off straight after. I had to take Mrs

302

Flintock-Smythe back to her London house. She was very upset. Then I had to go back to the track and deal with the, the body. With Douglas." His voice broke then.

More slaps on the back. No more words.

"I'd better go and see Kate, now."

They all concurred quietly and Jem nodded his thanks, swallowed the rock in his gullet and went to the hut they called home.

Agnes opened the door and touched her finger to her lips. Her eyes were red-rimmed. "Hello, Jem, love. They're both asleep in the bedroom. It's been a rough night. Come here, lad, and let me give you a hug."

Once again, Jem was enfolded in the arms of one of the Beagle family. He trusted Agnes completely. She let him cry for as long as it took.

"Jem, you're home." Katy stood in the bedroom doorway, still in her white nightgown with a shawl around her thin frame. She looked like she hadn't slept for a week.

Agnes gave him a handkerchief and he blew his nose. He must be strong. He squared his shoulders and went to his wife. They held each other tight. A little wail escaped from the crib. Agnes went past them, scooped Lily up and took her outside into the garden, wrapped in a blanket.

Katy, dry eyed but with puffy eyes that had obviously already shed many tears, tugged his good arm and drew him to the fireside. He sat on the big comfy armchair and held out his arms. She sat on his lap. She felt too light, too ethereal. He held her tight and she didn't protest, but squeezed him back. They didn't speak but sat like that for an hour, until Agnes returned with the baby.

CHAPTER FORTY ONE
Summer 1927

Much as she loved her mother, Katy was glad that Agnes decided to go back to her own house on Jem's return. Al was reinstated the very next day and it was lovely to have him home again. She'd never appreciated her little family more. They told Al about Douglas very gently but the little boy took it hard, as they all had. She chided herself constantly about the many times she'd moaned about Douglas's carefree attitude to life, his carelessness about detail and disregard for what their customers thought. Now, with a shock, Katy realised how much his lighthearted breeziness had helped them all. Douglas's laughter had carried them through so many difficult days. His absolute confidence and belief in their enterprise had underpinned everything they'd ever done. And so had his generosity. Katy felt as if the sun had gone behind dark clouds and would never shine again.

Jem told her about Mrs Flintock and the double shock almost took the wind out of her. She had no idea how they would cope now.

Al, with the adaptability of children, devoted himself to Lily's welfare, fetching nappies and talcum powder with a new seriousness. It softened the blow of losing Agnes back to the lodge. Quite apart from the sapping grief, Katy was still drained of energy from being unwell after the baby's birth and the broken nights feeding Lily didn't help her regain her strength as fast as she'd like. She was so grateful for all the help she was getting but she longed to be able to fend for herself again. More than anything she wanted to go over that sports Austin; make sure there had been no mechanical failure to cause the crash. She had to find out for herself if the car had killed Douglas but the day disappeared in a haze of baby feeds, snatched sleep and keeping the family fed.

Jem went up to the manor to see Nanny Morgan. He returned as white as sheet, having also seen Cassandra's

304

mother. Lady Amelia had told him she blamed the garage for the tragedy. That made Katy even more determined to scour the Austin for faults. She had to know the truth before Cassandra came home.

Jem was more preoccupied with their finances and confessed he was at his wits' end about it. That night, while Katy took Al off to bed, Jem went to the office in the workshop and brought back the account books.

"I haven't told you yet, Kate," Jem said, when she returned, "but both Austin and Morris have turned us down flat and I still haven't heard from Stockhead. It would be disrespectful to Douglas to rush an answer out of them but I don't know how much longer we can carry on paying Len and Jack just from what we make at the garage. We can cover Billy's wages from the garage's turnover, but not theirs - or have much over for us."

"Well, we can advertise the brake seals in the Motoring Magazine. We might get some takers that way, mightn't we?"

"We might, but it wouldn't be enough. I still owe Mr Wood for the factory shed and Mrs Flintock's promised money, that should have covered it, won't be coming after all. Look, here's a sum of what we've spent so far. You can see, it comes to some thousands. I didn't tell you before because of the baby and you being ill but we're at breaking point, Kate. I've made an appointment with the bank for tomorrow. Just to tide us over," Jem added when Katy betrayed her feelings by shaking her head.

"But Jem, what if someone invents the same thing, gets it produced before us, beats us to it? We'll be in hock up to our armpits and how would we pay it back?"

"It's a risk we'll have to take, Kate, my love. We've no choice now, but to push on through. And we've got to clear our outstanding debts. There's no other way we can raise the capital."

Katy was glad the garage was busy the next day, it stopped her thinking about what was happening with Jem's interview at the bank. Al had gone to school and Agnes had stayed at home at the lodge. With no-one to stop her, Katy went to the workshop, taking Lily with her. The smell of diesel and petrol greeted her like an old friend, except her real old friend wasn't there; would never be there again, never saunter in with a joke on his lips and a tune to whistle. She ignored her fatigue, placed the baby in her cot in the office, with Felix, the cat, to watch over her, and set to sanding the rust off an ancient spare running board she'd been meaning to restore for ages. Len and Jack promised to take turns checking on Lily, in between their workshop chores. Katy had developed a second sense when Lily needed her anyway, and by some strange telepathy always woke in the night just before the baby cried. Katy lifted the metal on to the workbench by the front window, so she'd see Jem the minute he got back and scratched away at the rust, wishing, if she worked hard enough, she could rub out recent events.

Jem was back by lunchtime and she ran out to meet him.

"What did he say?"

"Come into the office, where we can be private," was Jem's ominous reply. They hurried past Billy, who was serving petrol. They walked into the little cubby hole and Jem shut the door behind them. Lily murmured and then went back to sleep. Felix, stirred, rose from his curled up position next to the crib and sat up to have a thorough wash.

Amongst the litter of papers and files stacked up but not yet dealt with, Jem told her, "We've had to take out a mortgage. Payments are monthly and the term is twenty years. The land and the garage are the combined equity; we don't have anything else."

"Oh, no, Jem, we always said we'd avoid that. If we can't pay, they can take everything away from us, everything we've worked for."

"I know, but it's the only way. We already had the money we paid Cassandra for the extra twenty acres under loan, so Mr Wentworth has amalgamated the debt into one

306

mortgage. As it's a twenty year agreement, the payments aren't as bad as I'd thought they might be but they are not small. Of course, we won't have to pay for the loan that we have to cover now, but it makes the interest amount to a substantial sum over the full term of the mortgage. We're going to struggle to pay it every month and we're going to have to start turning a profit almost at once but at least we can go ahead, Kate. And, frankly, we have no choice because we have to clear the debt we've already accrued. We've got to sell those brake seals, Kate, we've simply go to, or we're sunk."

So they'd have to risk everything. She couldn't bear to lose Katherine Wheel.

It was more than a garage, it was their home.

***

"Seems Miss Cassandra's back." Agnes popped in the next morning, laden with two apple pies and a bottle of elderflower cordial. "Your father told me last night. He never saw her but everyone who has, says she's still in a terrible way."

"I'll go and see her today, Mum. Will you mind Lily for me?"

"As long as you're not too long. My heart goes out to that young woman. All she's got now is those two little girls and, God help her, Lady Amelia. I never did hold with these motor cars."

Another stab of guilt went through Katy at her mother's words. She gave Lily a feed and passed her over.

"And don't you go walking home, neither," Agnes said, as she took Lily in her arms. "You're not strong enough. Get your father to bring you home in the gig.

They needed to return the Sunbeam to the manor, so after telling Jem where she was off to and refusing his offer to come with her, she drove it up to the big house.

Her old boss, Mr Andrews, let her in. He wore a black armband on his already black coat. Pale mauve

307

chrysanthemums graced the table in the magnificent hall but to Katy, they just reminded her of funerals. No doubt that was the point. The whole place was sombre and very quiet.

"I've come to see Miss Cassandra."

"She's kept to her room, since she's come home, Mrs Phipps."

"Could you ask her if she would see me?"

"I'll try. Wait here."

Katy stood in the hall, feeling lost in its cavernous space. She always had disliked this echoing chamber, especially when she'd had to wash its marbled floor as a housemaid. That seemed a lifetime ago now. It *was* a lifetime ago. Douglas's short lifetime. She remembered when she'd thought Jem was dead in the war. No-one knew better how Cassandra was feeling.

Mr Andrews appeared on the left hand gallery above the sweeping staircase and beckoned with a gloved forefinger for her to ascend. Her shoes made no sound on the carpet but she was convinced the banging thumps of her heart must surely be overheard.

Mr Andrews melted away down the stairs with silent footsteps. Katy knew which door was Cassandra's, having been her personal maid before Cassandra married the man she'd now lost. She knocked but there was no answer. She turned the handle and entered the room, surprised at the transformation within.

When she had been the one helping Cassandra into her satins and silks, the room had been dark, oppressive. Now it was furnished in the latest modern style and its pale blue walls and curtains made it look double the size. Douglas's money and influence. He'd lightened up all their lives.

Cassandra was sitting by the big bay window that overlooked the orchard. She didn't look up or even notice Katy's approach and jumped when Katy addressed her.

"Cass?"

Cassandra's face was ghastly. Grey, drawn, with not

a scrap of make-up. Her hair hung down in chaotic wisps, uncombed and unwashed. She wore a man's dressing gown. Katy could guess who that had belonged to. A tray of uneaten food sat on a small table next to her. A cup of tea bore a scum of milk that had long ago cooled on its surface.

Katy knelt down in front of her friend and took her icy hands in hers. Cassandra stared back at her with unseeing, unfocussed eyes.

"Cass, what can I say? I'm so sorry, my dear."

"Nothing to say."

"No. We'll miss him so much."

"You'll miss him? Huh. If it wasn't for the girls, I'd jump out of this window right now. I don't want to go on living without him. He was my whole life."

"I know."

"No, you don't."

"Yes, Cass, darling, I do. I thought I'd lost Jem in the war, remember? I did try to kill myself."

"Pity you hadn't. Douglas would still be alive then."

Katy was stung into silence. Cassandra had voiced the very thought that ran through her brain day and night. If she hadn't invented the seals, hadn't wanted to run a garage, hadn't accepted Douglas's help, he would still be alive.

"I know."

"Why did you make him drive that day?"

"I didn't, Cass. He loved racing. You know that."

"Yes, he loved racing. We had a row. Before the race. He was angry. Bloody Denis Finch had taunted him about our earlier engagement, before the war. Years ago! As if it mattered. And I lost my temper. We hardly ever rowed. And that's how it ended. If I could speak to him now, Kate. Tell him how much I loved him. Why did I go off in a huff? I tried to see him before the race started. I wanted to say sorry. That I loved him. I didn't even say good luck!"

And Cassandra broke down into wracking sobs. All

Katy could do was hold her, and she did that a for a very long time.

CHAPTER FORTY TWO
Summer 1927

Death and trouble comes in threes, her mother told Cassandra, with all the smug certainty of the unafflicted. Did Lady Amelia not miss her dead husband too? Cassandra had lost her father, then her mother-in-law and now her husband. If it wasn't for Lottie and Isobel and the new life she carried, she'd happily make it four.

Mr Leadbetter, the family solicitor, had taken over the arrangements for the funeral, with the help of Mr Hayes. She wanted it to be private, family only, and so it was, inside the church. She hadn't reckoned on the crowd of locals who gathered in the churchyard outside to pay their respects to their American interloper. Why was she surprised? Everyone who'd met Douglas had liked him, with the sole exception of her mother. Why the hell was she still stuck with her?

Lady Amelia had taken this new bereavement as a personal injury. Having never shown Douglas any affection while he was alive, she now deified him. Cassandra found it revolting and couldn't bear to be in the same room with her mother, not even for five minutes. Lady Amelia's maudlin laments were as loud as they were insincere.

So, she kept to her room or the nursery. At least Nanny Morgan's sympathy was genuine and she didn't know what she would do without her strength and kindness. The girls were bereft, each in their own ways. Isobel was very tearful and withdrawn; Lottie, true to her character was in a constant angry rage, demanding why her daddy had died. Why hadn't he taken more care? How could he leave them alone like this? To which Cassandra had no answers.

Someone, she didn't know who, had decided to get the funeral over with quickly. She hadn't been home a week when Mr Hayes steered her into the village church in Lower Cheadle and sat her down in the front pew. Nanny

311

Morgan had decided that it would be too much for the girls, who stayed up at Cheadle Manor. Lottie had fumed and railed against it, but Nanny Morgan had held firm.

The vicar kept the service short, as requested, but she could barely stand at the end. All the faces passed in a blur when she followed the coffin out. All except Katy's, whose pale face was dominated by her strange blue, almost violet eyes. Those eyes followed her down the aisle. Cassandra wanted to rake them with her fingernails. If it hadn't been for Katy's vaunting ambition, Douglas would not lie, cold and lifeless, in that horrid wooden box. As she passed Katy, she paused and gave her a look of such hatred she hoped it would scald her.

She felt Mr Hayes' arm stiffen under hers and his step faltered. Katy blinked and swayed but Jem caught her. How could Katy still have a husband, when she had killed hers?

There was no wake. She wanted to see no-one. Unlike the day of the race, the late August day was fine, incongruously, defiantly fine. Cassandra went to the orchard before going up to the nursery and sat on the love-seat. At least that day when they had sat here together, she'd told him how much she'd loved him. Surely he'd still known that when he took that fatal risk? Or did he drive stupidly because of her? Was it, actually, her fault, and not Katy's? She hated herself just as much as Katy. She hated everyone and everything. She hated this wretched love-seat. Too small for two, yes, but oh, so big for just one. And it would be only her, for the rest of her life.

Another week passed, unnoticed. Papers were signed in Mr Leadbetter's presence. He confirmed there was no more money coming from America. Nothing. Not a cent. Mr Hayes offered to go and tell Katy and Jem that their funding had officially finished.

"I know you are grieving, Miss Cassandra, but we must inform Katherine Wheel Garage of the change in their circumstances. It is only right when they are running a business."

"Then I'll go myself."

"But, Miss Cassandra! You're not well enough. At least let me accompany you."

"No, Mr Hayes, you are very kind but this is one task I intend to do on my own. Katy and Jem are personal friends," her demonic inner voice changed the verb to were, "so it's right and proper that I tell them in person. I'll be fine. My tears are over, Mr Hayes. I'm just numb. You're probably the one person who understands how I feel, after losing both your boys in the war."

"I do understand, Miss Cassandra, which is why I wish you'd let me come with you. You're still in a very vulnerable state. Begging your pardon, but you're not yet in a stable state."

"Maybe not, but that's what I'm going to do. I shall go down there today."

Katherine Wheel garage looked disgustingly normal, as if nothing had happened, as if the world hadn't turned upside down because of it. She hated the very buildings; the signs that shouted its wares and services; the shiny motorcars with 'for sale' placards written in Douglas's bold hand. Cars he would have sold and then generously shared the profits with Katy and Jem. The people who used to be her friends.

Cassandra parked the Sunbeam by the cars for sale on the forecourt at the side, blocking them from any customer's view. Why should she help them anymore? Douglas wouldn't benefit from it.

It was raining again and the workshop door was shut. Billy was serving a butcher's van with petrol and touched his flat cap when he saw her get out of the car. He took some money from the van driver, who then drove off. She marched up to the lad and asked where everyone was.

Billy removed his cap and gave an awkward little bow. "I'm very sorry for your loss, Mrs Flintock-Smythe. We was all very fond of Mr Douglas."

"Thank you, Billy. Where's Mrs Phipps?"

"She's round the back, ma'am, in the yard behind the

workshop."

Cassandra nodded at him, not trusting speech and stepped briskly round the workshop. She stopped in her tracks when she saw what Katy was doing.

A tarpaulin roof had been rigged up on poles above Douglas's wrecked racing car. The blue sports Austin, that Douglas had painted to match her favourite colour, sat, crushed and broken, under the flapping canvas. Its radiator grill was squashed right in and its front wings lay in grotesquely bent shapes on the ground. All four wheels were off, their tyres stacked against the workshop wall. Katy crouched over one wheel arch, spanner in hand, wearing her habitual boiler suit, with a gay red scarf wound around her black curly hair.

"Trying to hide the evidence of your crime?" Cassandra spat out the words.

"What?" Katy looked around, frowning. Seeing who it was, she dropped the spanner and came towards Cassandra with her blackened hands outstretched in welcome.

Cassandra took a step back. A fierce, destructive anger consumed her. Katy looked thin and drawn but basically healthy. How many years of good life lay ahead of her, with her loving Jem at her side?

"How lovely to see you, Cassandra. Won't you come inside? Would you like some tea? How are you?"

"I don't want anything from you and I've come to tell you that you won't be getting anything from me again, either. You've shot yourself in the foot, Mrs Phipps. Douglas's money, that you made so free with, has gone with him. You won't get a penny more. I thought you ought to know."

"I don't care about the money, Cass. I care about you. We loved Douglas and miss him terribly."

"But you care about your business more, don't you? That's why he's dead, after all. Dead, dead, dead!"

"Cass, please. We never meant for this to happen, not for the world. I'd chuck it all away to have Doug back.

314

Please believe me."

"No, I don't believe you. Why are you working on the car? Trying to cover up what killed him. Because you did kill him, just as much as if you'd bloody shot him."

Katy gasped and lifted her dirty hand to her mouth. "Don't say that, Cass, please don't say that. I feel guilty enough as it is."

"So you should feel guilty! It's all your fault. I'm a widow because of you." Cassandra couldn't stop herself; she reached out to snatch Katy's gaudy scarf from her head. She wanted to tear those black curls away too. Her hands curled into claws; she'd scratch those beautiful eyes from that white face while she was about it.

A pain sprang into her belly so fiercely, it took her breath away and drew her hands back to her stomach. She clutched at her mid-riff as a huge contraction engulfed her and she fell back against the wall.

"Oh, my God, you're bleeding!" Katy was holding her.

She wanted to throw her off but she felt so weak and the pain consumed her. She felt a warm trickle down her legs and saw a line of blood running down into her shoe. The baby. She was losing his baby. How could this new cruelty be happening? The last thing she saw was Katy's face looming at her. She tried to swipe at it but she didn't have enough strength. The broken carcass of the car blurred behind Katy.

Then everything blurred, and went black.

CHAPTER FORTY THREE
Autumn 1927

"I'm sorry, Mr Phipps, but if you can't even make the first payment on your new mortgage, we are left with no other option but to foreclose on your land and business. We are a business too, you know, not a charity. It's not as if you've made a single contribution. If you had some years of repayment under your belt, we might be more lenient, but this is a brand new agreement and you're already unable to meet your solemn commitment.

"Here, read the contract for yourself." Mr Wentworth passed the lengthy document across his leather-bound desk.

The words swam before Jem in a meaningless smudge of indecipherable jargon.

"Look, Mr Wentworth, you know there's been a tragic accident and my partner has died. That's why I came to you in the first place. Please, just give me another month. I'm sure I will have heard from Stockhead by then. I'll advertise the brake seals elsewhere, in the motoring magazines, at Brooklands, and I'll write to Fords in America. I'll write to every car manufacturer I know. I'll make sure we get into production, sir."

"I'm sure you mean well and I can see that you are sincere, Mr Phipps, but rules are rules. Head Office stipulate that the first payments of any mortgage must be met."

"A week then? Just give me a week. I'll go to Stockhead myself, if I have to, and get a decision out of them. Everything's ready. We can start production today, if there is a demand. And we know the product is a good one. It didn't cause the crash and my wife, I mean, our chief mechanic, has tested the brake seals over and over."

Mr Wentworth put his fingers together to make a steeple and looked at Jem for a long moment. His bushy grey eyebrows met in the middle of his frown. He took off his pince-nez glasses and placed them carefully down over the large mortgage document. Jem looked at the fancy italics of the first line, thinking how like the beginnings of a sentence in the bible they looked. That was full of rules too.

Jem held his breath.

Mr Wentworth cracked his knuckles and replaced his glasses. "I'll tell you what I'll do, Mr Phipps. I won't say anything to Head Office just yet. I'll give you your week but no more. If I don't hear from you within seven days, I'll have to send the bailiffs round. I can bend the rules, but only so much."

"A week?"

"It's my best offer. Take it or leave it."

"I'll take it. Thank you Mr Wentworth. I'll be in touch as soon as I can."

"Make sure you do. I want your business to succeed, Mr Phipps, I really do."

Jem left the bank in a daze. He couldn't think straight. A week.

As soon as he got home, he telephoned Mr Mayhew at Stockhead. A secretary answered his extension. "Mr Mayhew's not in today, Mr Phipps. He's on leave."

"What? He can't be. Look, is there anyone else I can talk to about the hydraulic brake system?"

"Oh, I don't know. I'd have to ask Mr Mayhew about that."

"When will he be back?"

"Tomorrow, I think."

"You think? You don't know? Aren't you his secretary?"

"Now listen here, Mr Phipps. I don't have to pass messages on, you know."

"I'm sorry, sorry. It's just that it's really important." Don't tell them your business is at stake as well as your home, your family, your workers. Jem reeled his thoughts in. "Forgive my rudeness, Miss?"

"Miss Armitage."

"Miss Armitage, I would be grateful if you could

317

pass a message to Mr Mayhew that I need to speak to him urgently about the seals for the hydraulic brakes. My name is Jem Phipps, from Katherine Wheel Garage in Wiltshire. I saw him recently at Brooklands race track. Have you got that written down?"

"Yes, I've got all that. I'll tell him, Mr Phipps. Good day to you."

And the line went dead. Jem spent the rest of the day frantically writing letters to every car manufacturer he could think of. He looked up parts manufacturers in the dealer's books too and wrote to each of them. He sent Jack off in the van to post the wad of letters. He didn't want Martha Threadwell interrogating him about the avalanche of mail he was despatching to all and sundry. Or explain about the accident all over again to another living soul. Some things were best not dwelt on.

Not that he expected to hear from any of the recipients within a week. He fobbed Katy's enquiries off about the mortgage payments, saying that Mr Wentworth had given them an extension. She was so tired with the baby and work she didn't pursue it and he was left to worry in private. In fact, she hardly spoke at all these days, not since Cassandra's last visit.

At a quarter to nine o-clock the next morning, he rang Stockhead again and Miss Armitage answered Mr Mayhew's extension. "He's not in yet, Mr Phipps. It's very early. I suggest you try again after ten o'clock."

At one minute past ten, Jem got through. "Mayhew here, can I help you?"

For one ghastly moment, Jem couldn't speak.

"Hello?"

He cleared his tight throat. "Good morning, Mr Mayhew. Jem Phipps here, from Katherine Wheel Garage."

"Ah, yes, got a message you wanted to speak to me. Sorry I wasn't in yesterday. Played golf with a chap from Vauxhall Motors. Beat me hollow." Mr Mayhew gave a light laugh.

Jem ground his teeth. "Sorry you lost, sir, but I wanted to know if you've given our idea for the rubber seals for your hydraulic brakes any more thought?"

"Oh, yes, you're the chap whose partner was killed at Brooklands. Not the best advertisement for safe braking. Very sad turn of events."

"I can categorically assure you, Mr Mayhew, that we have gone over the car since the crash and have established that the brakes were not the cause. They were functioning perfectly at the time of the accident and, most importantly, have not leaked brake fluid once since they were installed."

"Really? Hmm, interesting. Yes, well, I was impressed with their performance on the track but the accident put a different complexion on the matter and I'd need convincing that they were genuinely safe."

"Not a problem, Mr Mayhew. I would be delighted to show you their performance. I could come over to your office or you would be very welcome to visit us here. If you decided to come, we would cover all your expenses and I would be proud to show you our workshop and demonstrate how we make the seals. It's all already to go, sir."

"And you're in Wiltshire, is that right?"

"Yes, sir. It would only take you a couple of hours to drive."

"Hmm, let me look in my diary. I'm rather busy this week. I could see you at the end of next week - maybe Friday?"

"Next week isn't so convenient for me, Mr Mayhew." Sweat had broken out on Jem's forehead. "This Wednesday would be best for me. I could put you up at the local inn in Woodbury. They do a marvellous steak and ale pie."

"But Wednesday is tomorrow!"

"No time like the present, sir."

"Steak and ale pie, hey?"

"The best in the world."

"Alright. I'll be there before midday. And don't forget to book the hotel room."

When Jem put the receiver down his hand was slippery with perspiration and shaking. What a relaxed life some people led. It was obviously a damn sight easier to be employed by a big company than be mad enough to try and establish a small, new one.

He booked the room at the George and Dragon and made sure they had steak and ale pie on the menu the next evening. Then he dashed across to the home hut to tell Katy.

"That's great, Jem. Well done." Her voice was as flat as a pancake. Jem wondered why she wasn't more excited, then remembered she had no idea about the risk of foreclosure. He decided to keep it that way.

He couldn't sleep that night. He'd gone to bed late, after sweeping every inch of the new factory shed, counting the bales of rubber, checking the equipment, the books and tidying the office. Nothing must be left to chance. It was all down to him now.

It was a relief when dawn broke. He got up early and cleaned spotless corners in the shed. At eleven o'clock a shiny new Vauxhall drew up outside and he went to meet it.

"I hope you had a good journey?"

Mr Mayhew had turned up in good time. Jem took that as a promising sign and was grateful the anxious wait for his arrival was over. The September day was blustery but warm and mercifully dry. Katherine Wheel looked its best in the breezy sunshine. Jem desperately hoped it would help to make a good impression, especially as he hadn't had a single reply from any other takers for brake seals.

"Come in, sir, and I'll make you a cup of tea. The kettle's already boiled. The little office was tidier than it had ever been. Even Felix had been banished in honour of the occasion. Mr Mayhew favoured a pipe and lit up while Jem made the brew.

"Interesting place you've got here. Were these Nissen huts left over from the war?"

"That's right, sir."

"And you don't have any problems with the curved roofs?"

"Not a bit, sir. Here's your tea. Would you like to take it into the new shed, where we'll be producing the seals?" Jem couldn't wait much longer.

"You're in a hurry, aren't you?" Mr Mayhew sucked on his pipe, making the embers glow red. Jem hoped he wouldn't drop any of those near all the flammable liquids in the workshop. The sooner he got him into the factory shed, the better.

"Just keen to show you our new enterprise."

Jem marched the older man into the new shed, where Len and Jack were primed to carry on producing the seals that, as yet, no-one wanted. Jem introduced them both and they shook hands.

Mr Mayhew downed his mug of tea. "Right, Mr Phipps. Show me what you've got."

Jem didn't need telling twice. He explained every aspect of the seal production and demonstrated how they fitted on to a Stockhead hydraulic brake, set up for the purpose on the workshop bench. To his credit, Mr Mayhew listened with intense concentration and asked informed, intelligent questions. So it wasn't all golf and late mornings. Perhaps he did earn his money.

At the end of the tour, Mr Mayhew refilled his pipe. Once lit, he drew deeply on the sweet-smelling tobacco and turned to Jem.

"Well, Mr Phipps. I must say I'm very impressed with your set-up. Your staff seem efficient and competent; your equipment is up to date and first class, and the design of the seals appears sound. I'll need to clear it with my manager, but I think we can arrange a contract to take supply of your seals. Together, I think we can revolutionise the braking systems in this country. We've imported the system from America and we know the design works. It was only the containment of the fluids that stopped us going into full production and, of course, full promotion, but you seem to have cracked it. I'm confident we can have an excellent working relationship."

Jem pumped his hand, until Mr Mayhew's pipe rattled against his yellow teeth. "That's marvellous, sir, it really is. How long do you need to confirm the decision?"

The bank's ultimatum was never out of Jem's mind.

"Oh, a week or two and I should have an answer."

"Not before?"

"Got to clear it with my seniors, you know."

Should he come clean? Jem decided not. He didn't want to beg. Keep things professional. "If you could let me know by the end of next week, it would be very helpful."

"Leave it with me, Mr Phipps. I'll see what I can do. I can see you're as keen as mustard. Now, about that steak and ale pie?"

Katy gave a weary smile when Jem came back from the inn in Woodbury, full of beer and pie, much later.

She hugged him tight, making his packed stomach feel very uncomfortable. "That's wonderful, Jem. You've done it, my love. We can swing into action at last. Oh, I wish Douglas could share in this success."

So did Jem, more than anything. He owed it to Douglas to make it all work but it would take at least a month to see any money from Stockhead. And what the hell was he going to say to the bank in the meantime?

It wasn't just indigestion that kept Jem awake that night. He stared at the curved ceiling of his bedroom and listened to the wind whipping through the gaps in the corrugated steel panels. He'd have to sell something. The cars for sale on the forecourt. He'd have to take them back to their makers and make a loss on them. He didn't have time to wait for a customer to turn up. They had no other saleable assets and they already used up their land equity on the mortgage. He told Katy he was returning the Austins because they'd partly belonged to Douglas and she'd accepted it tearfully, too upset to ask more.

Austin were pretty sniffy about it but took the two baby Austins back for half their value. He drove one and put the other on the trailer the next day and took them to the depot from where Douglas had bought them. Clutching the cheque he got in exchange, he took the train home and was back after Katy had gone to bed. Good, that was another disappointment he wouldn't have to spill, just yet. He'd have to share the dividend with Cassandra but that would have to wait.

The next day was Friday, the last working day of the week, the last day before foreclosure. Jem parked up in Woodbury as the town hall clock, which stood opposite the bank, struck nine the next morning.

Mr Wentworth personally banked the cheque. It was ten shillings short of the full mortgage payment. Jem tipped out his pockets but was still half a crown shy.

"Oh, for goodness sake, lad, I'll make up the difference. You can buy me a pint when you've made your first million."

Jem had never seen Mr Wentworth smile before. It transformed him.

CHAPTER FORTY FOUR
Autumn 1927

Cassandra dragged herself out of bed one autumn morning and looked out at the golden leaves in the apple orchard. Misty rain was falling, and hung in pearls on the cobwebs stretched between the knarled branches. As she stood there, a single leaf fluttered down and lay, damp and lifeless, on the rough grass. Time was passing and the rhythm of life had beat on unchecked without her. She could put off seeing her estate manager no longer, even though she still wanted to spend every day under her bedcovers, hoping to find the imprint of Douglas's body on the barren sheets.

Reluctantly, slowly, she dressed. Maisie had given up offering to help her as she hadn't put on more than a dressing gown since Douglas had died. His dressing gown. It was an effort to draw on a skirt, blouse and cardigan and she grabbed the first ones that came to hand. She no longer cared what she looked like. She couldn't face breakfast but went straight to the office above the stables, before she thought better of it, and crawled back into the refuge of her once-shared double bed, as she longed to do.

Mr Hayes's eyes looked both surprised and sympathetic when he saw her. Cassandra dropped her eyes before his compassion undid her and stood at the window, so she could look away if tears came.

"Good morning, Mr Hayes. I'm sorry I haven't been to see you, I couldn't see anyone for a while but life has a way of carrying on, even when we don't want to, doesn't it?"

"It does that, Miss Cassandra, and there's nothing we can do about it."

"I knew you'd understand, Mr Hayes, otherwise I wouldn't be here. I've not seen anyone else for weeks but I felt I had to come and ask about the state of our finances. Mr Andrews came to see me yesterday, saying some tradesmen are clamouring to be paid but the housekeeping accounts are very low."

"I'm sorry you've been bothered with that, Miss Cassandra. I've tried to spare you from worry and Mr Andrews should have consulted me first."

"I thought you had, but I can't hide forever, however much I want to, so tell me the worst."

"I wish I could give you good news, Miss Cassandra, but the estate is struggling. We've still not paid off all of the death duties from your father and without Mr Douglas's income, the books don't balance."

"What's the solution, Mr Hayes?"

"We need a large injection of capital, Miss Cassandra, and a steady income above and beyond the farm and cottage rents."

"What can we sell?

"We could let North Farm go."

"But old Stubbs couldn't afford to buy it off us."

"No, we'd have to sell it on the open market."

"And what would happen to Stubbs?"

"I'm afraid he'd have to find somewhere else to live. One of the empty cottages perhaps?" Mr Hayes shuffled his papers.

Something clicked in Cassandra's brain at the thought of old Farmer Stubbs out on his ear, his large family in the street, homeless. Her grief stepped aside and she started to think again. It was almost like taking a holiday from her pain.

"I couldn't do that to him. His family have lived there for generations. My father was very fond of him. Plus we'd miss his arable harvests."

"Good point, Miss Cassandra."

"No, I'll tell you what we'll do, Mr Hayes. We'll sell the London House. No-one uses it. I never want to go there again. Just reminds me of Douglas's death. And there's all those staff we keep on who have nothing to do. It should raise a substantial sum. What do you think?" Cassandra blotted out the memories that crowded in when she pictured the beautiful house overlooking Hyde Park. It would be a blessing never to see the damn place again.

"That's a big decision, Miss Cassandra. One you should discuss with your mother."

"Do I have to?"

"I think it would be for the best, yes."

"Oh, alright, but get it valued in the meantime, will you, Mr Hayes? Get someone in London to view it and let us know how much it's worth."

"Very well." Mr Hayes nodded his agreement. "It should fetch a fair price, Miss Cassandra and provide a very good buffer for many years to come."

"Yes, I agree, and I'll make sure Mother does too."

"I hope you can, Miss Cassandra." Mr Hayes's ability to convey his sympathy in few words was a great comfort. Her life without Douglas seemed devoid of any other solace. Except for her girls. Lottie had school to distract her but Isobel's spirits were still very low.

Finding her energy, absent for so long, had increased, rather than lessened after the interview with Mr Hayes, she went to the nursery. She couldn't tackle her mother just yet. "What are you up to today, Isobel?"

Her youngest daughter was playing spillikins in front of the fire. A game she'd loved to play with Albert Phipps. The coloured wooden sticks piled up in an untidy heap and Isobel delicately withdrew a pink one. The pile collapsed and she burst into tears.

"Oh, darling, don't cry, it's only a game." Cassandra gathered her into her arms.

"Not crying 'bout game, Mummy."

"What is it then, sweetheart? Are you missing Daddy again?"

Isobel nodded, making the curls on her neck bob up and down. Cassandra kissed them. Isobel smelt so innocent. She breathed in her scent.

"Daddy wouldn't want you to be sad, little Bella. He was always joking, wasn't he? We must do all the jokes ourselves now. Let's read a book together, shall we? Something that makes us laugh."

She picked up 'Winnie-the-Pooh', Isobel's favourite.

The little girl settled herself on her mother's lap and sucked her thumb. Lady Amelia had told Cassandra that it was a weakness she shouldn't indulge but Nanny Morgan had shaken her head and told her nothing that comforted her daughter should be denied. Cassandra, longing for a comforter of her own, could not disagree.

When the story was finished, Isobel shut the book. "Why we never see Al, Mummy?"

Cassandra had been dreading this question. It had been so long since Douglas's funeral that she had wondered if Isobel would ever ask. Now she couldn't remember the answer she'd prepared for the occasion.

"Mummy?"

Cassandra searched for a solution. "Well, Al's at school now, like Lottie, like you soon will be and he's busy. He's got a new little sister too, don't forget, and I expect he has to help look after her. Her mother doesn't have much time for looking after either of them." It was no good, she couldn't keep her adult hatred out of the situation.

"But I love Al." Isobel's simple answer was simply unanswerable.

"Time to see Nanny Morgan, Isobel. I've got to talk to Grandmama about something important." Cassandra lifted Isobel off her lap and stood up.

Isobel's chin wobbled.

"Come on, I think Nanny Morgan was sorting out the laundry cupboard." Cassandra had to close her heart to Isobel's distress. She had enough trouble managing her own welling tears.

Cassandra found her mother in the drawing room, eating sweetmeats, as usual, before a roaring fire. The October day was cold but she still found the room stuffy. Or was her claustrophobia due to her proximity to the woman who'd borne her? She wouldn't examine that now.

"Hello, Mother. How are you today?"

"Oh, Cassandra. I'm to be graced with your presence

for once, am I? I am fortunate. No-one has seen you for weeks. I know you've been bereaved but really, staying in your room will only deepen your grief. It's high time you started to think about other things. Do you genuinely want to know about my health?"

"Not really. I came to talk to you about money."

"Money? Whatever for?"

"Because, Mother, we can't live without it."

"What on earth do you mean?"

"I mean, since Father's death duties, we've had to sell a lot of assets - you know - his hunters, the hounds, a few cottages here and there. Now that Douglas has died, I don't have his income to fall back on and we've still got quite a bit of tax to pay."

"Oh, Cassandra, why are you bothering me with all this dreary business? Surely Hayes can deal with this sort of thing?"

"I'm sorry to take up so much of your valuable time, Mother, but we've reached the point where we have to take drastic action. In short, we have to sell the house in London."

"What? But what if we have a function to attend? What about when the girls come out and we have to give them their first Season?"

"They'll have to find husbands another way, or better still, get careers of their own."

"Work? I'll have no lady of this household grubbing about for employment, like some servant girl."

"All the more reason to release some capital. Frankly, Mother, we have no choice. If I have your permission, I'll tell Mr Hayes to go ahead with the sale. We only have a skeleton staff there but, even so, they are receiving wages for doing nothing and we can no longer justify the expense."

"That is true, I suppose. Oh, dear, I think I have one of my headaches coming on. Well, Cassandra, do what you must but I do not approve. I don't know what your father would have said. It's quite scandalous."

"Father would have wanted to keep the manor going, just as I am trying to do. Alone."

Cassandra could remain patient no longer. She got up and went back to the estate office above the almost empty stables and told Mr Hayes to put the London house on the market.

"Right you are, Miss Cassandra. I've been wondering what to do with the proceeds. I think that the best idea would be to put the bulk of the capital into stocks and shares. That way, we can have a steady income from the interest which will enable us to plan ahead and manage the estate."

"I agree, Mr Hayes. I think that's an excellent idea. The most important thing is to keep the estate in good heart, just as Father wished. What else is there for me to do now?"

Mr Hayes coughed. "I'll set things in motion then."

***

Cassandra never visited the house in Hyde Park again. She'd always loved going there, getting a bit of London gloss and glamour, but it no longer held any allure for her. It was sold by end of the month and she didn't even feel a pang.

More heart-rending had been Isobel's crying when Lottie went to the dame school every day. Isobel was lonely, she knew that, but had no solution for it. They hadn't seen young Al or his parents for weeks and she didn't want to renew the friendship. Oh, Katy had tried to contact her many times, after the miscarriage, but Cassandra had refused to see her on every occasion. Refused every note, every telephone call until, eventually, and to her great relief, Katy had given up. Even Jem had called one day, but she'd been out visiting the cottages for the first time as a widow and had been glad to miss him. It would have been hard to keep up the pretence of coping in front of his honest, kind face.

All she wanted was to be left alone to get on with her many duties. Happiness was something she no longer looked for. She only found that in her memories and she visited those often, reliving that halcyon week at Cape Cod, remembering the romantic voyage home on the ocean liner, when she had been expecting Lottie and she and Douglas were newly-weds. Before Katy and Jem had even thought about their damn business. Even the week at Cape Cod had been cut short by Fred's attack on Katy. That woman ruined everything and always came out unscathed.

She'd heard the gossip about the garage. You couldn't avoid it in a small place like Cheadle. Apparently the factory was up and running, churning out those bloody rubber seals that had cost Douglas his life.

Good luck to them. No, she didn't even wish them that.

CHAPTER FORTY FIVE
Winter 1927

Katy sat in the workshop office, poring over the accounts, hardly daring to believe the tally she reached after adding up the figures. She still hadn't got used to the success of the factory. Once Stockhead had agreed to take their brake seals, they hadn't looked back. It had been touch and go with the bank to start with, but now those monthly payments were met every time, and easily.

She'd even made designs for different seals with other uses than brakes. With all the new inventions for refrigerators and washing machines, there would be no end of demand for rubber seals to keep water in or out. The sky was the limit.

Jem popped his head around the door.

"Jem - come in and see this profit and loss ledger. I want you to check I haven't made a mistake because I can't quite believe how much we've made this month."

Jem grinned and sat down next to her. He ran his finger down the columns before looking back with a happy nod. "Looks right to me, Kate." A shadow passed over Jem's face. "If only..."

"I know, if only Douglas were here. I still miss him so much, every day, and Cassandra even more. Jem, do you think we might ask Cassandra if Isobel and Lottie could come and visit on Al's birthday? Like the old days? I feel I've got to try to see her again. Even if she slams the door in my face, I can't bear this rift. She must be so lonely up there, rattling around the manor with only her girls and her dreadful mother for company. I think it's time I made another attempt to see her." Katy's mood had suddenly deflated.

"Hmm, doubt she'd come. Those days are long gone, my love. I can't see Cassandra wanting to see us yet. I'd leave it awhile, if I were you. She's still grieving and that takes time."

"Maybe you're right. Goodness knows I've tried

often enough but I don't like feeling estranged from my best friend like this and Al is missing the girls too."

"I know, love, but we can't bring Douglas back, whatever we do."

They fell silent, all their joy in their bright future expunged by the past that had robbed them of the man who had helped create it.

***

Having had the idea about Al and Isobel's shared birthdays, Katy couldn't let it go. Her personal grief for Douglas and her guilt about his death, ate away at her. She would be working away in the garage, or feeding Lily, and Douglas's face would swim into her mind's eye, laughing. It shocked her every single time, remembering she'd never see him again. She had to try and contact Cassandra; had to try and reconnect with those poor little girls.

She broached the subject over supper later that day.

"We must think about how to celebrate your birthday on Christmas Eve, Al."

Al must have been reading her mind because his reply echoed it so closely.

"What I'd really like, Mum, is if Isobel and Lottie could come, like they used to. I miss them." Al's face was solemn.

Katy looked at Jem, who nodded back.

"Alright, your Dad and I have been thinking the same thing. I'll ask their mum if they can come. I don't know if they will, mind, but I miss them too, Al, so I'll try."

"I'll come with you, shall I?" Al's face lit up.

"I don't know if that would be a good idea, son," Jem said.

"I'll think about it, is all I'll say for now, love." Katy wondered if perhaps taking Al might be the one way Cassandra would agree but using children as blackmail didn't seem fair. No, Cassandra must come because she wanted to.

She talked it over with her mother. Agnes came every afternoon to mind Lily so that Katy could work in the garage or the factory but they always shared a quick cup of tea and a bite of lunch together beforehand.

"I've been meaning to find the time, and the courage, to go up to the manor and ask Cassandra and her girls to come to Al's birthday party. Weeks have passed and I've not managed it. She hasn't wanted to see anyone, but I can't rest until I try again."

"She won't be in no mood for a party, my girl!"

"But, Mum, don't you see? I have to find a way to break the ice and make contact with Cassandra. I can't think of a better way to reach her, can you? And I've left it so long. The party will be the perfect excuse for me to visit. Al is desperate to see the Smythe girls again and he and Isobel always used to share their birthday party."

"And do you really think she'll want you flaunting your success at a time like this?"

"I have to go and see her, Mum. I've got to sort things out between us. We can't go on being estranged like this. She's the best friend I've ever had and she needs me now. I'll be diplomatic, Mum, but it's exactly at times like these that you need your friends, don't you?"

"If she still thinks of you as her friend after what happened to poor Douglas."

Stung into silence, Katy acknowledged the truth of this.

"That settles it. I'm going up there this afternoon. You'll mind Lily, won't you?"

"Of course I will, same as always, and - I'm glad to see you try, Katy, love."

Katy left the rest of her sandwich uneaten and went to get changed. She chided herself for the weeks she'd wasted, determined not to let one more second slip by without seeing her old friend. She peeled off her stained boiler suit and replaced it with her new heather-coloured tweed coat and smart hat with a feather in it. She wouldn't

333

get past old Andrews dressed like a car mechanic.

She parked on the drive in front of the wide terrace, just in case she might need a quick getaway, and leapt up the steps, two at a time.

Mr Andrews, now grey at the temples, looked her up and down before saying, "Why, it's Katy Phipps, isn't it?"

"Hello, Mr Andrews. It has been a long time, hasn't it? May I come in?"

"I'm not sure," he began, but then she saw Cassandra climbing the stairs behind him and pushed past him into the hall.

"Oi! I never said you could come in!"

Katy ignored Mr Andrew's outraged face. "Cassandra! Please wait?"

Cassandra turned around. Katy was shocked at how much she had aged. Cassandra's long flyaway hair had been cut short but not very well. She wore a brown cardigan and a black skirt. The whole effect was drab and unbecoming. Katy searched for a word to describe her friend. Defeated, yes, that was it.

"What is it? Who's there?" Cassandra screwed her eyes up, as if she was getting short-sighted.

"Cass, darling, it's me, Kate."

Cassandra frowned. Surely she knew her friend? Then her face cleared in recognition. Katy's heart lifted but Cassandra turned away and continued climbing the stairs.

"Cassandra. Please listen to me, just for a few moments." Katy caught up with her. They stood on the same step, halfway up the wide, sweeping staircase. Katy could see her friend's brown eyes now; see the despair within.

She stretched out a hand and touched Cassandra's sleeve. Cassandra's entire body went rigid.

"Take your hands off me."

"But Cassandra!"

Cassandra shook her off. "I'm extremely busy. Why don't you leave me alone!"

334

But Katy wasn't going to be put off so easily. She gripped both Cassandra's arms with her own. "Not so fast! Look, Cass. I'm so sorry I haven't been here before. I realised you needed time to yourself after Douglas died so I stopped pestering you."

"How dare you come and pester me now?"

"Cass! Look at me! I'm your friend! Please, let me help you. I'll do anything I can but don't shut me out, not now."

"I wouldn't *be* alone, if it wasn't for your damn garage! Your money-making factory!"

"I know, I know. I'm so sorry for Doug's death, believe me. I loved him too. We both did."

Cassandra threw off Katy's hands and shoved her, hard.

Katy wobbled off the step and had to grab the banister to stop herself falling down the stairs.

"No, you have *no* idea, Kate! Do you know what it's like to be this alone? To bring up your children - alone? To go to bed, every bloody night, alone? No - you're in the thick of your little empire, aren't you? And, you've got your Jem to share it with. Children, money, a man to hold you at night? What do you know about my life anymore?" Cassandra's face was twisted up; distorted and unrecognisable.

"I do understand, Cass, really I do. Don't you remember how I thought Jem had died in the war? I tried to kill myself, Cass. I know the depth of the despair you feel. I think of dear Douglas every single day. I'd cut my arm off if it would undo that awful crash. Please, please believe me! I'd give anything to have Douglas back."

"Why are you talking about my Daddy?" Lottie was holding Isobel's hand. The two girls had their coats on, and stood in the open doorway, glistening with rain, next to the butler.

"Mrs Phipps is going now." Cassandra jerked her head in the direction of the door, where Mr Andrews still stood, looking shocked and uncertain as to whether he should close it or not. Katy walked towards the door, hoping the children couldn't see how much she shook.

She threw her earlier scruples away and bent her knees, so she was Isobel's height. "Would you like to see Al again, Bella? We're having a party on Christmas Eve, on your birthdays, just like we used to. We'd love it if you could come. Al would love it if you could come."

"Me, too?" Lottie said..

"Of course, Lottie, but you must ask your Mummy for permission."

Lottie nodded, in her serious way. "Can Mummy come too?" How grown up she had suddenly become.

"I'd love it if she did. Do you think you could persuade her, girls?"

She was rewarded by timid smiles. Had these two smiled since they'd lost their father? To look at them, she suspected not. Tears welled up in her eyes. She hugged them quickly, turned and waved back at Cassandra, still standing on the stairs like a broken statue, and fled.

CHAPTER FORTY SIX
Winter 1927

"I'm not going without you, Mummy. You've got to come, for Bella's sake."

Cassandra leant back against her pillows and looked at her eldest daughter's solemn face. Lottie was sitting on the end of her bed, cross-legged like a pixie. Lottie's eyes were exactly like Douglas's and normally she couldn't get enough of them. Today, they were fierce and uncompromising.

"But I haven't bought Al a present."

"Al won't care about that. His mummy and daddy are going to be rich, the servants say, hadn't you heard?"

"No, I hadn't heard that." She had of course. Even she couldn't avoid the rumours flying around that the Phipps were going up in the world as fast as her estate was falling down from it. And if Douglas hadn't died, neither would be happening. Life was cruel beyond measure. So cruel, she'd quit it tomorrow, if it wasn't for these girls they'd created together.

"I want to see him. So does Bella. And it's her birthday, so you've got to say yes, Mummy. It's the Birthday Law. Daddy always said you could have whatever you wanted on your birthday and this is what she wants."

"So *you* say. I haven't heard Bella say it." And if it wasn't for bloody Katy Phipps, Douglas would be here to speak in person; be here to share in his beautiful daughter's birthday.

"That's because she doesn't want to see you crying."

Cassandra sighed. It wasn't always easy having an intelligent child. Nothing escaped Lottie's observational powers. She was like a detective in one of those Agatha Christie novels her mother was always reading.

"If Bella asked you, as the birthday girl, would you go?"

The ultimate threat.

"Lottie..."

"Would you refuse her dearest wish on her birthday, Mummy?"

"Oh, for heaven's sake, child! Alright. We'll go."

Visiting the Phipps was the last thing she wanted to do but she couldn't refuse those pleading blue eyes, so reminiscent of Douglas's. She'd never been able to deny him anything either. Oh, what wouldn't she give to see him again, hold him again?

"Hurray! You can come out now, Bella."

Isobel stepped out from behind the curtain of the big bay window of Cassandra's bedroom. How had she sneaked in there? She must have heard everything. Chastened, Cassandra gave Isobel her birthday present. A pencil case. That was it. And she was mortified that neither of the girls complained about it. Honestly, some days their maturity made her ashamed.

"We don't even know what time the party is, do we?" Maybe she could wriggle out of it, after all.

"Yes, Mummy, look. Al sent me a card in the post, and there's this invitation inside."

So they had it all sewn up, these blasted Phipps, leaving her with no way out.

"I see. Right, you'd better have an early lunch and then get dressed in your best clothes."

She drove the girls herself later that frosty afternoon, in the old Sunbeam. On the forecourt at Katherine Wheel Garage was a sign, with a bunch of balloons attached to it, saying 'PARTY THIS WAY'.

The jolly sign smote Cassandra's heart and she bit her lip. Pain arrested the pricking tears obscuring her vision.

"Come on, you two. Let's get this over with."

She slammed the car door after the girls had jumped out and marched them up to the new front porch that had been built since the last time she'd visited the Nissen hut. While Cassandra hesitated, Lottie lifted the shiny brass knocker and rapped it three times.

The door opened. Al stood there. His face broke into a wide grin. "You've come!" His young voice sounded husky. Surely he wasn't old enough for his voice to break?

Al swallowed. She could see his Adam's apple bob up and down. "Come in," he said, in a stronger voice.

Lottie stepped over the threshold and held out the card she'd made. "Happy Birthday, Al." She leaned in and kissed his cheek, which went bright red.

Isobel had to stand on tiptoe to deliver hers and then put her little arms around his waist and hugged him. "I've missed you, Al."

"That'll do, you lot." Cassandra couldn't stand all this mawkishness. Jem appeared in the new, improvised hallway and switched on the electric light, which didn't yet have a shade. The bare bulb chased the shadows away.

"Cassandra, it's so good to see you, my dear." Jem kissed her cheek. "Let me help you with your coat. It's cold out there today. Do you think we'll have a white Christmas tomorrow, girls? If we do, you must come and build a snowman in our garden." He bustled them into the living room, where a coal fire blazed in the old range.

Katy stood in the centre of the room, looking both nervous and very glamorous. She was wearing a new satin dress. Its cerise colour suited her complexion perfectly and she'd obviously had her hair done. A little baby gurgled on a rug at her feet.

Cassandra felt intimidated and ill at ease. She hadn't bothered to dress up and wore her black skirt with a pale pink blouse and a green cardigan that didn't quite go with it. She hadn't even thought about clothes until this moment.

"Kate, you look...different."

"But, Cass, I'm just the same. I've missed you."

Katy held out her arms.

"I, I can't stay. I'll just leave the girls here and come back for them later."

"No, you won't, Mummy." Lottie had her hand in the small of Cassandra's back. She pushed her into Katy's embrace.

Cassandra froze in Katy's arms. Trapped. It was all a trap.

Katy released her but held her hands. "Don't hate me, Cassandra. I know your heart is breaking. We all miss Douglas so much and we always will. But look at these children. Don't they deserve to be happy? Let's be friends, if only for their sake?"

Cassandra looked at the children. All of them were staring at her with sad eyes, even the tiny baby, who didn't even know who she was. What would Douglas have told her to do?

"Please, Mummy, please stay." Isobel tugged at her cardigan.

Cassandra sighed. "Just for an hour, then."

THE END

AUTHOR'S NOTE

During the 1920's the sales of cars boomed and many garages like the Katherine Wheel sprang up throughout Britain. Fortunes were made from inventions but the company who hit on the idea for rubber seals for hydraulic brakes (manufactured by Lockheed) was in fact Chrysler.

As ever, Speedwell, is a work of fiction and, as stated in the acknowledgments, many liberties have been taken from real life and changed to fit the story.

Speedwell is a tribute to all those brave drivers who sacrificed their lives pushing themselves and their cars to the limit in the early days of motoring.

Speedwell is the third book in the **Katherine Wheel Series** and completes the story - for now. A fourth book, set in the 1940's may conclude the series but has yet to be written.

Daffodils is the first book in the trilogy and follows Katy and Jem into the First World War, http://amzn.to/19iDLtI (US) http://amzn.to/141yEIG (UK). It starts slowly. Life changes little in Cheadle. Petty scandals, gossip and the huge gap between the haves and those who serve them continue to dominate their small world. Daffodils drags Katy and Jem out of their narrow lives and catapults them into the wider arena of a global conflict. Most books follow what happened to the soldiers and so does Daffodils, in part. It also follows the gallant women who provided the backbone for the army, not just the nurses, but the gender defying mechanics and drivers who managed the vehicles and ambulances. Women took on very different roles which shook up the world they returned to, once the world-wide fight was over. But in essence, Daffodils is a love story, whose tender heart is almost torn apart through this tumultuous time.

Peace Lily http://amzn.to/1vHCMhc (US) http://amzn.to/1zxG8aL (UK) takes up their story in 1919. After the appalling losses suffered during World War One, three of its survivors long for peace, unaware that its aftermath will bring different, but still daunting, challenges.

Katy trained as a mechanic during the war and cannot bear to return to the life of drudgery she left behind. A trip to America provides the dream ticket she has always craved and an opportunity to escape the strait-jacket of her working class roots. She jumps at the chance, little realising that it will change her life forever, but not in the way she'd hoped.

Jem lost not only an arm in the war, but also his livelihood, and with it, his self esteem. How can he keep restless Katy at home and provide for his wife? He puts his life at risk a second time, attempting to secure their future and prove his love for her.

Cassandra has fallen deeply in love with Douglas Flintock, an American officer she met while driving ambulances at the Front. How can she persuade this modern American to adapt to her English country way of life, and all the duties that come with inheriting Cheadle Manor? When Douglas returns to Boston, unsure of his feelings, Cassandra crosses the ocean, determined to lure him back.

As they each try to carve out new lives, their struggles impact on each other in unforeseen ways.

Alex Martin's first book, **The Twisted Vine**, http://amzn.to/UzYbI8 (US) http://amzn.to/XHVZeD (UK) is set deep in rural France and is based on her own adventure of picking grapes back in the 1980s, before mobile phones and the internet were even invented, hard to imagine now! Like the narrator of the story, Roxanne Rudge, she was escaping a relationship that had gone disastrously wrong. Like her, she was trying to rediscover who she was while getting a suntan and deepening her love of this beautiful country. She too drove all over the French countryside, often lost (in more ways than one), bruised her knees and grazed her hands toiling away on steeply sloping vineyards. Luckily for her, She did not meet a sinister man like Armand le Clair or uncover the dark secret within a the elegant walls of a Burgundian Chateau, though she did drink plenty of the resulting wine!

There is also a little collection of 3 short stories, as a taster of Alex Martin's work. It's called **Trio** and is also available from Amazon http://amzn.to/1BKwhM4

You can keep up to date on her blog at
Alex Martin, Author at The Plotting Shed at:
http://bit.ly/1H5OtqT

http://alexxx8586.blogspot.co.uk/

Comments and reviews always welcome

62798275R00209

Made in the USA
Charleston, SC
19 October 2016